P
Way
Book One of The Vampire Earth

"*Way of the Wolf* is a winner. If you're going to read only one more postapocalyptic novel, make it this one."
—Fred Saberhagen, author of the *Berserker* series

"I have no doubt that E. E. Knight is going to be a household name in the genre."   —*Silver Oak Books Reviews*

"E. E. Knight has managed to create a compelling new world out of the ruins of our existing one. It's a major undertaking for a new author. . . . He does it with style and grace, and I would highly recommend checking out the book as soon as you can."   —Creature Corner

"E. E. Knight has offered up a novel that is at least the equal to anything out there now, and surpasses many other works."
—atFantasy.com

"I read the last hundred pages in one sitting. I just couldn't put it down."   —ebook-reviews.net

WAY OF THE WOLF

BOOK ONE OF *THE VAMPIRE EARTH*

E. E. Knight

A ROC BOOK

ROC
Published by New American Library, a division of
Penguin Group (USA) Inc., 375 Hudson Street,
New York, New York 10014, USA
Penguin Group (Canada), 10 Alcorn Avenue, Toronto,
Ontario M4V 3B2, Canada (a division of Pearson Penguin Canada Inc.)
Penguin Books Ltd., 80 Strand, London WC2R 0RL, England
Penguin Ireland, 25 St. Stephen's Green, Dublin 2,
Ireland (a division of Penguin Books Ltd.)
Penguin Group (Australia), 250 Camberwell Road, Camberwell, Victoria 3124,
Australia (a division of Pearson Australia Group Pty. Ltd.)
Penguin Books India Pvt. Ltd., 11 Community Centre, Panchsheel Park,
New Delhi - 110 017, India
Penguin Group (NZ), cnr Airborne and Rosedale Roads, Albany,
Auckland 1310, New Zealand (a division of Pearson New Zealand Ltd.)
Penguin Books (South Africa) (Pty.) Ltd., 24 Sturdee Avenue,
Rosebank, Johannesburg 2196, South Africa

Penguin Books Ltd., Registered Offices:
80 Strand, London WC2R 0RL, England

First published by Roc, an imprint of New American Library,
a division of Penguin Group (USA) Inc.

First Printing, September 2003
10

Copyright © Eric E. Frisch, 2003
All rights reserved

Cover art by Koveck

RoC REGISTERED TRADEMARK—MARCA REGISTRADA

Printed in the United States of America

To Mom and Dad, who believed

Have you ever dealt with people who have lost everything in just an hour? In the morning you leave the house where your wife, your children, your parents live. You return and you find a smoking pit. Then something happens to you—to a certain extent you stop being human. You do not need any glory, money anymore; revenge becomes your only joy. And because you no longer cling to life, death avoids you, the bullets fly past. You become a wolf.

—Russian General Aleksander Lebed,
veteran of Afghanistan

One

Northern Louisiana, March, the forty-third year of the Kurian Order: The green expanse once known as the Kisatchie Forest slowly digests the works of man. A forest in name only, it is a jungle of wet heat and dead air, a fetid overflowing of swamps, bayous, and backwaters. The canopy of interwoven cypress branches shrouded in Spanish moss creates a gloom so thick that twilight rules even at midday. In the muted light, collapsing houses subside every which way as roadside stops decay in vine-choked isolation, waiting for traffic that will not return.

A long file of people is moving among moss-covered trunks to the piping cries of startled birds. At the front and rear of the column are men and women in buckskin, their faces tanned to the same weather-beaten color as their leather garments. They carry sheathed rifles, and all are ready to use their weapons at the first hint of danger. The guns are for the defense of five clusters of families clad in ill-fitting lemon-colored overalls at the center of the file. Patches of brighter color under the arms and along the inner thighs suggest the garments once glowed a vivid optic yellow and are now faded from heavy use. A string of five pack mules follows behind them under the guidance of teenage versions of the older warriors.

At the head of the column, well behind a pair of silent

*scouts, a young man scans the trail. He still has some of the
awkward gangliness of youth, but his dark eyes hold a canny
depth. His shoulder-length black hair, tightly tied at the back
of his head, shines like a raven's feathers even in the half-
light. With his dusky skin and buckskin garb, he could be mistaken for a native resident of this area three centuries before:
perhaps the son of some wandering French trapper and a
Choctaw maiden. His long-fingered hands wander across his
heavy belt, from holstered pistol to binoculars, touching the
haft of his broad-bladed parang before moving on to the can-
teens at his waist. A scratched and battered compass case
dangles from a black nylon cord around his neck, and a stout
leather map tube bumps his back from its slung position. Unlike his men, he is hatless. He turns now and again to check
the positions of his soldiers and to examine the faces of his
yellow-clad dependents as if gauging how much distance is
left in their weary bodies. But his restless eyes do not remain
off the trail for long.*

    If they come, they'll come tonight. Lt. David Valentine re-
turned to that thought again as the sun vanished below the
horizon. He had hoped to get his charges farther north of the
old interstate before nightfall, but progress had slowed on
this, their fourth day out from Red River Crossing. He and his
Wolves shielded twenty-seven men, women, and children
who had hazarded the run to freedom. The families were now
adapted to the rigors of the trail, and followed orders well.
But they came from a world where disobedience meant death,
so that trait was understandable.

    If they had been traveling by themselves, the detachment
of Wolves would already be in the Free Territory. But Valentine was responsible for seeing the Red River farmhands
brought safely north. Four hours ago, the yellow-clad group

had crossed the final barrier: the road and rail line connecting Dallas with the Mississippi at Vicksburg. Then Valentine had driven them another two miles. Now they had little left to give.

It was hard to quiet his mind, with so much to think about on his first independent command in the Kurian Zone. And quieting his mind, keeping lifesign down, was literally a question of life and death with night coming on. Being a Wolf was as much a matter of mental as physical discipline, for the Reapers sensed the activity of human minds, especially when fearful and tense. Every Wolf had a method of subsuming consciousness into a simpler, almost feral form. But burdened with new responsibilities and with night swallowing the forest, Valentine struggled against the worries that shot up like poisonous weeds in his mind. The Reapers read lifesign better at night. His charges were giving off enough to be read for miles even in the depths of the Kisatchie. If his Wolves' minds were added to the total, the Reapers would home on it like moths drawn to a bonfire.

A trilling call from ahead broke into his anxieties. Valentine raised his arm, halting the column. Garnett, one of his scouts, gestured to him.

"Water, sir, in that little holler," the scout reported as Valentine came up. "Looks safe enough."

"Good. We'll rest there for an hour," Valentine said, loudly enough for the column to hear. "No more. We're still too close to the road to camp."

The faces of the farm families brightened in contrast to the deepening night as they drank from the spring trickling down the side of a shallow ravine. Some removed shoes and rubbed aching feet. Valentine unscrewed the cap on his plastic canteen, waiting until the families and his men had a chance to drink.

A faint yelping echoed from the south. Wolves dived for cover behind trees and fallen logs. The yellow-clad families, who lacked the ability to hear the baying, shrank together in alarm at the sudden movement.

Sergeant Patel, Valentine's senior noncommissioned officer, appeared at his elbow. "Dogs? Very bad luck, sir. Or . . ."

Valentine, careering along in his runaway train of thought, only half heard Patel's words. The families broke out in noisy consternation.

"Silence," Valentine rasped at the civilians, his voice cracking with unaccustomed harshness. "Sergeant, who knows this area best?"

Patel's eyes did not leave the woods to the south. "Maybe Lugger, sir. Or the scouts. Lugger pulled a lot of patrols in this area; I think her people lived westaways."

"Would you get her, please?"

Patel pointed to and brought up Lugger, a seasoned veteran whose limber, sparse frame belied her name. She held her rifle in hands with alabaster knuckles.

"Sir?" she breathed.

"Lugger, we may have to do some shooting soon," Valentine said in an undertone, trying not to alarm the unsettled civilians. "Where's a good spot for it?"

Her eyes wandered skyward in thought. "There's an old barn we used to use on patrol. West of here, more like northwest, I reckon. Concrete foundation, and the loft's in good shape."

"How long to get there?"

"Under an hour, sir, even with them," she said, jerking her chin toward the huddled families. Their yellow overalls now looked bluish in the darkness. Valentine nodded encouragement.

"Solid foundation," she repeated. "And a big water trough. We used to keep it filled with a rain catcher."

Make a decision.

"No help in that direction. Mallow's more to the east, but it will have to do," Valentine said. Mallow, the senior lieutenant of Zulu Company, had remained in the borderlands with a cache of supplies to help them make it the rest of the way to the Ozark Free Territory. He considered something else. "Think you could find the rendezvous at night?"

"God willing, sir," she responded after a moment's cogitation.

"Take a spare canteen and run. Ask Mallow to come with everything he can."

"Yes, sir. But I don't need my gun to keep me company. I think you'll need every bullet you got before morning," she said, unslinging her rifle.

Valentine nodded. "Let's not waste time. Tell Patel where to go; then run for our lives."

Lugger handed her rifle to the senior aspirant, spoke briefly to Patel and the scouts, then disappeared into the darkness. Valentine listened with hard ears to her fading footfalls, as fast as his beating heart, and thought, *Please, Mallow, for God's sake forget about the supplies and come quick.*

As his men dusted the area around the spring with crushed red pepper, Valentine approached the frightened families.

"They found us?" asked Fred Brugen, the patriarch of the group. Valentine smiled into their dirty, tired faces.

"We heard something behind us. Could be they cut our trail—could be a dog got the wrong end of a skunk. But as I said, we have to play it safe and move to a better place to sleep. Sorry to cut the halt short."

The refugees winced and tightened their mouths at the

news, but did not complain. Complainers disappeared in the night in the Kurian Zone.

"The good news is that we're really close to a place we can rest and get a hot meal or two. Personally, I'm getting sick of corn bread and jerky." He squatted down to the kids' level and forced some extra enthusiasm into his voice. "Who wants hot-cakes for breakfast tomorrow morning?"

The kids lit up like fireflies, nodding with renewed energy.

"Okay, then," he finished as he filled his canteen, forcing himself to go through the motions nonchalantly. "Everybody take one more drink of water, and let's go."

The aspirants somehow got the pack mules moving, and the column trudged forward into the darkness. With curses matching the number of stumbles brought on by confusion and fatigue in the night, the column continued north. Valentine led the way. A rope around his waist stretched back to Sergeant Patel at the tail end of the file. He bade the families to hold on to it to keep everyone together in the dark.

One scout guided him, and a second brought up the rear, in close contact with two fire teams shepherding the column's tail, their phosphorous candles ready. If the enemy was close enough for their dogs to be heard, the Reapers could be upon them at any moment. Valentine resigned himself to the orders he would give if they were set upon in the open: he would abandon his charges and flee north. Even a few Wolves were more valuable to the Free Territory than a couple of dozen farmers.

Valentine, continuing on that grim line of thought, decided that if he were a battle-hardened veteran from the campfire stories, he would stake the farmers out like goats to a prowling tiger, then ambush whatever took the bait. The death of the defenseless goat was worth getting the tiger. Those win-at-all-costs leaders from the Old World history books would never be swayed by sleepy voices repeatedly asking, "Is it much farther, Momma?"

"Close up and move on. Close up and move on," Valentine said over his shoulder, hurrying the column. Wolves picked up tired children, carrying them as easily as they bore their weapons.

They found the farm exactly as Lugger had described. Her Wolf's eye for terrain and detailed memory of places and paths would astound anyone who did not know the caste.

The barn was a little bigger than Valentine would have liked with only twenty-two guns. *No time to be picky, not with the Reapers on our trail,* he thought. Anyplace with the trees cleared away and walls would have to do.

Garnett entered with blade unsheathed, covered by his comrades' hunting bows and rifles. The parang—a shortened machete used by the Wolves—gleamed in the mist-shrouded moonlight. A few bats fluttered out, disturbed from their pursuit of insects among the rafters. The scout appeared at the loft door and waved the rest in. Valentine led the others inside, fighting a disquieting feeling that something was wrong. Perhaps his Indian blood perceived something tickling below his conscious threshold. He had spent enough time on the borders of the Kurian Zone to know that his sixth sense was worth paying attention to, though hard to qualify. The danger was too near somehow, but ill defined. He finally dismissed it as the product of overwrought nerves.

Valentine inspected the sturdy old barn. The water trough was full, which was good, and there were shaded lanterns and oil, which was better.

Patel posted the men to the doors and windows. Cracks in the walls of the time-ravaged structure made handy loopholes. The exhausted families threw themselves down in a high-walled inner corner. Valentine trotted to the hayloft lad-

der and began to climb. Someone had repaired a few of the
rungs, he noticed as he went up squeaking wood. The barn's
upper level smelled like bat urine. From the loft he watched
his second scout, Gonzalez, backing into the barn, rifle
pointed into the darkness.

"Gonzo's got wind of 'em, sir," Garnett reported from his
perch at the upper door. "He always gets bug-eyed when
they're around.".

Three Wolves from downstairs joined them in the loft and
took positions on each side of the barn. Valentine glanced
down through a gap in the loft floor to the lower level, where
Patel talked quietly to Gonzalez in the dim light of a screened
lantern. Both glanced up into the loft. Gonzalez nodded and
climbed the ladder.

"Sir, the sarge wanted me to show you this," he reported,
extending a filthy and stinking piece of cloth drawn from his
pocket.

Valentine reached out to take the rag, when a chorus of
shrieks sounded from down the hill in the direction of the old
road. He spun and ran to the wide loft door.

Garnett cursed. "Ravies, goddamn Ravies!"

The banshee wailing out of the midnight mists turned the
back of his neck into a bristle-brush. *They're here!* He bent to
the gap in the floor and called out to the Wolves. "Keep to
your posts, look to your fronts! The Ravies might be a ruse.
They could be on top of the hill already."

He ran to the ladder and clambered down the rungs two at
a time, driving a splinter into the flesh opposite his thumb in
his haste. Wincing, he unsnapped the leather strap of his
parang sheath and drew his revolver.

"Uncle, the flares!" he shouted, but Patel knew better than
to wait for an order. The veteran sergeant already stood at the
gaping southern door, lighting one. A Wolf opened a lantern

door so he could thrust it in. The high-pitched shrieking grew louder, until it filled the night.

The firework burst into flame, illuminating the barn with blue-white light and sharp black shadows. Patel wound up and threw the burning flare down the slope they had just traversed. Before it landed, he lit another and hurled it into the darkness, as well. Other Wolves copied him, tossing phosphorus candles in each direction.

Valentine stared down the hill, transfixed by a mob emerging into the glare. Running figures with arms thrashing as if trying to swim through the air swept up toward the barn. Seemingly endless supplies of wind powered their screams. Their siren wail was paralyzing. They were human, or what amounted to human, considering their minds burned with madness, but with the wasted look of corpses and sparse streams of unkempt hair. Few wore more than tatters of clothing; most ran naked, their skin pale in the light of burning phosphorus.

"Don't let 'em in close enough to bite. Drop 'em, goddammit!" Patel bellowed.

Shots rang out in the enclosed lower level of the barn. Ravies fell, one rising again with blood pouring from his neck, to stagger a few paces and fall once more, this time for good. Another had a bullet tear through her shoulder, spinning her around like a puppet with tangled strings. She regained her balance and came on, screaming all the while. What looked like a scrawny ten-year-old boy stepped on one of the flaring candles without a glance.

Valentine watched as the human wave approached, dribbling bodies as the Wolves' bullets struck. He knew the Ravies served as a distraction for something else lurking in the night. He felt the Reaper stalking his mind, approaching from the darkness, even if he could not see its body.

The Reaper came, full of awful speed and power. A cloaked figure charged into the light, seeming to fly over the ground in a blur of motion.

"Hood!" a Wolf shouted, squeezing off a shot and working the bolt on his rifle. The caped and cowled figure, still twenty feet from the barn, made a leap and crashed bodily through the old planks and beams as if they were papier-mâché.

The Reaper landed on all fours, arms and legs splayed like a spider. Before a gun could be turned in its direction, it sprang at the nearest Wolf, a shovel-bearded wedge of a man named Selbey. It was upon him before he could bring up his gun. The Hood's satchel-size mouth opened to display pointed ebony teeth. Large, inhuman jaws sank into Selbey's arm, thrown up in defense. The Wolf's scream matched those from outside as the thing opened its mouth to bite again.

Chaos reigned as the refugees began running. Wolves at the exits had to restrain them, taking up precious seconds when they should have been employing their guns. One Wolf pumped shot after shot, working the lever-action rifle from his hip, into the Reaper pressing Selbey to the detritus-covered floor. The Reaper fed, immune to the bullets hitting its heavy robes.

Valentine grabbed a candle flare from Patel's two remaining at the south door. He thrust the candle into the lantern, waiting for it to sputter into life. It caught after an eternity, and he ran toward the Hood.

The thing raised its blood-smeared face from its twitching victim to receive the burning end in its eye. It howled out its fury and pain and slapped the candle out of Valentine's hand with the speed of a cougar's paw. The flaming wand fell to the ground as the thing rose. Behind it, the Reaper's menacing black shadow filled the wall of the barn. Death reached for

Valentine, who struggled to draw his blade from its sheath in time.

A bullet caught the Reaper in the armpit, staggering it. A heavier leather-clad missile hurled itself onto the Hood's back. Patel's body blow brought it down, and using every ounce of his formidable strength, the sergeant managed to keep it on the floor until Valentine brought his machete onto the back of its neck. The blade bit deep into flesh and bone, but failed to sever the head. Oily, ink-black ichor poured from the wound, but still the thing rose, rolling Patel off with a heave. The sergeant fought on and bore down on one arm, ignoring the deadly teeth opening for him. Valentine lashed out again with his machete, catching it under the jaw. The Reaper's head arced off to land with a thud next to Selbey's lifeless body.

"Jesus, they're in, they're in!" someone shouted.

A few Ravies, ghoulishly white in the glare of the candle, clambered through the gap in the wall created by the decapitated Reaper. Valentine shifted his parang to his left hand and reached for his pistol. The empty holster turned the movement into comic mime as he realized he had dropped the gun while getting the candle. But other Wolves drew their pistols, snapping off a shot at the shrieking forms.

The screaming grew into a chorus: a Ravie plunged in among the families. Valentine rushed to the corner to find the howling lunatic pinned against the wall by a man who'd had the presence of mind to grab an old pitchfork when the fight started. The Ravie had both hands on the haft of the weapon, trying to wrench the tines out of her belly, when Valentine came in, swinging his parang to strike and strike and strike again until she sank lifeless to the floor, at long last silent.

The screaming outside had ceased. The Wolves opened ammunition pouches and took bullets from belts and bandoliers. A final bullet or two ended the spasms of the few crawling, crippled targets still living and therefore still dangerous. The men in the loft called downstairs, in anxiety over their comrades. Valentine ignored the chatter and saw with a kind of weary grief that one of the wives had been bitten by the impaled Ravie. He went to check on Patel. The husky sergeant was on his feet, one arm hanging limp and useless, Valentine's pistol in his working hand.

Patel handed the pistol back to the lieutenant. "Quiet, up there! And keep your eyes peeled," the sergeant shouted at the uncomprehending floorboards above. He held his hurt arm closer to his body, grimacing.

"Broken collarbone, I think," he explained. "Could be my shoulder is out, as well. Are you okay, sir?"

"Hell, Patel, enough is enough. Next it'll be 'I hope you liked your drink.' Let's get that arm in a sling, for a start." Valentine motioned an idle Wolf over to help his sergeant. He saw another of his men bandaging the Ravie bite on the woman as her anxious family crowded around. "We've got a widower there who doesn't know it yet," he said, sotto voce. His sergeant nodded with sad understanding, and Valentine thought of Patel's family. They had been taken by the Raving Madness five years ago.

The lieutenant walked through his shaken command, checking on his men, and came into the corner sheltering the escapees. He shot a significant glance at his Wolf attending to the woman; the man caught the hint and nodded. "The bleeding's stopped already, sir."

"Quick action, Mosley. Grab someone and get that"—he pointed at the lifeless Ravie—"out of here."

The candles outside were sputtering out. Valentine walked over to the ladder, intending to check with Gonzalez upstairs . . .

. . . when the floor suddenly tilted beneath his feet. Thrown to the floor, he saw an albino-white arm open a heavy trapdoor in an explosion of dirt, dried leaves, and twigs.

The barn had a cellar.

The Reaper got halfway out the trapdoor as the bullets zipped over Valentine's head. His Wolves, still keyed up from the fight, aimed their guns with lethal accuracy and pumped bullet after bullet into the yellow-eyed creature. Under the point-blank cross fire from five directions, the black-robed shape jerked wildly and fell back into the basement.

"Grenades," Valentine bellowed. Three of his men gathered at the trapdoor, now shooting down with pistols.

Striking matches or using the lanterns, two Wolves lit fuses on the bombs and hurled them down the square hole. Valentine grabbed the trapdoor and flung it shut. The rusty hinges squealed their complaints.

The first explosion threw the door forever off its aged fastenings, and the second boomed with an earsplitting roar. Smoke mushroomed from the square hole.

A Reaper sprang from the gap like something a magician had conjured from the smoke, arms nothing but two tarry stumps, and head a bony mask of horror. Even with its face blown off, the Reaper was on its feet and running, seeming to favor them with a splay-toothed grin. The guns rang out again, but the creature fled through the exit, knocking Patel aside like a bowling pin in the path of a cannonball as the sergeant attempted another body blow. A tattered and smoldering cape streaming out behind it as it ran, the Reaper disappeared into the darkness.

Some of the children had hands over their ears, screaming in pain. Valentine tried to shake the drunken sensation that had come over him, but it was no use. The acrid air of the barn was too thick to breathe. He staggered to the doorjamb and vomited.

An hour later, with the barn cleared of bodies except for the unfortunate Selbey, who lay in his poncho in the empty blackness of the blasted cellar, Gonzalez again shared his discovery with Valentine. His scout, after asking for permission to speak privately in the loft, presented him with a filthy strip of cloth.

Valentine examined the excrement-stained yellow rag with tired eyes.

"Uncle smelled something, sir, you know? He told me to check the area where we heard the bloodhounds real careful after everyone pulled out. I found this in the bushes where the Red River people . . . er, relieved themselves, sir," Gonzalez elaborated, half whispering.

He read the semiliterate scrawl by lantern light: "N + W, barn, about twenty gun, yrs trly."

Betrayal. That explains a thing or two. But which one is "yrs trly"? Valentine wondered. He remembered a couple of the farmhands had hurried to the bushes as they assembled for the flight to the barn. He hadn't thought anything of it at the time: the fear in the night had turned his own bowels to water, as well.

He gathered three Wolves from downstairs and explained what he wanted to do when the sun came up.

Mallow and his reserve platoon trotted up to the barn, just beating the sun. He suppressed the urge to hug the panting Lugger, who looked as tired as Valentine felt.

The senior lieutenant responded to Valentine's report with a low whistle. "One in the basement, huh? You had some bad luck, rookie. But it could have been worse. Good thing the

Kurian pulling the strings wasn't good enough to work more than one at a time." Mallow shook Valentine's hand, then offered the junior lieutenant a congratulatory swig of busthead from a silver flask.

Valentine tippled gratefully, remembering his mother's warning about men who drank before noon. Well, the sun wasn't up yet, so it didn't quite constitute morning.

"The Kurian had a little help, sir. Someone was sending the Hoods love notes. They knew we'd make for that barn; they brought up the Ravies and had everything ready."

"Aw, Christ," Mallow groaned. "Some clodhopper thought he'd be up for a brass ring, huh?"

"Seems like."

"What a welcome to Free Territory. One of their own dangling from a tree. No, I'll let them handle it back at the fort."

"I lost a Wolf, sir. They'll want quick justice." Valentine had hoped they would settle for a formal trial later, but the looks on his detail's faces when he told them why he wanted the farmers searched made him doubtful.

Mallow's face clouded over. "They'll obey orders, Valentine, or they'll see some quick justice. Tell 'em that, if you must."

"Yessir."

Mallow stepped inside the barn. The sky to the east was pinkening, ending the longest night of Valentine's young life. He nodded to his waiting Wolves, and they roused the sleepy farmers and began checking pockets and packs.

They had barely begun when the guilty party revealed himself. A sixteen-year-old boy, the one whose mother had been bitten the previous night, bolted for the gaping south doors. Two of Mallow's Wolves interposed and restrained him. Valentine found a charcoal pencil wrapped in more rags of cloth, as well as a small compass.

"A kid, whaddaya know," one of the men sighed. A couple of others swore.

The boy broke down, alternating threats and curses in between sobs. His ashen-faced father held his distraught wife. She already trembled with the weakness of the first stage of the disease that would claim her life within two or three more days, when she would have to be shot like a rabid dog. Mallow and Patel ignored the grieving parents and questioned the boy in time-honored good cop–bad cop fashion.

"Who put you up to this, boy?" Mallow asked, leaning to put his face below the boy's downcast eyes. "What did they promise you? If it were up to this guy here, he'd snap your neck with his good arm. I can't help you unless you talk to me. Tell you what, you leave another note, only write on it what we tell you, and you won't get hanged. Can't promise anything else, but you won't hang."

The boy's fear exploded into anger. "You don't get it, do you? They're in charge, not you. They make the laws. They run the show. An' when they get tired of you, you'll be emptied an' the Grogs'll have the leftovers! Them that don't want to die gotta go along with orders."

Valentine, sick with fatigue, stepped outside to watch the dawn. As the yellow-orange sun burned through the morning haze, he wondered what doom of fate had selected him to be born into such a fucked-up time.

Two

Northern Minnesota, the thirty-ninth year of the Kurian Order: He grew up in a pastoral setting among the lakes of upper Minnesota. David Stuart Valentine was born during one of the interminable winters in a sturdy brick house on Lake Carver. The scattered settlements of that area owed their survival not so much to resistance as to inaccessibility. The Kurians dislike cold weather, leaving the periodic sweeps and patrols of this area to their Quislings. The Reapers come only in the summer in a macabre imitation of the fishermen and campers who once visited the lakes between May and September.

In the first few years after the Overthrow, myriad refugees supported themselves amid the abundant lakes and woods of what had been known as the Boundary Waters. They exterminated the remaining disease-infested Ravies hotzones, but the settlers refused aid to would-be guerrilla bands, as most of them had already tasted Reaper reprisals elsewhere. They wished nothing more than to be left alone. The Boundary Waters people were ruled only by the weather. A frantic period of food storage marked each fall, and when snow came, the families settled in for winter, ice-fishing for survival, not sport. In summer they retreated into the deep woods far from the roads, returning to their houses after the Reapers were again driven south by the cold.

Young David's family reflected the diaspora that found refuge in the region. He had a collection of Scandinavian, American Indian, and even Asian ancestors in a family tree whose roots stretched from Québec to San Francisco. His mother was a beautiful and athletic Sioux from Manitoba, his father a former navy pilot.

His father's stories made the world a bigger place for David than it was for most of the children his age. He dreamed of flying across the Pacific Ocean the way some boys dream of being a pirate or building a raft and drifting down the Mississippi.

His early life came to an abrupt stop at the age of eleven, on a cool September day that saw the first frost of the northern fall. The family had just returned from summer retreat to their home, but a Quisling patrol or two still lingered. Judging from the tire tracks that David found later, two trucks—probably the slow, alcohol-burning kind favored by rural patrols—had pulled up to the house. Perhaps the occupants were also liquor fueled. The patrol emptied the larder and then decided to spend the rest of the afternoon raping David's mother. Attracted by the sound of the vehicles, his father had died in a hail of gunfire as he came up from the lakeshore. David heard the shots while gathering wild corn. He hurried home, accompanied by a growing fear that the shots had come from his house.

David explored the too-silent house. The smell of tomatoes, which his mother had been stewing, filled the four-room cabin. He found his mother first, her body violated, her throat slit. Out of spite or habit, the intruders had also killed his little brother, who had just learned to write his own name, and then his baby sister. He did not cry—eleven-year-old men don't cry, his dad said. He circled the house to find his father lying dead in the backyard. A crow was perched on the former pilot's shoulder, pecking at the brains exposed by a baseball-size hole blown out of the back of his skull.

He walked to the Padre's. Putting one foot in front of the other came hard; for some reason he just wanted to lie down and sleep. Then the Padre's familiar lane appeared. The priest's home served as school, church, and public library for the locals. David appeared out of the chilly night air and told the cleric what he had heard and seen, and then offered to walk with the Padre all the way back to his house. The saddened priest put the boy to bed in his basement. The room became David's home for the remainder of his adolescence.

A common grave received the four victims of old sins loosed by the New Order. David threw the first soil onto the burial shrouds that masked the violence of their deaths. After the funeral, as little groups of neighbors broke up, David walked away with the Padre's hand resting comfortingly on his shoulder. David looked up at the priest and decided to ask the question that had been troubling him.

"Father Max, did anyone eat their souls?"

Every day at school they had to memorize a Bible verse, proverb, or saying. Often there was a lot of writing down and not much memorizing. Sometimes the lines had something to do with the day's lesson, sometimes not. The quotation prescribed for the rainy last day of classes had an extra significance to the older students who stayed on for a week after the grade-schoolers escaped the humid classroom for the summer. Their special lessons might have been called the "Facts of Death." The Padre hoped to correct some of the misinformation born of rumor and legend, then fill in the gaps about what had happened since the Overthrow, when *Homo sapiens* lost its position at the top of the food chain. The material was too grim for some of the younger students, and the parents of others objected, so this final week of class was sparsely attended.

The Padre pointed to the quotation again as he began the afternoon's discussion. Father Maximillian Argent was made to point, with his long graceful arms and still-muscular shoulders. Sixty-three years and many long miles from the place of his birth in Puerto Rico, the Padre's hair was only now beginning to reflect the salt-and-pepper coloring of age. He was the sort of pillar a community could rest on, and when he spoke at meetings, the residents listened to his rich, melodious, and impeccably enunciated voice as attentively as his students did.

The classroom blackboard that day had fourteen words written on it. In Father Max's neat, scripted handwriting, the words THE FARTHER BACKWARD YOU CAN LOOK, THE FARTHER FORWARD YOU CAN SEE.——WINSTON CHURCHILL were written with Euclidean levelness on the chalkboard. Normally Valentine would have been interested in the lecture, as he liked history. But his eye was drawn out the window, where the rain still showed no sign of letting up. He had even used the leaky roof as an excuse to shift his desk to the left so that it pressed right against the wall under the window, and the chipped white basin where his desk usually sat was now full enough with rainwater falling from the ceiling to add a plop every now and then as punctuation to the Padre's lesson. Valentine searched the sky for a lessening of the drizzle. Today was the final day of the Field Games, and that meant the Cross-Country Run. If the Councilmen canceled the games because of weather, he would finish where he now stood in the ranking: third.

The youths came from all over the Central Boundary Waters to compete against others in their age group each spring as part of the general festivities that ended the winter and began the great Hideout. This year Valentine had a shot at winning first prize. Second and third place got you a hearty handshake and an up-close look at the trophy as whoever came in first received it. The prize for boys aged sixteen to eighteen was a real over-under shotgun, not a hunting musket, and fifty bird-shot shells. A good gun meant a bountiful hunting season. The Padre and David needed all the help they could get. The Padre taught more or less for free, and Valentine didn't earn much at his job chopping endless cords of firewood for the neighbors. If Valentine won, he and Father Max would be dining on goose, duck, and pheasant until well after the snow flew.

"Mr. Valentine," Father Max said, interrupting David's mental meal. "Please rejoin the class. We're talking about a very important subject . . . your heritage."

"Funny," whispered Doyle from a desk behind. "I don't remember him saying anything about what a stupid son of a bitch you are."

Plop, added the basin to his right.

The Padre cracked his knuckles in a callused fist; profane jokes out of Doyle were as natural as water dripping into the classroom when it rained. He evidently chose to ignore both, keeping his eyes fixed on David.

"Sorry, Father," Valentine said with as much contrition as a seventeen-year-old boy could summon.

"You can apologize to the class by reviewing what you know about the Pre-entities."

Another whisper from behind: "This'll be short."

The Padre shifted his gaze. "Thank you for volunteering two hours of your free time to school maintenance, Mr. Doyle. The roof and I are grateful. Your summary, Mr. Valentine?"

Plop.

Valentine could hear Doyle slump in his seat. "They go back to before the dinosaurs, Father. They made the Gates, those doorways that connect different planets. The Interworld Tree. It's how the Kurians got here, right?"

Father Max held up his hand, palm outward. The thumb was missing from his right hand, and his remaining fingers were misshapen. They always reminded Valentine of tree roots that could not decide which way to grow. "You are getting ahead of yourself, Mr. Valentine. Just by sixty-five million years or so."

The Padre sat down on his desk, facing the eight older students. The classroom should have contained forty or so, had all the teenagers within a long walk attended. But education, like survival, depended on initiative in the disorganized Boundary Waters.

Valentine settled in for a good listen, as he always did when the Padre parked himself on the desk in that fashion. The rest of the class, not having the qualified joys of living with the Padre, did not know as he did that when the Padre perched there, he was imitating another teacher from his own youth, a determined San José nun who had woken a hunger for learning in the ganja-smoking teen he still had trouble imagining the Padre had been. His mind insisted on wandering off to the games.

"We know so very little about these beings, the Pre-entities, except that they predate everything else we do know about life on Earth," the Padre began. "I was telling you about the Doors yesterday. No, Mr. Doyle, not the Old World rock-and-roll band. I know we think of these Doors as a terrible curse, the cause of our trouble. Everything we know would be different if they had never been opened. But long ago they were marvelous things, connecting planet after planet in the Milky Way as easily as that door over there connects us with the library. We call the builders of this Interworld Tree the Pre-entities, because we are not even sure if they had bodies—in the sense that you and I have bodies, that is. They probably didn't need our little chemical engines to keep going. But if they did have bodies, they were big. Some of the Doors are said to be as big as a barn.

"We know they existed because they left the Interworld Tree and the Touchstones. A Touchstone is like a book that you can read just by laying your hand on it. They don't always work correctly on our human minds, however; there are always a few who touch them and go insane from the experience, which I find easy to believe. But a person with the right kind of mind who touches one has what we might call a revelation. Like the downloads I was telling you about when we were talking about the Old World's computer technology."

The Padre looked down and shook his head. Valentine knew the Padre had a love–hate relationship with the past; when he was in his cups, he would sometimes rave about the injustices in the Old World, which had the ability to feed and clothe all of its children but had chosen not to. This might lead to tears over missing something called McDonald's fries dipped into a chocolate shake, or overpriced souvenir T-shirts.

"The Pre-entities existed by absorbing energy; a very special kind of energy, produced by living things. Plants make it at a very low level. All animals, us included, possess it to a greater extent. This energy, which we call a 'vital aura' for lack of a better term, is determined by two factors in an organism: size and intelligence. The latter predominates. A cow, despite its size, gives off a smaller vital aura than a monkey. A monkey being the 'brighter' of the two in more ways than one, if you understand."

A student held up her hand, and the Padre stopped.

"You talked about this before, but I never got if the aura

was your soul or not. Is it, I mean?" Elaine Cowell was a thirteen-year-old, but so bright she stayed for all the lessons with the older teens.

The Padre smiled at her. "Good question, Miss Cowell. I wish I had an absolute answer. My gut feeling is that a vital aura is not your soul. I think your soul is something that belongs to you and God, and no one else can interfere with it. I know some people say it is your soul that gets fed on, but there is no way we can ever know that. I think of the vital aura as being another special kind of energy you give off, just as you give off heat and an electromagnetic field."

Elaine fixed her gaze at an invisible point sixteen inches in front of her face, and Valentine sympathized. She was also an orphan; the Reapers had taken her parents five years ago in Wisconsin. She now lived with an aunt who scratched out a living weaving blankets and repairing coats. The others sat in silence. Whenever the Padre discussed the Facts of Death with the older students, their normal restlessness vanished.

"So why aren't they still around? I thought that energy stuff was what made the Kurians immortal?" another student asked.

"Evidently our Creator decided that no race can live forever, no matter how advanced their science. When they started to die, we think it caused a terrible panic. I wonder if beings who are nearly immortal are more afraid of death, or less? They needed more and more vital aura to keep going, and they cleaned out whole planets in their final years, trying to stave off the inevitable. They probably absorbed all the dinosaurs; the two events seem to have happened at the same time. In their last extremity, they ate each other, but it was all for nothing. They still died. With no one to maintain their portals, the doorways began to shut down over the thousands and thousands of years that followed. But pieces of their knowledge, and the Interworld Tree itself, survived for a new intelligence to find later on."

Thunder rumbled outside, and the rattling of the rain increased.

"So we call the Pre-entities Kurians now?" a young woman asked.

"No. The Kurians come from a race called the Lifeweavers. They found the remnants of the Pre-entity civilization. They pieced some of their history and technology back together and made use of what they could understand, like the barbarians who moved into Rome. We get the word *Lifeweaver* from their own language; it refers to those of the race who visit other worlds and interpopulate them. Just as man takes his livestock, crops, and orchards with him when he migrates, but is willing to adapt if something better is found, so did the Lifeweavers in their colonization of the Interworld Tree. Lifeweavers live a long, long time . . . many thousands of years. Some believe they were created by the Pre-entities as builders, but it seems strange that beings with a vital aura as strong as theirs would have survived the extinction throes of the Pre-entities.

"These Lifeweavers reopened the portals to our Earth about the time we were discovering that food tasted better if it was cooked first. Our ancestors worshiped them. Most of them were content to be teachers, but it seems a few wanted to be more. A Lifeweaver can appear to us as a man or woman, or an elephant or a turtle if it wants, so they must have seemed as gods to our poor forefathers. They can put on a new shape as easily as we can change clothes. Maybe they threw thunderbolts for good measure. I think they inspired many of our oldest myths and legends.

"They adopted us in a way. As we grew more and more advanced, they took a few of us to other worlds. I've been told humans are living on other planets even now. If so, I pray their fortune has been better than ours. The Lifeweavers could do anything they wanted with DNA. They could make useful creatures to suit themselves, or modify a species as they required. We know they liked making beautiful birds and fish to decorate their homes; some of these still live on our planet today."

The Padre smiled at them. "Ever seen a picture of a parrot? I think they tinkered with them a little bit." He paused in thought.

Valentine had seen pictures of parrots. Right now the only birds in his mind were pheasants, tender young pheasants rising in a flutter of wings. He could see them in his newly won shotgun sight. He'd heard the Kolchuks' lab–pointer pair had had another litter; maybe he could still get a puppy.

The Padre droned on.

Doyle held up his hand, serious for once. "Sir, why tell us all this now? We've known about vampirism and so on since we were kids. Okay, maybe some of the hows and whys were wrong. What difference does it make how any of it got started? We still have to hike out every summer—and every fall, a couple of families don't come back."

The Padre's face crumbled. He looked ten years older to Valentine.

"No difference, no difference at all. I wish every day of my life something could make a difference. Mr. Doyle, class, you are young, you've lived with it your whole lives, and it is not such a weight for you. But I remember a different world. People complained a lot about it, but in hindsight it was something like Eden. Why talk about this now? Look at the quotation on the board. Churchill was right. By looking back, we may often see the future. I tell you this because nothing lasts forever, not even those who will do anything to become immortal. They're not. The Kurians will eventually die, just like the Pre-entities. Once an old king paid to have a piece of knowledge carved deep in the side of a monument, something that would always be true. The wisest man of the age told him to carve the words 'This, too, shall pass.' But who shall pass first, us or them?

"We will not live to see it, but one day the Kurians will be gone, and the Earth will be clean again. If nothing else, I want you to take that certain knowledge from me and carry it with you wherever you go."

The rain left shortly after the rest of Valentine's school-mates did. He hurried to empty the various bowls, basins, and pails brimming with rainwater from the leaky roof, then headed for the kitchen. Father Max sat at the battered table, staring at the bottom of an empty glass. He was already recorking the jug.

"David, telling that story always makes me need a drink. But the drink I have always wants another to keep it company, and I should not do that. At least not too often." He replaced the jug in its familiar spot on the shelf.

"That stuff's poison, Father. I wouldn't use it to kill rats; it'd be too cruel."

The old man looked up at David, who poured himself the last of the cow's vintage from the morning milking. "Isn't the race today?"

Valentine, now dressed in faded denim shorts and a leather vest, bolted a piece of bread and washed it down with mouth-fuls of milk. "Yeah, at four or thereabouts. I'm glad the rain stopped. In fact, I better get moving if I'm going to walk the trail before the race."

"You've been running that trail since April. I'd think you'd know it by now."

"All the rain is going to make the footing different. Might be muddy going up the big hill."

Father Max nodded sagely. "David, did I ever tell you that your parents would have been proud of you?"

Valentine paused for a second as he laced his high moccasins. "Yes. Mostly after you've had a drink. It always makes you soft."

"You're a bit of the best of both of them. You've got his quick thinking and dedication, and enough of your mother's looks and humor and heart to soften his edges. I wish he—they—could see you today. We used to call the last day of school *graduation,* you know that?"

"Yup. I've seen pictures and everything. A funny hat and a piece of paper that says you know stuff. That would be great, but I want to get us that gun." He moved to the door. "You going to be in the public tent?"

"Yes, blessing the food and watching you collect first prize. Good luck, David."

He opened the patched, squeaky screen door and saw two bearded men coming up the path from the road. They were strangers to him. They looked as though they had spent every moment of their adult years in the elements. They wore buckskin top to bottom, except for battered, broad-brimmed felt hats on their heads. They bore rifles in leather sheaths, but they did not have the shifty, bullying air that the soldiers of the patrols did. Unlike the soldiers charged by the Kurians with keeping order in the Boundary Waters, these men moved with a cautious, quiet manner. There was something to their eyes that suggested wary wild animals.

"Father Max," Valentine called into the house without taking his eyes off the men. "Strangers coming."

The men paused, smiling with tobacco-stained teeth. The

taller of the two spoke: "Don't let the guns scare you, boy. I know your people."

Father Max emerged from the house and stepped out into the rain-soaked yard with arms outstretched. "Paul Samuels," he half shouted, walking out to embrace the tall man in his gangly arms. "You haven't come this way in years! Who is this with you?"

"My name's Jess Finner, sir. I've sure heard about you, sir."

The Padre smiled. "That could be good or bad, Mr. Finner. I'd like you both to meet my ward, David. He's the son of Lee Valentine and Helen Saint Croix."

"I knew your father, David," said the one named Samuels. Valentine saw memories lurking in the brown pools beneath his wrinkled brow. "Bad business, that day at his place. I saw you after the funeral. Took us four months, but we got the men that—"

"Let's not dredge up old history," the Padre interrupted.

Valentine caught the looks exchanged between the men and suddenly lost interest in the race and the shotgun.

The Padre patted his shoulder. "We'll talk later, David— that's a promise. Get going! But give my regrets to the Council at the public tent, and get back here as soon as you can. We're going to crack the seal on one of the bottles from the woodpile, and then you may have to put me to bed."

"Not likely," Samuels guffawed.

The Padre gave David his "I mean it, now" look, and Valentine headed off down the road. He still had time to look over the two-mile course if he hurried. Behind him, the three men watched him go, then turned and walked into the house.

The smell of cooking food greeted him at the campgrounds. The public tent, a behemoth, six-pole structure that saw weddings, baptisms, auctions, and meetings at the start of every summer, was hidden in a little glade surrounded by lakes and hills, miles from the nearest road and out of sight from any patrol in vehicles. The Hideout Festival featured sports and contests for the children and teenagers. A wedding or two always added to the celebratory atmosphere. The adults learned crafts; held riding, shooting, and archery competitions; and then feasted on barbecue each evening. Families brought their special dishes for all to share, for in a region of dreadful, cold winters and summers spent in hiding, there were few chances for large gatherings. With the festival's conclusion, the people would scatter into the woods and lakes to wait out the summer heat, hoping that the Reapers would comb some other portion of the Boundary Waters in search of prey.

The race felt less a sport and more of a chore to Valentine by the time he reached the crowd. The people, horses, wagons, and traders' stalls normally fascinated him, but the arrival of the two strangers held his thoughts in a grip that startled him. His desire for a ribbon and a shotgun in front of an applauding crowd seemed meaningless when compared with meeting a man who had known his father.

He resigned himself to running the race anyway. The course looped out in a horseshoe shape around Birch Lake. Usually a mud-rimmed half-swamp by mid-May, Birch Lake had swollen with the heavy rains until its fingers reached up almost to the public tent.

Valentine greeted Doyle and a few other acquaintances from school. He had many acquaintances but no close friends. As the Padre's live-in student, responsibilities in keeping the house and school running prevented him from forming attachments, and if that weren't enough, his bookish habits made him a natural outsider on the occasions when he did mix

with the boisterous teenagers. He wandered off into the
woods along the two-mile trail. He wanted time to be alone
and to think. He had guessed right; the ground on the big hill
to the west of Birch Lake was slick with clay-colored mud.
He stood on the hill and looked out across the rippled surface
of the lake toward the public tent. A thought sprang from the
mysterious garden in his mind where his best ideas grew.

Fifteen boys participated in the race, though only a handful had enough points from the other Field Game events to
have a chance at the prize. They were dressed in everything
from overalls to leather loincloths, all tan and thin, tangle
haired and wire muscled.

"One to be steady," invoked Councilman Gaffley to the
rocking assortment of racers. "Two to be ready, and you're
off!"

A few of the boys almost stopped a hundred yards into the
race when Valentine made a sharp right turn off the trail,
heading for Birch Lake. He sprinted out onto a long spit of
land and thrashed his way into the water.

Valentine swam with lusty, powerful strokes, sighting on a
tall oak on the other side. This neck of the lake was 150 yards
or so across, and he figured he would be back on the trail
about the time the rest of the boys skidded down the muddy
hill.

And he was right, lunging dripping wet from the lake and
pounding up the trail before the lead boy, Bobby Royce, could
be seen emerging from the woods. David broke the string at
the finish line with a muddy chest to a mixture of cheers and
boos. Most of the boos came from families who had their
boys in the race. A frowning Councilman grabbed it off him
as if it were a sacred icon being defiled and not a piece of ratty
twine.

The other boys hit the finish line two minutes later, and the debate began. A few maintained that the important thing was to race from point A to point B as quickly as possible, and the exact route, land or water, didn't matter. The majority argued that the purpose of the race was a two-mile run cross-country, not a swim, which would be a different sport altogether. Each side increased its volume under the assumption that whoever made the most noise would win the argument. Two old men found the whole fracas hilarious, and they pressed a bottle of beer into David's palm, slapping him on the back and pronouncing him a first-rate sport for getting Councilman Gaffley so huffy he looked like a hen with her feathers up.

A hasty, three-councilmen panel pronounced Valentine disqualified from the race, but the winner of a special award in recognition for his "initiative and originality." Valentine watched Bobby Royce receive the shotgun and shells and wandered out of the tent. The barbecue smell made him hungry all over again. He grabbed a tin tray and loaded it from the ample spread outside. The homemade beer tasted vile. *Had beer been this bad in the Old World?* he wondered. But somehow it complemented the smoky-tasting meat. He found a dry patch of ground under a nearby tree and went to work on the food.

One of the backslapping oldsters approached him, cradling a varnished wooden case and dangling two more bottles of beer from experienced fingers.

"Hey there, kid. Mind if I sit with you a bit?"

Valentine smiled and shrugged.

Almost seventy years of creaky bones eased themselves up against the trunk of the tree. "Don't have much of an appetite anymore, kid. When I was your age, give or take, I could put away half that steer. Beer tastes just as good, though," he said, taking a pull from one of the open bottles and handing the other to Valentine.

"Listen, son, don't let 'em get you down. Gaffley and the rest are good men, in their way; they just don't like the unexpected. We've seen too much unexpected in our days to want any more."

Valentine nodded to the old man, mouth working on the food, and took a companionable pull from the fresh beer.

"My name's Quincy. We were neighbors, once. You were a squirt then. Your ma used to visit, especially when my Dawn was in her last illness."

Valentine's tenacious memory, jogged, came to his rescue. "I remember you, Mr. Quincy. You had that bicycle. You used to let me ride it."

"Yeah, and you did good, considering it didn't have any tires. I gave it away with everything else when she passed on. Moved in with my son-in-law. But I remember your mother; she used to sit with her. Talk with her. Tell jokes. Get her to eat up. You know, I don't think I ever thanked her, even the day we put my wife in the ground. . . ."

The old man took a long pull at the beer.

"But that's water under the bridge, we used to say. Ever seen a real bridge, boy? Oh, of course you have, the one on old Highway Two is still up, isn't it. Anyhow, I'm here to give you something. Seeing you with your hair all wet and shiny made me think of your mom, and since those old dorks won't award you the prize you deserve, I thought I'd give you one."

He fumbled with the greenish latch on the case and raised the lid. Inside, nestled on formed blue velvet, rested a gleaming pistol.

Valentine gasped. "Wow! Are you kidding? That gun would be worth something at the wagons."

The old man shook his head. "It was mine. Your daddy

probably had one just like it at some time or other. It's an automatic pistol, an old United States gun. I've kept it clean and oiled. No bullets, though, but it's a nine millimeter, which ain't too hard to find ammo for. I was going to give it to my son-in-law, but he's a putz. He'd just swap it for liquor, most likely. So I brought it here, figuring I'd trade it for some books or something. All at once I wanted to give it to you, where maybe it would do the most good. It's not too handy for hunting, but plenty comforting on a lonely road."

"What do you mean, Mr. Quincy?"

"Look, kid, er—David, right? I'm old, but not particularly wise. But I got old by being able to read people. You've got that look in you; I can tell you're hungry for something besides your food. Your dad was that way, too. You know he used to be in what we called the navy, and they went all over the world, which just suited him. After that, after all the shit came down, he did other things. He fought for the Cause just like the Padre. Did things he maybe even didn't tell your mother. You are a rolling stone, too, and all you need is a little push. What that push is gonna be, I can't say."

Valentine wondered if he had been pushed already. He wanted to talk to Paul Samuels, wanted to talk to him alone. He might as well admit it to himself, he had been thinking about asking to go with the men when they left the Padre's.

"This world is so cocked up I sometimes can't believe I'm still in it. You can do two things when something's wrong: fix it or live with it. All of us here in the Boundary Waters, we're trying to live with it, or hide from it, more like. We've gotten good at it. Maybe we should never have gotten used to it, I don't know, but there were always hungry kids to feed and clothe. Seemed better to hide, not rock the boat. But that's me, not you. You're a smart kid; that little stunt at the lake proved it. You know that the ones really in charge don't bother with us because we're not worth the trouble. Living with the Padre, you probably know that more than most. It's only a matter of time before they get around to us, no matter how deep in the woods we go. It's them or us. *Us* meaning human beings. Getting rid of them is work for the Cause."

David swallowed his food, but swallowing his mixed emotions was a much tougher proposition. Could he just take off? His vague plans for living in a lakeshore cabin in the company of books and fishing poles no longer applied or appealed, ever since Samuels and Finner had mentioned killing the patrollers who had turned the only world he'd known into piles of butchered meat. Odd that this old neighbor spoke as though he were privy to secret, half-formed thoughts. "Are you saying I should leave, join the resistance, take up the Cause?"

"A few of the boys your age are. It happens every year. Folks are quiet about it. If word of a son or daughter leaving got to the patrols, there'd be trouble. So it's usually 'Joe got married and is living with his wife's folks near Brainerd,' or some such. The councilmen discourage it, but Gaffley's own daughter ran away two years ago. Letters arrive every year, but he won't show them to anyone."

In a fit of contrariness, perhaps to show Quincy that he wasn't as astute a judge of human nature as the old man credited himself for being, David shrugged. "I can't say what I'll do, Mr. Quincy. I was thinking of going up to Lake of the Woods, building a boat . . . I love fishing, and they say next to no one lives there."

"Sure, son. And maybe twenty years from now, a patrol will come through, just like—"

"Hey," Valentine flashed, "that's not . . . fair."

"But it keeps happening. Just this spring, out by Grand Rapids. Eight people, that one. The way I hear it, it's a lot worse down south. Especially in the cities, where there's nowhere to hide."

Valentine was about to say, "That's not my problem," but held his tongue. An orphaned eleven-year-old had not been the Padre's problem that September afternoon so long ago, either. The Padre had faced the problem, took responsibility, because that is what decent people do.

It was an anxious young man who hurried to the Padre's that evening along familiar paths, carrying a burlap bag full of leftovers, an old empty pistol, and a head full of choices. The faces and animals at the public tent, the shores, hills, and trees—all pulled at him with promises of safety and security. *The woods are lovely, dark and deep . . .* He went into the backyard, checked on the animals, and began to chop wood. Turning cordwood into kindling always cleared his mind, even if it left his body wet and rubbery. He had been doing this chore for the Padre, and for a number of the neighbors in trade for sugar or flour, since his arrival five years ago. The solid feel of the ax in his hands, the *thwock* as the blade sank into the dried wood, absorbed the things that bubbled up from the dark corners of his mind.

He stacked the splintered results of his labor and went inside the house. He found the three men sprawled in the smoke-filled library around an empty bottle and a mostly empty jug. A small bag full of letters, including a couple from a young lady named Gaffley, sat on the Padre's nicked-up table, and a much larger bundle of letters lay tucked in one of the men's satchels, ready for the long return trip south. The one called Finner paged raptly through a battered volume titled *Classic Nudes through the Photographer's Lens*.

"David, you missed some boring catching up. And some even more boring drinking," Father Max said, not bothering to rise from his barely upholstered chair. "Did you win the race?"

"Sort of. It doesn't matter." He told the story. When he got to the part about being disqualified, Finner blew a raspberry. "I'd like to hear how you knew my father, Mr. Samuels."

Samuels looked at the Padre. "It's always Paul when I'm off my feet, son. When I was a kid about your age, give or take, your dad and I used to come up together from down south, just like me and Jess do now. We liked to keep in touch with the folks up here, and this old fraud. Well-lubricated philosophy sessions, you might say."

Valentine began distributing the bounty from the public tent. The men dug in with the enthusiasm of days spent on the road eating only what the wilderness provided.

"You fight them, right? The Kurians, the Reapers, the things they make? And the patrols, right?"

"Patrols are what we call the Quislings up here nowadays," the Padre interjected.

"Well, not all at once, son," Samuels answered. "In fact, we spend more time running scared from them than we do standing and fighting. We can hit them here and there, where we don't stand too much chance of getting hit back. When we're not doing that, we're trying to keep from starving. Ever drunk water out of a hoof print to wash down a couple handfuls of ground-up ants? Slept outside in the rain without even a tent? Worn the same shirt for a month straight? It really stinks, son. And I don't just mean the shirt."

Valentine stood as tall as he could, trying to add a couple of inches to his six feet one. "I'd like to join up, sir."

Father Max broke loose with a whiskey-fumed laugh. "I knew you could talk him into it!"

*   *   *

A week later, Father Max saw the party off on a warm, sun-dappled morning. He gave David an old musty-smelling hammock. It had uses other than rest; the Padre showed him how to roll his spare clothing up in it, then tie it across his back. By the time that was finished, other recruits who had collected over the past days began to shoulder their own burdens. Most carried backpacks bulging with preserved food. Valentine found that there were mouthfuls of words to be said, and no time or privacy to say them.

"God be with you, David," the graying old man finally said, tears wetting his eyes.

"I'll write. Don't worry about me. Jacob Christensen said he'd help out around here. He wants to teach the younger kids, too, so you don't have—"

The Padre held out his gnarled hand for a handshake. "Yes, David. I'll be fine. Soon you'll have more important things to worry about than getting the cow milked and the chickens fed. But the day I quit teaching the kids their ABC's is the day I'll be resting in the ground."

Samuels and Finner also shook hands with the Padre. How the men looked so alert was beyond Valentine; they seemed to be up every night drinking and talking, then visiting the trading wagons and surrounding homes in the day. David guided them, leading them on backwoods paths to the households that matched the names on the mail. One visit stood out, when Samuels had called on an old woman to deliver a few personal effects from her dead son, who had been a friend of Samuels's. Some intuition must have revealed her son's fate; she seemed neither surprised or grief stricken, and wasn't even preparing to leave her home for the summer. That night there had been more drinking and less laughter in the library.

Valentine began to learn on the first day of the journey south. He learned just how sore his legs could get. Though he had walked all day many times in his life, he had never done so with better than forty pounds of food, water, and possessions on his back at a pace set by a demanding sergeant. Other volunteers joined the group as they walked, one whom he knew. Gabriella Cho had gone to the Padre's school for a number of years; her rich black hair had fascinated him as he struggled through the awkward rites of puberty. Necessities at home kept her out of school past the age of fifteen. She had blossomed into a woman since Valentine had last seen her two years ago.

"Gabby, so you're coming, too," Valentine said, relieved to be finally taller than the doe-eyed young woman.

She looked at him once, twice. "Davy? Yeah, I'm taking the big trip."

"We missed you. Father Max had to start asking the rest of us the tough questions. It wasn't the same since you left."

"No, nothing's been the same since then," Cho responded. When she replied to further questions with one-word answers and downcast eyes, Valentine ended the conversation.

They spent the first evening at an overgrown crossroads more than a dozen miles south of the Padre's. They made camp and spent the next day talking, waiting, and nursing sore muscles. Another soldier showed up, escorting four more recruits. Two of the men were twin brothers, six-foot-six-inch blond giants. Valentine was surprised to learn their names were Kyle and Pete rather than Thor and Odin.

They repeated the process as they hiked south and west in easy stages—*easy,* that was, in the estimation of the men who bore the title *Wolves.* To Valentine, each day proved more exhausting than the last. By the time they reached the outskirts of Minneapolis, the group had swelled to thirty soldiers and over a hundred young men and women.

Lieutenant Skellen met them at a boat they used to cross the Mississippi. The lieutenant wore an eye patch so wide, it could have just as well been labeled an eye scarf, which mostly covered a crescent-shaped scar on the left side of his face. He had a dozens more recruits with him. Like the sergeant's they were in their teens or barely out of them, wide-eyed and homesick among new landscapes and unfamiliar faces. The travelers made a wide loop west around the Twin Cities, into empty lands teeming with prairie plants. One day they skirted a hundred-head herd of mountains of hair and hide, and the Wolves informed Valentine he was looking at his first buffalo.

"Ain't no weather can kill those big shaggies," Finner explained to his charges from the Boundary Waters. "The cows and wild horses gotta find low wooded spots when the snow is blowing out here, but them buffalo just form a big circle and wait it out."

Valentine picked up much more on that journey south. He learned he could make a compass by stropping an old double-edged razor blade against the back of his hand. Charged with static electricity, he suspended it from a string in a preserve jar to shield it from the wind. The little piece of metal found north after wavering indecisively like a bird dog sniffing the breeze. The recruits learned how and where to build a fire, using reflectors made of piled logs to hide the flame and direct the heat back toward the camper. He was taught about trench fires in high wind, and to always roast game skewered on a spit beside a fire, not over it, with a pan underneath to catch every drop of valuable fat. They learned how to make flour not only from wheat, but also with the flowerheads at the end of cattails and even with bark. Valentine pounded masses of bark in a pan of water, removed the fibers, and allowed it to settle, then poured off the water and toasted the pulpy starch on a stick. Even with salt it did not taste like much, but he found himself able to eat just about anything as the long weeks of walking wore on. Even more incredibly, he gained weight—though he was hungry from dawn to dusk.

When their packs emptied, they didn't always have to live off the land. They stopped at isolated farmhouses and tiny, hidden enclaves where the residents fed them. "I can't fight them, no sir, but I can feed them that does the fightin'," one goat-whiskered farmer explained, passing out bags of beans and corn flour to the hundred-odd campers on the banks of his stream.

He practiced with his pistol. The Wolves passed a hat around and collected two dozen bullets from the men with handguns that used the same ammunition as his. Some of the Wolves carried up to three sidearms in order to have a better chance at using bullets acquired from scavenging the deceased after a fight. He plinked away at old paint cans and weathered, paint-stripped road signs. It was during one of these marksmanship sessions in an old barn near camp that Valentine made an effort to talk to Sergeant Samuels. He had just knocked down a row of three aluminum cans, their colored labels illegible with the passage of years, and he was feeling pretty full of himself.

"You should try it with your left hand," the veteran suggested.

That cleaned the self-satisfied smile from Valentine's face in a hurry. "Why, Sergeant?"

"What if your right arm's busted, kid? What if someone just blew your hand off? I know, most instructors say it's a waste of time. Me, I think it's good to use your off hand. Makes your brain and body work different than it's used to."

Valentine set one of the cans back up, the sharp cordite smell tickling his nostrils. Feeling awkward, he raised the gun to eye level, feet shoulder-width apart. He sent the can flying with the second shot.

"May I?" Samuels asked.

Valentine passed him the gun. The sergeant examined it professionally.

"This was your dad's?"

"No, Sergeant. A—I suppose he's a neighbor—he gave it to me."

Samuels whistled. "A gun like this? It's in great shape. He must have thought a lot of you." He handed the gun back to Valentine.

"More like he thought a lot of my parents," Valentine mused. He paused for a moment, not sure how to phrase the question. "You seemed to think a lot of my father, too. I never knew about his life before he met my mother. He just said he traveled. "

Samuels glanced out the missing barn doors. The campsite was nearly empty; a heavy patrol was out under the lieutenant, and most of the recruits were taking advantage of the afternoon off to wash clothes and bathe in the nearby river.

"Yeah, David. I knew him. Not from way back, from before the skies filled with ash, that is. We met in Michigan, soon after all this shit started. I was younger than you then, maybe fifteen. Your dad and I were in this outfit; we called ourselves the Band. Fighting sometimes, hiding mostly. Cops, army guys; we had some coast guard sailors from Lake Michigan, even. The uniform was a hat with a piece of camouflage material sewn on it somewhere. God, what a hungry, sorry-looking bunch we were."

He shook his head and continued. "Even when we were blasting away at the Grogs, we couldn't really believe it. It was like something out of a sci-fi movie. No one knew shit about what was going on. I used to cry every damn night, it seemed to me. My parents were in Detroit when the nuke went off, you see. I learned one thing: tears make you feel better, but they don't change anything. You'll still be hungry when they dry up. Still be lonely."

The two men, one mature and weathered, the other a few years past puberty, wandered out of the barn and watched the sun descend into the western haze. Samuels nodded to a couple of the Wolves carrying out camp duties, and sat down on the corpse of an old green tractor. The space where the engine once sat gaped, an open wound with wires dangling.

"So you were both Wolves then?" Valentine omitted the *sir*, since they were both sitting.

"That came later. God, we didn't know what to think. The rumors we heard. Stuff about government experiments. That the Apocalypse was here and Satan walked the earth. People getting rounded up into camps like in the Nazi movies. Creatures from outer space. Turned out the truth was even weirder than the rumors, of course.

"Seems to me we were trying to make for this Mount Omega—there was talk that the vice president was there with what was left of the government and the joint chiefs. Only problem with it was no one knew where Mount Omega was. And then we came across the Padre.

"The Padre was working for someone named Rho. Not that he'd given up on Holy Mother Church, of course. He said this Rho was very special and was advising us on how to fight these things. We weren't interested. He said Rho was holed up in a safe place with food, liquor, women—I can't remember what all he promised us. None of us were interested in that, either. We'd been almost trapped and killed by those kind of promises before; the Quislings were already running us down. Then the Padre said this Rho knew what was going on. That got us. Especially your father. Some of the guys said that it was another trap, but I went with your dad, because he'd done a good job looking after me.

"It turned out this Rho was a Lifeweaver. He looked like a doctor from TV, really distinguished and everything. Guess you know who the Lifeweavers are, living with the Padre as you did. He gave us this speech about doors to other planets and vampires and vital auras and how the Grogs were things cooked up in a lab. We didn't buy any of it. I remember some of the guys started singing 'Row, Row, Row Your Boat,' sort of having fun with him. We thought he and the Padre were a couple of fuckin' nuts, you know? He said something to the Padre, and then, I swear to Jesus, he turns into this big gold eagle, with flames for wings. Circled over us like the *Hindenburg* going up. None of us knew whether to shit or shoot, I can tell you. Your dad told us to quiet down, and it turned back into a man again, or the image of one.

"Believe me, after that we listened. He told us about a group of Lifeweavers on a planet called Kur. They'd learned from some Touchstones the secret of how to live off vital auras. To beings with a life span of thousands of years, the chance to have a life span of millions must have been temptation, too much temptation. They violated the Lifeweaver law, their moral code, and started absorbing aura. They were trying to become immortal. In the interest of science, of progress. According to Rho, what they accomplished instead was to turn their world into a nightmare. They became what we call vampires, beings that are, to us, immortal. They do this through taking the lives of others. These rogue Lifeweavers, the Kurians, became the mortal enemies of the rest of their race.

"The Kurians smashed Lifeweaver society. They'd been transformed from researchers and scientists into something else. Cold. Ruthless. They used their skills to destroy all opposition. Overwhelmed, all the Lifeweavers could do was shut the portals to Kur. I guess it was in an attempt to keep the infection from spreading. But it was too late. A few Kurians had already escaped and were using the Interworld Tree to attack the whole Lifeweaver order. More doors were shut, but that only cut the Lifeweavers off, stopping them from organizing an effective resistance. It was like a houseful of people each hiding from a pack of killers in separate locked rooms instead of banding together to fight."

The sound of galloping hooves interrupted the story. A rider on one of the three horses in the group pulled up in the yard.

"Sarge," the rider said, walking his horse in a circle, "the lieutenant says there's a Grog column out east of here, heading this way. Mounted on legworms. Four legworms, twenty Grogs altogether. Not coming right for us, but definitely looking. You're supposed to gather everyone up and get to the Highway Forty-one bridge. If the lieutenant hasn't shown up by tomorrow, you're supposed to get everyone to Round Spring Cave."

"Got it, Vought. Now ride on down to the river and get the kids in gear. Slowly, don't scare them out of a year's life like you did me." The courier moved his roan off at a more sedate pace. "Damn, but the Grogs are far out from Omaha. Maybe someone saw us outside Des Moines. Lot of Quislings live in this area nowadays."

The sergeant gathered up the six Wolves remaining at the camp and issued orders. He motioned Valentine over.

"Sarge?"

Samuels pulled at the beard sprouting on his chin. "Valentine, we're going to be marching tonight. We're going to stick to an old road because I want to get some miles south of the Grogs, but that means I've got to have scouts and a rear guard.

I'm shorthanded, what with the lieutenant and his group out. That means you're getting what's called a battlefield promotion. I'm going to put you in charge of the ass end of the recruit column. Make sure everyone keeps up. It's going to be six kinds of dark tonight with these clouds, so it won't be easy. Lucky for us, we've been slacking all afternoon. Can you handle that?"

Valentine threw out his chest. "Yes, Sergeant!" But nervous sweat was running down his back.

Already a few recruits were returning to the area around the old barn, some with wet clothes plastered to their bodies. They broke camp. Usually the shouts and curses of the Wolves trying to get their green levy to move faster came from simple habit, but this time the words were in earnest.

They moved off into the deepening night. Before, they had done only night marches when arcing around Des Moines. The Grogs out of eastern Nebraska patrolled this area. They could follow a trail in day or night by sight, by ear, or by smell.

They moved at a forced march with Valentine bringing up the rear. They walked, and walked fast, for fifty minutes, then rested for ten. The sergeant kept up a punishing pace.

Complaints started after the fourth rest. By the sixth, there was trouble. A recruit named Winslow couldn't get to her feet.

"My legs, Val," she groaned, face contorted in pain. "They've cramped up."

"More water, less hooch, Winslow. The sarge warned you. Don't come crying to me."

The column began to move. Gabby Cho, who had been keeping Valentine company at the rear, looked at him wonderingly. Valentine waved her off. "Get going, we'll catch up."

Valentine began massaging Winslow's quadriceps and

calves. He tried to stretch one leg, but she moaned and cried something unintelligible into the dirt.

Insects chirped and buzzed all around in the night air.

"Just leave me, Val. When it wears off, I'll jog and catch up."

"Can't do it, Winslow."

He heard the three Wolves of the rear guard approach. It was now or never.

"Up, Winslow. If you can't walk, you can hobble. I'll help you. That's an . . . order." He reached out a hand, grabbed hers, and tried to pull her up. "But I'm not gonna carry you; you've got to move along as best you can."

The Wolves, rifles out of sheaths, looked at Valentine with raised eyebrows. They thought the situation humorous: a cramp-stricken recruit and would-be noncom trying to get her up by issuing orders with a voice that kept cracking.

"What's going on?" asked Finner, who was in the rear guard. "You two picked a helluva time to hold hands in the moonlight."

"She wants us to leave her," he explained.

"No, she doesn't," one of the Wolves demurred.

"Okay, Winslow," Valentine said, drawing his gun. "I've given you an order." *The word still sounds odd,* he thought. "And you're not obeying it. I'm not leaving you to get found and . . . made to talk about us or where we're going." *Do people really talk like this?* "So I guess I'll have to shoot you." He worked the gun's action and chambered a bullet.

"Val, you've got to be joking."

He looked at Finner, who shrugged.

Laboriously, she got to all fours. "See, Finner, I can barely crawl!"

Valentine's bullet struck the dirt a foot to the left of her ear, sending pebbles flying up into her face.

She ran and he followed, leaving the three Wolves chuckling in the darkness.

Samuels met them at the rear of the column. "Christ, Sarge, he tried to kill me," Winslow said, telling her end of the story. The sergeant planted a boot in her scrawny behind.

"Keep up next time, Winslow. Valentine," he barked, fist and palm crashing together.

The two men waited while the file drew away. "Don't ever use your gun, except as a last resort on the enemy. Not out of consideration to that non-hacker, but 'cause the Grogs can hear like bats. You get me?"

"Sorry, Sergeant. Only thing I could think of to get her moving. Her legs were cramped up, she said."

"Next time, kick 'em in the ass, and if that doesn't work, you come get me."

"I thought you said I was responsible for keeping them moving, sir."

Sergeant Samuels considered this, then fell back on old reliable. "Shut up, smart-ass. I didn't give you permission to pull a gun on anyone. Get back in line. Keep 'em moving."

Finner, drawing near with the rear guard, had a few words with the sergeant. Samuels doubled the column, returning to the front.

"Hey, Valentine," Finner said, jogging up to him. "Don't worry about it. You tried to get her on her feet, when most guys in your spot would've turned to us. Don't let the sarge BS you about the gunshot; a single shot is tough to locate unless you're next to it. Plus, that thing doesn't make all that much noise. I told the sarge that if I thought there was a problem, I wouldn't have let you do it."

"What did he say?"

"He said I shouldn't think too much, it was dangerous for

a guy like me. He added a few comments about my mother, too."

A cloud, shaped like a snail with an oversize shell on its back, began to cover the rising moon.

"I think he'd take a bullet for you though, Jess."

"Damn straight."

The lieutenant was not at the rendezvous. The tired recruits and tireless Wolves rested for four hours. At dawn, the sergeant sent Vought on his horse with three Wolves to scout the other side of the two-lane metal bridge spanning the Missouri. The land sloped upward as the wooded hills began beyond. Safety.

One of the rear guard, at a copse of trees half a mile up the highway, waved a yellow bandanna.

Samuels clapped Valentine on the back. "C'mon, son, you deserve to see this after last night. Everyone else, get across the bridge."

He jogged off northward along the edge of what was left of the road, and Valentine followed.

They reached the stand of trees. One of the Wolves had a spotting scope resting in the crotch of a young oak, pointed down the highway. Valentine could make out figures in the distance, but he was unwilling to believe what he saw.

Samuels looked through the scope. "They must have got wind of us last night. Not sure how many of us there are, so they're going back to report. Take a look at this freak show, Valentine."

He put his eye to the scope.

The Enemy.

They were apish figures sitting astride a long pencil of flesh. The mount was like a shiny, slug-skinned millipede. Hundreds of tiny legs moved too fast for the eye to follow, reminding him of a finger running across a piano keyboard. The riders, five in all, had armorlike gray skin that reminded Valentine of a rhinoceros's hide. Their shoulders were wide— almost two ax-handles across. They carried guns that looked like old Kentucky long rifles held pointed into the air like five waving antennae. Valentine wondered if he could even aim one of the six-foot weapons.

"They're even uglier from the front. Those are fifty-caliber single-shot breechloaders, Valentine, and they're handy with them," Finner elaborated. "They can blow your head off at a thousand yards if you're fool enough to be visible and not moving."

"Those are Grogs?" Valentine couldn't tear himself away from the eyepiece.

The sergeant retrieved the scope. "Those legworms are fun to stop, too. Brain is at the tail end, kind of like Finner here. Nothing up front but a mouth and some taste buds, I guess. Also like Finner here, come to think of it. Nothing short of a cannon will keep a legworm from coming at you. Good thing they're kinda slow."

"We try to pick off the riders, but the lead one always has a big riot shield, thick as tank armor," another Wolf said. "We have to get them from the side. One thing you do not want to ever see is about fifty of them coming at you in line abreast."

"That happened at the Battle of Cedar Hill," the sergeant put in. "We lost."

They made it across the Missouri on a Sunday. The sergeant led them in a prayer of thankfulness that their long journey was almost complete.

The next few days had briefer, harder runs mixed with walks and ten-minute breaks. They stayed away from the roads, and the Grog patrols stayed out of the hills, as each side considered this border region bushwhack ground. Around the campfire one night, Samuels told Valentine a little more about his father, how the Lifeweaver Rho had created a special body of men to fight the Reapers and their allies: the Hunters.

"He told us that these things had come to Earth once before, and some of Rho's people had taught men how to fight them. We'd forgotten it, except maybe as legends and myths garbled over the years. They took certain men and made them a match for what they were up against. Rho said he could do the same now, if we were willing to accept the bargain. But it would change us forever; we'd never be the same people again. Your father was willing. Soon he had the rest of us convinced. That was the beginning of a lot of hard years, son. But when you get to the Ozarks, you'll see it was worth it."

The lieutenant was waiting for them at Round Spring Cave. It was a road-hardened group that was welcomed by the officers in charge of training new blood in the Ozark Free Territory.

A welcoming banquet was spread out under the trees. Six weeks' worth of traveling on foot made the feast even more welcome. There was fresh bread, watermelons the size of hogsheads, meat from the fatted calf, the fatted hog, and the fatted chickens under the summer sky. Valentine ate an entire cherry pie at one sitting for the first time in his life. Another little cluster of would-be soldiers had arrived the day before, youths gathered from the Missouri valley in the Dakotas. They swapped good stories and bad in the pseudo–hard-bitten fashion of youth.

Gabby Cho shared a picnic table with Valentine under a spread of pine trees. The fresh, clean scent reminded him of Christmases before the death of his family. Valentine was experimenting with iced dandelion tea sweetened almost to syrup. The tea, ice (in summer!), and apparently plentiful sugar were all novelties to him.

"We made it, Davy," Cho said. She looked a little older now to Valentine; she had chopped her long black locks after the second day of hot marching out of the Boundary Waters. "I wonder what's next. You're in with these Wolf guys. Any idea what's up?"

"Not sure, Gab. I'd like to spend a few days sleeping."

Cho seemed unsure of herself. "Why'd you join up?"

Valentine shot her a questioning look. Cho had remained distant on the whole trip south whenever any personal topic arose. She politely rebuffed the other recruits' attempts to get to know her. .

He rattled his ice in the pewter mug, enjoying the sound and the cool wet feel. "You probably think revenge, because of the whole family thing. You know about what happened, right?"

"Yes, David. From some of the guys at class. I asked the Padre about it once. He told me to ask you, but I didn't want to do that."

"Well, it's not that."

Are you sure? a voice in his head asked.

"I know now my dad was with these Wolves. Maybe he would have wanted me to do it, too. He must have thought it was worthwhile; he spent a lot of years at it." He paused at a rustle overhead. Squirrels, attracted by the masses of food, were chasing each other around in the tree branches, sending flecks of bark falling onto the pair below. They were cute, but they made a decent stew, too.

"I want to make a difference, Gab. It's obvious, something's not right about the way things are. You know the Jefferson stuff we used to read, about being endowed by our Creator with inalienable rights? It's like those rights of ours have been taken away, even the right to live. We have to do something about it."

"As simple as that?"

"As simple as that, Gabby." He finished off the iced tea. "What about you?"

"Did you know I had a baby?" she blurted.

Valentine absorbed the news in awkward silence, then cleared his throat. "No, you just disappeared from school. Went north with your family, I thought."

"We kept it quiet. The father was a patroller. . . ." She read Valentine's eyes. "No, it wasn't like that. I knew him. His name was Lars. Lars Jorgensen," she said, giving him the feeling that she had not said the name in a long time.

"He used to give me stuff. Nice clothes, shoes. I never thought to ask where it came from. Looted stores in Duluth, I figured. One day he gave me a watch, a real working watch. I could tell there had been engraving on it, even though he had tried to scratch it off. I told him not to give me any more presents. He disappeared when I told him about the baby coming."

"Who's got the kid? Your mom, or—?"

"Scarlet fever got her. Last winter. Remember the outbreak? It hit around where you were living, too. It took . . ." Her words began to fade.

"Jesus, Gabby, I'm so sorry."

She wiped her eyes. "I think about it too much. I talked to the Padre after it happened. I thought maybe I didn't take care of her right, not on purpose, but because of how I feel about the father. I just didn't know. The Padre put it down to a lack of qualified doctors. Or if they're good, they don't have the equipment or medicines."

She took a cleansing breath of the Ozark air. "The Padre said that lots of people he knew put this kind of thing behind them by helping others. He gave me a lecture about the need for strong bodies and good minds, got talking about the Cause. Well, you know him."

"I wonder if I do. He didn't talk like that to me."

"I think he knew you would go south when the time was right," she said, smiling her old "I've got the right answer" smile from school. "I wanted to tell you all this for some reason. I feel like someone has to know the real me here."

The recruits got the word from Capt. "Steam Engine" Fulton. He gathered them on a little slope in a ring of trees. In this natural amphitheater, he informed the mass of youths from Minnesota, the Dakotas, and a smattering of Great Plains outposts that they would form a reserve regiment for now. They would receive uniforms. They would be armed and taught how to use those weapons. They would be paid. But for now, their main duties would be as a disciplined labor force, to be moved about the Free Territory helping the residents at harvest, improving roads, and learning about how things were organized on the Ozark Plateau. The harder they worked, the more there would be to eat over the winter.

The bloody minded and the phony tough guys groaned at the news. But Valentine grinned at Cho. A gun, a uniform, and something he had heard about but never seen: a paycheck. He couldn't wait to get started.

Three

The Ozark Plateau, the fortieth year of the Kurian Order: An island of sanity in the eye of a hurricane of death, the scattered farms and towns of the Ozarks are a civilization under siege. The heartland of the region is bordered by the blasted ruins of Little Rock to the south; in the west by a line extending from the western Ouachitas and Fort Scott to Springfield, Missouri; in the north by the far-flung foothills of the Ozarks and the Mark Twain Forest; and to the east by the Saint Francis River. Known by some as the Ozark Free Territory, and by the more military-minded as the Southern Command, the region supports three quarters of a million survivors. They are mostly farmers and ranchers connected by a network of poor roads and unreliable rivers flowing through the worn-down remnants of America's oldest mountains. Heavy stands of oak, hickory, and pine give these hills a bluish tinge, fed by cool streams winding through limestone gorges. The small mountains have bare patches of exposed felsite and rhyolite, rocky scars that symbolize the flinty hardness beneath the exterior of the inhabitants.

New farming centers have sprung up to replace the old. Little clusters of homes huddle together like medieval villages, stone walls with narrow loopholes facing the world; doors, windows, and porches facing the neighbors. The squatty settlements, perhaps built by men whose motto is

"Built for Safety, Not for Comfort," are linked by walls that do not divide home from home, but separate houses from the Outside. Corrugated aluminum barns and Quonset huts in the center of the ring of homes shelter livestock and machinery from the elements and thieves.

Some areas are electrified, and a substantial portion use natural gas. A ham radio network maintains communication. Telephones are back in action, but service is unreliable. The suspicious and tough-minded residents dislike strangers, and they sleep with rifles and shotguns handy. Pack traders traverse the area with stock on muleback or in gaily painted wagons, bringing basic necessities and few luxuries. Both necessities and luxuries are paid with barter, sometimes with greenbacks. Perhaps a measure of the success and fortitude of the inhabitants of what used to be southern Missouri and much of Arkansas is their acceptance of paper currency as being worth something. But as gold coins can be changed at two thousand or more dollars to the ounce, perhaps paper money's value is not what it once was. A regular judge advocate general, civilian relations (called the "Jagers" in a tone suggesting the word has an obscene connotation) Court rides circuit and brings some measure of order and law to the lives of the residents.

A few towns operate in the region, home to the artisans and technicians that keep society together. There is still singing in Branson, and a riverboat casino is in operation on the White River, paying out prizes in a system of Byzantine complexity. A governor resides in Mountain Home, Arkansas, trying to keep the roads open and mail running on shoestring budgets.

The Soldiery, as the residents know them, are concentrated in the Ouachita Mountains to the south, and in the broken Ozark ridges to the north. Ceaseless long-range patrols circle *the area, picking up information and refugees from all points of the compass. Strong cavalry reserves train constantly in the center of the region, ready to go to the border to slow invasion or destroy a raid. Although the Ozark Free Territory is relatively safe, it is not impregnable, as small holders and settlements in the boundary areas learn the hard way.*

The uniform combined the comfort of burlap with the durability of cheesecloth. How innocent cotton minding its own business could be turned into such a scratchy, sagging patchwork amazed Valentine. And the rifle! It was a single-shot breechloader, operated by a lever that flipped out the expended case of the bullet (woe to the recruit who failed to collect the hot brass thimble!) as it opened the chamber for the insertion of another round. At least, that was the theory. In practice, a few shots heated the action sufficiently to soften the thin brass encasing the heavy bullet, and Valentine became better at clearing jams than shooting the quickly fouled weapon. It kicked like a mule and aimed with the ease of a steel shovel. However, it had few moving parts and was within the manufacturing capacity of the Ozark Free Territory. The pay was the biggest joke of all. The recruits received multicolored military scrip, usable at the scattered-to-the-point-of-inaccessibility Southern Command Trading Post commissaries and accepted by a few pack traders desperate enough to take it in return for merchandise that failed the caveat emptor test everywhere else.

Fulton pushed them through two months' worth of drill in an exhausting six weeks. A few recruits bristled at the discipline and gave it up after the first week, either trying the dangerous trip home or finding work on the farms and ranches of the Territory. The majority finished their training under the supervision of bellowing NCOs. They ran and memorized the simple Common Articles that governed them and the Territory. They ran and sat through lectures about recent United States history, about the other knots of the resistance in Oregon, Arizona, the Appalachians, and New England. They ran and practiced with their rifles, as well as the captured support weapons and the simple cannon produced in inadequate factories. They ran and learned about camp life: brain tanning, drying and smoking meat, planting, foraging, and where to find medicinal herbs. They ran and learned about running.

Labor-Private Valentine learned to recognize the divisions of Southern Command: Guards, Militia, and Hunters. The largest body of professional soldiery was the Guards. They provided a solid core for the defense of the Ozark Free Territory. Sometimes the NCOs and officers were veterans of the Lifeweaver-trained Hunters. The Guards reinforced the Militia, the first line of defense for most communities. Most able-bodied adults, especially in the border areas, belonged to the Militia. They drilled with the Guards one day a month and stood ready to assemble at the call of drum, whistle, or siren. The Hunters carried war into the Kurian Zone. Trained by the Lifeweavers, they were divided into the Wolf, Bear, and Cat castes, each with a unique duty to the Cause. At talks given by members of the castes, Valentine learned that the Wolves carried out long-range patrol duties and maintained communication between the other Commands across North America. The Cats, rarely seen in the Territory, served as spies and saboteurs across the country, often leading double lives deep in the Kurian Zone. The Bears fought as the shock troops of the Cause, the Reapers' most fearless and skilled enemies. A Hunter usually started as a Wolf, and some of the best stayed as Wolves rather than moving to a different caste. There were a few that knew all three of the Hunter's Arts, as they named the Lifeweavers' disciplines. But all fought and sacrificed to-gether to bring mankind back to a place in the sun.

Valentine experienced the uneasy symbiotic relationship between the military and civilians when the labor regiment broke up into work squads and were dispersed to the sur-rounding farms for the harvest. The military could not under-stand why civilians seemed to begrudge every mouthful that went into the bodies of the men prepared to give their lives to protect them. The civilians failed to see why so much of what they produced, barely enough to feed the community in a good year, disappeared into a machine that often failed to keep them safe, and showed flashes of competence and effi-ciency only when gathering the agreed-upon 15 percent tithe.

The harvest came and went in a whirlwind of dawn-to-dusk labor. Valentine, in charge of Cho and eight other re-cruits between visits by an overworked officer, helped a dozen hardworking families in an enclave near the Arkansas–Missouri border. They built and repaired houses and barns, helped get in the crops, and then butchered and preserved the summer-fattened livestock. Most of the grain and corn filled a pair of silos at the center of the little defen-sive ring of homes called Weening, but they also hid a reserve in a series of clay-lined pits set between Weening's barns. They covered the pits with tarps and dirt, and hoped the vil-lage dog and cat population would protect the edible buried treasure from scavenging rodents.

Harvest Feast followed the weeks of frantic work. For three days the recruits participated in athletics while daylight lasted, then joined the farmers at long tables laden with roasts, hams, turkeys, chickens, side dishes, and desserts of every de-scription at dinner. Valentine sat next to Cho and gorged him-self, then retired distended to the Militia barracks above the town stable for the nightly farting contest.

With the food put away, literally and figuratively, a brief period of repair and maintenance ensured that the blockhouse homes and barns would keep their inhabitants in some measure of comfort for the winter. All the while, the oaks and hickories of the area turned red gold, until a period of dry, windy days whipped the leaves from their tethers and left the twigs dead and empty.

Rumor suggested that Valentine's team would soon pull back into winter camp in the Ouachitas. The labor crews in some of the neighboring villages had either left or were getting orders to do so. The farmers' generosity began to run out as soon as the last root cellar was filled and barrel of salted pork nailed shut. A family named Ross gave Valentine a padded overcoat stuffed with goose down and coated with a waxy waterproofing. Valentine had spent some of his few spare hours that fall raising the Ross children out of semiliteracy in well-remembered Father Max fashion, first reading to the kids from borrowed books and then having the children read the passages back to him.

Weening abutted Black River, a sandbar-clogged stream that flowed through a tunnel of black gum, oak, and river birch. Each night, even as the evenings grew cooler, Valentine waded out into one of the chilly, deeper pools for a bath. He had added another inch to his frame in the year since joining the Cause, and his long-limbed physique was leaving its boyish scrawniness behind. Lean muscle coiled up his arms and across work-widened shoulders brushed by his glossy black hair. His square-cut face was harder, and his bronze skin darker than he had ever seen before, but his eyes retained a youthful twinkle. Life in the Free Territory suited him: the work among the people of Weening was rewarding, and he had the memory of the Ross children swelling with pride as they sounded out compound words for him and their parents. He was happy.

One November evening, with a chill in the air promising an even cooler dawn, he waded into the scrotum-tightening current for his nightly bath. A few frogs started up their musical croaking, but it was far from the ear-filling chorus of the summer nights. A heron, standing sentinel on a snag in midstream, eyed him suspiciously as he plunged into his twilight revivification. He resurfaced with a "Cooeee!" torn from his lungs at the exquisite shock.

"Val, you're going to stop this nonsense by Christmas, I hope," Gabriella Cho called from beneath the tresses of a riverbank willow. "I'm all in favor of men that bathe. In fact, I wish you'd give lessons. But the river, in this temperature?"

He laughed, breathing hard in the cool water. "I can't pass up the chance for a swim in November. We couldn't do this in the Boundary Waters, not at this time of year. You should try it."

She stepped into the veiled moonlight, holding a wicker laundry basket. "I'll stick to dipping a piece of me at a time in a washbasin, thank you. It's slower, but I can do without the double pneumonia. Anyway, I brought you a treat, you nut."

Valentine waded up and out of the stream, toes pleasantly digging into the cool sand. He felt no embarrassment at being naked in front of Cho; they'd shared too many rough camps for him to worry about modesty. She knelt, unwrapping one of the bundles from her basket and then standing up again with the air of a magician performing a trick. The brick-heated towel she draped around his shoulders warmed him deliciously.

"Thanks, Gabby, this feels great! To what do I owe the royal treatment?" He began to dry himself off, goose-pimpled skin luxuriating in the welcome heat.

Cho retrieved the other towel, stepped behind him, and affectionately tousled his hair. "It's winter quarters for us soon. I hear they're going to split us up into apprenticeships or something in camp."

"That's the rumor," he agreed as she dried his back with a series of strong strokes. He found it easy to be agreeable with his skin tingling the way it was.

"You've filled out a little, Davy," Cho observed. "You used to be such a reed. Too much time cooped up in Father Max's library."

Valentine felt a spark. *Are you going where I think you're going?* he wondered, applying it equally to the direction of the conversation and her rubdown. Now aware of how close she stood behind him and drinking in her rich feminine scent, he thought with a little nervous thrill how easy it would be to turn around and embrace—

A shriek from the buildings on the other side of the belt of trees broke the moment like a thrown brick shattering a window.

"Fire!" echoed a second, more intelligible yell.

By the time Valentine pulled his pants on and stepped into his boots, a *ting-ting-ting-ting* sound rang from the metal tube in the gate watchtower that served as Weening's alarm gong.

"Flames, Val, and— *Jesus, what's that?*"

Something flapped across the night sky over the stream, bigger than a vulture, banking to make another pass over the ring of houses.

The two friends ran for the River Gap, a narrow alley between two homes that served as the smaller of the two entrances to the village. Cho ran three paces ahead of Valentine, who was still fumbling with his pants.

A shot flashed from one of the long rectangular windows just under the roof of the house overlooking the River Gap.

Cho staggered as the whipcrack hit Valentine's ears, a leg yanked out from under her as if someone had pulled it with a trip wire.

Valentine waved his arms above his head. "Don't shoot, don't shoot, it's us!" A second shot whistled past his ear.

He dropped to the earth, crawling for Cho. He found her writhing in the undergrowth, clutching her injured left leg. Oath after oath spat from her contorted mouth.

"Val," she gasped. "Val, my leg's broken, I think. Help me—Oh Christ, it's bleeding bad."

"Don't shoot anymore!" Valentine shouted into the flame-lit night. He pulled off his belt and cinched it around her thigh as a tourniquet. "Send help out here, damn it, you shot her!"

More shots rang out from somewhere, not aimed at them, thankfully. Valentine tried picking Cho up, but an agonized scream dissuaded him.

A scared-witless voice called from the window: "That you, Mr. Valentine?"

He started to reply with profanity strong enough to blister paint, but cut it off. "I'm coming in, we need to get some help out here. Dorian Helm, right?"

"Yessir. I'm sorry, but when you came up so—"

"Never mind. C'mon out here, I want you to keep an eye on her. Get a good look at what happens when you shoot without knowing what you're shooting at."

"Tell him to bring some water," Cho groaned up at him. "David, the bleeding's slowed. Please, God, let them have chloroform or something."

"And water, Helm. A canteen, anything," he shouted at the house. No response. He turned back to Cho. "I hope he heard me. Just hold on for a little while; the two of you stay under these trees. Those flying things are busy lighting fires."

"Knock a couple down for me, Val. What a dumb way to

get hit," she said from behind closed eyes. Her lip was bleeding; she must have bitten it in pain.

"Hang tough, Gab. Back in a few."

The Helm boy, sixteen at most and wide-eyed with fear, let him in the tall metal gate that barred entrance to the west gap.

"Mr. Valentine, I'd never . . . ," the Helm boy began, but Valentine had no time for him after seeing that the kid had recovered his wits enough to bring a blanket out for Cho.

He reached the center of Weening without further shots aimed at him. Smoke streamed from the top of one of the silos, where two men climbed an exterior ladder, laden with blankets wrapped around their shoulders. Flames licked at the side of the main barn, the largest building in the center of the ring of walled houses.

Two of his fellow reservists stood before the shed that contained their rifles. They were taking potshots at the bat shapes circling above. He ran for the shed, hunched over in expectation of claws digging into his head or shoulders any second. He retrieved his rifle and thrust a handful of cartridges into the pocket of his beltless pants, which threatened to drop to his ankles.

"They're throwing Molotov cocktails, I think, Val," Polluck, one of the would-be soldiers in Valentine's squad, warned. "You can see them burn as they come down."

"How many of them are there?" he asked, searching the skies. Thirty feet away, some of the residents worked the hose attached to the powered pump, directing a thin stream of water at the fire threatening the barn. At the other side of the village, a mountain of a farmer, gray-haired Tank Bourne, held his automatic rifle at the ready under his porch. The weapon looked like a toy pressed against his massive shoulder. Bourne aimed a shot at a shape arcing around the barn, diving at the firefighters, short leg-claws extended like an eagle after a fish. Valentine and his comrades' guns rang out at almost the same instant. The volley of shots brought the attacker crashing to earth.

Another flapper appeared on the slanted roof of the Bourne house, crawling down the shingles with leather-draped arms toward Bourne. Valentine chambered a fresh round, sighted, and fired. Bourne heard either creature or bullet, and came out from under the porch roof. Bourne pumped shells into the abomination. It turned over and rolled off the roof.

"That's two down," Valentine said, his heart pounding in his ears.

"The main hayloft's on fire!" someone shouted from the water pump.

Framed in the growing red-orange-yellow light of the burning hay, an ungainly shape waddled toward the upper doors from deep inside the loft. Tottering on short bowlegs, it pulled itself along with long arms like a webbed spider monkey. Two triangular ears jutted like sharp horns from its angular head.

Tank Bourne rested on one knee, feeding a fresh magazine into his rifle. Valentine and the reservists shot, apparently without effect as the bat-thing launched itself into the air. With a series of audible flaps, like clotheslined sheets whipped by the wind, the beast disappeared into the smoke above.

Bourne waved them toward the already burning barn. "We have to get the stock out of there!"

The hay, now well alight, threatened to take not only Weening's central structure, but much of its livestock, as well. Bourne, Valentine, and a handful of men dashed inside, throwing the lower doors all the way open. Rising heat whipped the wind inside. The men pulled, pushed, and cajoled the stupefied cattle, which stood frozen in their stalls,

away from the flames. Weening's few horses needed little encouragement, but added to the Noah's Ark confusion in the
great barn's lower level as they danced and collided in their
rush for the door. Once they coaxed a few cows into moving,
the rest took to the idea with a will and followed the horses,
bellowing their panic into the night air.

The pair who dared climb the ladder, covered by every
available gun, fought the fire on the roof of the silo. Valentine
prayed there wouldn't be an explosion. Bullets felled two
more bat-things as they tried to pluck the men from the
heights. They extinguished the most immediate threat to the
village. Layers of corrugated iron and shingles bought enough
time for the coughing men to beat the fire into submission
with water-soaked blankets.

As the gunfire died down, women and children emerged to
help combat the blaze with bucket chains and another canvas
hose. The main barn could not be saved, but the smaller buildings, coops, and pens that stood near it in the center of town
stayed wet thanks to brave souls who dared the heat of the
burning barn to douse them with buckets of water.

Bourne, rifle held ready at his chest, still watched the
skies. "Those Harpies haven't been in these parts in years," he
told Valentine. "When I was with the Bears, we caught a couple hundred of them in daylight. Burned them out of an old
bank they were sleeping in. We shot them out of the sky in
daylight easy. They're big, slow targets, compared to a duck
on the wing."

"Slow?" Valentine asked.

"Yes, they're better gliders than they are fliers. Especially
if they are loaded with grenades. They're pretty smart, at least
enough to know when to attack and when to try to get away."

"Would they fly in the day?"

"I doubt it, too much chance of a patrol seeing them."

Valentine felt his pulse quicken. "They hit us within an hour of sunset. How far could they fly in that hour, Mr. Bourne?"

Tank looked at him, bushy eyebrow raised in interest. "I see where you're heading, young man. Hmmm, they'd be flying against the wind out of the east. I don't think they'd be more than fifteen miles away. Ten's more likely."

Valentine belatedly remembered Cho. "I've got a wounded man on the west gate. Can you help me get her in? After that, I want to find out which way they went when they flew off."

"There's a stretcher in the tack shed where you keep your gear. I'll help you bring her in, but we don't have a doctor anywhere hereabouts."

They found the young Helm boy propped up against a tree, eyes gaping and empty. His neck had a ragged hole in it just below the Adam's apple. The wound looked as if someone had probed his chest cavity with an oversize drill.

Cho was missing.

Whatever took place at the west gap had happened so fast that the boy couldn't even get off a shot with his carbine, which lay fully loaded and broken in half on either side of his body.

"There's a Hood nearby," Bourne observed coldly. "Poor kid, he was dead before he knew what was happening."

"Could Cho still be alive?"

"Maybe. It fed off Dorian here. Broke his neck then went for the blood. Chewed a hole in his neck and stuck its tongue right into his heart. Ever seen a Reaper tongue? Pointed at the end, like a big rubbery syringe."

Guilt hammered at Valentine with a string of precisely aimed blows. *You left Cho unprotected in the open, watched by a kid who shouldn't even have been responsible for cover-*

ing the west gate from a loophole. You pulled him out of his house and left him in his own backyard to get his heart pierced. Two people are dead because you couldn't stand hurting an injured buddy by moving her. Nice work, Valentine. The Kurians need a few more like you giving orders.

All the more reason to make them wish they had tried someone else's friends, a stronger part of him countered.

At the watchtower over the main gate, three farmers gulped at the roasted hickory nut drink called *coffee* for lack of a more accurate term. Valentine asked them for their best guess about which direction the Harpies were last seen flying and got three slightly different answers. The consensus seemed to be a little north of east.

Most of the town still worked to keep the blaze from spreading. The exception was the Helm family; the father retrieved his son's body while Mrs. Helm sat on the steps of her porch with her arms around her other two children, dully watching the flames consume the great barn.

Valentine climbed down from the watchtower. Bourne and the other eight reservists waited by the Militia stable tack shed. Recently turned earth next to the little wooden shack exposed two stout cases. Bourne gingerly examined the contents of one of the open cases.

"How is it, Tank?" Valentine asked.

"Still usable. We turned it this summer when we blasted the new drainage ditch from town. Quickest way I know to get rid of tree stumps."

"If I promise not to ask where you got it, will you spare us some of that bang?" Valentine knew the dynamite had probably been lifted from a Southern Command supply cave, perhaps with the aid of a small bribe to the resident quartermaster.

"If it means paying the Harpies back in their own coin, I'll tie up a couple of five-stick bundles and have them fused before you can say *nitroglycerin*. Part that worries me though, kid, is you wanting to take off right now. Wandering around in the dark with a Hood around, looking for something you aren't sure where it is—well, it's like playing blindman's buff in a room full of buzz saws."

Valentine squatted down and looked at the dynamite. "I want to hit them while they think we're still busy with this fire."

"Yeah, I buy that. One thing you got going for you, anywhere these things are holed up, it's sure to smell like a well full of dead skunks. They shit as much as pigeons, and you up everything proportional. I know they eat like crazy and their handlers aren't too particular about what they feed them."

Valentine's entire team volunteered for the duty, but in the end he took two. He asked two others to borrow horses and ride for the nearest Command post. The rest would guard against further attack in case the Harpies came back to finish the job. He just prayed the Reaper didn't decide to come back.

Valentine took Gil DelVecchio and Steve Oran with him. Steve Oran, a brassy young man who enjoyed hunting, had ventured many times into the borderlands east of Weening in search of game. Oran had the best knowledge of the land and excellent eyes. He'd once explored as far as the Saint Francis River, which marked the belt of uninhabited land surrounding the Ozark Free Territory. Gil was a powerfully built farm boy from the Missouri Valley in the Dakotas. He exuded strength and could be relied on to keep his head in a fix. DelVecchio had been one of the two men to climb the silo: his sweaty skin was still stained with soot.

The three forced down a quick meal as they loaded up two days' supplies in rucksacks. With weapons, ammunition, dynamite, and almost no camp gear, they could move quickly even in rough terrain. Valentine brought his pistol, with six bullets left in the magazine, and the best compass and map Bourne could provide.

They hiked out the main gate a few minutes after midnight, turning down an offer by the other Helm boy to go along as guide. Valentine told him he would help his family more by fighting the fire that threatened their house. He mentally added that while the killing machine that took his brother was probably elsewhere by now, perhaps striking again in the confusion of another Harpy attack, there were too many other risks in the eastern dark for Valentine to chance losing both of a mother's sons the same night.

The Reaper was much on Valentine's mind as the three men moved east. Oran picked the trail; Valentine followed several paces behind, making sure he stayed on course; and DelVecchio walked just behind, rifle ready for instant use. The Hood obviously worked with the Harpies, but would it decide Cho was a valuable prize to be taken for questioning? Her nondescript uniform differed little from any other impoverished resident's, and she carried no weapon. She was grabbed as a weak target that could not put up much of a fight, to be consumed at a later time.

Valentine prayed Cho had lost consciousness from pain and shock. He could not bear the thought of his closest friend being carried east to a dreadful end, screaming out her pain the whole way.

By three in the morning the men reached the wide Saint Francis River. A few ruined buildings that had been reclaimed by the wilderness more or less stood on its hilly banks. Valentine looked into the skull-like emptiness of a brick house, the interior nothing but humps of collapsed roof and saplings, and thought of the world-that-was. Fifty years ago, little cabin cruisers and fishing boats must have floated up and down the river, its banks under control and sandbars dredged. But with man occupied elsewhere, Nature had reclaimed her own. At a rest halt, he began to despair of their hunt. The Harpies could be anywhere.

"Val, there's a light on the river," Oran reported.

The three climbed a little promontory and looked north at the distant speck of light. It was near the western bank of the hundred-yard-wide river, but whether it came from boat or shore could not be seen at this distance. Who would be fool enough to burn a light right at the border? *A guide for the returning fliers?* Valentine wondered, suddenly hopeful.

They decided to check it out. Valentine and Oran readied their rifles and picked their way north, keeping under cover. When they got close enough to see that the light in fact came from a boat, they rested for a few minutes before creeping forward again.

"It's a small barge and a towboat," said Oran, who had the best night vision of the three, and therefore used the binoculars. They lay in a little hollow, peeking at the river from behind a fallen tree. "Looks like five men visible on the towboat. One's got a gun. No one is on the barge. It's riding light, must be practically empty. The light is on the barge, electric, not a lantern."

The towboat was attached to a ruined concrete piling projecting out of the lake, perhaps the last remnant of a dock.

Oran leveled the binoculars at the barge. "They got it anchored at the front and back. If anyone's in it, they're staying hid."

A gust of wind off the river made the men wrinkle their noses. They exchanged glances.

"I think we've found the nest," said Valentine.

They hashed out a plan. Valentine would take a bundle of dynamite and swim to the ship from the north end of the barge. When he set it off, the other two men would start sniping at the tugboat, with hope that it would be lit by the burning barge, and use the other bundle of dynamite on it from the shore. Gil said he was sure he could throw the bundle the thirty feet from the shore to the boat.

"Here, Val," DelVecchio said, pulling a hand ax from his belt. "You might need this. Who knows what might be in that hull?"

The weapon was light and handy, more of a fighting tomahawk than a tool. "Thanks. We'll meet back here," Valentine ordered. "If you're being chased, just go west like hell, don't wait for me."

"Hope you don't puke easy, if you're going close up to that thing," Oran commented, tension written in boldfaced capital letters on his face.

"Let's not waste any time. I want to get this over before dawn. Maybe that Hood sleeps in the barge."

Valentine stole past the lounging figures on the tug. If five men were up and around at this hour, perhaps ten more might be crammed below. Or were they out, somehow helping the Harpies? Once he had the bulk of the barge between him and the towboat, he crawled through vegetation to the water. The dynamite, matches, and his pistol rested on his back, in a pack that might keep the water out for a moment or two, if he was lucky.

Valentine kicked off his shoes and crawled into the cold water. It reminded him of his bath, and how Cho had dried him off afterwards. He took the comforting wood handle of the tomahawk in his hand and half floated through the water toward the barge, moving like an alligator with just eyes and nostrils out of the water, the pack making a sea-monster hump on his back. He felt as alive and alert as if he had just finished a light breakfast after a long night's sleep, rather than having been awake for eighteen hours.

It was a good thing he hadn't eaten recently. When he slithered close enough to really smell the barge, a horrible musky odor mixed with a sharper turpentine-like smell assaulted his nostrils. The hazy moonlight revealed details of the ancient barge, a mass of rust and paint and makeshift welds with M-33 painted on its side in three-foot-high letters. He shifted the tomahawk to his mouth, holding it between his teeth with straining jaws, and breaststroked into the river. He made for the stern anchor line. The gentle current assisted him with its chilly flow. He reached the cable, grateful for its hand-filling thickness. He climbed it, still gripping the ax in his teeth like a dog with an oversize bone.

The deck of the barge was as beat-up as its sides. It had a single hatch open to the sky. The battery-powered lamp, a conglomeration of what looked like a car battery and a truck headlight, pointed up into the night but seemed to bathe the whole top of the barge with an intimidating, revealing light. Valentine wished he had told Oran and DelVecchio to start firing when they saw him reach the barge; he could use something to draw the men's attention to shore. Still dangling, he gently placed the hatchet on the deck of the barge. Now or never.

He hoisted himself up on deck and crawled for the hatch. Expecting a shout at any second, he peered into the reeking hold. He could make out little in the dark, but there seemed to be floor six feet or so down.

He rolled over the edge and landed barefoot in sticky filth, ax ready. The hold stank like a slaughterhouse, and he had to fight down his gorge as he stood up in a cramped little area.

A gutter ran the length of the deck, filled with noisome excrement. The hollow interior was empty.

No. As his eyes adjusted, Valentine realized that a panting shape leaned against one wall. It was a Harpy, wrapped up in its own wings as though in a leathery cocoon. A trickle of blood pooled beneath its rump. Wounded, maybe dying. The debris on the floor included a mélange of bones. A cluster of human skulls decorated a metal pillar, part of the barge's rusting structure holding up the deck. The heads looked like a yellowish bunch of coconuts. There was a door forward out of the hold. A body lay at the bottom of stairs descending from the door: pale, naked, and headless. But it was nevertheless familiar.

Valentine had found Cho.

An awful kind of warmth filled his stomach. He no longer minded the reek. He padded toward the sleeping Harpy with slippery steps. He could make out slit nostrils and a toothy, pointed jaw decorated with bristling catlike whiskers protruding from the tent of folded wings. Wet drool dripped out with its rapid, shallow breathing. He raised the ax and buried it in the face with a bone-crushing blow. The thing never knew what happened, falling nervelessly sideways. Valentine leaped on top of it, bringing the blood-and-brain-soaked tomahawk down again and again with a series of wet smacks. Flecks of blood splattered his snarling features.

A familiar flapping sound came from the hatch, and the light reflected from the deck lamp was obscured by a winged shadow. Valentine crossed the hold to the forward stairs to the door, keeping clear of the hatch. He could sit there, light the dynamite, and blow a few Harpies to kingdom come.

Shots echoed from outside. DelVecchio and Oran must have panicked at the returning Harpies and tried to prevent them from reentering the barge. Valentine somehow ignored

Cho's body, took his pistol, and tossed the backpack onto the stairs. A Harpy flopped into the hold, one wing injured.

"Welcome home, fucker," Valentine cursed, putting a bullet into its stomach. The spent cartridge case pinged off the metal interior.

The Harpy screamed out a horrible, burbling kind of call. Language or pain, it brought answering shrieks from outside. Valentine knew he was drawing all kinds of ugly from the skies as well as the tugboat, but he wanted Cho's body to have a lot of company feeding the crayfish and gars. He heard, for the first time in his life, the chatter of a machine gun fired in anger. The tugboat crew must have a support weapon mounted on deck. He prayed that DelVecchio and Oran were smart enough to pull out now and head west.

He pounded on the roof of the hold, dislodging a shower of grit. "Dinner, dinner, come and get it!" he shouted.

The wounded Harpy pulled itself toward him, gremlin mouth open in vicious anticipation. Other flappers dropped into the hold.

Valentine took two steps backwards toward the door and found the bundle of dynamite and tin of matches. Grabbing a bunch of matches, he struck them against the rough side of the stairwell. They flared into life, illuminating the dank little closet space. Valentine lit the fuse, dropped the matches to the floor, and picked up his pistol. He fired a shot into the vague shapes collected in the hold. He placed the hissing dynamite on the first stair and pushed at the hatch.

Locked.

He bashed at the hatch with his shoulder, closing his eyes to the expected oblivion that would blow him to bloody fragments, but the rusted lock gave way. He threw the door open and dashed onto the deck, then dived for the water on the river side of the barge. He felt a bullet pluck at him as it passed through his shirt at the armpit.

He was under water when the explosion hit. The *boom* sounded muted, but its force thumped at him even through the cushioning protection of the river, knocking the breath from his body. He surfaced, gasping for air.

The shattered rear half of the barge upended as pieces of its hull splashed into the river all around. The towboat was a mass of flame, the machine gun silent. The Harpies' incendiary bombs must have been on the towboats deck in readiness for another attack. Valentine got his bearings and submerged again, swimming for shore. No doubt a few very unhappy Harpies still circled above. His fingers struck the river bottom.

As his brain cleared, he realized that he was unarmed. His pistol was at the bottom of the Saint Francis, dropped when the concussion from the explosion racked him, and the tomahawk was probably landing somewhere in Mississippi. He gathered himself and ran out of the water and onto the riverbank.

Picking up a river-smoothed rock in each hand, Valentine hurried under the protective overhang of the trees. He felt defenseless as a rabbit with raptors circling above but made it to the little hollow without trouble. What was left of the tugboat was floating downstream in flames.

He crept to the place where he had left the other two and whistled softly.

An answering warble came out of the darkness. The pair joined him.

"Quite a show, Val," complimented Oran, returning Valentine's rifle. DelVecchio put the other bundle of dynamite back in his pack. Bourne could use it on more tree stumps or trade it for corrugated tin to build a new barn.

It felt good to have a rifle in his hands instead of rocks. "Oran, you need a break. I'll take point on the way back. You can keep us on course, and Gil, you cover."

"Sure thing, boss."

The light of the burning towboat faded as it sank behind them, and the three started for home. Not knowing how well the Harpies could see, hear, or smell, they stayed under the trees. Nothing dived at them or circled above. Later they sang softly as they walked through the shadowed woods, like young athletes returning home from a successful match. Beneath the bare-boughed canopy, Valentine felt safe from any of the surviving Harpies. But the trees made the Reaper's attack that much easier.

It stepped from behind a tree, plucking the gun from DelVecchio's hands and sending it spinning into the night. With its other hand, it picked him up by his backpack, holding the giant young man at arm's length like a filled diaper.

Valentine and Oran spun around, flicking the safeties on their rifles. The Reaper put the frantic DelVecchio between them like a shield.

"Drop him," was all Valentine could think to say.

"No! Wait! No!" DelVecchio was screaming. "Don't let him . . . don't shoot."

you might as well shoot, foodlings, the Reaper whispered, its voice all hissing air and menace. *you'll all three be dead as soon as i take you.*

"God, let me go," DelVecchio gibbered. "Val, get it off me!"

Valentine thought his heart was going to break out of his chest, it pounded so hard. His tongue felt dry, and his eyes seemed misted over. Only a burning sensation from the region of his kidneys prevented him from fainting dead away. He waved at Oran, motioning him to spread out. The Reaper couldn't hold DelVecchio in two directions at once. Oran, eyes fixed on the hypnotic yellow eyes of the pale, black-clad figure before them, did not respond. Valentine stepped backwards, rifle at his shoulder.

The thing turned its gaze to Valentine, bringing Oran out of his trance. Seeing Valentine stepping away, he turned and ran off into the night, discarding gun and pack.

run! i'll catch you, the Reaper breathed after him. *hide. i'll find you.* It turned to Valentine, shifting its gaze in a quick, lizardlike movement. *shoot, and i'll pull your legs apart, one joint at a time, as easily as you'd yank off a fly's wings.*

Valentine continued pacing backwards, lowering the gun barrel somewhat. He stepped behind a thick tree trunk, aiming his gun.

The Reaper laughed at the gesture, a sound indistinguishable from a cat's spitting fury: *pha pha pha!*

useless. It looked at Gil, the young man quivering in its grasp. *you got one thing right, foodling,* the predator said into DelVecchio's ear as it drew the thrashing figure close. *i am a god!*

DelVecchio screamed as it turned him around, pointed teeth tearing a hole in his neck. Gil pushed and flailed against the creature's grip, screaming the blubbery underwater screams of a man with a severed windpipe.

"Sorry, Gil. Hope you'd do the same for me," Valentine muttered, exhaling and squeezing the trigger.

The .45 shell found DelVecchio's backpack. The dynamite exploded in pinkish-orange light, throwing Valentine on his back with a warm, irresistible punch. Valentine's ears roared, and his head filled with light as he plunged into unconsciousness.

*   *   *

It was almost dinnertime when the exhausted residents of Weening heard a shout from the guard tower.

"Walker coming in." A moment's pause while the watchers in the tower employed an old telescopic sight. "It's Valentine. Alone."

The residents gathered, the still-smoldering barn behind them, to greet the strange apparition.

Barefoot, pants in tatters, shirt reduced to a few ribbons, and pale with fatigue, David Valentine walked into Weening. He held his rifle in one hand and bulging backpack in the other. He examined the crowd, looking for a face.

"Mr. Helm," he croaked, reaching into his backpack. "We killed the thing that got your son. And Gab. And Gil. Steve, I don't know about."

He pulled out a skull covered in sticky soot from the fire he'd used to burn off the flesh and hair. In everything but color it resembled a human skull, with an oversize forehead and an unusually long jawbone. The charred bone was bluish black and looked as if it had been carved from a block of onyx.

Randall Helm refused the offering and instead put his arms around the weary eighteen-year-old and walked him home.

That evening Bourne opened a jug of homemade whiskey and he, Valentine, and Helm took turns solemnly chiseling the names GILMAN DELVECCHIO, GABRIELLA CHO, and DORIAN HELM into the polished obsidian skull of the Reaper, still a little warm from its hours in the boiling pot. By the time the jug was recorked, the skull was mounted, slightly askew and off-center due to alcohol-impaired judgment, over the main gate of the village.

It stands there still.

Four

Ouachita Mountains, February of the forty-first year of the Kurian Order: The snow is retreating up the rugged, rocky hills of the Ouachitas, but an Arkansas winter still sits firmly in the saddle. In the narrow valley between two low mountain ranges pointing like cleft fingers at the blasted ruins of Little Rock, a little collection of cabins marks the temporary home of Fort Candela. It is a fort in name only; the soldiers are scattered across twelve square miles of the valley floor. There is electricity most of the time and fresh food some of the time, but warmth and companionship by the cabin hearths always.

The erratic war is blessedly far from the men and women quartered in this valley. They concentrate on making and repairing equipment, cutting and sewing new uniforms, eating, drinking, gambling, and trading. And most important, training. This winter, like every other for the past twenty-odd years, recruits get paired up with seasoned veterans, until the green soldiers can do what the vets do and know what the vets know. Specialists and artisans travel through, giving lessons and once in a while taking on permanent apprentices if a recruit shows unusual ability at veterinary work, perhaps, or in making quality leather goods.

The officers in charge of Fort Candela make decisions and act on them. One recruit has hopelessly bad vision, another drinks too much, and another cannot keep up on practice marches. The culls are offered support jobs—honorable service in paid labor outfits—or are returned to civilian life. Those who do not try for home are absorbed by the labor-hungry farms and towns of the Ozark Free Territory, but a few malcontents become "bummers" and inevitably a matter for the law.

For the rest, the question becomes Guards or Hunters. Seven out of ten go to the Guards, the military regiments that provide a defensive core for the Ozark Free Territory. Guard service is rewarding: The soldiers get the finest uniforms Southern Command can produce, ample ammunition for marksmanship training, and frequent parties and barbecues, games and riding contests. Many of them are mounted, adding to their dash and swagger. They also get plenty of opportunities to mix with civilians. No New Year's dance is complete without a handsome contingent of young Guards in polished boots and crisp charcoal-gray uniforms, kepis with regimental-colored neckerchiefs hanging to precisely the base of their tunic collars. The Guards are the well-ordered, well-disciplined, reassuring face of Southern Command, who can and do fight, giving their lives in defense of wives, children, and sweethearts.

The others—the men and women who will become cold-eyed Hunters ranging outside the friendly reaches of the Ozark Free Territory to slay the minions and Quislings of the Kurians—are brought before the Lifeweavers.

A glossy black house cat named Sailor Tom ruled the cabin with an iron paw. Six men shared the bunkhouse nestled in a hollow between two spurs of Fourche Mountain, but none disputed the feline's claim to the warmest chair by the stone fireplace or the best tidbit from the steer quarter hung in the cool room. The heavy cat looked like a witch's familiar with a lynx somewhere in the family tree. He strutted around the cabin on muscular rear legs, half-wild and all attitude. Sailor Tom asserted his authority with a rising corkscrew growl that blossomed into a biting, clawing fury aimed at anyone foolish enough to ignore that first and only warning. He gained his nickname when one Wolf declared, "If that tom spoke English, you just know he'd be cussing like a sailor." The men tolerated the bad-tempered cat and pointed him out to recruits as an example of tenacity to be imitated. The men depended on stored food to get them through the winter, and Sailor Tom exterminated trespassing mice, rats, squirrels, and even rabbits with samurai spirit.

The cat's realm encompassed a two-room, sooty kingdom full of beds and furniture as roughly finished as the men who occupied them. A fireplace of watercourse stones dominated one entire wall at the "sitting" part of the bunkhouse, and a two-hundred-years-old-and-still-going-strong potbellied stove warmed the "sleeping" part, a musky warren of bunk beds and old blankets hung for gloomy privacy.

Four veteran Wolves and two recruits shared the cabin. Pankow, Gavineau, Big Seth, and Imai saw to it that neither David Valentine nor Marquez, the other Wolf Aspirant, enjoyed a moment's peace. Anytime they were not actually in the field or attending a lesson as part of their caste training, the four Senior Wolves dedicated themselves to seeing that the would-be Hunters idled as little as possible. Not just with training. Marquez found himself held responsible for the firewood supply and general cabin maintenance. The firewood might seem an easy task for a man in the middle of a forest, but the Wolves insisted he fell, and consequently haul, the timber from two miles away. If he so much as looked at one of the bushy pines surrounding the cabin, the trainers accused him of wanting to expose their temporary home to the enemy.

The Wolves assigned everything else to Valentine. "Every-thing else" included cooking, washing up, laundry, stocking the pantry, mending, disposing of Sailor Tom's half-eaten *corpus rodentia,* and the morning ersatz coffee. The men accepted a certain amount of slackness and inefficiency in all his responsibilities excepting the last. No matter that Valentine may have returned from a night orientation march exhausted at the first pink of dawn, if the coffee was not steaming and ready to be poured at the customary rising hour of 6 A.M., he was thoroughly cursed and punished. This required a fell run up Bald Knob, a forty-degree-grade hill bare of trees, under the disapproving eyes of the four coffeeless Wolves.

Valentine learned from all four, but his principal mentor was Evan Pankow. The child of a representative from Ohio, the then seven-year-old congressman's son had watched his privileged world disappear in a few insane weeks when the Raving Madness virus swept the United States. Young Evan was one of the few people immune to the virus. While this protected him from a death that claimed better than three quarters of the United States population, his genes were useless against the war and chaos that followed. He followed a stream of refugees into the tidewater of Virginia, where he got his first taste of the Kurian Order. He witnessed an albino man with yellowish eyes and a soft voice claiming to be a "crisis governor" kill an entire family in a hotel room. The boy, forever after avoiding the Reapers, was flown southwest by a woman who had also witnessed the "crisis governor" in action. Pankow had lost his parents, and she had lost a son, leading the two to form an increasingly real mother-son bond.

The pilot's name was Jamie Kostos, a former journalist who wrote some of the first pamphlets examining the Kurian Order. Her early writings, accurate in fact but mistaken in analysis, brought her to the attention of the Lifeweavers. Through her, Evan became a student of the Lifeweavers and a Wolf.

In his twenties, Pankow helped found Southern Command. Now fifty, with a seamed face and world-weary eyes that reminded Valentine of a Karsh portrait of Ernest Hemingway he had seen in one of the Padre's books, Pankow devoted himself to training a new generation of Wolves to carry on the struggle.

One late-February afternoon, with snow camouflaging the mud surrounding the little cabin, Pankow lectured his Aspirant about, of all things, tea.

"It's way too easy, when you're outdoors and on the move, to just eat rabbits and such," Pankow said, running his ungloved hand across the soft needles of a mountain spruce. "Especially in cold weather, you get hungry for meat and fat, and forget about everything else. But you've got to get your greens. You know what vitamins are?"

"Yes, I do, sir. It's those letters, *A, B, C,* and so on," David responded.

"Yeah, well, when I was a squirt we got them in stuff like breakfast cereal, little candy pills: damn near everything said 'vitamin fortified.' Now it's not so easy, it being winter. Take these spruce needles. In the spring, the little buds taste pretty good; you can just chew them. But if we pull some of these needles and boil them up into tea, you get as much vitamin C as from an orange, even. Ever had an orange?"

Valentine shook his head.

"Too bad. Sweet and juicy like a watermelon, but tart, too. Anyway, your greens aren't a problem in summer; any fool can pull up a dandelion, chew its leaves, and roast the root, but winter's a different story. You don't get your vitamins, you end up losing teeth, getting fevers. You'll catch some virus and die even if the scurvy doesn't take you. Trappers in Canada used to die of it; rabbit fever, it was called. They were starving their bodies to death while stuffing themselves with fresh meat every night. So never just eat meat, on the trail or at home. Add a lot of greens if you value your eyesight and your teeth."

"We should just raid more food off the Kurians," Valentine suggested.

Pankow scowled. "That's not so easy. But before you can fight, you have to be healthy in mind and body. I know it seems hard, what we've been having you do, but soon your body's going to be like a whole new machine. We're trying to get you as strong as possible so nothing quits on you once you start keeping the Way of the Wolf."

"When will that be?"

"Not for me to say. Not for you to say, not for the captain to say. It's up to the old Wizard. He might be watching you now, he might be advising the governor in Mountain Home. One thing is for sure, no one who meets him comes away the same as he was before."

Back at the cabin, like a demon invoked by mention of his name, word from the Lifeweaver waited in the form of a small printed list. The cabin was empty save for Seth and Sailor Tom, both napping in front of the Franklin stove.

"Amu's called an Invocation," Big Seth explained from his modified bunk. Reinforced wooden wings accommodated his six-foot-six-inch frame and supported an elongated mattress of his own making. "Starting Saturday and running for a week. One hundred fifteen fresh Wolves in this batch, thank God."

"Nice to see the roster growing this year. Many's the summer we had less than the year before. Let's see the list," Pankow said, reaching for the typed sheet of paper.

"Marquez made it. Bad news, Valentine," he said, watching Valentine's face fall. "You made it, Valentine. In fact, you're last on the list."

Valentine felt ambivalent at Pankow's joke, but a little pride still crept into his voice. "At least I made it, even if I'm dead last."

"Don't take it that way, son," Big Seth interjected. "It isn't good or bad, being last. Just means they may want to take more time."

"Doing what? Tattoos, a Vulcan mind-meld, what?"

Pankow laughed. "Hell, Valentine, where did you come up with that? Little before your time, and they haven't done reruns in over forty years."

"My dad liked to read science fiction. The man who brought me up after he died taught me to read my dad's books. But what is this *transformation* you all keep hinting about?"

Big Seth and Pankow exchanged a look. Pankow shook Valentine's hand.

"You'll just have to meet Father Wolf and see for yourself. Magic, son, is a little hard to explain."

The week dragged on, and Valentine made it pass more quickly by devouring the few books in the cabin. A heavy snowstorm came, and the Wolves relaxed the tough schedule shared by the two Aspirants. Valentine gratefully retreated to his bunk. Pankow gave him a pamphlet written by his foster mother. Printed in heavy, slightly smeared type and cumbersomely titled *Fallen Gods: The History, Theory, and Practice of the Kurian Order,* it was fifty pages relating the history of the Lifeweavers, their schism over the use of vital auras to attain immortality, and the Kurian takeover of Earth.

The Kurians failed in their first effort to take Earth because it was chaotic, badly planned, and they had not even consolidated their victory on Kur itself, where knots of Lifeweaver resistance slowed them. Humanity owes these brave lost souls a four-thousand-year debt of gratitude. Mankind in its primitive, isolated state was less vulnerable to the spread of the Ravies plague and quicker to accept the word and help of the Lifeweavers.

We hunted the horrors that came over from Kur, closed the doors, and having eradicated the threat promptly forgot about it two hundred years before Stonehenge was built. Vampires became rumor, then legend, and the Caste of the Bear trickled down into human legend as the berserkers of the Norse sagas.

Certainly a Kurian or two remained on Earth, lurking in untraveled corners of the globe. And Kurian-designed spawn, now known generically as *Grogs* and individually through slang and names out of mythology, no doubt survived to trouble humanity now and again as it pushed back the borders of the unknown.

But though the Gates of the Interworld Tree were closed, the Kurians in their red-clouded underground world learned in the long years of their exile how to open new ones. When and where the first of the new portals were opened is a matter of some dispute. Even the Lifeweavers are unable to say. It could have been as early as the Dark Ages in the Balkans, or as late as the eighteenth century. Opening the portals requires enormous sacrifices of vital auras to achieve, but after the first Kur came through the new Gate or Gates, humanity aided the Kurians in this all too frequently.

Humanity took the first step toward its own overthrow. Over the years, the Kurians recruited human allies, perhaps by striking Faustian bargains. The Kurian moles gained positions of trust and authority in society.

With the new millennium, the dragon's teeth sown in the last hundred or so years of man's history were ready to grow. In the first week of June 2022, they sprang the trapdoor on the vital auras of Earth's seven billion inhabitants.

The door to the cool room opened noisily, and Gavineau entered the cabin. He walked over to the hearth, apparently not seeing Valentine, and took the jug of busthead down from its place on the shelf. Gavineau collapsed in the leather-webbed camp chair by the empty fireplace, took a long pull, and stared at the cold ashes. Sailor Tom took advantage of the warm lap, and Gavineau scratched the cat between the ears without looking at it. Valentine considered greeting him, but didn't wish to be given something to do. He returned to his booklet.

THE OVERTHROW

The world was already a miserable place in the spring of that cursed year. The New Depression was at its height. Stocks fell, jobs were lost, and consumer consumption fell in a corporate death spiral as the aging technoczars were revealed to have feet of clay. Financial institutions underreacted, the government overreacted, and a society living on borrowed time paid for with borrowed dollars failed. Hard times and hunger came to the Western world, which was all the more of a shock because the generation that survived the last financial collapse had virtually died out.

Ancient hatreds smoldered and burst into flame. Europe saw its first real war in generations over food tariffs; China used America's preoccupation with its economy to overrun Taiwan. Russia and Japan, both backing different factions in Europe and the Pacific Rim, started a naval war that the United States, in its last great overseas commitment, stopped by cordoning off the two powers.

Civil unrest over the use of American wealth and resources abroad with so many suffering at home erupted into violence. Paramilitary groups took a hodgepodge of economic, political, and even racial grievances to the ultimate court of violence. A few polarizing and charismatic leaders further unraveled the tattered American social fabric.

The Earth itself added its cataclysmic voice to the dissonant chorus of human suffering. A worldwide string of earthquakes and volcanic eruptions leveled cities and made ash-covered wastelands of regions near the volcanoes. Particles in the atmosphere changed the climate more to the Kurians' liking. As if the tectonic damage was not enough, a plague added to the chaos. People called it *rabies,* but its twenty-four- to seventy-two-hour incubation cycle and mind-altering effects made the cure seem more like a job for exorcists than doctors. Wild mobs tore through the cities in a biting and clawing frenzy that shattered civic order.

Not even suspected at the time was that both events were long planned. Kurian technology allowed the fallen Lifeweavers to use the Earth itself as a weapon, and the disease, which we know today as Raving Madness, had appeared on Earth in the first Kurian invasion. The pale, robed Reapers began to walk the night.

The Reapers strode into the maelstrom, alternately cowing and killing. They commanded legions of Grogs, genetically altered creatures designed to break up opposition. As fearless in battle as army ants, but far more cunning, the Grogs come in many shapes and sizes. The most common form is a large rhino-hided ape, with hands and brains capable of using weaponry from assault rifles to armored personnel carriers.

The military and civil forces of the United States, already unable to deal with the plague and widespread destruction, succumbed as spare parts, ammunition, and especially morale ran out. A few Kurian agents and collaborators in the command structure helped orchestrate defeat on a grand scale. In the final extreme, a scorched-earth policy destroyed military bases and their equipment to keep them out of the hands of the Kurians. A few nuclear and chemical weapons were used in the last gasp of the war, but this added to the suffering rather than slowing the Kurian takeover. The end came with a bang and a whimper. The president shot himself when he learned his family had caught the Raving Madness virus at a riot in Quantico, and the vice president fled with a few leading members of congress to Mount Omega after she read the president's final executive order. In it, the despairing president declared, like the captain of a sinking ship, that the situation was "every man for himself."

The United States, and as far as we can tell the rest of the world, belonged to the Kurians within a year.

* * *

Valentine could understand why Kostos ended her life a hard-drinking woman. The facts of life of the New World Order came more easily to Valentine, who had been born well after the Kurian takeover. No memories of the vanished security and assorted technological delights of the past haunted him, just a wistful curiosity. He sometimes felt a schism between himself and Pankow's generation, including even the Padre. They cherished and fought for the past, a flag with stars and stripes, a way of living that would probably never return. Valentine wanted to win back his future.

A creaking from the sitting part of the room and a disgruntled *miaow* from Sailor Tom made Valentine glance up from the old red pamphlet and look at Gavineau. The Wolf set the jug on the floor and shuffled over to his bed, a sad and sick look visiting his face with every intention of staying the night.

"You okay, Don?"

"Hey, Val," he slurred. "Didn't see you there. Pankow giving you some slack?"

"He rode up the Happy Trail today," Valentine explained. The Happy Trail Getaway was a saloon where the bartender was friendly to the Wolves and the girls were even friendlier, if the words were kind and the price was right, the price being anything from a new pair of shoes to an old song, depending on the charm of the man. "I think he's letting up on me with the Invocation a day away. All I had to do was draw him a hot bath and put an edge on the razor. He told me I couldn't eat anything, and just to take it easy. Wouldn't tell me why I couldn't eat, though."

"Valentine, Marquez is dead. Can't think of any other way to say it."

The Aspirant's thoughts about-faced and came to attention in a hurry. "What?"

Gavineau sat on his bed, a bunk away from Valentine's. A sheet of laundry hung between them.

"It just happens sometimes, boy," said Gavineau.

"He made it through the Invocation fine. It's not like you run an Indian gantlet or something," slurred Gavineau. "He got out of the cave and just lost it. It can affect you funny. I remember I got out of mine and all I could smell was wood smoke on everything. He looked around like he didn't know where he was and took off at a run. Jumped right off the damn cliff. I remember two years ago one kid quit eating after it. Wouldn't touch any food, always saying it was diseased or filthy or something. He starved himself to death, just threw up when we force-fed him. Usually the guys who come over funny are just jumpy for a couple of days, then they come round. Bad business with Marquez. A couple others volunteered to go down and get the body. I only saw it from three hundred feet up."

"My God, what made—?"

"Hey, David, don't let it get to you," he said. "He just wasn't wired right, and sometimes not even the Wizard can spot that. You'll be fine."

Gavineau's drunken prediction was something Valentine reminded himself of again and again as he climbed the mountainside with ten other Aspirants, the last set supposed to meet with the Lifeweaver known variously as Amu, the Wizard, and Father Wolf.

Named Winterhome Mountain, the 2,200-foot cap of rock and snow looked like a shark's tooth from some angles and a sagging tepee from others. The cave was a little more than halfway up, set back from Marquez's fatal cliff by a sloping meadow. Five goats grazed there, some stripping bark from the stunted mountain pine and others pawing at the lingering snow to expose dead bracken underneath.

Two totem poles flanked the crescent-shaped entrance to the cave. Carved wolf heads, ears erect and eyes alert, crowned the poles. Carved names covered the rest of the pole, some with dates written afterwards. Valentine decided these must be the tollpoles, mobile gravestones for Wolves who died in battle. *Not so bad,* Valentine thought, *a few hundred names for twenty years of fighting.*

Just inside the cave eleven more poles, filled with tightly packed names, formed an arch the recruits filed under like a wedding party passing under crossed swords. Valentine paused and ran a finger over the carved names on one of the poles. Would his name join the long list?

The tunnel widened into a teardrop-shaped cave with a curtain at one end. What might have been a tapestry decorated the curtain; Valentine couldn't make out much in the dim light trickling in from the entrance even after his eyes adjusted. The two Wolves guiding them motioned for them to sit.

"Just keep quiet, and let him work you one at a time," one of them warned. "After the ceremony, they'll be kinda twitchy, so keep still and quiet when they come out."

The curtain moved as a wet black nose appeared. A canine head the size of a champion pumpkin lifted the curtain, revealing blazing blue eyes that reminded Valentine of a husky from the Boundary Waters. A wolf that could be mistaken for a pony by its size strode into the ring of Aspirants sitting around the edges of a cave. It had striking white fur, with black tips visible only up close. It sniffed each man, stepping sideways on paws the size of horseshoes.

"Thank you all for earning your places in this cave," a rich, cultivated voice came from the wolf's mouth, which did not seem to be forming any words. The wolf quivered and blurred, to be replaced by a smiling old man. "Forgive the dramatic entrance; it's an illusion that impressed your ancestors. I continue it out of love of tradition. Ahem. I hope you all know who I am."

"Amu," said some of those present. "The Wizard," said a few others. Valentine just nodded. There was something noble and strong about the man, Valentine thought, but with just a hint of tired lunacy in his frosty blue eyes. Valentine for some reason thought of Cervantes's Don Quixote.

"My name is not as important as who I am, a matter entirely different from a simple name. For I am going to be your Father. You all have a biological father who started your life, and most of you believe in a spiritual father who will take you unto him after death. I am here to be a third Father. I will give you rebirth."

Eleven separate faces digested this.

"Yes, I am speaking in riddles. Riddles are simple, usually after you hear the answer. But I am a busy man and would prefer to deal with each of you individually. Michael Jeremy Wohlers," the Wizard said, standing in front of a husky, curly-haired youth. "I'll see you first."

The prospective Wolf shot to his feet, narrowly missing crashing his head against the ceiling. "How did—?"

"I didn't," interrupted the Wizard, opening the curtain and gracefully pointing with his chin to the inner cavern. "You did."

Valentine spent four increasingly sore hours waiting his turn. Hungry, anxious, cold, and confused seemed a strange way to go through this invocation ceremony. He watched each of the ten other recruits emerge one at a time from behind the tapestry and stare about at those remaining as if they had never seen them before. Pete, the Viking giant who came down from northern Minnesota with Valentine, looked around at the remaining Aspirants suspiciously, as if fifteen minutes ago he had not been shifting from one aching buttock to the other with the rest of them.

"Pete, how'd it go?" Valentine asked. The blond jumped away from Valentine like a horse startled by a firecracker. His head connected with the cavern roof with the audible *thump* of a dropped melon, and he crashed to the ground, unconscious.

"Told you to keep quiet. If he ain't up by the time you're done, you're carrying him out," one of the Wolves said.

Pete began to groan and rolled onto all fours. He retched, vomiting clear liquid across the floor of the cave.

"Oh, that's just fine," the second Wolf said. "Now the other three are sure to puke."

Pete staggered to his feet and lurched out of the cave, rubbing the back of his head.

And puke they did. As the last two returned to the cave, they each added their own puddles of bile to the floor of the cave before fleeing to the open air outside. Valentine wondered if this was the reason for the orders not to eat anything.

"You're up, kid," one said.

"Through the looking glass you go, Alice," added the other.

He pulled the tapestry aside and stepped through. Behind him, he heard one Wolf say to the other, "Glad this happens only twice a year."

The tunnel wound downward, illuminated by nearly guttered candles set into the irregular sides of the cave. Valentine counted twenty paces before a second heavy piece of cloth blocked his progress. He didn't know whether to just open it, say his name, or tap on the material. He cleared his throat.

"Come in, come in, Valentine the Younger."

He entered, bending beneath the low rock arch.

The cave was warm and well lit, with a clean, inviting smell, which Valentine identified as balsam. The warmth and light came from an apple-size glowing ball that floated a few inches below the cave's eight-foot ceiling. It was bright but somehow did not pain Valentine's eyes, even when he looked directly at it. The room reminded Valentine of the inside of an igloo, were the igloo constructed out of grayish ice.

Father Wolf sat cross-legged in the center of the room on a woven rug. The floor of the cave was a mass of pine needles and small branches, with more patterned rugs thrown over the boughs. Five four-legged wolves snored in a companionable heap near the door.

"My bodyguard, you might say," said Amu. "Long ago, in another part of your world, I traveled with twenty of them. It made more of an impression on those simple folk: they lived in fear of wolves. I have grown rather fond of them, and should our enemies discover me here, I would remask myself and slip out with them. Sit down, please."

Valentine sat, grateful for the cushioning needles and rug after the hard floor of the outer cave.

"What do you want me to do?" Valentine asked.

"The question would be better put as what do *you* want to do. Why did you leave Minnesota? You did not come south just for a change of geography."

"I want to do my part."

The Wizard smiled at this. "Simply put. I hear something a little different from each young man or woman. They want to defend hearth and home, liberate their enslaved fellow men, and kick the invaders back into their kennels.

"What is needed from you, and what you can give me if you are true to yourself, is an outlet for your hatred. Hatred makes for good killers. The word is anathema; your religions rightly discourage it because it makes poor mortar for a society. But, young Valentine, your race is being *eaten*. You should be consumed by hate; your every breath should be drawn to curse your enemies. It gives you energy and a purpose and a determination that only love matches. The more you love your fellow men, the more you should be aflame with hatred for your foe. Your culture is so full of the image of the reluctant warrior that it is an archetype. The man who kills regretfully, who goes into battle terrified but gets the job done and then shows mercy to his enemy afterwards. That kind of man will keep the Free Territory upright for a while. But he will not win the war. Not against this enemy.

"There is a beast in you that I'm going to help you release. If you agree, that is. I give fair warning, though. It means a vicious life and perhaps a hard end. You will live only to kill our enemies until you yourself are slain. Few of my warriors retire to marry as your father did. So if you want a role inside the human family, I'm giving you a chance to walk out of this cave and down the hill with your humanity intact. You can serve with honor in the Guards, living up to the image of noble crusader, or go back into hiding. There are many ways to do the right thing. Stay with us, though, and you will become the thing the enemy fears in the night. The prey will become the predator."

Valentine wondered how many refused the offer. How many men wanted to be killers? He had expected physical or mental tests, not a moral one. He thought of his father but could not make the connection between the Wizard's animalistic killers and the quiet man who was shot to death in his own backyard.

"Why don't the Lifeweavers fight? I would think that with

your technology, magic I've heard it called, you'd be able to beat the Kurians."

The Wizard seemed a little surprised. "Usually I ask the questions, but I will do my best to answer yours: We are not any good at it. It would be like you defecating in your pants. You could do it if you put your mind to it, but you would not enjoy the experience, and until you had a chance to clean yourself, you would probably be preoccupied. We toilet-trained ourselves far too long ago, we are not numerous, and my ability to change into a wolf does not mean I could bite like one.

"You *Homo sapiens,* on the other hand, are almost perfect killing machines. You are flexible, aggressive, intelligent, and inventive. We examined life-forms on twelve worlds, and you half-savages revert to your terrible earlier selves with greater alacrity than any other. So we help you fight your battles, and in doing so you fight our war for us. Or am I speaking in riddles again?"

"No, I understand. It's your method I question. Instead of arming us with some kind of advanced technology, you turn us feral. That seems a strange way to help us win a war."

The Wizard abruptly disappeared, only to emerge from the dome-shaped cave's other exit, carrying what looked like a small mirror on a stand. "I am sorry," he said to the startled young man. "I had to get this, and I didn't want to interrupt, so I left you talking to an image. You said you understood, David. It is clear that you do not. I'm giving you the most powerful weapon on the planet: yourself at your full potential."

"I thought I was supposed to make up my mind."

"You did, David, you did," he said, sitting again opposite the young man. "The moment you thought of your father, and his death, and wondered if he was the kind of man I want you to become. You may not have felt it, but to me your fury was white hot. You can hide your rage from yourself, but not from me. It is so big, I wonder where you put it so you can sleep at night."

The item the Wizard placed between them looked like a plate-sized round mirror. It hovered at face level between them, held up by the same mysterious force that kept the light globe near the ceiling. Valentine saw in it only his own reflection, but fuzzy and out of focus, conforming to his general outline.

"What is this?" he asked.

Amu's face appeared in the mirror. The Lifeweaver's visage melted and shifted as though his skin were made of clouds boiling in the wind. "You could say it's the surgeon's scalpel, David. I will use it to operate on you. There is a cup in front of you. Drink up."

Valentine looked at the woven rug. A wooden cup, round like a hollowed-out coconut, sat before him. Had it been sitting there all the time? Valentine sniffed at it suspiciously.

"Just a little something to facilitate the ceremony. It is tasteless."

Valentine drank. Just before consciousness faded, he looked into the mirror-thing. First he saw his face, then the Wizard's, then a wolf's. The images flickered together: Wizard-Wolf-Self-Wizard-Wolf-Self-Wizard-Wolf-Self. Only the eyes were all the same. But they were not his. Not Amu's. The Wolf's. Valentine found himself fixing on the eyes of the three faces as they morphed from one manifestation to the next, all sharing the same ice-blue stare.

The young Wolf awoke to an overwhelming farrago of sounds and smells. The pine needles, musty rugs, dried lichen on the walls, and living wolves all vied to overthrow his brain. He could hear their heartbeats as with a stethoscope. Their breathing sounded like a gale. *Too much! Too much!* his brain shrieked at him. He leaped up and hurled himself away from the sleeping pack as if flung by a catapult, bruising himself with the force of the impact against the wall.

David, stay calm. Your senses are just sharpened up a little, that is all, Amu's voice in his head whispered in a soothing monotone. *I will help you through your first days; then you will learn on your own. You must learn to switch your senses between two levels, "hard" and "soft." You have to learn how to hear with soft ears and smell with soft nose first. You will use the hard ears and hard nose later, to sense over distance.*

"Where are you?" Valentine asked, hearing the echo of his voice in the outer cavern where he had waited before being called.

I have linked us. I cannot understand you very well. I am not as gifted as some in this type of communication with human thought-shapes. I just get impressions about your emotions. You need to take a deep breath, fill your lungs with air, and relax. Draw everything back into your center. Soften your eyes, let them go out of focus; soften your ears, let them relax and listen to the sound of the empty air in front of you; soften your nose and smell the heat of the light cube.

Valentine tried to relax, but the smell and sound of the slumbering wolves kept beating down the barriers. He felt dazed.

You are doing very well. I think you are a natural. Try to walk out of the cave the way you came in.

The musty old tapestry at the door reeked abominably, and he hurried past it. His legs were suddenly working too fast and he crashed into the cavern wall like a mechanized toy bouncing off an obstacle in its path. He steadied himself, but the flickering candles sounded like whip cracks in his ears.

Center! Center! the voice implored. *No, you still don't have it. Let me help you.*

Valentine felt himself steady, the cacophony of sensations fading into the background. He made it to the other curtain, but as he pushed through it, the acidic vomit smell overthrew him. His gorge rose and joined the slick mess on the floor.

"Serves you right," one of the Wolves thundered. Valentine leaped forward in alarm, but could not keep control of his spastic body and missed the exit. He ricocheted off the unforgiving stone and came away bleeding at the forehead. The coppery-smelling fluid infiltrated his nostrils, took over his sense of smell.

Breathe, breathe, bring it back to your center. Try crawling outside. You are fine.

The young Wolf did not feel fine.

"Hell, I think Father Wolf turned him all the way up," he heard one man whisper behind cupped palm.

On hands and knees, Valentine crawled through the cave, toward the light outside. He could smell the blood trail behind.

"The Wizard thought that Marquez was something special, too. Sent him right off the cliff," the other muttered back.

Valentine, remembering what had happened yesterday, brought himself back down with a determined effort. The world seemed almost normal. He climbed to his feet.

Good, good. Outdoors can be a little much; just keep breathing into your center and drawing everything back to that place inside you. You will learn in time. A good bloodhound controls his nose without even realizing it, the way you focus your eyes. You will be able to do the same soon.

Valentine made it into the daylight. Clear blue filled the

sky overhead, a rarity on Kurian Earth. The snow seemed to gleam, and even across the valley, Valentine's visual acuity was such that he literally could not see the forest for the individual trees. It smelled as if he were standing in the center of the world's largest goat farm, despite the fact that the three goats stood a hundred yards away. Downwind.

He centered on his own. *David, try to find some goat droppings.* The voice in his head still made him uncomfortable. Although his nose told him he was in a sea of goat shit, he localized it with an effort and walked toward the still-warm source, pausing less and less frequently as he drew nearer. He found he could play with his ears as easily as his eyes. He located a creaking branch, and listened to one of the goats pull up fodder from beneath the snow.

There you are, he thought at the end of his pungent treasure hunt, standing over the rounded mass.

Now, David, you are doing excellently. Follow the trail the goats left. Not by using the tracks in the snow, but with your nose. Shut your eyes as much as possible. Hear and smell your way down the mountainside.

It occurred to him that none of the other Wolves had explored the field in this way. He would have known, since most of them had left within the last few hours and there were only a few irregular, staggering footprints in the field. He took a deep breath, closed his eyes, and began to smell for the trail left by the odiferous goats.

And fell flat on his face. A tree root hidden in the snow snagged his foot. Usually he was agile enough to catch himself if tripped, but his usual reflexes had gone AWOL. He had the disquieting sensation of being in a different body. The only memory he could compare it to was his rare all-day fishing expeditions in Minnesota: taking a small boat into a lake and then feeling a little unsteady on his feet when he returned to dry land.

He got up, closed his eyes again with an effort, and began walking with an unsteady tread like a drunk doing a Frankenstein's monster imitation. He found he could hear the location of trees by the sound of wind in the pine needles. He sensed a branch ahead and leaned back to avoid it, and fell flat on his back.

The goats showed a penchant for investigating clumps of thorny bramble. After a painful rake across his lips, he cursed and opened his eyes.

No peeking, Amu admonished.

Valentine sucked the blood from his punctured lip, took a deep breath, and tried again. He leaned forward and found the going easier with his hands placed ahead and his nose closer to the trail. Even when he bashed his head straight into a tree trunk, coming away with sticky pine bark tangled in his hair, he managed to keep his eyes closed. He found himself able to concentrate on the trail, letting the other senses fade into the background, like a reader absorbed in a book using just her eyes and her brain.

The odor became stronger, and he let out a yip like a foxhound. He began to lope, ignoring the bruises and scrapes as he bounced down the slope. He heard a panicked bleat from something ripe and warm, and he leaped. The goat collapsed under him, kicking.

The animal's struggles brought him out of his trance. He found himself with a mouthful of goat hair, feeling as if he had just woken from a vivid dream. He released the unfortunate herbivore.

"Sorry, Billy. I got carried away."

Terrible! the Wizard shouted into his brain. *Had you been following someone with a gun, they would have shot you like a frothing dog. You mustn't go feral. Do it again, but this time see if you can find one of your fellow Wolves as they disperse. Just follow him, don't let him see you. Open your eyes now and then if you must, but try to work with your former semidormant senses as much as possible. Practice, because when it's for real, there are no second chances, David.*

David Valentine, Wolf of the Southern Command, got his new, awkward, battered body to its feet, closed his eyes, and stalked on.

Five

The Yazoo Delta, summer of the forty-first year of the Kurian Order: The wet crescent between the Mississippi and Yazoo Rivers is one of the most uncomfortable pockets of the globe. The swamp-and-canebrake Delta, returned to its original waterlogged existence by the breaking of man's levees on the Father of Waters, is virtually empty of human habitation. The Yazoo's flow moves imperceptibly through the bayous, making it impossible to tell if a current exists at all among the soggy sloughs. The water is so choked by vegetation, it seems like earth, and the earth among the tangled roots of cypress, willow, and water oak is spongy and hard to separate from the water. From water beetle to cougar, the teeming wildlife lives an amphibian existence among the Spanish moss and cattail thickets. It is a patch of humid desolation, taking its name from an Indian word for "death."

This empty land is a fine training area for the young Wolves of the Ozark Free Territory. From the Yazoo Delta, they can keep an eye on Mississippi River traffic and explore outside its football-shape, 188-mile length into the burned-out shells of Memphis in the north and Jackson in the south. It is the most impenetrable and least guarded of all the empty borders of Southern Command, and the handful of Wolves in the Delta keep on the move, often going an entire season without supply or communication from the Territory.

David Valentine traveled here as a newly invoked Wolf and learned the Hunter's Arts under two unremitting teachers: Nature and a longtime Cat named Eveready. In nature, Valentine learned to apply the lessons of his winter on how to find food, water, shelter, and fire, what might be called the four primary elements of human existence. From Eveready, a man who accepted no rank in Southern Command because it would mean an end to his one-man war against the Kurians as well as his jealously guarded independence, he learned how to unify his judgment, senses, skills, and tools into a single weapon. The young Wolves under Eveready's tutelage practiced their art, improvising weapons to hunt everything from submerged alligators to treed raccoons. They took not only nourishment from their kills, but also hide, bone, and sinew for use in making clothing and tools. A few of the more atavistic-minded fashioned lucky charms from their trophies. Eveready, owner of perhaps the longest necklace of Reaper fangs in the Old South, encouraged the practice.

What Eveready taught even better was the art of concealing lifesign. His apprentices spent more time learning mental discipline than they did physical, mastering a form of self-hypnosis that cloaked their auras against the inhuman searching powers of the Reapers. Their skill at this determined whether they would hunt the enemy or be hunted like the game they brought home to camp.

The camp used a pair of ancient water oaks as its roof. The stumpier of the two oaks suffered a curious deformity; the main trunk ended twelve feet up and branched into six limbs that curved out of the trunk first sideways and then upward, resembling a cupped palm with too many fingers. The Wolves had rigged a patchwork of tents into these branches, making an area beneath that stayed dry as long as the wind kept down.

Wind would have been welcome in the humid air of the swamp, where runoff came to die. There was an air of death, decay, and corruption to the flooded Yazoo Delta that no graveyard could match. Mists and fogs haunted the neophyte Wolves, and mysterious wildlife voices croaked and hooted and gibbered from the bulrushes. Even their camp resembled an abattoir, with their packs and water bottles hung from the low branches like trophies on a gamekeeper's gibbet.

Valentine sweltered in his cocoon of mosquito netting in a shallow sleep brought on by heat exhaustion. His usually pleasant hammock had been transformed into a torture chamber by the temperature and humidity. Naturally he preferred to keep himself, like his clothing and his pack, off the ground and out of reach of the various multilegged crawlies and snakes that might be attracted to a warm, motionless body on the damp earth. Only the earliest hours of the morning brought a lessening of the heat. He would give anything he owned for a swim in one of Minnesota's clear cool lakes in this Delta summer. But even if he had been physically comfortable, he would still have passed a fitful night. The old dream about his family home had come back.

Eveready's predawn return cut off his old nightmare. The Cat had walked off into the east within an hour of picking the spot for their camp days ago, leaving orders to wait and not to use guns while hunting. Eveready declined to explain whether this was because of nearby danger or just the parsimony brought on by visiting a supply station twice a year.

"Everybody up," Eveready announced, laboring into camp with a heavy sack across his shoulder. His ancient M-1 carbine was slung across his chest, stock glowing with its usual loving polish of well-oiled wood. Burton, who had the third watch, started to pour water into the coffeepot. "Forget that for now, Burt," the Cat rasped. "You boys aren't going to want breakfast when you see what I've brung home. Hand me that water, boy."

Valentine tried to rub the gum from his eyes as he watched Eveready drink. Though the black-skinned man was a Cat, one of the caste whose members operated alone deep in Kurian-conquered territory, there was nothing catlike about him. Eveready was a grizzled old warthog: all tough-minded determination on a thick body beneath a thicker hide. Barefoot, with ragged black trousers that ended at calves as wide as horse hooves, the rest of his body resembled a barrel with arms added as an afterthought. Chest muscles strained from an equally ragged vest cut from the heavy ablative cloth that the Reapers wore, and his neck was festooned with dangling teeth pulled from the Hoods he'd exterminated. The Wolves had never seen him eat anything but oversalted game stews and apples—Valentine believed Eveready knew the location of every single apple tree and grove within a three-hundred-mile arc of the Yazoo Delta—and this eccentric diet had left him with ageless vitality and shining white teeth. He was bald as the man in the moon but hid the fact with a battered baseball cap with a Saints logo. Eveready could climb like an ape, float like an alligator, and leap like a deer, all without making enough noise to cause a mouse to startle.

Easing himself out of the hammock, Valentine shook his head and took a pull from the water bottle he bedded down with to save a trip out of the mosquito netting. He pulled on his moccasins after eyeing the insides. Though they had hung from his hammock, the ingenuity of the Yazoo wildlife at curling up for a nap where least expected had been brought home to Valentine by a painful centipede bite earlier in the summer.

"What did you bring us, Santa?" Alistar, one of the Wolves, asked.

The Wolves gathered, and Eveready dumped the stained sack in the center of the campground. At first Valentine thought it was a trick of the rapidly growing light, but the sack seemed to writhe as it hit ground.

"Valentine, get your chopper," Eveready ordered. Valentine retrieved his parang, a fourteen-inch broad hunting knife swelled at the center like a pregnant machete. It had a heavy wood handle with the tang capped at the end, combining the sharpness of a skinning knife with the utility of a hatchet.

Eveready used his own smaller clasp knife to cut open the bag, which Valentine saw with a kind of cold horror really was squirming on its own in the center of the ring of five men. The big Cat dumped the sack's contents.

"Fuck me!" Burton said, and pulled at the beard he had been growing all summer.

Flopping in the dawn was a pale humanoid torso. Where arms and legs should have been, only tarry stumps remained. A second sack fixed by cording circled around the neck and hid the thing's face. Burton half laughed, half retched at the sweet corruptive odor that made the Wolves take a step back. Sixteen-year-old Hernandez, the youngest of the new Wolves, crossed himself.

"Never seen one this close, boys?" Eveready asked. The four shook their heads, disgusted and fascinated at the same time.

"There are these big hunting cats in a place on the other side of the world, boys. India, it was called. Big stripy orange things called tigers. You wouldn't think they could sneak up on anything, unless you saw them moving through tall grass on our televisions, that is. But a momma tiger would teach her baby to kill by swatting something so it was half-dead; then the cub would kill it. Now that ain't exactly what I'm doing with you cubs, but I want you to get a good look at a Hood up close, minus his robes, in such a way that you'll live through the seeing of it. Sort of a National Geographic, courtesy of old Eveready."

The thing rolled on its back and made an inarticulate glubbing sound.

"Bastard can't talk too good," Eveready continued, reaching into his forage pouch. "I yanked this out." The Cat handed over the Reaper's limp, sixteen-inch-long tongue, and the Wolves passed it around dubiously. It reminded Valentine of a snake, scaly with a beaklike point at the end. "That's the straw it sticks into you. See the scales? They come up in you like barbs, keep you from pulling away. Not that you have much chance if this honey's got you in his arms."

"How . . . how did you bag it?" Valentine asked.

"I was scouting a little railroad town southeast of Big M's ruins. Holly Springs. Sources told me this fella came into town about midnight, doing the usual checkup with a company of Quislings out of Corinth. Any time a Reaper comes through, a few folks try to leave town real quick, and this thing goes after them when it was getting on toward dawn. The Quislings were too busy in the henhouses and pigpens to notice much. A hungry Reaper is hard enough to keep up with and maybe they didn't want to be around when he fed. So these refugees are heading for tall timber on horseback, and the yellow eye here is after them. He got one just as the sun came up, fed, and I caught up with him when he got all dopey from the drinking. It was a pretty bright morning for a change, so his eyes weren't working too well, either. I emptied old Trudy into him from about ten feet," he said, patting his carbine affectionately. "Shot a leg more or less off where it was showing under the robe, and took the rest off with my cavalry saber before he knew what hit him. I hacked around at his throat and pulled his tongue out from beneath the jaw,

Colombian-necktie style. Sacked him up, then caught up with the horse belonging to the poor bastard he caught. Then I about broke my ass getting west."

Eveready chuckled. "I wouldn't care to be that Quisling commander in Holly Springs. The Big Boss in Corinth will send some Hoods out to settle things, with me and them both."

"You covered some miles," Alistar said. "Where's the horse, rode to death? We could've traded it, at least."

Eveready shook his head. "There was some border trash camped out by a crick a few miles northeast of here. I gave the horse her head, just took the saddle and bridle off, and she scented the other horses and wandered off. I carried the saddle aways, but it was too much lugging the ghoul and all that leather, too. I didn't want to be too slow; this guy's friends might home in on him."

"Hard on the group by the crick, if the Reapers catch up with that horse," Valentine suggested.

"They ain't no friends of yours, son. That's why I've been warning you boys about these borderlands. No law and order. There's the bad order of the Kurian spaces, and the law of the Free Territory. In fact, you'd be surprised at how orderly some of those Kurian towns are. Everybody with identity cards and permission slips and papers just to go to the outhouse. But between 'em where we are is up for grabs, and these bastards will rob you and leave you for dead as soon as they'd say 'Good morning.' I figure any Hood pursuit is welcome to 'em.

"Now let's get down to business. Gimme your slaying blade, Valentine. Now watch this," Eveready lectured as if he were in a classroom with glossy black experiment tables instead of a patch of soggy ground forty miles from nowhere. He opened a vertical cut along the thing's stomach. "See how that black goo comes up when the air hits it? It's something in these things' blood that makes an instant suture. If you ever get any on your hands, get it off quick, and whatever you do, don't get it in your mouth. Put some of this stuff on a dog's tongue, and it'll kill the man holding the leash. It's not so bad though; even when you're hacking one up, the goo doesn't fly around that much. It's too sticky. Make sure you pull your blade out quickly, though; if you leave it in for a few seconds even, this stuff will sometimes glue it right in place. Take my word for it, you don't want that to happen."

The Reaper thrashed around in pain, and Valentine stuck his foot on its chest to hold it in place. The smell sickened him. He felt thankful for his empty stomach.

"The sumbitch is moving around too much," Eveready decided. "Let's finish him. But I want to look him in the eyes for a second," he stated, cutting the cords around the thing's neck with the sharp edge at the tip of Valentine's parang.

The Reaper's face was a mess. Two gummed-over bullet holes in the cheek and forehead stood out against the deathly pale skin. Black fangs snarled at them from above the butchered neck. Its eyes were not the pink of a true albino's but rather black, with slit pupils and yellowish reptilian irises. It hissed, glaring hatefully at the five humans around it. Valentine felt hard pressure against his foot as it tried to wiggle loose despite its injuries. Valentine looked into its eyes and felt lost in the black depths. Was there such a thing as blacker than black? He felt himself compelled to lift his foot off the thing's chest.

"Steady there, David. You look like you might keel over," a voice said from somewhere near the Gulf Coast.

Valentine tried to raise his eyes from the black slits, failed.

Don't give in to the darkness, a part of his consciousness urged. *It's only the black eyes of the crow, picking at your fa-*

ther's brains. He raised his eyes up to the lightening sky and planted his foot even more firmly on the mutilated torso.

"That's better, David," Eveready said, patting Valentine's shoulder. "You got to watch those eyes. For a second there, you looked like a bird staring at a snake. You weren't seeing the Hood, it was the Kurian behind it."

Eveready leaned over its face, taking a small cylinder from his pocket with his left hand. It was a crusty old battery, of a type invented just before 2022 that had a very prolonged shelf life. A symbol of a black cat leaping through an electric hoop could be seen on the casing.

"Here I am again, hungry Prince," Eveready taunted at the snapping face. "Old Eveready got another of your drones, you murdering pig. I know it feels good when your little bloodsucker here takes a life. How do you like it when I do this?" He waved the battery label as close to the snarling face as he dared and brought the curved blade down on the thing's neck with a grunt of effort.

The body quit moving under Valentine's foot. He glanced down, afraid to meet those baleful eyes a second time. A fresh wave of moldy-crypt odor wafted from the corpse of the Reaper, causing Burton to empty the remains of last night's dinner from his stomach. Alistar sank to his knees, trying not to join him.

Eveready thrust the parang into the dirt and picked up the head, cautiously draining the black syrup from the neck. Holding it by the scraggly black hair, he displayed the trophy up for the Wolves to get a good look. "See how the teeth are black? We call that stuff carbonite. It's not a scientific name or anything; I think it's out of a movie. Stronger than steel, and Kur builds the Hoods so they use the stuff for their skeletons, teeth, and nails. Stops bullets pretty good. I saw one take a faceful of double-ought from about two feet one time. The eye and nose holes are baffled, not open like in a human skull, so the sumbitch was just blinded, and mebbe couldn't smell too good either. But it kept coming for us. And while I left this bastard's fingers behind, they have these pointed black carbonite fingernails that can claw through a safe door, peeling it back layer by layer."

The Cat wedged the old battery into the Reaper's mouth and stuck the head in the crotch of a nearby tree. Its eyes rolled around in their sockets. "It's dead, don't let that unsettle you. Just nerve impulses or something."

Returning to the body, Eveready continued the autopsy. He began to peel back layers of skin with parang and skinning knife, sticking small broken branches through the skin to keep the wounds open. The black tar had stopped flowing with the creature's death, but an abundance of oily clear liquid seeped out of the cadaver. Alistar was still on his knees and looked about to go to all fours, and Hernandez was wiping his mouth with the back of his hand. None of them would eat that day, Valentine suspected.

"Okay, a whole bunch of a human being is taken up by equipment to process different kinds of food into our blood. These monsters don't need all that; they have as simple a digestive system as can be. But they have this big bladder inside; see that thing that looks kind of like a honeycomb?" He opened up the spongelike organ, bigger than a bovine liver. "Those little sacks fill up with blood like a camel's hump, and pass through this thing, which is kind of like a big placenta, to its bloodstream. And see those two thick cables going down its sides? Those are nerve trunks; it's got more than one. Yours goes up the backbone; if that gets snapped, you're dead. You can break its back and maybe it'll just walk funny, 'cause it's got these other nerve trunks. All wired to a couple of balancing organs in the head, gives them ungodly reflexes and agility. Little clusters of nerve cells at pressure points help that. Their spines are much more flexible than yours, like a cat's, and their knees are hinged so they can bend backward, coiling just about every major muscle in their bodies for a jump.

"Everything's heavier than ours: bone, skin, muscle. Makes them crappy swimmers. They can move through water, but they really have to thrash, so you can hear them coming with all the splashing. I keep telling the jokers in the Free Territory to dig wide moats around everything they build, something they can't jump over, but they don't want to make the effort. If you ask me, if a hundred Kurians got organized, they could go through Southern Command like a bullet through a paper target."

Valentine raised his hand. Since Eveready was showing this unsuspected schoolmarm side, it seemed the appropriate thing to do.

"Why don't they?"

"Overrun us, you mean? One of the things we don't know. We do know that each Kurian boss or Prince or Master or whatever has grown his thirteen Reapers to feed him and run his show. We think it hurts them when one of their puppets gets killed. There's some kind of special link that allows the vital auras absorbed by the Reapers to feed the Kurian that controls them. Over the years, the stories about Kur got confused, that is if our ancestors ever had them right to begin with. We combined the two creatures, the Reaper and its Master, into one vampire legend. But 'that's got nuthin' to do with nuthin'' as my old man used to say. The Masters don't like to have all their Reapers together in one spot. We think if all of 'em buy it, so does the Kurian. Those Kurians are selfish pricks, too. They don't risk their Hoods helping out other Kurians. You see it in the different ways their little principalities are organized. Maybe they even fight among themselves, like Mafia gangs—if you know what those were. We can only hope. They're not too creative. They don't seem to invent anything. The Lifeweavers got a philosophical answer to that; they say that the Kurians have degenerated over the millennia, becoming like addicts who can't see beyond the next fix. Nothing matters to them but keeping the vital auras flowing. Even when they invaded, they laid the groundwork well, but once it started, it was like the Oklahoma land rush: they all grabbed a spot and started harvesting . . . well, us.

"But all that is for the thinkers and strategists and leaders. You boys have got to be the killers, so just remember this one thing: the only damage that puts a Hood permanently out of commission is a central nervous system disconnect. That means severing the head or blowing it to bits. And since they duck faster than most folks can swing, let alone pull a trigger, it ain't easy. You got to get them when they're dopey, after they've fed or in good daylight. You get them out in the sun without their robes, they get so sick you can slice them up easy as pie. Sometimes they get laid up in a trance, either daytime or nighttime, and that's a good time to hit 'em, too. My theory is that a Kurian Lord can't really control more than one Reaper at the same time, and the others either go on pure instinct, feeding off whatever's around until they're gorged and pass out, or they fall into this trance while the Kurian is controlling a different Hood."

"Sir," Hernandez piped up. "You said there would be others on this one's trail. Are we gonna jump 'em?"

A small smile broke out across Eveready's ebony features. "Son, you got more balls than brains. You ain't even blooded Wolves yet. For the last time, save the *sir* stuff for the ones that have to hear it to believe in themselves. I'm here to teach you how to keep hid so the Reapers don't find you. Fighting a Reaper's a job for a team of Wolves. Yassuh, about ten-to-one odds is what you need. And that's ten well-armed, experienced Wolves. Even I don't take on an up-and-running Reaper if I can avoid it. I got all these teeth by being patient," he said, fingering the rope of polished fangs across his hairy chest. "You need to hit the enemy when he ain't looking for you, not when he is. A stand-up fight is work for the Bears, and even they die faster than the Lifeweavers can replace 'em sometimes.

"Nope, it's been a fun summer, but I want to get you all back across the Saint Francis alive and well. Hopefully a little bit wiser, too. School's just about out, boys."

Getting to the Saint Francis meant they first had to cross the Mississippi. Wide, muddy, and sandbar-choked at this time of year, the Father of Waters was no easy obstacle to overcome. Quisling traders and river patrols frequented it in battered boats and bulky barges, pulled by diesel tugs.

The afternoon after the grim session with the Reaper's body, the party started a leisurely journey westward. The Cat encouraged them to concentrate on keeping lifesign down, but Valentine's doubts prodded and pulled him out of his sublimation with hard staves. What if he failed to keep himself centered, as the Cat liked to call it, and drew the hunting Reapers to his comrades like sharks to a blood trail? The others seemed so confident, talking about how they would take their first Hood, discussing ambushes and cross fires and carefully planned traps. Valentine had barely survived his first encounter with a Hood, and heard again and again in his mind the terrible screaming of the steady, stolid DelVecchio as the Reaper's needle-tongue found his beating heart.

The plentiful wild rice and bullheads of the Delta fed the five men on their bayou-bridging journey to the river. The

Wolves had grown so experienced in navigating the trackless morass that they hardly thought twice about wading or swimming a bayou in pairs and trios, one group always covering the other as they moved southwest. They reached the great river on a hazy afternoon two days later. Upon sighting it, Valentine forgot his doubts in the breadth and majesty of the current. Or perhaps it was just the change in the air after the miasma of the backwaters.

"Two choices, boys," Eveready announced from a teamhuddle squat. "We build us a raft, or we go find the one we sunk after crossing over back in the spring. Might take a day or two to find the spot; we're just a little south of it now. If we build a raft, it means chopping wood, and that can be heard a long way off. Also, we won't stand a chance if we run into a patrol except to swim for it. If we go to the old boat and raise it, we'll have something a little more navigable. But I've got my doubts it'll even be there after all these months. The river men and patrols spend all their time along the banks, and chances are one of them already thumped it with a pole or a paddle even if it is still underwater."

The Wolves decided to vote, with Eveready as tiebreaker. Valentine was the lone vote for building a raft, as he saw little reward and a good deal of risk in blundering along the bank in search of the old aluminum fishing boat that had brought them across the first time. The others remembered a little too well the want-of-a-nail lecture they'd received before departing for the Delta. It concerned coming home with weapons and gear issued, under pain of having to spend the next year on stable and livestock duty.

So they turned north.

Traveling the banks of the Mississippi made even the bayous seem like afternoon picnicking. The flooded and unattended banks turned the great river into a twisting mass of horseshoe loops and tadpole floods. Eveready took what shortcuts he knew and always kept an eye to the river. Although they could spot a patrol boat long before the Quislings had a chance at seeing the Wolves, every appearance of one of the noisy, fiberglass cabin cruisers made them get under cover while it plodded back and forth across the river. The first day there were two such sightings, each one wasting over an hour.

Valentine was jumpy the whole march. The others noticed it and put his mood down to bitterness over the vote on how to get across the river.

"Ain't nothing here worth the bogeymen keeping an eye on," Hernandez asserted.

"C'mon, Val," Alistar added. "With that old gumbo stirrer up on point, we've never even been spotted, let alone walked into an ambush." The gumbo stirrer in question waved from the crest of a small hillock ahead. Eveready had spotted something, and the Wolves obediently waited as the Cat went in for a closer look at whatever it was.

The sun was at the final landing in its descent of the staircase at the horizon. Valentine wondered at the simplicity of the age Eveready and his own father had been born into, when a red sunset meant only a beautiful end to another day rather than the beginning of eight hours of shadowed threat.

Valentine tried listening with "hard" ears as Eveready moved up the crest of the little hill at a level so just the Cat's head could be seen from the reverse slope of the hill where the object of his attention lay. Eveready's sure footfalls snapped no branch or twig detectable to Valentine's senses, raised to atavistic acuity. Eveready stopped, having found the best vantage, and stood for a full quarter-hour, staring motionless into the lengthening shadows.

Burton, who had already acquired the veteran's knack of

sleeping at any opportunity, was softly snoring by the time Eveready returned. Alistar jostled him into wakefulness with a push of his moccasined foot.

"Is it that dogleg pond where we sunk the boat?"

"It's a boat, all right," Eveready said. "But not ours. Big wooden canoe, pulled up and overturned. There weren't any leaves or twigs or anything on it, so I bet it's just been there a day or two. And I'd just about bet Trudy against one of your Free Territory buckchits there's oars sitting under it."

The Wolves exchanged grins, but Valentine's was forced, almost more of a grimace. Good boats didn't just get left on their own, even if they were wooden canoes. A canoe would be an impractical boat for a long patrol, and a tiring one for a trip upriver. And he knew, without knowing how he knew, that his uneasiness came from something having to do with the canoe in the same way that a plague-sheet hanging on the door of a house meant death inside. Something cold and fearful tickled at his mind.

"I say we move quick, before the owners come back," Alistar said, rubbing his palms against each other.

"It's a risk, but I'd like to be across tonight," Burton agreed. Hernandez just nodded, and the three turned to Valentine.

Eveready's eyes met his. "It's a gamble, David, but I think it's okay. You feeling all right? You look like something you ate doesn't agree with you."

Trust the Cat, who lived by and for his stomach, to chalk up Valentine's unease to indigestion.

"Just a feeling. Old Padre, the guy who raised me, used to call it a *vibe*. There were good ones and bad ones. I guess I'm getting a bad one. This place doesn't feel right."

Alistar made a sound that might be interpreted as clucking. Eveready ignored it. "Son, when I used to have hair on my head, if it went up, I backed off. I wouldn't be alive today if I didn't pay attention to the part of me that was quivering like a bowl of Jell-O. Which reminds me. When the four of us are back at Newpost Arkansas, I'm going to do some trading at the butchers and make you all some apple Jell-O. My momma's own recipe, with custard crème on top."

"We'll hold you to it," Valentine said, steadiness returning to his voice. "Let's have a look at this boat of ours."

From Eveready's little hillock, it looked easy enough. The canoe was pulled up, well out of the river's reach, on a little backwater of the river. A long peninsula of land, probably an islet at some times of the year, pointed westward beyond the boat: rising and then falling away rapidly like the profile of a wooded sphinx.

Valentine, after a quick look at the overturned boat, gazed at the spur of land pointing into the river. Something about that ominous shape troubled him. But if Eveready, veteran of thirty years' guerrilla fighting against the Reapers, thought it was safe, why shouldn't he trust the wisdom that had not yet put them into danger?

Later, he castigated himself for his silence. The Wolves spaced themselves out and readied their weapons. Eveready unslung his carbine.

"I'm going to take a little look-see. You four relax, stay centered, keep your lifesign down, breathe deep. We got lucky. It'll be dark as we're trying to cross, and the moon won't be up for a while. But I want to make sure, just in case Val's radar is working better than my own."

Valentine nodded, struggling with an encouraging smile as he tried to put into practice what Eveready preached. He envisioned his body glowing with a warm red aura. As he centered himself, he envisioned that aura changing color to blue. Then he began to contract the blue, drawing it inward with each breath. As he inhaled, the blue glow shrank to a small, softly glowing ball in the center of his body. The world around him seemed to fade.

Eveready approached the boat in two great loops, moving to the low edge of the sphinx-peninsula and then back to the base of their own hill before scouting the boat more closely. He even pointed his rifle under it as he approached, but as the last of the daylight faded into twilight's gloaming, he waved the Wolves down.

The canoe was wider than most, well fashioned out of overlapping planks. Someone had put a great deal of time and effort into making it; the wood shone with a polished luster. Two men could sit abreast on its two fore-and-aft seats, and there was room for their packs under the thwarts. The canoe would have held twice their number. Four oars, matching the wood, lay underneath. They decided that the four young Wolves would row two to a side, and Eveready would sit in the center with rifle ready. Darkness grew as they inspected their prize.

"Let's get out into the current quick," Eveready ordered. "If someone starts shooting, the wood is thick enough to stop a bullet fired from anything but point-blank, so just dive into the bottom and let the river take us away. I'll row by myself if I have to. This old Reaper vest stopped a bullet in my back before. Southern Command, in its wisdom, saves this stuff for the Bears, when they can get our guys to turn in the spoils of war, that is. Many's the old Wolf that has one of these under his leathers where the officers don't see it. Not that I'm advising you young men to break regulations, now."

While Eveready stood guard, the four Wolves overturned the heavy canoe and slid it down the gentle gravelly slope. Hernandez pushed a driftwood log out of the way and hooked his hand on to the bow of the canoe as the team heaved their transportation into the Mississippi.

"Hey, did you see this?" Hernandez asked.

Valentine peered through the blue-black night at the bow of the canoe. An insigne had been branded into the wood, scarring the delicate grain with four black bent bars. Something about the spiderish design tickled Valentine's capacious memory. . . .

"That's a swash-sticker, I think. Only it's backwards," Alistar said, in a hushed tone.

"The Germans and Japanese had them on their planes and stuff in World War Two, right?" Burton added, uncertainty in his voice. His schooling, like that of his comrades with the exception of Valentine, had been sporadic.

"Just the Nazi Germans," Valentine said. "But Alistar is right, it's the wrong way around."

Eveready came down from his post. "Into the boat, boys. Try not to splash around when you row. I don't like being this close to the bank."

"Eveready, this mean anything?" Valentine asked, pointing at the palm-size design on the bow.

Eveready squinted his aging eyes at the swastika. Good as his distance vision was, he struggled with his "reading eyes." For the first time in the entire summer, the big Cat looked afraid. "It means trouble. Let's not waste time; we don't want the owners to find us." He clicked the safety off on his ancient gun. Another first, and far more unsettling.

They clambered into their allotted places and took up the oars. A few lusty strokes took them away from the bank. The canoe seemed to glide on a sea of oil.

"Breathe and row, breathe and row," Eveready half chanted, kneeling in the center of the canoe. Valentine glanced at him from the right forward seat. He and Burton, the most muscular of the Wolves, provided the power for Alistar and Hernandez at the back. Eveready searched the sphinx-shape to their right, rifle at his shoulder.

Valentine relaxed into his breathing and rowing. Reducing lifesign was a matter of falling into yourself, concentrating on a single tiny point in the center of your being, like a candle glimmering in the middle of an enormous lake.

The candle flickered.

He felt his hackles rise, a curious corkscrew electricity running up his backbone, as if Death had run a playful forefinger up his vertebrae. A cold, hard spot appeared in his mind, coming from the head of the sphinx. Unable to say what it was, he knew only that he feared it.

"Eveready," he said, voice low in his concentration. "The very top of the hill. Maybe by that big windfall trunk . . . I think something's up there."

The matchless night vision of the Cat searched the hilltop peak as the boat shot toward open river. Valentine dug his oar blade into the water as if trying to dig a hole for the boat to hide in.

"Val, I think you're right. It's up there, but not moving. A Reaper. Hard ears, boys. This is a sound you need to know."

Fingernails on the blackboard. The cry of a stricken hawk. Sheet metal squeezed in a compactor. Each would remember the banshee wail differently, loud and fresh and terrifying, to their dying day.

"Madre de Dios," Hernandez gasped, missing a stroke. "Shit!" he added, "I'm sorry, I dropped my oar."

"Use your rifle butt!" barked Valentine.

Other, distant wails answered the ghostly cry.

"Five," counted Eveready. "One for each of us. Hope that's luck, not planning."

The clouds thickened and dropped, bringing the horizon to

a few feet from their faces. Aghast, Valentine brought his palm to the sky, barely able to see its outline.

"How the hell . . . do they do that?" Burton asked, puffing between strokes.

"I'd rather know how they knew we were going to hit this stretch of the river," Valentine said as he paddled.

Even in their current perilous situation, Eveready had lessons to teach. "They're disrupting your minds, not the weather. This could even mean a Kurian himself is around or working us from his Seat of Power. I've heard they can make a city seem to go up in flames, or a building catch real fire, just by willing it.

"They're reading us somehow. One or more of you might be giving off lifesign. While the swamp is full of it, if one of them were close to us, they might have picked up on ours, kept their distance, and just plotted where we were going. We'll never know for sure. The good news is that while they can swim the river, it'll take 'em a while. We can be across and separate, and head for the New Arkansas Post like hell. They'll go after whoever they can pick up on, and with luck the rest of us will make it back."

"Jesus, that's cold," Burton gasped.

"Makes sense to me," Alistar said.

Valentine swallowed his fear. "Can't do it, Eveready. We're Wolves—"

"I was a Wolf before you were born, son, and—"

"Then you should know," Valentine interrupted right back. "We stay as a team, whether it's two or two hundred. Only the dead get left behind."

"Whoever's giving off lifesign is dead already, Val," Eveready argued, trying to pierce the black curtain behind them. "Maybe not tonight, but some other trip in the future."

"We don't know they're reading lifesign. Maybe they

tracked us the old-fashioned way. There are sniffer-Grogs, I'm told."

"Sorry, kid. I've got experience, and you don't. Gotta be lifesign."

Valentine broke the glum silence. "I say we put it to a vote. Every man for himself, yea or nay. If we decide to stick together, we put you off on the west shore. Alone, the way you like it." Valentine feared he might have pushed the old Cat too far. Maybe the vote would go four to one against him again, but he needed to try.

"No, no votes. Not with five Reapers on your tail," rasped Eveready.

"This isn't about you anymore," said Burton. "It's for us to say."

"Have it your way. Idiots. You know, if one Reaper catches up with you four, *just one,* you'll all be dead in twenty seconds. Five seconds each."

"Okay, lets take a breather," Valentine ordered, turning himself around in the boat to face his fellow Wolves. "Tradition. Youngest first. Hernandez? Every man for himself: yea or nay."

Valentine expected the sixteen-year-old to glance around at the others, or at least Alistar, for approval. But he looked squarely into Eveready's eyes. His hero. The man he called *sir* despite Eveready's repeated commands to knock it off.

"Nay."

Valentine's heart leaped. He could have hugged the skinny youth. "Alistar?"

The tawny youth, who thought himself the leader of the Wolves through this summer, shook his head at Valentine, a half-sneer on his face. "Yea."

"Fuck you, Al," Burton spat. "Nay. And fuck you again, in case you didn't hear me the first time."

"Nay," added Valentine, trying not to grin in triumph. "Alistar, you can get off with Eveready, if you like."

"You bet your ass I like."

"Can we get moving, Valentine?" Eveready asked.

The four rowed with renewed vigor. Valentine, feeling the energy of vindication in his limbs, dug his paddle deep into the water. Burton poured out his fury on the other side, and the canoe sped through the night.

Within five minutes, the western shore loomed out of the darkness. Alistar buckled on his pack, and Eveready jumped out and held the canoe steady. Hernandez started to put on his pack.

"Wait, Hernandez. We're staying in the boat," Valentine ordered.

"What's that?" Eveready asked.

Valentine put his oar behind his back and stretched. "Burton, let's switch places so I can use some different muscles. Eveready, you said they don't swim too fast, right? We head downriver, with the current. We'll hear any patrol boat. Go all night if we have to, then start moving overland at dawn."

"Hell, kid, if you had a plan, you should have said so. You're still taking a risk that the Reapers don't have another boat."

"You said five. This boat fits five easy. Can you still draw one off?"

Eveready smiled, apple-whitened teeth the brightest thing Valentine had seen all night, like a beacon of hope. "If one is still following me by sunrise, it won't live to see another nightfall."

"Alistar, last chance," Valentine called to the receding figure.

"You'll be bled out before dawn, Valentine," Alistar said. He turned. "Hernandez, this is your last chance, too."

The teen shook his head. "Sorry, Al. The pack stays together."

Alistar tightened his straps, managing to put contempt in the gesture. "Hope you make it anyway. I'll wait for you at Arkansas Post."

Eveready stepped closer to Valentine. "David, give me your gun."

Valentine reached into the bottom of the boat and brought up the single-shot breechloader. "Why's that?"

"We're gonna swap. I don't know if you have more guts than brains, or more brains than guts, but Trudy can pump five shots into a Reaper faster than you can count. You shot her pretty good this summer. You may need her tonight."

"Aren't you worried you'll never see her again?"

"Just don't let some Quisling mother take her off your body. Bury her at sea when she's empty. You know what I mean?"

The men exchanged rifles and ammunition. "I know what you mean. See you in hell, Cat."

"I'll be waiting, Wolf." Eveready shook his hand, then gripped his fingers in a curious gesture. "David, if you make it, tell your CO about how you sensed that Hood. That's unique. They'll want to know more about it, and you."

"I'll worry about getting home first. Take care!"

Eveready, still standing in the water, turned the canoe and pushed them southward.

"Get running, Alistar, it's every man for himself," Eveready said. "You heading north or south?"

Valentine listened with hard ears.

"I thought we could make the run together," Alistar said, deflated.

"Not a chance. I have to move fast and alone if I'm gonna

draw one of these off. Take off, boy. I hope you make it, but I can't have you around me."

As they drew away, Valentine heard a shout from the Cat's muscular throat, perhaps strong enough to be heard across the river by the Hoods' ears:

"Halloo! Hoods, come on over. Eveready's in the house, and he wants to par-tay. Bring it on, you balless bastards. I got forty-five sets of teeth around my neck, motherfuckers. I wanna make it an even fifty!"

The canoe glided southward, propelled by current and oars. Valentine realized he was achingly tired; they had marched all day on light food. Water was not a problem; the center of the big muddy gave them all they could desire, clear and cool.

"Hernandez, turn in. Just relax for a couple hours in the bottom of the boat. Burt, you'll be after him. Take the stern for now. I'll take the third shift."

Hernandez almost collapsed into the center of the boat, asleep in a few seconds with his head pillowed on his pack.

"Jeez, he didn't even put his blanket down," Burton observed, after gaining the stern.

Valentine paddled on. "Anyway, you give off less lifesign when you're asleep. Just in case it was him."

"I thought it was me," Burton said.

"Funny, I thought the same thing," Valentine admitted. Both men chuckled. The canoe shot southward.

Splashing . . . an overactive imagination at work?

"Did you hear that, Burt?" Valentine whispered.

"Hear what?"

"Hard ears, Wolf. To the left. Didn't he say they made a lot of noise swimming?"

Burton quit rowing as both men concentrated their ears to

the left. Over the wind and noise of the river, a vigorous splashing could be heard.

"Oh, hell. Sorry, Burt. Looks like I guessed wrong,"

"Let's pump it, Val. We still got a chance. The fucker's a ways off, still. Hernandez," he said, knocking the sleeper with his foot. "Nap time's over, you got to do some rowing."

Hernandez yawned, pushing one arm into the sky and rubbing his eyes with the other. "Jeez, that felt great. How many hours did I sleep?"

"About two minutes. Get up here and row," Valentine ordered.

"What?"

Burton tossed the oar toward him. "Reaper is swimming for us. Don't drop your oar this time."

Propelled by terror, the three men pushed themselves to a stroke every two seconds. Valentine used his hard ears to locate the splashing, which began to fade first to the left, and then astern.

"We're leaving him behind. I think," Valentine said through gritted teeth.

A few minutes would tell the tale. Valentine counted strokes. At 214, he realized the ominous splashing was getting louder.

"Hell, a Hood," Burton swore, puffing. "How fast is it going?"

"Faster than us," Hernandez said.

Valentine could not resist looking over his left shoulder every few seconds. The moon was up, but high, thin clouds muted its three-quarter face. Their strokes began to slow as exhaustion set in. Valentine saw a pale figure, arms whirling like paddle wheels, splashing along behind them.

"I can see it now," Burton said, resigned.

A horrible image of the Reaper closing remorselessly on

them flickered through Valentine's mind. It would swim underwater the last few feet, push up and turn over the boat, then tear each of them to bits in the water. He looked back at the steadily gaining swimmer, moving through the water at a speed no Olympian could match, pale back visible in the moonlight.

It had removed its robes to go faster through the water.

"Take a rest," Valentine ordered, picking up Trudy. The magazine held thirty rounds. Another magazine rested in a leather pouch on the offside of the stock.

"What do you mean, take a rest? We gonna shoot ourselves?" Hernandez asked.

"I'm going to take a crack at him with Trudy," Valentine explained. "It took off its robes to go faster through the water."

"Jesus help you shoot straight," Hernandez babbled.

Valentine carefully tucked himself against the stern. He sat down, bracing his back against Burton's seat. He brought the rifle to his cheek and set the sights for a hundred yards. The two other Wolves panted as Valentine tried to quiet his own respiration and steady his trembling muscles. *Exhaustion or fear?* he wondered.

Breathing out, he fired three times, pausing for a second between each shot. The thirty-caliber carbine shell had a fair kick, but braced as he was, knee against the side of the canoe and back braced by the bench mounted behind him, the recoil was negligible.

Machinelike, the Reaper swam on. At this distance, Valentine couldn't make out splashes to see if he was hitting. He let the distance close another twenty yards, then fired three more times.

The Reaper dived.

Valentine scanned the surface of the water. How far could it go without air?

The wooden stock felt comforting against his cheek. He lowered the barrel slightly.

The thing breached twenty yards closer, and Valentine shot five times, missing in his panic. It disappeared underwater again.

Calm, calm, his mind told his body, but the body refused to cooperate. He quivered, unable to control the nervous tremors.

Jesus, it's close. The fierce, pale face surfaced twenty yards away, gulping air. Valentine shot, splashes erupting within inches of the head. One shot tore a black gash in its cheek. The head disappeared.

"Now, row, row for your lives!" Valentine shouted. He braced himself for the expected upheaval, as the thing tried to make it under the boat.

The canoe gained speed. Barely an arm's length away, the Reaper breached, coming halfway out of the water like a porpoise. Its mouth was open. Black teeth gleamed in its hellish fury.

Trudy spat as fast as Valentine could pull the trigger. Black holes appeared in the Reaper's chest as the spent cartridges bounced off the wooden sides of the canoe and into the water. The thing fell backward, thrashing more feebly. It rolled over and floated, facedown.

Valentine looked wonderingly at the smoking weapon and said a silent prayer for Eveready's safety. Trudy had saved their lives.

Valentine angled the canoe toward the western shore with the earliest light. There was always the chance that a river patrol would stop them. From here on, getting back into the

Ozark Free Territory was just a matter of bearing northwest for a couple of days.

Burton looked back into the river. "I don't believe it. He's still coming."

The Reaper swam on, using a sidestroke motion. So bullets were useless, after all. Valentine suppressed an urge to press the barrel of the rifle under his chin and blow his own brains out in defiance.

"Let's get ashore," he said, defeated.

The others carried their packs in one hand, rifles in the other. Valentine pushed the canoe off into the current and climbed up a short ledge to the riverbank proper. Burton was already heading toward a fallen tree.

The Wolves knelt down behind the log, too tired to run. *Two single-shot breechloaders and a full magazine in Trudy,* Valentine thought. *Plus our parangs. Enough?*

The Reaper paddled toward shore, leaving a wake that aimed at their tree like an arrow.

The haze dissipated into a cloudless morning. The sun shone yellow and bright, inching above the horizon.

Valentine looked at the sky in wonder. Only rarely, outside of winter, was it this clear overhead.

"We're saved. Saved by the sun," Valentine breathed.

The Reaper reached shallower water. It, too, raised its head to the sun, but in pain rather than praise. Thin black hair lay plastered over its chest and shoulders. Bullet holes formed a reverse question mark shape on its chest, and one arm hung askew.

Valentine stood up, copying Eveready's taunt. The Reaper cocked its head, shutting its eyes to squeeze out the daylight.

"Are you coming for us?" Valentine shouted.

The Reaper straightened. Its ears were working better than its eyes. It staggered, hammered by naked sunlight.

not today, it seems. but some night, in a lonely place, you'll be taken, it hissed.

"But not by you," Valentine said, raising his rifle.

The thing dived backwards, disappearing beneath the water.

In some ways, Valentine thought, *it's almost better than killing it. It ran. It was afraid.*

They made New Arkansas Post in four days. The little wooden fort on a bare hill overlooking the Black River was built like something out of an old-time western, right down to the sharpened logs serving as crenellated walls. More supply depot and stable than actual fort, it still contained the welcome sight of a cantina.

Eveready was waiting for them on the cantina's porch in a rocking chair, happily munching an apple, finishing everything but the stem. Two new fangs hung from his necklace. He chided Valentine about not finding the time to properly oil Trudy's stock after exposing her delicate wood to water.

Lewand Alistar was posted as missing a week later. His family received notification the following spring, during the recruiting swing through the Council Bluffs area of Iowa.

Six

Pine Bluff, Arkansas, fall of the forty-first year of the Kurian Order: At the beginnings of the fertile, flat corner of south-eastern Arkansas, the crossroads town of Pine Bluff thrives. Strategically located on the chord of an inhabited arc covering the borderlands in that quarter, a permanent garrison regiment of Guards frequently offers its hospitality to Wolf patrols into Louisiana and Mississippi.

Independent farmers from as far away as Drew County come to barter with the Southern Command Commissioners. The town itself boasts eight churches, a high school, blacksmiths and boatwrights, teamsters and tailors. The Guards stable their horses at the old Livestock Showgrounds, and no less than a full regiment known as the Bluffs protects the Old Arsenal, the largest and arguably the best munitions plant in the Free Territory. The Old Arsenal produces everything from bullets to bombs, protected by the heaviest concentration of pre-Overthrow machine guns in Southern Command. In town, the Molever Industrial Wood Products plant has switched from making pallets to sturdy wagons and river barges, and numerous craftsmen exhibit their wares each weekend at the Sixth Avenue Street Market. On evenings each weekend, the Saenger Theater Players sing, dance, and act out famous scenes from old movies and plays. The aged theater's cool limestone and Florentine decor make an opulent break from

*the meanness of everyday life. Shakespeare makes an occa-
sional appearance on the billboard, but more often a tear-
streaked heroine shakes her fist at the sky against a fiery red
backdrop, vowing never to be hungry again, or a pair of
lovers affirm deathless devotion as they cling to wreckage behind billowing sheets meant to represent an icy sea.*

*There is a sense of stability, order, and permanence to the
place that the settlements on the other borders lack. The
tracts of relatively empty Louisiana and Mississippi wetlands
protect it from quick forays, and the Guards are experienced
at fighting river-borne incursions. Their clothes are a little
better, the food is a little more varied, and the buckchits are
more welcome here than in the remoter regions of the Free
Territory. There is a regular newspaper and more regular
mail, and even a social stratification of sorts has taken hold,
for better or worse. The complacency here is a true achieve-
ment, one paid for in blood on the other borders.*

*David Valentine received orders to join Zulu Company at
Pine Bluff shortly after making his report to the officers at
New Arkansas Post. With the gift of an aged horse from the
post commander, a haversack of food from the supply sergeant, and a parting bag of apples from Eveready, he rode
west up the scenic, if broken-down, western highway. Once
known as US Highway 65, now called the Arkansas River
Trail, it is one of the better all-weather pikes of the Free Territory. Making easy stages out of respect for his slow-stepping
mount, Valentine reached the shores of Lake Pine Bluff.*

Valentine smelled the sentries before he saw them. The tobacco and wood-smoke odor meant there were men in the little earthen bunker even if nothing could be seen in the gloom
beneath the head logs. A pair of horses stood side to side
swishing flies in the morning breeze inside a little split-rail

corral overlooking the broken road. Valentine sniffed again and suspected halfhearted enforcement of latrine discipline in what, to the Guards anyway, must seem wilderness.

Head bobbing and ears forward, his horse quickened its walk. The roan gelding was old and wise and knew the smell of horses on a good diet.

A slight figure in a charcoal-gray uniform, comfortably barefoot with riding boots off, appeared from the dugout and waved. Valentine turned his horse with a gentle nudge of his moccasined heel.

"Good morning, stranger," said the youth, teal blue kepi and neckerchief proclaiming his membership in the Bluff Regiment. "What's your business up in town?"

Valentine brought up his forearm, palm outward, in the old Indian greeting. Not quite a salute, but friendly enough.

"Good morning," responded Valentine, but as most of his mornings began at the first pink of dawn, it seemed a little late for the salutation. "I'm three days out of New Arkansas Post with orders to report to the Commanding Wolf. Whereabouts can I find Captain LeHavre?"

"I need to see your orders," the sentry said, holding out his hand.

"They're verbal. The Wolves don't use much paper, Bluff."

"Then I can't let you through. We can send a message to get one of your Wolves in for escort, but I don't have authority to let you through."

More like too much authority and too little brain, Valentine thought. A good empiricist, he decided to test the theory. "Is that so? What's up the road that a man with a single-shot rifle on an old horse might take out, anyway?"

The soldier patted his rifle stock.

"Maybe you're a spy, come to look at the arsenal. Count

the machine-gun posts, map out the tanglefoot paths. Maybe you're going to set fire to a barge full of black powder and blow up everything on the dock—"

"Enough of that, Johnson," a stern female voice called from the bunker. "If he is a spy, he can turn around now. You just told him all he needs to know." A middle-aged, uniformed woman came out of the bunker and approached the road in the measured, confident stride of NCOs the world over. "We heard a Wolf was coming in from downriver. I figured you'd be on foot by now; any horse old Gregory would part with has got to be on its last trip. Is there news?"

"Not that I'm aware of. You're wrong about the horse, he's a nice ride, long as you don't ask more than he wants to give. Good thing, too, since I'm bareback," Valentine said.

"You'll find LeHavre up the road a few miles, just into town proper. The Wolves always camp at Old Harbor Woods, right at the north bend in the river. There's a brick entrance off the road, says it was a golf course. Still is, actually, on the sheep meadow. Don't have time for the game myself. You'll see your little tepees around the old clubhouse. Tell Captain LeHavre that Brit Manning says hi. We were at Webber's Falls together."

"You were a Wolf?" asked Valentine, not even knowing in what state to look for Webber's Falls on a map.

"No, but owing to your caste, we were ready for them when they tried to push into Fort Smith. Exactly ten years ago May. We bushwhacked them from the north while they were in the middle of ferrying across. So many Grogs ended up in the river, they say the Arkansas ran red. It didn't really, but it was still pretty hot there for a while. Two companies got caught on the wrong side of the river, and his Wolves saved our auras. You might say I thanked him personally afterwards," she reminisced, a sly smile crossing her weathered features.

"I'm sure he'll remember."

"You want some coffee, son? Just chicory, but it's hot. I'd offer you some lemonade, but my four boys here drank it all first two days we were here, and the rinds haven't soaked long enough to make another batch."

"No, thank you, Sergeant Manning. At my horse's pace, I'll be lucky to make the town by dinner." Valentine offered a true salute, crisply returned. "Thank you for the directions."

Captain LeHavre's steady green eyes evaluated Valentine from his pulled-back hair to his stained knee-high moccasins, fingers drumming against his thigh. The company commander wore the look of a busy man who accepted only efficiency.

The captain and Valentine both stood in the sole leak-free room in the old Harbor Clubhouse. Its dark paneling hinted at a previous existence as either an office or a small library. Two comfortable armchairs and a table, piled above and below with a honeycomb of plastic milk crates, almost filled the warm little room. Black-and-white photographs, most bearing the marks of poor film stock, hung in rough frames.

LeHavre flaunted the swarthy good looks and heavy mustache of a romance novel pirate or ruthless western outlaw. His athletic build, spoiled slightly by the hint of a paunch, set off his forest green buckskins, so dark they looked almost black in the dim light of the windowless office.

Offering Valentine a warm handshake in the worse-for-weather main entrance to the clubhouse, LeHavre invited his new Wolf to the "records room." Both men sank into the armchairs with the appreciation of the rarity of such comfort.

"You might call this our cave," LeHavre explained with a

casual wave toward the laden table. "These papers are the closest thing we have to a headquarters. The milk crates just make moving easier. The rest I leave to the clerk. Coffee, tea, beer?"

"A beer would be very welcome, sir," Valentine responded gratefully. "It's been a long summer."

LeHavre rose from the chair without using his arms, almost a levitating trick. "I'll bring two cool ones from the basement," he said.

Valentine looked around at the pictures, wondering about a man who would treat a wet-behind-the-ears recruit like an honored guest. In less than a minute, a breathless brown-skinned girl, seven or eight years of rubber-band energy and frizzy hair, bounced into the room with a clasp-stoppered bottle. LeHavre followed the little dynamo. "Meet David, Jill. David hails all the way from the Land of Ten Thousand Lakes. Which state is that, tadpole?"

"Minnesota," she said, showing a proud smile as she handed over the bottled beer. "Hi, David. Did you swim in those lakes?"

"Er, some of them. Why, do you like swimming?"

"Does she like swimming!" LeHavre interjected. "I check her feet whenever I can to make sure they aren't growing flippers. Don't I, tadpole."

"Uncle Adam!" she squealed.

"David came on a horse. Can you take him to the corral? He looks like he needs a brushing."

"Can do!" Jill said. "Nice to have made your act-tense, David."

"Acquaintance," LeHavre corrected.

"Likewise, I'm sure," Valentine responded, shaking her hand.

"Acquaintance," the girl repeated, a furrow crossing her

brow. She solemnly returned the handshake and stepped backwards out the door.

"That's Jill Poole. Her father was a lieutenant of mine. He died in a fight about three years ago. I look in on her mom whenever we're in the area. She runs a nice little boardinghouse right by the river. Fine woman; she keeps a firm hand on the boatmen who stay. It's not quite a marriage, but I think of Jill as my daughter. She's fearless around the men. Most of them remember Poole, and they indulge her. She loves making beadwork. Most of the Wolves in Zulu Company have a bracelet or something of hers."

LeHavre opened his bottle. "To the people we're fighting for," he toasted.

"Prosit," Valentine responded, imitating a memory of his father. The cool froth flushed the dry road away.

"My apologies, Valentine. I'm sure you want to know about the outfit you've been ordered to join. Zulu Company is one of ten companies in the Arkansas Regiment, which makes up the smaller half of the Wolf Brigade. There's only three thousand or so Wolves in all of Southern Command, counting Aspirants and reserves, and we're the most numerous of the Hunters. We're in reserve now. But don't expect to spend a lot of time dancing at regimental balls. Maybe two thirds of the regiment is together when we're wintering in the Ouachitas. We don't often fight shoulder-to-shoulder; the last time was when we stopped a Grog incursion out of St. Louis. That's when Poole bought it.

"Zulu Company has four platoons of about thirty men each, as of this month. Fifteen support personnel, mostly older Wolves who aren't up to running fifty miles a day anymore, seven wives and two husbands who can keep up with the camp, and four transport teams of four men, making me responsible for a little over one hundred fifty lives. I have twelve senior NCOs, but I'm short a lieutenant out of the three I should have. You want the job?"

Valentine swallowed his mouthful of beer, which had turned into a grapefruit descending his throat. "Me, an officer? Sir, I'm not even twenty yet."

"Napoléon was a lieutenant of artillery at sixteen, David."

"And Alexander the Great was a king breaking up rebellions at twenty, sir," Valentine interjected. "But I'm not either. I've never read a book about tactics."

The captain set down his beer and crossed the room to the desk. "Valentine, I've got a folder here. In it is what we call your 'Q file.' Don't ask me what the *Q* means, because I don't know. It's got your reports, about what happened on that barge, and it's going to contain your report on the Mississippi crossing, once the copy works its way here. There are some words from Wolves like Pankow and Paul Samuels. I also knew your father, slightly. I was younger than you are now in those days, and I'd give my right nut to be half the man he was. I heard he was murdered when you were still a boy."

LeHavre returned to the chair. "David, I know from people I trust that you've got brains and guts. You also take responsibility; most people try to hide from it. You've shown some initiative in going after the enemy, and Eveready told me that you're smart about avoiding a fight, too. Which takes a certain kind of courage."

Valentine listened to LeHavre's summation of his record as a Wolf. But LeHavre didn't know about the fear and horror inside the Harpy barge that had unmanned him into lighting his bomb without thinking it through. Or the stupid theatrics with a gun (a valuable pistol now submerged in the muddy river bottom thanks to his forgetting to hang on to it in the water) to get a cramped recruit on her feet. Or the luck of a clear sunrise that saved them on the shores of the Mississippi.

"And one more thing, David. Our very own Wizard, Amu, recommended you to me. That counts for something; he reads people like a book. Don't misunderstand me, please. Being an officer is a tough tackle. You drink last, eat last, sleep last, and usually die first. No one notices your good decisions, and you have to bury your bad ones and then write home to somebody's parents that their son stopped a bullet carrying out your orders. Getting them to fight is the least of your worries; the Wolves know their business. But getting them ready for a fight, choosing where and when, and then getting them back safely takes a special kind of person."

"Why did you become one, sir? An officer, I mean."

LeHavre sighed and pulled down the last of his beer. "Long story, David. I wasn't even a sergeant, just a vet in charge of four kids younger than you. Our platoon went into the wrong town. Quislings had a hell of a fine ambush set up. They'd killed just about everyone in what had been a friendly stop and filled it up with their people. Somehow they scared a family we knew into greeting us and making everything seem normal. Everyone was tired and hungry, so we dispersed for dinner and sleep. That's when they hit us. The lieutenant and sergeants got it first—it seemed like the lead was flying from every direction but up. I made it out and got some other survivors together, dogs at our heels and Reapers screaming from the hills. I've never been so scared before or since—been pretty damn close a few times, though—but we made it back. I carried a wounded Wolf the whole way, but she didn't weigh much over one-fifteen. So they made me an officer. Funny thing to do for a guy who spent three solid days running from the enemy.

"But that was a good number of years back. The Free Territory's changed from a backwater cluster of hard-luck farms to a real patch of civilization. The Kurians haven't had any luck stomping us. We're not as big as some of the groups out east, even. I understand there's a band of Hunters ranging the Green Mountains of New England up to Canada and down through the Smokies about twice the size of us, and the freehold in the Pacific Northwest has more square miles. But out east, they're more of a wandering guerrilla army; they don't have a spot to really call home. And in the west, well, it's only a rough confederation out there. A couple of the strongmen paying lip service to the Constitution and Bill of Rights. A few even think the Hunters and the Lifeweavers are part of the same disease as the Kurians. You'd think the days of men fighting anything but the Kurians and their Quislings are over, but I'm sad to say it just isn't so."

The captain shook his head, eyes downcast. "Curse of Babel, I guess. We just won't work on the same team sometimes. But back to the here and now. Can I count on you, Valentine?"

Has anyone ever counted on me? Valentine wondered. He thought of the gangly little girl, Jill, and her unknown mother. *Can they count on me? Will I be able to prevent some black-fanged monster from making lifeless husks of them?* He remembered the little Poole girl's response to LeHavre's request. Maybe LeHavre liked to be answered that way.

"Can do, sir," Valentine said, hoping the enthusiasm did not sound too forced.

The captain walked him out into the pleasant afternoon. The worst of the summer's heat had faded, and the clouds were piling on and thickening overhead. Five-pole tepees filled what was probably once a lawn and putting green.

"Zulu Company is spending time in reserve, Valentine," LeHavre repeated. "Your last winter you stayed in true winter camp. Four companies get to do that, another four are in reserve, leaving just two companies to stay in the Outlands.

They'll be spread thin, patrolling and relying on the Cats for notice of anything major outside the borders. If something happens, or a good opportunity to hurt the Hoods comes along, we go out of reserve. But that doesn't mean we'll be sitting on our rears. As of today, you're Acting-Lieutenant Valentine on my authority. The colonel will confirm after your course work gets done. We're not the Guards, the civilian government doesn't have to give its rubber stamp. I'm not giving you a platoon yet, though you'll get your bars right away. But back to your duties. You're going to be in charge of the support staff, transport teams, and the Aspirants. When you aren't doing that, you'll be running back and forth from the Officer's Training College, which holds classes at the old UA Pine Bluff Campus on the west side of the lake. If you want my advice, you'll memorize Sun-tzu and study the nineteenth-century campaigns of the Apaches and Comanches, and some Civil War histories of Bedford Forrest and Stonewall Jackson. Just read enough about the rest to pass your tests. You'll learn a lot about how to fight when you're outnumbered and outgunned. When you're reading about the Chiricahua, try not to remember that they were on the losing side. It'll be a hell of a schedule for you, but be grateful for it. We've got officers all over the place who are just jumped-up sergeants, and thought they're hell on wheels with the men, but sometimes the lack of formal training leads to problems."

"When's this going to start, sir?"

"It started the minute you accepted your commission, Lieutenant. The War College is always more or less in session. One more thing: Eveready said you got some kind of premonition that there were Reapers around. Answer me straight, was it a lucky guess, or did you really catch wind of something?"

Valentine thought for a moment before answering. "I can't

account for it, sir. It wasn't based on anything I actually sensed, more of a 'by the pricking of my thumbs—' "

" 'Something wicked this way comes'?" finished LeHavre. "That's interesting. Reapers make horses and dogs nuts, too. Well, the nearest thing we have to a center for study of the Kurians, by us humans anyway, is at the college here in Pine Bluff. They'll be interested in your story. There's a half-dozen people researching the New Order; they like to come out and talk to us after we've seen them up close. They always want to know which Kurian sent which Reapers—as if we can tell. Let's get you quartered, and you can go meet them tomorrow when you enroll yourself at the OTC."

The following day, after a delicious cool night in a cot in the warmth of the junior officers' tepee, which he had to himself because his tentmate was on a training patrol, Valentine rode through the bustling little town to the college campus. It was an uninspiring collection of solid little 1950s buildings dominated by a curious stunted tower: a clock that some tinkerer had restored to its function decorated it. Uniformed Guards sitting outside one brick building revealed the location of the War College. As he had business there, Valentine decided to make the OTC his first destination. Exchanging friendly nods with the lounging Guards outside, he followed an old black-and-white plastic sign with a red arrow. A chalkboard outside the open office door read:

THIS WEEK:
MAJ. JONAS BRATTLEBORO—MEDICINE IN THE FIELD
(TUES, WED, PM 114)
LT. P. HAYNES—BLACK POWDER TO THE STEEL-
JACKETED BULLET
(FRI, AM 106 /PM RIFLE RANGE)

Valentine entered the office. A breeze came through the open windows, but it was still uncomfortably hot, and the room had the sour smell of old paper. A young female Guard in a white cotton uniform Valentine identified as a cadet's, her face as fresh as this morning's flowers, rose and smiled.

"You must be the new Wolf from Zulu Company, sir. Nice to meet you, Acting-Lieutenant Valentine," she said. "My name is Cadet Lambert, but the guys here call me Dots. Because I'm kind of a born picture-straightener. I dot all the i's and cross all the t's."

"You're well informed, Lambert. I didn't know you Guards paid that much attention to the Wolves."

"There's one other Wolf studying here right now, sir. She's from Tango Company over at Fort Smith. She stays at the Poole Boardinghouse; she's a little older than you. Her name is Carol Pollisner. Usually the Wolves mustang up and don't have to do much formal classwork. Speaking of which, I have your packet all ready."

"Thank you, Lambert. How the hell old are you, if you don't mind me asking? You look about twelve." He took a heavy pack of paper wrapped up in a tied linen folder from her hand.

"I'm fifteen. But I passed the Guard physical, and I ran the table on the written test. I'm the Colonel Commanding's staff assistant until I turn eighteen. I actually prefer Dots, sir."

Valentine whistled, knowing the number of push-ups required to pass a Guard Cadet physical. He opened the linen folio.

"The OTC is mostly self-taught," Dots explained. "There's a reading list, and written test on each book. You have to do six months' worth of lectures unless you can pass out of the subject by taking an oral exam. The classwork is easier unless you're some kind of genius. Each week's lecture schedule is on the blackboard outside. Once you do that, and have your Certificates of Diligence, Responsibility, and Sobriety, you take the final oral exam. They hold those whenever there's three captains or above around. In fact, your Captain LeHavre is going to be serving on one a little later this month. I hear he's merciless on Grog Recognition. If you don't know where to shoot a Harpy to bring it down with one bullet, you're recycled."

"What's this thesis?" Valentine asked, looking at the graduation requirements.

"That's one of Colonel Jimenez's pet projects. Hope you can write. He wants a fifty-page paper on any subject, strictly nonmilitary. History's okay, as long as you keep off the wars and battles covered in the reading list. A week after you turn it in, you get questioned about it, so you better know whatever it is you're writing about. I did mine on the great mariners, Columbus and Cook and so on. A week later he was grilling me about how Columbus enticed his men to make the voyages, and how Captain Magellan might have avoided getting killed. I think Jimenez just does it to keep himself sharp."

"Thanks, Dots. I'll read this over. I'll start on the lectures this week, if LeHavre will spare me."

"The library's on the top floor. You can check out books if we have two or more copies available, but that covers almost everything on the reading list," she said, already making notes in her desk book.

"Which building is the student union, Dots?"

She looked up with a raised eyebrow. "Going to visit the Creeps, huh? There's a campus map in your packet, but it's just across the quad. It's a good place to learn about the Grogs, but I wouldn't let them talk you into trying for any bounty money."

"Bounty money?"

"For all sorts of stuff. Reaper clothes or artifacts. Written records stolen from the Kurian Zone. They offer big money for live prisoners, but if it's Quislings, they have to be officers. Their dream catch is a whole, live Reaper. They had one once, but it got out. LeHavre will look the other way if you grab a clipboard now and then, but don't ever try to throw a rope around a Reaper or he'll probably shoot you himself."

"Thanks for the tip, Dots. I have a feeling I'll be saluting you someday."

She looked pleased at the compliment. "If you need any help, I'm here every day. I live in the old dormitory."

Valentine exited past three Guards, who had quit skylarking and were talking over a broken-backed copy of *War and Society*. There were fewer than when he had entered; it seemed a couple of the number had duties elsewhere.

The stone on the student union read L. A. DAVIS STUDENT UNION and 1952, but someone had hung a carved wooden sign that read MISKATONIC UNIVERSITY over the door. Valentine entered the unlit building, which smelled of bad plumbing. A stairway leading up had a sign reading APPOINTMENTS ONLY, and a second notice board, which at one time had been behind glass, read BOUNTY INQUIRIES, PLEASE RING over a small hand bell. Valentine climbed the stairway.

The second floor was a warren of rooms, some with doors completely missing and others with darkened windows. A faint, Poe-esque tap-tap-tapping sounded from an inner chamber. Valentine hunted the source of the sound, which he eventually realized was a typewriter. It came from a central office with three overburdened desks, festooned with pin-filled maps and drawings of Grogs.

Under a bright electric desk lamp, a rotund and hairy man typed with two fingers and an occasional thumb. The mountain-man mass of hair on his head and face made his age hard to guess, but Valentine put the man in his late thirties, as his temples and chin were just beginning to be flecked with gray. He wore large, octagonal tortoiseshell glasses that had probably been originally worn by a woman. A bare chest that would have done a grizzly proud, fur-wise, bulged out of a sleeveless jeans jacket.

Valentine knocked on the doorjamb and broke the typist's concentration.

"Hi, can I help you?" the man asked in a friendly tone.

"I think I'm supposed to help you," Valentine said. "Are you one of the people who researches the Kurians?"

"Yeah. I sometimes think *research* isn't the right word, though. We're more like witch doctors trying to explain why a volcano erupts and throwing in the odd virgin to see if that helps. I think we used to put 'New Order Studies Institute' on our documents, mostly because it acronymed out as *NOSI*. But whoever we are, we're them."

Valentine entered the office, making his way around the desks and floor-filling mounds of binders to reach the scientist. As the latter stood up to shake hands, Valentine noticed that his pants were around his ankles.

"Oh, sorry," the man said. It was difficult to tell if he was blushing behind the beard. "Warm up here, you know. I swear that lightbulb puts out more calories than candlepower." He brought his trousers up to their conventional position.

"David Valentine, Wolf. Originally out of Minnesota. Pleased to meet you," Valentine said, taking the hairy-knuckled paw.

"David Walker O'Connor. From Indianapolis, myself. Ran away at the tender age of thirteen. I was brought here just because I knew about current conditions in Indiana, more or less, and stayed on. I read you took a Reaper outside of Weening about a year ago. What have you got for us now?"

"Do I talk to you? It's about a feeling I got when a Reaper

was around. A couple weeks ago. A Cat named Eveready thought it was important enough that I should tell you."

O'Connor scratched himself under his shovel beard. "Let's go into the cellar. I need a break and a drink. You like root beer?"

"Yes, thank you. In fact, it'll be a treat. I've only had it once or twice."

The researcher grabbed a notebook and led the way out of the tangle of airless offices. The two descended into the cellar. At the base of the landing, a classic pawnshop barred door and window prevented further penetration. O'Connor pulled a ring of keys from his pocket and selected one. The door opened with a squeal from the hinges.

With the flick of a switch, O'Connor turned on a single bulb. Its pathetic forty watts did little to help the darkness and nothing at all to alleviate the musty smell coming from piles of clothing, trunks, and assorted boxes and crates heaped with artifacts.

"A lot of it is junk, but it all helps put together a story," his guide explained.

Something shuffled out of the shadows: slab skinned, inhuman, peering at them with a gargoyle face. Valentine startled, reaching for his absent weapons.

O'Connor put a comforting hand on his shoulder. "Easy, Valentine. This is Grishnak. As you can tell, he's a Grog. A couple of the Team found him after a battle, badly wounded. We patched him up, fed him. He's something of a mascot. He puts up with all our little experiments, don't you, Grish?" He thumped it affectionately on the arm.

The Grog cocked its head from side to side, half closing its eyes.

"Does it talk?" Valentine asked, touching its thick horn-skin.

"He gets by with a few meaningful grunts. He's a bit of a firebug; we can't let him have matches or a lantern or anything. Loves to watch things burn; they all do from what we can tell. He's a living table-scrap disposal. He thinks corncobs are a real treat. Potato peels, too. Would you like a root beer, Grish?"

Valentine looked at the half-dozen badly healed bullet wounds in the creature's leg and abdomen. A long knife scar also ran across its shoulder and down its armored chest. It unrolled its tongue.

"Grish loves root beer. Let's sit down."

Valentine listened to the small noises of the empty building. "There's more than just you to this Institute, I suppose?"

An icebox devoid of ice sat next to a slop sink, and a card table stood under the inadequate lightbulb. Shelves held a few dishes and cups. O'Connor drew three drafts from a scratched plastic barrel resting in the icebox. "There's one other scholarly fellow like myself around now, and he keeps even stranger hours. We have a couple of would-be students, but they have to scratch a living so they work in the day." The Grog held out both hands for its sweet drink and scuttled off into the shadows with its cup.

"Just as well. He's kind of messy when he drinks from a cup. I think Grishnak is pretty dumb even for a Grog. They have a language, but they don't use writing. They send little rune-stones in hollow bone tubes to communicate over distance. And the beads in their hair are kind of like military decorations, family totems, stuff like that. But back to the Institute. The rest of the team is in the field. Our elder sage is up around Mountain Home. I don't know if you heard, but five or six Reapers are on the loose up north, well within the Free Territory, and they're causing quite a problem. They're moving around faster than word of them travels, and every time it seems like they're cornered, they slip out. There's bad weather up north, and that's hurting things."

He solemnly opened his notebook and licked the end of his pencil. "Okay, Valentine, what's the story?"

Valentine relayed the events at the Mississippi crossing for the second time in as many days. O'Connor scribbled.

"And you can't link the hair-raising feeling to anything you heard, saw, or smelled. You're positive?"

"I guess I can compare it to . . . let me see . . . the feeling you get when you're next to a window on a very cold winter day. Like the heat is being pulled out of your body. I can't put it any better than that. Or a feeling I got once crossing under a high-voltage line in the dark; I knew something was above me, but I couldn't say what. How would you describe an itch to someone who has never had one?"

"I couldn't. You've smelled a Reaper, right? Since your invocation as a Wolf?"

Valentine nodded, relishing the smooth sweetness of the root beer. "Very up close. Eveready held an impromptu dissection of one before we pulled out of the Yazoo. Smelled like an offal heap."

O'Connor thought for a moment. He leaned back in the tube-steel chair, causing it to creak. "There've been a couple of incidents like yours. Not just Wolves, either. A few people have a sensitivity to Reapers. A lot of animals are the same way. We think it's because of smell, but we've seen too much weirdness in the last forty years to discount anything, including psychic powers. If it keeps happening, try to figure out at what range you sense them, if it makes a difference whether there are more than one, whether they can be distinguished as individuals, stuff like that."

"Can they tell who's who by our lifesign?"

"According to the Lifeweavers they can't, unless they're really close and it's a good read. Lifesign varies with mood, whether the person has just eaten, stuff like that. Of course you guys learn to disguise it. Distance seems to matter most of all. Like you can recognize movement from a long way away, tell a man from a woman at a certain distance, and then distinguish individuals up close. Of course it helps if you've run into the person a couple of times. But back to your question, I think they can tell who's who under certain circumstances. There've been incidents where the Reapers have gone after a specific person. I don't know if it was bullshit or not, but we had a report from New Mexico about Reapers gathering from miles off to hunt one of the Wolves out there. I guess his squad split up, and they all went after the one. Of course, lifesign reads better in the desert, there's less interference from plants and animals, and they might have just been chasing the best signal. Odd coincidence that it was someone who had done them a lot of damage, though."

"By the way," Valentine added, remembering. "There was a funny design on the boat. Kind of a bent *X*."

"That's good that you noticed it. Can you remember it well enough to draw it?"

Valentine reached for the pencil and beneath the researcher's notes traced out the design.

"You're sure it faced that way. Not like this?" He drew a Third Reich swastika.

"No, it was facing the other way. Is it important?" Valentine asked.

"Hard to say. It's been showing up lately, so I did some checking. That symbol can be found on temples in the Asian subcontinent, on Buddhist artifacts, as well as over here in American Indian cave paintings. It appears in the ruins of Troy, on Egyptian walls, even in China. I will say this: whoever used it in prehistoric times sure got around."

Seven

Arkansas, spring of the forty-second year of the Kurian Order: Valentine spent the winter months in diligent pursuit of his commission as lieutenant. While learning about interior lines and maneuver in the face of the enemy in the classroom, he became acquainted with the idiosyncrasies of oxen and pack mules in the field. He would wheedle six different calibers of ammunition out of the arsenal during the day and construe Clausewitz at night. He finished a thesis on the argument for objective reality, defending Socrates against Protagoras and Gorgias after earlier arguing about the quality of the latest barrel of flour with the demanding camp wives.

An astute observer with a detailed memory, Valentine molded his conduct after the officers he respected. He admired LeHavre's methodical planning of every company movement, each leader knowing his assignment so well the captain would often issue just two orders in a day of march: "strike the tents" at dawn and "make camp" at dusk. The company functioned as a well-tuned machine from the moment its commander hit the ON switch. He appreciated Lieutenant Mallow's role as senior in amplifying and following up on his commander's orders, and copied Brostoff's devotion to his men in supplying their every want. If he also avoided Mallow's indecisiveness in the absence of clear and specific orders from the captain and Brostoff's binge drinking, it showed that he could learn how not to behave, as well. His men liked him and, what was more, respected him for the simple reason that he showed them respect.

The Guards attending the Officer's Training College chided him for his drab deerskin clothing and his shyness. He avoided the boisterous weekend outings, a fixture of college life since education began, and kept quiet in class unless called on. He remained silent about his experiences even with the other Wolves who dropped in occasionally as students and lecturers. He grew to know the scholars of Miskatonic Hall, read some of their raw files concerning the Kurians, and listened more than he talked. These traits, but especially the last, proved rare among the alternately bitching and bragging young Wolves.

Still, he felt lonely and fell into the trap of pretending to prefer being alone, thus leading to further loneliness in a vicious circle of solitude that young men of a certain temperament build for themselves and then inhabit. But apart from the lack of companionship, he enjoyed his time as an acting-lieutenant more than anything else in his life up to that point. The constant challenges, physical and mental, stimulated him.

Zulu Company saw action twice that winter, but owing to his studies and lack of experience, Valentine remained back at the reserve camp with the sick and other dependents, commanding a squad of equally discouraged Wolves and being responsible for guarding the cumbersome wagons and baggage. Marksmanship contests for the noncombatants and rehearsing musical follies to welcome back the returning Wolves provided comic relief for the men's tensions, and every time one of his squad smuggled a woman into an isolated tepee, he pretended not to notice. By the first silent green explosion of spring, Zulu Company moved from Pine Bluff to the Ouachita River, returning to active duty.

*   *   *

"Sorry, Valentine, you're staying behind again." Captain LeHavre put down his piece of chalk. The slanted rays of the falling sun gave his features a warm golden cast.

Behind him, the blackboard (which was actually green) had a rough map of southeastern Arkansas and the Louisiana borderlands. Dotted circles traced locations the other two platoons would explore on the long-range patrol consuming the rest of the month. Next to the young Wolf, Brostoff and Mallow exchanged comments in an undertone.

"Questions, gentlemen?" the captain asked.

"What are you leaving Val, sir?" Brostoff asked.

"His whole platoon. Just because he's staying doesn't mean he'll be unoccupied. In a sense, while we're out, he's the first line of defense of Southern Command. Once the rivers fall a little more, a hard-riding column could raid this place without us cutting their trail, let alone sighting them. The river needs watching, too. He needs men for patrols, running supplies down from Regiment and out to our caches, mapping and surveying these border farms."

"Bartering for rice, too, Valentine," Mallow said. "We'll all be sick of the stuff by fall."

"Beats going hungry. Time was there wasn't much more than trappers out here," LeHavre added. "Now there are some farms—plantations more like—and if we can get them organized, we might count the land out to the Mississippi ours. It would take a couple thousand men to garrison it properly, though, and unless they provide some irregular forces, that's not going to happen. You're a good talker, Valentine. Sound out a few of these locals and see if they'll accept arms and ammunition for a patrol service."

Valentine and his platoon saw the other two thirds of Zulu Company off the following dawn.

"Give my regards to the gators," one of Valentine's platoon japed.

"Leastways we'll be doin' more with our blades than whittlin'," countered one of the men from the southbound files, spitting sunflower seed shells.

Valentine's platoon worked the lines of the ferry the company constructed for the river crossing. Within weeks, the river would be wadable at a number of drifts, but LeHavre wanted to start exploring the southern borders with the Kurian Zone now.

Blooming dogwoods decorated the slow-moving river. Valentine rode across the river with the supply mules and surveyed the campsite from the opposite bank. Zulu Company's tepees and tents were hidden, set well back from the river. Even if the Quislings sent armed patrol boats up the river, they wouldn't know the Wolves were there once the raft and lines were hidden.

"You might think you've got the easy duty, but it's a serious responsibility," a voice said from behind.

Valentine turned. LeHavre emerged from the foliage, weighed down by map cases, a telescope, and the company's only submachine gun. The clouds had thickened, and the forest was a canopy of shadow.

"This is a tricky corner you're in, Valentine. The Kurians could float up the Ouachita, raid in from Louisiana, or come across the Mississippi. They have a big garrison at Vicksburg and the barges to float them. Your first job is to protect Southern Command by looking out for that kind of thing. If they come in strength, send as much information back to Regiment double-quick. Cause trouble for 'em if you can, but your men are worth more than Quisling conscripts, so make sure you don't get cornered. I've left you here for a reason, not because you're the junior. Fact is, another time I'd stay myself."

"Yes, sir. Hopefully it'll be a quiet summer."

A third man joined them, the bulky senior NCO, Sergeant Patel. "Everything's across, sir. Scouts are out and the column is ready to go."

"Thank you, Sergeant. I'll be along in a moment." He turned back to Valentine.

"Count on us being gone six weeks. I'll send you on a short patrol when we get back, so you can get some experience. I'm going to leave Brostoff out all summer watching the rivers, but I'll be back with Mallow and his platoon."

"The chickens will be fat by then, and I'm sure I can find some good-size watermelon."

"So young, and you already know how old soldiers think. Take care, Mr. Valentine," LeHavre said, returning Valentine's salute with his usual grace. "Don't let anything happen to Southern Command while I'm gone."

Valentine forced a confident smile when LeHavre winked.

With the patrolling Wolves departing and the day fleeing, Valentine supervised the team dismantling the ferry. They floated the lines and stakes back to the camp-side and rolled the raft out of sight.

"There's a new occupied farm two miles north of here, Lieutenant Valentine," Sergeant Quist reported. "Will we be paying them a visit?"

"Keep the men out of the henhouse, if you value your rank, Quist. You know how the captain feels about that sort of thing," Valentine said, clouding over like the sky above.

"Didn't mean that, sir. They know better. I meant a social call. Get things off on the right foot. We'll be moving up and down the river, and we don't want a gut full of buckshot by accident. He might want to trade for some grub, too."

"I see. I'm sorry, Quist, wrong conclusion. I'll make it the first thing tomorrow morning. I'll take Bozich; having a woman along will seem less threatening. Michaels is the senior Aspirant now, right? I'll take him, as well. You'll have to handle things while I'm gone, Sergeant."

It began to rain, and Valentine walked the perimeter of the camp. He enjoyed a warm rain, the feeling of privacy it afforded. He smelled the sentries' tobacco smoke even in the wet before seeing them, considered issuing an order against smoking on duty, then rejected the idea. The veterans knew when it was safe to smoke, and the newbies could be taught. Shelter, food, firewood, and security occupied his mind as he wandered through the drizzle, an ear always cocked for sounds in the camp. He used his nose as much as his ears, smelling which way cooking smoke and latrine odors drifted in the prevailing winds. There were Grogs who could hear and smell better than the Wolves. He would have to set stillwatches on the river, build some kind of redoubt in case of sudden attack, and arrange for safe storage of ammunition and food supplies. Some kind of netting in the overhead trees might be a good idea, he thought, remembering his encounter with the Harpies in Weening. That made him think of Gabby Cho, and his good mood vanished like a lump of sugar in the rain.

The farm Quist had spoken of consisted of a single wellbuilt barn, still under repair. Only a foundation remained where there had once been a house. The barn stood above a wet inlet from the Ouachita, and rice paddies flourished in the cleared land.

Valentine led Bozich and Michaels up the path from the river. Bozich had a hard face but warm eyes; LeHavre was thinking of making her a sergeant. She was the most diminutive of the Valentine's Wolves, but had stamina in inverse proportion to her size and carried a carbine with a telescopic sight. Michaels still had pimples and wheezed sometimes, but a little asthma would not necessarily disqualify him from future service. More important, he took his duties as senior Aspirant seriously.

The Wolves smelled cows and goats in the barn, but no pigs. It appeared that the farmers, whoever they were, lived above their animals, and pigs were not ideal livestock for sharing accommodations.

Dogs barked, and a tousle-headed girl in the yard scrambled up a ladder at their approach, calling "Momma! Momma! Momma!" like a wailing siren. A hairy face appeared at one of the lower windows, and the Wolves stopped.

"It's sojers," somebody yelled. Valentine's ears picked up at the sound of a shotgun breech being closed.

Two men emerged, both bearded, one a little more grizzled than the other. The elder held the shotgun Valentine had heard. Both wore faded rags, patched and clean but obviously pre-Kur salvage.

"Y'all out upcountry? Command boys?" the younger asked, within jumping distance of the barn door.

"Course they is," the armed one said. "Wearin' skins an' deer-booties."

"We're camping a couple miles downstream. Thought we'd pay a call," Valentine said, hand well away from his holster.

One of the barking dogs decided nothing interesting was going to happen and flopped on its side with a sudden motion, almost as if it had been shot. Bozich and the Aspirant snickered, and the dog's owners exchanged a look.

"That dog beat all. Goes to sleep like he's droppin' deyad," the unarmed man said, showing a gap-toothed smile.

The ice was broken, and the men called out their families. Concrete Barn Farm, as the occupants styled it, consisted of two brothers, Rob and Cub Kelly. Their families and another unmarried young man worked the rice paddies, gardens, and fishing streams.

"We-uns think what's ours is ours," Rob Kelly, the younger of the brothers, said later, as the men and their wives sat with Valentine's team on the foundation of the house. Perhaps it had once been a front porch.

Cub nodded in agreement. "Couldn't take it up by y'all. Taxation, regulations. Law stopping by with empty bellies. Don't plant, don't pitch, but want it all the same. Paw took we-uns outer there."

Bozich opened her mouth, but Valentine shook his head.

"You're on your own down here, that's for sure. Lonely country, though, should the others come through."

Rob Kelly's wife tightened her mouth.

"Our boys keep good watch," the younger Kelly said. "We-uns too small fer them to bother with. We-uns jes' tell Steiner and his Beasts if'n anythin' dangerous shows up."

"Who's this Steiner?"

"His-uns got a few places in country. Half day's hard walk."

"I've got a box of shells for that twelve-gauge if one of your sons will take me to him. Looks like you could use some paint for that barn, too. I might be able to find some."

Cub Kelly looked suspicious. Of course Valentine had seen only two expressions on his face, suspicious and taciturn. He made up his mind and nodded to his brother.

"We-uns got a deal, sojer-man."

Cub Kelly's scarecrow-lean, half-naked son Patrick spoke as little as his father. All tan skin and searching eyes, he guided Valentine through a series of swamp trails. The boy carried a sling and a bag of rocks the whole way. Valentine watched the youth kill a watchful hawk atop an old utility pole. He retrieved the limp mass of talons and feathers, saying, "Sumpin' fer the boilin' pot."

Bozich whistled at the sight of the Steiner place. A cluster of buildings sat on a mound in the center of miles of rice paddies. The whitewashed buildings were in good repair, with aluminum-covered roofs surrounded by walls, and the walls in turn surrounded by a wide moat.

The Wolves observed it from a little hummock of land marking the end of the trail and the beginning of the paddies. A small cemetery filled the hill, neat little crosses in rows, interspersed with rock cairns. Some of the graves were tiny, in clusters, telling the usual tale of high infant mortality in a rural region, lying next to cross after cross with DIED IN CHILDBED burned into the wood. After a moment's study of the community's dead, Valentine turned back to the living.

"Have you heard about this?" he asked Bozich.

"We knew there were some big plantations out here, but this beats all. These aren't border squatters—this is years of work, sir."

"Wonder how you get in? Drawbridge?" Valentine said.

"A boat on a line, sojer," Master Kelly said.

"Thanks, son. You can take your hawk home to the pot now. Tell your pa he needs anything, we're always ready to trade."

"Sure, sojer," the boy said, tying his sling around the legs of the hawk and trotting back into the brush.

"There's the boat," Michaels said. "Under where the wall goes down to the water."

Valentine surveyed the walls with his binoculars. The stone for them had been quarried; they were fitted together with no small skill. He saw another head, binoculars held to the eyes, staring back at him. "They've seen us, too. No use looking timid, let's go find the landing."

The three Wolves zigzagged across the earthen dikes separating the rice fields. It occurred to Valentine that anyone attacking the compound would have to take a circuitous route to rush the walls if they did not want to flounder through the mud.

"Think these folks'll feed us?" Bozich asked. "The Kellys weren't too hospitable."

"We'll learn soon enough," Valentine said. "Michaels, you stay outside of rifle range. There's a funny smell to this place."

Bozich sniffed the air. "Smells kinda like pigs . . . I hope, Mr. Valentine. Really clean ones?"

"Smells like Grogs to me. Doesn't look like there's been a fight. But be ready for anything. If night comes, Michaels, and you don't hear from us, you skedaddle. You hear shooting, you skedaddle. Understand?"

"Yes, sir. I'll bring help."

"You'll tell Quist to alert Southern Command is what you'll do."

Dogs barked as they approached, not just the yips of mongrels, but the deep baying of hounds. A man appeared at the wall. He looked at them from behind a firing slit.

"Hi-yi, strangers. Whatever you're selling, we don't need any."

"We're buyers, not sellers. We'd like to speak to Mr. Steiner. We don't have an appointment."

"You don't have a what?"

"Never mind, can we come in?"

There was a pause.

"He says he'll come out."

Steiner was a sizable man with a shock of red hair growing out of freckled skin. After a glance at the visitors, he rowed himself across in a small flat-bottomed boat.

Valentine guessed him to be about thirty-five. He wore rawhide sandals and a short wide-necked tunic that made Valentine think of pictures he had seen of Romans. It looked cool and comfortable.

"My guess is y'all are Wolves out of Southern Command. If you're looking to buy rice, I already sell mine up in Pine Bluff. I've got an agent there. And don't go quoting your Common Articles, this spread isn't part of Southern Command's ground. We built it, no help from you, and we hold it, no help from you. Last jumped-up bushwhacker that tried that ten percent routine walked up threatening and ran off yelping."

Valentine held the man's gaze. "You think you hold it, no help from us. How long you'd keep it if the Free Territory weren't still standing is another question. But I'll concede the point to save an argument."

"I'm done talking," said Steiner.

"Quite a spread you've got here. You must have room for fifty families or more. Is this a refuge if the Kur come through?"

"That's our business, Running Gun."

"We're a couple of tired Running Guns, Mr. Steiner. Hungry, too. Part of my unit is camped near the Ouachita, and I'm just trying to get to know the neighbors. I'm impressed. I've never seen a settlement quite like this in the borderlands. I'd like a better look."

"It took a lot of hard years, mister."

"Valentine, David. Lieutenant with the Arkansas Wolf Regiment."

Steiner considered. "Mr. Valentine, we don't take strangers in normally, but you seem a better sort than your usual Command type. I'll offer you a tour and a meal, but I don't want your men showing up weekly, making speeches about how totin' a gun for Southern Command entitles them to a fried chicken dinner. You'll see things not many in your outfit have seen, or want to see."

They took the little dinghy to the island. More corrugated aluminum covered the wooden gate. Valentine wondered if Steiner knew his aluminum wouldn't do him any good against white phosphorus bombs.

They passed through the gate—

And froze. A pair of Grogs stood inside, cradling their long rifles. They wore tunics similar to Steiner's and pulled back rubbery lips to reveal yellow teeth.

Bozich gasped, reaching for her carbine.

"Wait, Bozich, leave the gun," Valentine barked, putting his hand on her barrel to keep her from raising it. His heart pounded, but the Grogs kept their guns in a comfortable cradled position.

"Don't worry," Steiner said. "These aren't the usual Graybacks. They're friendly."

"I've seen a tame Grog before."

"These ain't tame," Steiner said, flushing. "They're as free as you and me."

Valentine looked at the homes. The village resembled Weening in its circular shape, but there were no barns, just henhouses and goats. A water tower stood in the center of the village, and the community focal point appeared to be the troughs where the women did the laundry. A female Grog (with just two breasts; Valentine had heard they had four teats, like a cow) pressed the water out of her wash with a bellowslike tool. People and Grogs stopped to stare at the strangers.

Steiner invited them up onto a porch of a small house and

bade them them to sit down on a comfortable-looking wooden bench.

"Mr. Valentine," Steiner began, "a long time ago I came out of Mississippi with a Grog named Big Joke. He helped me and my wife escape a labor camp, and we found the Free Territory. Some of your Wolves picked us up in the border region, took both of us prisoner. Prisoner! After weeks of trying to get to this 'bastion of freedom,' I had to go before a judge with the Grog who saved my life and beg for both of ours. I'm either convincing or she was liberal, and we were released as citizens of the Free Territory. Big Joke and I learned quick that there was no place for Grogs in your towns. The person— and he is a person, even if they think a little different than us—I owed my life to couldn't get a job, a bed, or a meal for love or money. Best he could do was 'work for food' on the docks. So my wife, Big Joke, and I headed south and found this land in the midst of these swamps. I'd spent years draining swamps and building paddies in Mississippi for *them,* so doing it a couple years for me came easy. A few others came down and joined us. That was the beginning of a lot of hard times, but we got this built."

"You lost your wife early on. I'm sorry."

Steiner's brows came together. "How—?"

"We came in past the cemetery. I saw a LaLee Steiner, who seemed about the right age. 'Evergreen' was a tribute to her?"

"No, it was her last name. I lost her to a fever, after she gave birth to my son. Two years after that some Southern Command Johnny shot Big Joke dead from ambush. He had been out hunting. I tried to understand. A Grog in the borderlands poking around with a crossbow. If I didn't know better, I'd shoot first and ask questions later myself. But y'all got to start knowing better."

"How's that?"

"Your Southern Command. Old thinking. Maybe it's because it was built by a bunch of military types. They're trying
to preserve a past, not create a future. The Grogs are here, and
they're here to stay. I'm sure there are hundreds of thousands,
if not millions, by now. Seems a long way off, but if we ever
do win, what'll we do with 'em? Kill 'em all? Not likely. Put
'em on reservations? Good luck."

"Southern Command is trying to stay alive," Valentine
said. He silently agreed with Steiner about Southern Command, but he could not publicly criticize it, especially in front
of Bozich. "They don't have the luxury of looking too far
ahead."

"Not that living with Grogs is easy. They have a lot of fine
qualities, but their brains work different. They're the most
day-by-day thinkers you ever saw. If they plan three days
ahead, it's an act of genius. How'd you like to wake up every
morning surprised? That's what they do, in a way. Though
they're smart enough at solving a problem once they understand it. You two hungry?"

"Yes, sir," Bozich said, turning from the sight of Grog
children playing with a young dog. Valentine looked out; the
Grogs were mimicking the dog's behavior, gamboling on all
fours and interacting with it through body posture better than
a human child could.

Steiner took them in to the dim house. The homemade furniture had a rough-and-ready look, though someone with
some skill with a needle had added cushions.

"Sorry it's dark. We save kerosene, and anyway it just
heats the place up." Steiner rekindled the fire and placed a pot
from the cool-room on the stove.

"Hope you like gumbo. It's the staple here. The rice-flour
buns are pretty good."

Steiner offered them a basin to wash in while the stew heated.

"I get the impression you're responsible for more than just this settlement."

The redhead laughed. "I'm still trying to figure out how that happened. Once this place got going, and we had wagons going up to Pine Bluff and back, some of the other small-holders started tailing along. With them and the Grogs guarding our wagons, it made quite a convoy. We have some great stonecutters and craftsmen here, and the locals just started trailing in, especially once we got the mill going. They started coming to me for advice, and the next thing I knew I was performing weddings and deciding whose lambs belonged to whom."

"King Steiner?"

"The thought's crossed my mind. Seems like the worry isn't worth it, but then when you get a baby or two named after you, it appears in a different light."

It occurred to Valentine that Steiner hadn't mentioned his son. He had already pressed the man on the sorrow involving his wife, and the grief in his eyes then made him hold his tongue now.

The food went into wooden bowls, and the Wolves scooped the spicy gumbo into their mouths using one rice-flour bun after another.

"Guess they call you Wolves 'cause of how y'all eat," Steiner said.

"Ain't the first time someone's said that," Bozich laughed, gumbo coating her lips.

Valentine finished his meal and helped his host clean off the dishes.

"Steiner, if you don't want to live under the Free Territory, how about you live with it?"

"With it?"

"Like an alliance."

Steiner shook his head. "What do I need Southern Command for? We do all right by ourselves."

"You might need guns and ammunition."

"We make our own shells and shot. Better than yours, mostly."

"Someday this swamp might find itself with a Kurian column in it. What then?"

"They'd lose more than they'd gain taking this place."

"We could give you a radio, and Southern Command would answer a call for help in this part of Arkansas. Anything coming through here is on its way to us."

The redhead looked doubtful, then shook his head. "Don't want a garrison, thanks."

"No garrison. We could build a hospital . . . well, health center anyway. A full-time, trained nurse and a doctor. Not just for here, but for all the farms in the area. Might mean a few less crosses in your cemetery. You could do even more for these people, if you'll just give the okay."

"Who are you, son? You have that kind of pull?"

"I'm an officer with Southern Command. I can offer whatever I think appropriate to the locals as long as it'll be used for us and not against us. Maybe I'm overstepping what they expected, but if they're going to grant me that authority, I'll use it. We put a health center up near the Saint Francis a year or so back. Why not here? Every gun you have means one more gun Southern Command can put on another border. You feed, clothe, and arm yourselves. That's a savings in money and organization. I'll put it all on paper, assuring your independence. No ten percent tithe. You'd never have to defend anything but your own lands."

Steiner probed his teeth with his tongue and stared out the window at the wash troughs.

"Mr. Valentine, you have yourself an ally."

Lieutenant Mallow stared openmouthed as the sergeants quieted the excited comments of the men of First Platoon. Captain LeHavre shook his head, a wry smile on his face as the ferry pulled him and the weary men across.

LeHavre had sent a runner two days ago to let Valentine know the patrol was coming in, tired and hungry. The river was still deep enough to make refloating the ferry necessary. Valentine alerted his new ally at the swamp fortress to gather his militia for a meeting and review.

On one side of the landing Valentine had his platoon drawn up, at least the men who weren't working the lines and mules pulling the ferry across. On the other, Colonel Steiner stood at the head of three hundred men, women, and Grogs. Each wore a dark green bandanna tied around the neck, the only common item to the tatterdemalion Militia Steiner had christened the "Evergreen Rifles." To Valentine, the name had a certain amount of irony, as under half the group's members had firearms, mostly shotguns, and the rest carried spears, bows, pitchforks, and axes. A hundred more rifles were on their way from Southern Command, as Valentine had added several impassioned letters to the paperwork requesting heavier weapons, a health center, and a radio for the local residents. From the Wolf camp, smells of barbecue and cooking drifted out to the river. The first semiofficial gathering of the Evergreens would be celebrated with a feast.

LeHavre jumped off the ferry and splashed ashore.

"What's all this, Mr. Valentine? Grog prisoners, or a posse?"

Valentine saluted. "Welcome back, sir. Those are local

Militia. Their commander and I are still going around to some other homesteads. We hope to get five hundred together before the summer is out. He's an influential man in this area."

"Leave it to you, Valentine. I leave you with a little over twenty men, and I come back to hundreds. What are you handing out, free beer?"

"Just free-*dom,* sir."

Eight

The battlefield, August of the forty-third year of the Kurian Order: Burned-out motors and wagons fill the streets of Hazlett, Missouri. Some of the brick buildings still stand, but of the wooden houses only stone chimneys remain, standing as monuments to the homes that had been.

A few soldiers still poke and rake among the sooty ruins, their smoldering houses finally quenched by the morning's downpour. The salvaged Grog weaponry and equipment lay in three heaps: destroyed, repairable, and intact. Expert scroungers added to this mechanical triage as they gleaned further material from the surrounding woods and the road back to Cairo, Illinois.

The only bodies in evidence lay in neat, unshrouded rows lined up outside a wooden barn a half-mile outside the town proper, conveniently close to a water spring. The maimed and wounded inside, groaning their agony out on pallets, old doors, and even hay bales, envied the corpses now past all suffering. Two-man teams of battlefield surgeons, faces gray with fatigue and smocks brown with hundreds of bloodstains, fought exhaustion and sepsis.

The gravediggers adhered to their own priorities. The first day after the battle, they put to rest the dead of Southern Command: Bears, Wolves, Guards, and Militia. The second day, the dead Quislings were buried in a long common grave, dug *by the prisoners spared after the fall of Hazlett. Finally on this day, the third after the battle, the gravediggers set alight a great pyre of Grogs, who shared the flame with putrefying dead horses, oxen, and mules inside a ring of firewood. Exhausted from the labor of dragging the bigger corpses out of sight and smell, the officer in charge decided to rest his detail before attending to the row of this morning's bodies outside the field hospital. The doctors couldn't save everyone.*

Thus the miasma of burned flesh introduced Lt. David Valentine to the tableau of a battlefield. Three companies of Wolves, including Zulu, marched up from reserve near the southern border. Sent to help deal with the incursion, they arrived too late to do anything but shake their heads at the destruction of the little town and join in the services held over the bodies of the slain.

Chuckwagon tales told by the survivors of the Battle of Hazlett described a push into the valuable mining towns of the area from the tip of Illinois. The Quislings and Grogs made a fortress of the little crossroads town, and only a concentration of every available Bear in eastern Missouri backed up by Wolves and a Guard regiment forced them out again. It might have been worse, but Valentine learned that a company of Wolves had ambushed reinforcements at the Mississippi, sacrificing themselves to keep the road to Hazlett closed. Out of a hundred Wolves, a bare sixteen now licked their wounds on the banks of the Whitewater River.

It was this destruction of Foxtrot Company that led Captain LeHavre, the senior Wolf officer in the area, to call Valentine into his tepee one afternoon. Zulu Company was preparing to return below the state line again, as an incursion in the northeast might mean an even larger one in the southwest.

Valentine wondered, as he answered the summons that afternoon, what the news would be. LeHavre always hit his officers, whenever possible, with bitter medicine early in the morning and saved the sugar for evenings. So an afternoon conference might be a trail-mix assortment of sweet and sour.

He found LeHavre by a commissary wagon, sharing a cup of coffee with an unknown, clean-shaven Wolf.

"David Valentine, meet Randall Harper," the captain introduced. "Sergeant Harper here is part of the Command Staff. A courier, to be exact."

The young men shook hands. Harper seemed a little young to be a sergeant, particularly on the Command Staff, but then Valentine was even younger to be a lieutenant. The courier had a lazy eye, which made looking into his face unsettling, but he wore a cheerful smile that brightened his whole face to such a degree that Valentine liked him from first sight.

"Pleased to meet you, sir," Harper said.

"Valentine, you are going on a trip. I need some young legs to accompany Harper here on a four-hundred-mile jaunt. All the way up to Lake Michigan, as a matter of fact."

"I've got two bags of mail and one of dispatches, sir," Harper added.

"Why me, sir?" Valentine asked, risking a rebuke.

"Normally an officer from Foxtrot Company and another Wolf would go, but as of these last few days, Foxtrot doesn't exist anymore and probably won't for another year or so. There's only acting-lieutenants in the junior position in the other two Wolf companies, and I don't know enough about them to pick one. And you're from the Great White North, so I thought you'd like a trip back up. I was going to send you up with Paul Samuels anyway on one of his recruiting sweeps, but this'll be a better experience for you."

"Mounted or afoot, sir?"

"With a little luck, you'll be mounted all the way. Three horses plus a spare is what you have, right, Sergeant?"

"Yes, sir," Harper answered. "The fourth will carry the mail and some oats. Or if we lose one, it'll be a remount."

"So a third man is going, sir?" Valentine asked. "Who will that be?"

LeHavre patted Valentine on the shoulder. "Take who you want, Valentine. Except for Patel. I need him, and he's too old to cover forty miles a day for long stretches anymore."

Valentine mentally ran down the list of Wolves in Zulu Company.

"I'll take Gonzalez, sir. He has the best nose in the company, and he's first-rate with his hunting bow."

"Take him with my compliments, Lieutenant. Let me know your needs. I realize the company wagons haven't caught up with us yet, but I can probably scrounge you up about anything. Questions?"

The only questions that came to Valentine's mind implied evading responsibility, so he remained silent.

LeHavre finished his coffee. "You two get together with Gonzalez and talk it through. I know you've made the trip a couple of times, Harper, so tell as much about the route to the other two as you can, just in case. You leave at dawn."

Harper accepted the possibility of his death, suggested by the *just in case,* with the same sunny smile. "Gladly, sir."

That evening, Gonzalez joined them in an informal campfire conference.

"Seems like a lot of effort to deliver a few letters. How often do you do this?" Gonzo asked.

"Two or three times a year. Southern Command tries to stay in touch with the other Resistance pockets, at least the big ones. This is information we don't want to broadcast on the shortwave. That's why if it looks like we're going to be taken, you need to pour the fluid in the flasks onto the dispatches and burn 'em."

"If the Reapers are closing in, I'm going to be too busy to start any fires, Sarge."

Valentine mopped up his stew with a slab of bread. "How long are we going to be gone?"

"Depends on the horses, and then the sailors. If we can come up with feed now and then, about two weeks per leg. But there's no guarantee the ship will be in Whitefish Bay on time. The Lakes Fleet has troubles of its own. Luckily the Kurians don't pay much attention to the ships, unless they get too close to a city they care about. We'll just have to wait if they aren't there."

"Ever had any problems running the mail?" Valentine inquired.

Harper's smile returned. "A few close shaves. We should keep toward the Mississippi until the Wisconsin border or so. About all you have to worry about there is border trash, but they're mostly scared of everything. Wisconsin has the real Kurian lands we have to cross. Their pet humans farm that area pretty good, and of course the Reapers farm the humans. The shortest route would be up through central Illinois, but that's thickly settled, and unless you have a death wish, you'll want to keep away from Chicago."

Valentine and Gonzalez bade farewell to their company in the predawn gloom. LeHavre offered a final word of advice to his junior lieutenant.

"Keep your eyes open, Mr. Valentine," LeHavre said, solemnly shaking his protégé's hand. "We never know enough about what is happening in the Lost Lands. Try and pick up any information you can, even if it's just impressions."

"Thank you for the opportunity, sir."

LeHavre winced. *How many young men have you sent to their doom with those words on their lips?* Valentine wondered.

"You can thank me by coming back, David."

The three Wolves mounted their horses, the excited animals stamping and tossing their heads in their eagerness to be off, and rode into the misty dawn.

During the first leg of the journey, they kept to the rough terrain of the Mississippi Valley. They conserved the strength of horse and rider, walking their mounts and stopping often. On the second day, they crossed the Mississippi in a hollowed-out old houseboat, well camouflaged with dirt and plant growth on its battered sides. The trio of old Wolves who took them across laughed as they listened to the secondhand story of the Battle of Hazlett over the labored *putt*ing of the aged diesel engine.

"That'll learn 'em," one of them cackled as he brought the houseboat out of its hidden cove and into the current at the "all clear" signal from his observer. "Hank and I, we've been puttin' up signs all over the west bank for miles readin' 'Trespassers Will Be Prosecuted' and 'No Solicitors Invited,' but them Grogs don't read too good."

Once in no-man's-land, the Wolves traveled cautiously. They camped for the night when they found the right spot, not when the sun set. Daybreak never found them in the same location in which they bedded down. Each night Valentine ordered a camp change of at least a half-mile, and lost sleep was made up with a siesta each afternoon during the worst of the late summer heat. They set no watch, but relied on their senses to rouse them from their light slumber in the event of danger. They always cooked their meals before dark, knowing better than to call attention to themselves with the light of a campfire.

By the third night out, they were swapping life stories. Valentine had heard Gonzalez's before, but listened again to his scout's words as he lay in his hammock under a cloud-masked moon.

"I was born in Texas in 2041, out there in the western part. My parents were part of a guerrilla band called the Screaming Eagles, which my father told me was an old army unit and my *madre* said was a music group. They used to do a war cry. . . . I would do it, but it's too loud for these parts. Too loud for the Ozarks, too. I don't remember much fighting when I was young. I think the Eagles stole cattle off the Turncoats. That was what we called the Quislings out there. Sometimes in the summer we went as far north as Kansas and Colorado, and in the winter we would be in Mexico.

"I was about twelve when the Turncoats got us. It was in Mexico. We were in this kind of bowl-shaped valley, a few old buildings and tents, with the cattle all spread out. They got some cannon up in the hills somehow, and pretty soon there were explosions everywhere, with men on horseback pouring down from the mountains. My father fought them, but I'm sure he was killed with the rest. There were just two passes out of the valley, but they had hundreds of men with guns hidden in the rocks. I don't think anyone made it out that way. My *madre* got me and my baby brother out over the hills. One of the Turncoats caught up to us. He attacked her, but I picked up his gun and shot him in the foot. He grabbed the gun out of my hands and was going to shoot me, but my *madre* brought a boulder as big as a football down on his head and killed him. God knows how she found the strength to lift it; she was a small woman."

Gonzalez fingered a small silver crucifix around his neck.

"We walked for days and would have died, but a rainstorm saved us. We hid for a while in a Turncoat village. An old man who was kind to us arranged for my mother to move into eastern Texas where his son lived. My mother lived with his son and had a child with him, but she never loved him as she did my father, even though he was very good to us. She gave him two daughters, but when I turned sixteen, she said, 'Victor, you must leave this land, for the people here have forgotten themselves and God.' We heard rumors about a place in the mountains where the Hooded Ones could not go, and I found this place on my own, but I fear it went bad for my stepfather, who let me run away. But I know my *madre* still lives because I still live; her prayers protect me and keep me alive. With what I have seen, I cannot pray as she does, so when she dies, I will die, too."

Valentine told his story next, leaving out the fact that his father had been a Wolf. He described the cool beauty of the Boundary Waters' woods and lakes, and the challenge of living through a Minnesota winter.

"I hadn't seen much geography until I became a Wolf," Harper began. "I was born to a big family near Fort Scott. My pa was an officer in the Guards, and he tried to keep me in school, but I wouldn't have it. Everyone made fun of this eye of mine; you know how kids are. At nine, I tried to be an Aspirant, but they wouldn't let me. I hung out in Wolf camps whenever I could; my pa was away a lot, and my ma—Well, she had her hands full with the other children. They let me become an Aspirant at thirteen, finally. I was invoked when I was fifteen, and I was in the middle of it at Cedar Hill and then Big River. They made me a sergeant after all that. I was a champion distance runner, so I got put in the couriers. I made a trip to the Gulf in 'sixty-three, and did the run to Lake Michigan twice last year. I crossed Tennessee this spring going to the Appalachians, and that's the worst run I've ever been on. Took me forever to find resistance people in the Smokies. These trips should be run by just couriers, but we've lost so many out West over one thing and another that Command is short on messengers."

"I was wondering why you showed up with two empty saddles," Valentine said.

"Well, I'm grateful of your company. Mr. Valentine, you seem to be a right smart officer, afraid of all the right things, if you'll excuse me for saying so, sir. And Gonzalez—you, sir, have the most righteous set of ears in the Free Territory. I'm glad you're along to count the mouse farts, you know?"

Gonzalez proved just how good his hearing was somewhere east of Galena, Illinois. They had been traveling for a week when someone began trailing them.

"There are three or four riders coming up behind," Gonzo reported. "Haven't caught sight of them yet, but you can hear them. I don't know if they're right on our trail or just keeping with the old road."

The three Wolves rode parallel to an old road, now overgrown but still too far from tall timber for their purposes. Valentine debated the choices. An ambush would be easy enough to set up, but he balked at shooting down strangers in cold blood. Anyone close enough for the Wolves to hear would probably have cut their trail by now and would know someone was ahead. The idea of being trailed worried him.

"Do you know who lives around here?" he asked Harper.

"This far off the river? A few farmers scratch a living out here. On other trips we've crossed the trails of pretty big groups on horseback. I don't like thinking worst case, but this is just the kind of area a pair of Reapers might hunt."

"Yes, but they wouldn't be on horseback. And they wouldn't make enough noise for Gonzo to hear them," Valentine argued. As usual, someone else's opinion helped him form his own, for better or worse. "Let's go up the bluffs. If they're casual travelers, they won't follow. If they come up after us, we can get a good look at what we're taking on before we start shooting."

With that, the Wolves made a sharp turn east, moving into the wooded hills away from the overgrown road. Valentine removed his lever-action rifle from its sheath. Soon they were struggling up a steep slope, leaning far forward in their saddles to help the horses' balance.

As they ascended the hill, Valentine searched right and left. No rock pile or fallen trunk presented itself. Valentine cursed his luck at riding for the one uneroded hill covered with uniformly healthy timber in all of western Illinois.

Gaining the summit, the Wolves at last found a deadfall they could hide behind. The breeze blew fresh from the west hard enough to whip at the horses' manes and make the men clutch at their hats. They rode past the fallen log and looped back; tracks heading straight for an ambush spot would be investigated more cautiously. Valentine asked Harper to hold the four horses out of sight behind the crest of the hill.

Dismounted, with weapons in hand, Valentine and Gonzalez walked back to the fallen log. Gonzalez held an arrow to his bowstring. With luck, the trackers had a single scout out front who could be silently dispatched with a feathered shaft.

"Keep your bow ready, Gonzo," Valentine said in a low tone. "I'm going to get in that oak above our trail. If there's just two scouts, I'll drop on one. When you see me leap, try for the other with the bow. If it's three or four, I'll let them ride past, and I'll backshoot them."

"Let me go up the tree, sir."

"I'm not much with a bow, my friend. I doubt I could hit a horse at this distance, let alone a rider. Just stay cool and wait for my signal."

Valentine scrambled to his perch among the thick limbs of the grandfather oak. He hugged the tree limbs like a lizard, pulling a leafy branch toward his face for concealment. Whoever the trackers were, they had four scouts ahead on horseback. Valentine listened with hard ears past them, but his nose helped even more. A large group of horses and men were somewhere out of sight, upwind to the west. He smelled some tobacco, and cannabis, as well.

As the scouts walked their horses up the slope and into view, Valentine decided this was no Quisling patrol. The shabbiness of man and beast, from worn-out boots to collapsed felt hat brims, indicated either the worst kind of Quisling irregulars or simple bandits. They carried rifles, but some of the guns looked like black-powder muzzle-loaders.

Whatever their deficiencies in equipment, the four scouts knew their jobs. One concentrated on the trail, two a little behind him searched the terrain ahead, and the fourth stayed far back in case of trouble. One of the middle scouts didn't like the look of the hilltop, and they pulled up to a halt. Binoculars and small telescopes emerged from their patched overcoats.

One of the four Wolf horses, scenting those below, let out with a high, questioning neigh. The scouts spun their horses and plunged down the hill.

Valentine mouthed obscenities.

A good second line of defense, Valentine maintained, is

running like hell. He jumped from the tree and, waving to Gonzalez, ran up toward the four horses.

"It's border trash, I think. A lot," he explained to Harper as they mounted.

Valentine led them at something less than a flat-out gallop along the ridgeline. Their horses had covered a lot of miles in the past week, but perhaps were of sterner stuff and in better health than the beasts of the ragamuffins below.

He reveled in the mad inconsequence of it all. Their pursuers might catch them; he and the two Wolves might die, and the world would change or care not a whit. But it felt glorious to pound through the woods on a running horse, his legs tight in the stirrups and hands far up the horse's neck. Clods of dirt kicked up by the horses' rhythmic gait flew up behind like birds startled at their passing.

Harper is having trouble with the spare horse, the sane part of his mind reminded him. Valentine spotted a clearing on a prominence ahead and turned his horse toward it, slowing the pace to a trot and then a walk. Reaching the bare spot, they saw a ruined house, roofless and empty.

"We covered some miles," Gonzalez gasped. "Where the hell is the road?"

"Somewhere down to the west of us," Valentine said, waving vaguely at the descending sun. Trees obscured the road's probable location. "Let's take a breather and see how our friends are doing."

The overlook gave them a good view of the hills to the south. Valentine and Harper listened to the steady drum of hooves in the distance.

"Aw, shit," Harper said. "I always figured a Reaper would get me, not some grubby thugs."

Valentine looked at the house. There were good walls there, and only two doors to cover. The horses would fit inside. "Okay, so their horses are fresher than ours. We've still got three guns and a good spot to shoot from."

He could now see distant riders galloping along the trail. He stopped counting after estimating fifty. "Let's get inside our new home and get ready to greet our guests."

Behind the house a pump stood on a concrete patio. "Oh, pretty please with sugar on it," Harper said, working the handle. It moved a little too easily; nothing came from the rusty metal spout but noise.

The main room of the house was filled with collapsed roof, but they were able to bring the horses through the back door into a room slightly lower than the larger one. The paneless windows were set so a man at the front could cover the main door, more or less, but the western exposure of rooms off the main one would have to go unguarded. Valentine posted himself at the front window, Harper at the side, and Gonzalez at the rear door. They manhandled an empty refrigerator into the doorway to the main room.

"We ought to be able to hold out for about two minutes now," Harper said.

"There's always the chance we'll make the price too steep for them," Valentine said, filling a pocket with cartridges.

"I was sick of riding anyway," Gonzalez said.

"That's the idea," Valentine responded. "If we can get them to wait until dark, we just might be able to slip out. Head for steep hills and thick woods. Maybe all they want is the horses. I know we can outrun them on foot, even carrying the mail. Whoever they are, they're not Wolves."

Their pursuers approached their refuge with caution. A thin man with a ragged straw hat bearing a single black feather in the brim trotted up toward the house, carbine at his hip. He turned his face suspiciously, first looking at the ruined dwelling with one eye, then the other. Valentine sighted on his dirty undershirt.

"That's far enough. What's on your mind?" Valentine shouted.

The thin man's long face split into a grin. "You boys want parley?"

"We're willing to let lead fly if you want it that way. Might be better for both if we talked first."

Straw Hat turned his horse and disappeared downslope. Valentine counted the minutes; every moment toward dusk helped their cause.

He heard horses moving through the woods below the hill. The pursuers were fanning out to surround the house. It sounded like a lot of riders.

Three heavy figures on tall quarterhorses approached the house. Even beneath beard and dirt, Valentine thought he saw a family resemblance. Their scruffy beards were black as coal, save for the center rider, who had two narrow streaks of gray running down his beard. Their hats also bore black feathers tucked in the left side of the hatband like that of the point man.

"Hello, the house," center rider called. "You wanted a parley, here it is."

"May I know to whom I'm speaking?" Valentine hollered back.

The man glanced at his younger associates. "Sure, stranger. My name's Mr. Mind Your Own Damn Business. This is my son Or I'll Tear Off Your Head and my nephew And I'll Shit Down Your Throat," he yelled. "That satisfy the rules of ettycute?"

A few guffaws broke out from below. "Charming," Harper said. "Why don't you plant him, Lieutenant?"

Valentine kept his concentration on the rider. "Thank you,

Mr. Mind. Looks like you got us four in a box. Is there a way for us to get out of it without a bunch of you winding up dead?"

"Maybe there's four of you and maybe there's three. One of your horses is riding light, so maybe you got a woman or a kid in there to think about," the negotiator called back.

"All we're thinking about is how many of you we can take with us. The consensus is twenty. If you're smart enough to know what a claymore mine is, you'll agree that it's at least that."

"Son, we can smoke you out of there easy. You'll be better off to take my terms: leave us your rifles, and give us the horses and tack. You can keep all your food, all your water, and your handguns, if you got 'em. And your lives. Even your self-respect, knowing that you met the Black Feather Troop and lived to tell about it."

"You want the guns, you just try and get 'em," Valentine shouted back, trying to keep the calm assurance of Captain LeHavre in his voice. "You'll get plenty of the business end. How about this: We'll give you the horses and the tack, and walk out of here after you pull out."

"No bargaining! I'm giving you five minutes to talk it over. You're up a dry hill in a building you can't even cover all the sides of. Bring out your rifles, and we let you walk out and keep heading north," he demanded with the assurance of a man holding four aces.

Valentine knew he was beat on card strength, but he believed they wouldn't live to see the sunrise if they walked out of the house without their rifles. The men turned to him, having reached the same conclusions and wanting to go down shooting.

"Gonzo, Harper, get out your blades. There's something we have to do."

"Cut the horses' throats?" Harper asked.

Valentine decided there was still a chance at bluff. "No, we have to whittle."

Five minutes later, but with over an hour of daylight left, Valentine stepped out of the door with the three rifles in his arms. He inflated his lungs, threw out his chest, and let loose with a high-pitched shriek. The three Black Feathers startled at the cry, which didn't seem to echo off the hills so much as pass through them.

"Come and get your guns," Valentine called hoarsely, advancing a cautious pair of steps away from the door. His holster was empty; Harper covered him from behind with the revolver.

"You made the smart move, son," Mr. Mind said, trying to keep the satisfaction out of his voice. The three rode forward to claim the repeaters.

Valentine carefully placed them on the ground and stepped back.

The older man dismounted, covered by the guns of his younger relations. He knelt to pick up one of the guns. "So, there are only three of you. I thought so. These are mighty fine—"

He made a surprised choking sound and pulled his hands away from the rifle as if it were a rattlesnake shaking its tail.

Carved into the stock of each rifle was a small insigne, a reversed swastika identical to the one Valentine had seen on the canoe and discussed with the researcher at the Miskatonic.

He looked up at Valentine, lips trembling. "Where'd you get these?" he asked.

"Our Masters gave them to us. Their mark is on the saddles, as well. I even have a tattoo. We're scouting for them, you see. Eight of them moving west as we speak. So take them, but we'll have them back by morning. In good condition, too: They'll only be dropped once."

"Now, son, we had no knowing you had anything to do

with the Twisted Cross. Hell, we're no enemies of yours. You might say we're on your side. Just this spring we caught a Cat out of the Ozarks. Real little spitfire; the boys ganged her, and we cut her throat, of course. You can ask Lord Melok-iz-Kur, in Rockford. We pay for what we take there with good silver, turned in runners even."

Valentine smiled. "It seems we've just had a misunderstanding here. No one was hurt, no one need know, Mr.—"

"It's Black Craig Lorraine, sir. At your service. If there's anything we can do to help you along, anything at all . . ." The Black Feather was almost groveling.

"Come to think of it . . . ," Valentine mused.

Valentine returned to the house, holding the rifles. "He folded." Harper handed the pistol back.

"Eh?" said Gonzalez.

"They're letting us go. In fact, they're giving us some supplies. Problem is, they're cannibals, so I had to promise them Gonzalez, since he's the plumpest of us."

"Bad joke, Val," Gonzalez said. "That was a joke, right?"

That night the Wolves rode north with guns, horses, and a new shoe on the spare horse. They were also weighed down by bags of corn, grain, and food from the supplies of the Black Feathers.

"Jesus, Lieutenant," Harper said, voice tinged with admiration. "When you did that Reaper scream, I about crapped my pants. You could have warned us."

One of the Black Feathers, part of the dispersing ring to the north, waved in a friendly fashion. Gonzalez eyed him warily.

"That was a joke, right, Lieutenant?"

Nine

Milwaukee, August of the forty-third year of the Kurian Order: The burned-out corpse of a city that once held nearly two million people rots across some eighty square miles on the shores of Lake Michigan. From the steep hills overlooking the great lake in the east to the Menominee and Root Rivers in the west, the city is nothing but hollow shells of buildings, the upper stories now housing bats, hawks, pigeons, and seagulls. The lower levels shelter everything from rats and coyotes to vagrant humans. Green has covered pavement throughout much of the city. Crickets chirp and grasshoppers leap along Locust Avenue, and Greenfield Avenue is precisely that: a green field where cattle are moved along to graze.

The new center of the city is the railway station, where the more favored soldiers and technicians house themselves in a ring around the Grand Avenue Mall. A hobo jungle of casual labor lives around and under the spaghetti-strand warren of overpasses that make up the old Interstate 94/43 juncture. Two Kurian Lords run the city, one from the Grog-guarded 1950 bomb shelter under the Federal Building, and the other from Tory Hill on the grounds of Marquette University. The Miller Brewing Company is still in business, producing but a trickle of the pilsner torrent it once did. Under new management, of course.

*   *   *

Lake Michigan awed Valentine with its quiet majesty. It had nothing of the crashing drama of the ocean shoreline he knew from books. The expanse of water covering 180 degrees of the horizon in almost a north-south line impressed him nonetheless.

He and Randall Harper camped together north of White-fish Bay. They had left Gonzalez in a secluded barn far outside the city limits with the horses after a cautious but uneventful crossing of southern Wisconsin. The only difficulty had been from a pack of guard dogs at a lonely farming settlement who chased them out of a field where they were stealing corn for the horses. The dogs contented themselves with barking rather than biting, and the Wolves had hurried back to their mounts without injury to anything but their dignity.

Now each night they stood behind a four-foot-tall, decorative stone wall in an overgrown park overlooking the lake, waiting for a boat from the White Banner Fleet to show three lights, one flickering, which they would answer with two.

"What exactly is this Flotilla?" Valentine asked his companion.

Harper, comfortably seated with his back to the stone wall, took a puff of one of the noxious cigarettes he smoked. "They're sympathetic to the Cause, even if they don't fight the Kurians tooth and nail. They're smugglers, gunrunners, traders. When they fight the Quislings, it's more because somebody got double-crossed, or they asked for too big a payoff. The Hoods hate going out into blue water, I'm told, so they leave it to the Quislings and some amphibian Grogs. Naturally the Quislings take bribes whenever they can get away with it. But the Flotilla always fights the Grogs whenever they get the chance. It's a real blood feud. I guess these Grogs are more partial to human flesh than most."

"Oh, I think I've heard of these. Big Mouths, Snappers, or whatever. They have jaws that open right to left, instead of up and down, right? Kind of fish-frog things?"

"Yep, slimy skin, like an eel. They're a problem in summer. They go dormant in winter. The real danger's in the spring, when they lay their eggs, you gotta keep away from the shores of the places they inhabit. They forage miles inland for food. They like the water a little shallower though, so they're not such a problem here. Up by Green Bay it's another story, though. And Lake Erie is stiff with them, they tell me."

Valentine thought of all the times that he had taken a boat out into the lakes of the Boundary Waters, collecting fish for dinner. Strange to think of fish emerging and hunting ashore. "So why does the Fleet carry our mail for us?"

"The Hunters in upstate New York give them guns and ammo, that's why. Rope, lumber, paint, turpentine, engines, gasoline—all sorts of stuff. We're lucky. We're just delivery boys; we don't have to worry about payoffs. But I got a little grease for the wheels in my bag; it's sort of expected."

Valentine shrugged. "Whatever it takes. You'd think they'd be on our side."

"They are, they are. In fact, I guarantee that you'll like 'em. Those sailors got a million stories. Of course, most of it's lies and brag, but it's still fun to listen to."

"I'll bet," Valentine said.

The next night the boat arrived. Valentine almost missed it, having wolf-trotted back to Gonzalez's barn to check on things at the main camp. Both the horses and his scout looked better for a few days' rest. Gonzalez had explored the area, finding some apple trees and rhubarb growing nearby. The scout had collected a basket of green apples and an armful of rhubarb, and was sharing his findings with the horses. "I saw some tomatoes near there, too. I'll get 'em tomorrow, sir," he reported.

"Just make sure you're not raiding somebody's field. We might end up dealing with something worse than dogs. I don't want any locals to suspect we're here."

"No tracks, no sign, and best of all, no Reapers," Gonzalez reassured him.

"I hope not. Sleep light. I'll take some apples back, if you have no objections, Mr. Bountiful," Valentine said, filling his pockets.

"Of course, Lieutenant. Give a few to the sarge with my compliments."

It was a tired lieutenant who returned to the overlook that evening, having covered fifteen miles on foot in the course of the day. Two hours after sunset, the three lights appeared on the dark lake.

"Thar she blows," Harper quoted, choosing a curious allusion. Valentine was mentally reciting *two on the land and three in the sea, and I on the outskirts of Milwaukee will be.*

Harper poured his flammable liquid on two piles of wood, twelve feet apart on the lakeside of the overlook wall, and set them ablaze. One light on the boat began winking on and off, as somebody opened and closed a hooded lantern.

"Are you satisfied it's them?" Harper asked.

"Yes," answered Valentine, trying to make out the lines of the little ship.

"Then let's go down to the beach, sir, and deliver the mail," Harper said, kicking out his fires.

The ship bobbed in the small swell of the lake. The waters of Lake Michigan did not roar as they struck the shoreline, but instead gently slapped it. The lake almost seemed playful on this idyllic summer evening, and something about the cool water in the warm evening breeze made Valentine forget the dangers of the night. The men waded out, weighed down with their waterproofed message bags, moccasins tied around their necks.

A tiny dinghy met them, its sides a bare sixteen inches out of the water.

"Climb in sideways," a boy's voice said from the stern. "You'll capsize me if you try to vault in."

The Wolves threw their packs into the dink and rolled into the little boat. It settled in the water appreciably with their added weight.

Valentine looked into the stern, at the figure with the paddle. What he had thought was a young boy was in fact a young woman dressed in shapeless white canvas. She had a round face and merry eyes, looking at her passengers over freckled cheekbones.

"Nice night, eh, boys? Captain Doss sends her compliments to the representatives of the Ozark Free Territory and invites you aboard the yawl *White Lightning*," she said, flashing an impressive set of teeth.

"The what *White Lightning?*" Valentine asked.

"Yawl," she repeated. "You know nothing of ships, soldier?"

"Not much," Valentine admitted.

"It's a little thing, but seaworthy as a porpoise. A ship not very different from ours made it around the world with only a single man on board. Over a hundred years ago, that was."

"Good to see you again . . . Teri, is it?" Harper said, contemplating his soaked deerskin breeches.

"I thought you looked familiar. Aaron . . . no, Randall Harper. Met you twice before, I recall. But I didn't see you this spring."

"I had the overland route. I don't want it again," Harper explained.

"Well, the captain will be glad to see you. So who's this with you?"

"Lt. David Valentine. He hails from Minnesota."

She reached over to shake Valentine's hand. "Pleased to know you, Lieutenant. Teri Silvertongue, first mate of the *White Lightning*. Will it be possible for you gentlemen to be joining us as guests this lovely evening?"

"I can't think of anything I'd like more, Miss Silvertongue," Valentine said, imitating her courteous phraseology. He wondered if Silvertongue was a nickname.

"We go by *Mr.* in the flotilla, man or woman," Silvertongue corrected. "Just as you do in the Wolves. Will you take an oar, sir?"

"I beg your pardon, Mr. Silvertongue. Sergeant Harper here didn't tell me the ship had a female crew, let alone how you expected to be addressed. Likes to keep a good thing to himself, I guess," Valentine explained, shooting a glance at Harper. He paddled for the white blob outside the gentle surf.

"Oh, there's plenty of men in the Flotilla," Silvertongue explained. "The commodore of our fleet just has a soft spot in her heart for any woman with a sad tale. It's the only soft spot she has; the woman has steel in her backbone and flint in her heart in all other matters excepting her 'poor foundlings,' as she calls us. But yes, it's three women on the *Lightning*. But it beats life on land. The Capos just want us for breeding stock, and their gunbelt lackeys seem to think they have the right to get the job started on any girl who tickles their fancy."

"Capos?" Valentine asked.

"That's what we call the Reapers out east, handsome boy."

The dinghy reached the ship, and Valentine got a good look at the *White Lightning*. Her lines had kind of an off-balanced beauty, with an oversize central mast set well forward and a smaller, secondary mast projecting from far astern.

Captain Doss wore a smart white semi-uniform to greet her guests. The captain had beautiful, dusky skin and the angular features of a storybook pirate queen. Her short black hair matched even Valentine's own mane in its glossy sheen.

A third woman, who helped Valentine and Harper into the *White Lightning,* stood over six feet tall and had the long, graceful limbs of a ballerina. "Give me the bags up," she said perfunctorily, and Valentine realized he had heard a foreign accent for the first time in his life.

Once on board, the *White Lightning* seemed smaller than it had looked from the dinghy. It was wide-waisted; the top of what was obviously the cabin area filled the middle third of the ship. It had a wheel to steer it—someone had spent a lot of hours carving and polishing the spokes—placed in front of the rear mast. All the woodwork, save the planks of the deck and the decorative wheel, was painted a uniform light gray.

The captain introduced her crew. "You've met my first mate, Mr. Silvertongue. My second mate, who works so hard I don't need any more crew, is Eva Stepanicz. She crossed the Atlantic four round trips before ending up in the Lakes."

"It will be more times, once I have goods enough for my own ship," she said.

"You mean gold enough?" Harper asked

"No, sir. Goods. In Riga is agent of tradings, who pays most for paintings brought back from America. I am here collecting arts."

The captain smiled. "It's hard not to indulge someone so determined. And she's a hard bargainer. I don't know a Picasso from an espresso, but I think our Mr. Stepanicz has enough to start a gallery."

"But I'm forgetting my manners," Harper said, reaching into his haversack. "Captain, compliments of my last trip through Tennessee," he said, handing over a pair of elaborately wrapped and sealed bottles of liquor. In the muted light, Valentine couldn't read the black labels, but they looked authentic.

"Sergeant Harper, you just bought us a new coat of paint, and maybe some standing rigging. My thanks to you, sir."

Harper pointed to the three bags of correspondence. "You'll also find a box of cigars for each of you in those bags. If you don't smoke them yourselves, a little good tobacco helps grease the Quisling wheels, I believe."

"You southern gentlemen are too kind. I wish those Green Mountain Boys would show the same courtesy," Silvertongue said, with a curtsey involving her overbaggy trousers.

"Enough playacting," Captain Doss interrupted. "I'd like to be anchored off Adolph's Bunker by midnight. You Wolves want to pay a call on Milwaukee? Get a little taste of life in the KZ?"

"We're always interested in the Kurian Zone. But would that be wise, Captain?" Valentine asked.

"Well, Lieutenant, the pathfinder look would have to go. But we've got some extra whites in the slop chest. The Bunker's a rough spot, but I've never heard of the Reapers going in there. The owner never makes trouble; in fact, I've heard he turns troublemakers over to them. I'd like a little extra muscle showing for the deal we need to do. I'll make it worth your while."

Valentine thought for a moment. "Is this deal anything the New Order would object to?"

"If they knew about it, Lieutenant," Doss said, looking at the wind telltale. The tiny streamer fluttered east. "You might say we're fucking with the Quislings."

"Count us in, then."

*   *   *

An hour later, the yawl tacked into Milwaukee's harbor. A single decrepit police boat, piloted by a Quisling whose sole badge of rank was a grimy blue shirt, motored alongside and illuminated the *White Lightning* with a small spotlight.

Captain Doss held up a hand and flashed a series of hand signals that would have done a third-base coach proud. The Quisling nodded, satisfied.

"Just arranging what you might call the port charges," Doss explained to Valentine. The Wolves now wore white canvas shirts and trousers, as well. While more tattered than the mates' uniforms, they still found it a pleasant change from sweat-stained buckskins. During the run south, Valentine had questioned the captain about the Lakes Flotilla and its habits, and had learned a little about how the sails were balanced. Valentine sponged information off anyone he met, his mind always ready to learn something new.

They pulled up to the main civic pier, a cracked concrete affair that sloped toward Lake Michigan at a twenty-degree angle. Valentine noticed that the captain pivoted as she brought the ship in so that its bow pointed out to the lake.

"The Kurians aren't too big on infrastructure repairs," Silvertongue commented as she tied the *White Lightning* to the dock. A few boats, none of which matched Captain Doss's in lines or upkeep, bobbed along the pier.

"Stepanicz, you've got the first anchor watch. Don't give me that look; after the deal, I'll take over for you. If we're not back in two hours, or if anything goes down, you raise sail. There's a good wind for it tonight."

"Aye, aye, sir," she answered, drawing a sawed-off shotgun from the chart locker. She broke it open and inserted two loads of buckshot.

"And if our broad-shouldered young men would each grab one of the barrels lashed to the mast in the cabin—Silver, help

Mr. Valentine with the knots, would you—we can be about the rest of this night's business."

Adolph's Bunker looked like a transplant from the Maginot Line. Whatever its original purpose, its builders had wanted it to last. They constructed it from heavy concrete, with narrow windows imitative of a castle's arrow slits. The bleached white of the concrete and the irregular rectangular slits gave it the countenance of a toothy skull. It lay on the lakeshore, set well away from the dead and empty buildings frowning behind.

"Why is it called Adolph's Bunker?" Valentine asked as they approached the squat, brick-shaped building. The ten-gallon cask grew heavier with each step.

"The guy who runs it is a dictator, for starts," Captain Doss said.

Silvertongue turned and looked at the men, each laboring with a cask on his shoulder. "There's a feeling about the place. It's a piece of sanity in an insane country. Or maybe a slightly different insanity within the insanity, take your pick. It's popular with the Quislings. When we found out we had to meet you this week, we contacted a Chicago big shot, so we could kill two birds with one stone this trip."

"As long as our bags get delivered," Valentine said, trying not to breathe too hard under his awkward burden.

"This trade will make getting your bags through a lot easier," Doss said.

The building seemed hollow and dead as a shucked oyster. Valentine surmised that the clientele liked to do their drinking in dark and quiet, when he realized that music, too loud to be the product of any instrument, was filtering up from somewhere beneath the building. He switched to hard ears and listened to the beat of ancient rock and roll and the gabble of voices echo up from a stairwell. Captain Doss turned to a set of narrow concrete steps that disappeared along the side of the building down into the earth. A knobless metal door opened out onto a small landing. Doss squatted down and said something into the hole. It swung open.

As he descended the stairs, Valentine plastered a drunken smile across his face, trying to live up to his role of eager sailor. The captain entered, nodding to someone. Valentine looked at Harper, and the two Wolves exchanged shrugs. Silvertongue turned to the men. "Don't worry, they're going to frisk you for weapons and smokes. Just put your hands on the wall and read the sign."

A Grog roughly the size of a Volkswagen Beetle barred their way. Over its yard-wide shoulder Valentine watched the captain and then her mate being frisked and sniffed by a dog-man right out of an H. G. Wells nightmare. When it finished with Silvertongue, the smelly roadblock at the door stepped aside and Valentine passed into the noise of the Bunker.

He mimicked Silvertongue's stance, placing his feet twice his shoulder width apart and putting his hands to either side of a sign, stenciled in paint onto another concrete wall just inside the door. To Valentine's left, a sumo-size man sat inside a wire cage, idly scratching his stubble with a Saturday night submachine gun.

As the dog-man gave him the once over, Valentine read the stenciled letters:

THE RULES

ADOLPH'S WORD IS LAW

NO SMOKING ANYTHING WE DIDN'T SELL YOU

NO DRINKING, UNLESS IT'S OURS

YOU'RE ONLY AS GOOD AS YOUR BARTER

YOU'RE ONLY AS BAD AS WE LET YOU BE

VISIT OUR GIFT SHOP
CONFUSED? SEE RULE 1

Valentine retrieved his keg and joined the women. He looked around the bar, trying to avoid staring like a corn-fed hick fresh off the back forty. Electric light and noise overwhelmed him. Prerecorded music played by machine was a rare treat to Valentine, and he gaped at the source. A box of neon and chrome against one cinderblock wall blared CD SELECTION & SOUND, as the reflective lettering on the glass proclaimed. A bar almost filled the wall opposite the jukebox, and a mismatched assortment of tables, booths, and benches stood about the sawdust-covered floor. The base of a flush toilet peeped from beneath a curtain in the corner farthest from the bar. A sour-smelling urinal next to it trickled water down the wall and into the soggy shavings beneath. An alcove, separated from the rest of the room by a layer of wire netting similar to the guard-cage at the door, advertised itself as CURRENCY EXCHANGE—GIFT SHOP—MANAGEMENT.

He was relieved to see the rest of the occupants of the Bunker were human, albeit a poor genetic cross section. Two bartenders stood only a hair shorter and slimmer than the Grog at the door, stuffed like a pair of pointy-headed sausages into red T-shirts with black lettering reading THE BUNKER. A desiccated weed of a man in a green visor sat behind a desk in the alcove-cage, smoking a cigarette from a long black holder. Gliding between the tables, laden tray miraculously balanced as she dodged and weaved, a nimble barhop waited on the customers. Clad only in a Bunker logoed baseball cap, bikini top, and a thong, she looked the happiest of anyone in the room. Valentine ran a quick estimate in his head and decided her hat contained more material, and covered a higher percentage of her body, than everything else she wore combined—high heels included. The patrons, dressed in ill-fitting black-and-tan fatigues or blue merchant marine overalls, drank, talked, and smoked in huddled groups.

The captain led her little party in single file to the Currency Exchange—Gift Shop—Management cage.

"Why, if it isn't the *White Lightning* herself come to pay me a visit," the gnome croaked, cigarette clenched between yellowed teeth. "And Teri Silvertongue! Ahhh, missy, what I wouldn't give to be young again! Any time you get sick of high seas and low wages, you just come see me."

"Thanks for the offer, Ade," Silvertongue said, exposing her rack of teeth in a forced smile. "But I catch cold kind of easy."

Captain Doss stepped up to the slot midway up the cage and placed a small leather pouch on the owner's desk. "Brought you some makings for your coffin nails, Ade. Do me a favor and die quick, would you?"

"I'll outlive you, Dossie. You got a couple new hands?" The owner ran his eyes quickly up and down Harper and Valentine, perhaps assessing their creditworthiness or potential as troublemakers.

"Just a little extra muscle for this run. Speaking of which, has the Duke arrived yet?"

"Take my advice, Cap. Slow down and enjoy life a little. But yeah, his party is in the card room. You buyin' for your crew, or are you gonna pull another Captain Bligh like last time?"

Doss shook her head. "After the deal, Ade, after the deal." She gestured to the other three, and they filed toward a door next to the long wooden bar. Valentine counted three casks and some thirty-odd bottles of assorted poison, all unlabeled. He watched one Quisling, crossed rifles of a captain on his epaulets, purchase a shot and a beer chaser by placing a pair of bullets on the bar. The Quisling tossed off the shot, face contorted as though he had poured an ounce of nitric acid down his throat.

Valentine tried not to think about the fact that he stood in a room with thirty people, each of whom could win a brass ring by turning him over alive to the Reapers.

Doss knocked on the door marked PRIVATE. It opened a crack, and half of an ebony face looked at her through a narrowed eye. The door shut again, but just for a moment.

The guard opened the door, and the crew entered a spacious, well-ventilated room. Three men and a woman sat around a felt-covered table. Cards and chips lay before three of the players; the fourth, a man, only watched. Valentine's eyes were drawn to him by his outlandish clothing if for no other reason.

The Duke of Rush wore a red uniform heavily trimmed with gold braid. Half high school marching band outfit and half toreador costume, it gaudily set off his pale skin and black hair. A brass ring, the first Valentine had ever seen, hung from a golden chain around his neck. Bored blue eyes stared up at the crew of the *White Lightning*.

The Duke's male henchmen wore the simple navy-blue battle dress of Chicago Quislings, and the card-playing woman an elegant blue cocktail dress glittering with real gemstones. No guns were evident, but the black man who opened the door toyed with a butterfly knife, opening and shutting it with quick flicks of the wrist.

"Captain, we expected you hours ago," the Duke said in an educated accent. "You know how I hate it when my own parties start late. What were you up to, running guns to insurgents?"

Doss let a simper mask her face. "No, trying to find something to wear. You always make such an entrance. I decided it would be better to let you enter first."

"You don't need to dress for this dive, Captain. The only reason I'm wearing my best is that the purported reason for this trip is social. I spent the day calling on the Kur here and arranging beer trucks for Chicago. But our business is going to be much more lucrative. May we see the merchandise?"

The black man put aside his butterfly knife long enough to push a chair forward for Doss. She sat. "Put the bills on the table, and you'll see it," she said.

The Duke gestured to a lieutenant, who opened a leather satchel and drew out a sheaf of papers. Captain Doss pulled out a magnifying glass and went through the pages one at a time, examining the wax seals covering printed red-and-blue tape.

"Eight firearm permits, good," she counted to herself. "Five labor vouchers . . . twelve supply vouchers, sixteen . . . eighteen . . . twenty passports. Three dockyard releases . . . Hey, wait a second. The dockyard releases aren't signed and sealed, my friend!"

The Duke smiled. "Sorry, Captain. An oversight on my part. I'll make it up to you next time, okay?"

"Afraid not. We're keeping a bag. You want it, get these filled out properly, and you can have it," she said firmly.

"Oh, very well. Have it your way, Captain. We'll take one bag less now, and I'll see if I can get the sign-offs for your next run. Though it breaks my heart that you don't trust me. Now bring out the snuff, and we'll see if your color is worth all this."

Valentine and Harper, on cue, placed their barrels in front of Silvertongue, who popped the lids with a knife of her own. It was full of clumps of brown sugar. She upended the barrels one at a time and dumped the sugar on the floor. Glass test tubes filled with white powder soon emerged from the sugar. She gathered up two dozen tubes and placed them among the cards and chips on the table.

Captain Doss took two of the tubes and pocketed them.

The Duke wiped his mouth eagerly. "Test it, my dear."

The woman in the cocktail dress pulled a vial of clear liquid from her small handbag. She uncorked one of the tubes, licked a toothpick and coated it with the powder, then stirred it in the vial, which turned an azure blue.

"They don't call me the Duke of Rush for nothing," the Duke quipped. Valentine forced a laugh, but the captain and her mate ignored him.

"Can I take the bills now?" the captain asked.

"Of course, Captain. But I think this calls for a celebration. The drinks are on the Duke tonight, and your crew is invited, of course."

Doss rose from her chair. "Sorry, Duke. You know how I get when I'm away from my ship."

"I should be going, too. Maybe next time," Silvertongue said, bringing crestfallen expressions to the Quislings.

Harper patted Valentine on the shoulder. "Duty calls."

"It's not calling that loudly," Valentine demurred. "Captain, may I stay for a while?"

Captain Doss shot him a questioning glance. "Just be back by dawn. And I mean dawn, Tiny, because we sail with first light with or without you."

"Thank you, Captain. I'll be there."

"Finally one of your little flock shows some sense, Doss." The Duke laughed as the other sailors exited. "Ask anyone in Chicago, no one parties like the Duke. What's your name, son?"

"Dave, Mr. Duke. Dave Tiny."

The Duke clapped him on the back. "Glad to meet you,

Tiny. I'm always making friends with traveling people, never know when they'll show up with something worth trading."

A knock sounded at the door.

"Duke, it's your other appointment," Butterfly Knife said.

"Oh, yeah. Tiny, you keep quiet; you might find this interesting. You'll see something you won't see sailing with Doss, that's for sure. I need to get a little dispute resolved."

The man with the butterfly knife opened the door, and two neatly dressed men and a woman entered.

"Thanks for the invite to the party, Duke," the tallest of the three said. Valentine noted he wore a wide brass ring similar to the Duke's, on his finger rather than on a chain.

"Good you could make it, Hoppy," the Duke said with a smile-snarl. "You seemed kind of preoccupied during my business call. Thought you might be tired of my company."

Valentine felt a shiver, but it had nothing to do with the nasty glint in the Duke's eye. There were Reapers outside. He thought of making up an excuse to leave, but decided to obey the Duke's order to remain silent.

"Glad you brought your assistant, but you didn't have to bring the muscle, Hoppy. This is just a friendly social gathering.

"Gail Allenby takes care of my professional life," Hoppy said. "Andersen here is responsible for the physical one. He uses a knife just as well in the kitchen as in an alley, by the way. I'll have you over for dinner tomorrow and prove it."

"I trust the cutlery will be well washed," the Duke responded. "Thanks for the offer, but I have to get back to Chicago. We need to get something straightened out, Hoppy. When it's done, you might not want to honor that invite anyway."

Someone screamed in the main part of the bar, and Valentine heard chairs tip over. Butterfly Knife opened the door again, and a Reaper entered the room, glancing around with wary yellow eyes. A muscular man in a sleeveless shirt followed. Then a female figure—at least, it appeared female to Valentine—slowly came in. She wore a black-and-gold woven robe and a heavy hood, her face hidden behind a shining mask. The mask was decorated only by a narrow eye slit; the rest was silvery, polished mirror-bright. She did not so much walk as float across the floor on legs unseen under the robe; Valentine heard no footsteps as she moved. A second Reaper remained at the open door, its back to the room, facing the rapidly emptying bar.

"Thank you for coming, Lord Yuse-Uth," the Duke said, his face calm and serious.

Valentine looked at Hoppy, who seemed to have lost three inches and twenty pounds since the Reaper and its Master Vampire had entered. He focused all his attention on the blanching man, hoping the Kurian would not probe his thoughts.

"Lord, what need brings You here?" Hoppy stammered.

"I asked Her to be present," the Duke said. "You've been cheating me, Hopps."

"Never!"

"Past couple months I've been noticing our beer running dry a lot. We opened up some kegs, found plastic balls inside. Not many, but enough to skim off ten percent or so. I had my men spill a keg after we made our purchase today: balls again."

Hoppy, who was apparently the factory manager, thought for a moment. "Maybe someone at the brewery is up to something. I had no knowledge of this, Duke. I'll make it up to you."

"I'm withholding payment. You've got ten percent less bodies coming north this shipment, and another ten percent less for the previous two." The Duke turned to Kurian. "With winter coming on, that's going to be fifty, sixty less auras for the Milwaukeee Families, my Lord."

The man in the sleeveless shirt spoke. "Lord Yuse-Uth says that the brewery will make it up next year. Her need is for the full allotment of auras."

"I don't like to say no to a Lord," the Duke said, "but my own Lords may have some say in the matter. Does She want a faction-war? That'd cost Her more. I'll split the difference, twenty-five fewer auras and you can make it up to me next year."

The mirrored face turned to look at the Duke. "Agreed. The ring is revoked." Valentine was not sure if the grating voice came from the mask or between his ears.

The Reaper grabbed Hoppy's arm and reached for the ring on the third finger of his right hand. It took the ring, pulling off the finger as well with a sickening snap of tearing cartilage. Hoppy screamed. His bodyguard stood frozen, staring in awe at the Reaper.

"He is no longer under Lord Yuse-Uth's protection," the Kurian's speaker said, watching Hoppy try to squeeze off the blood flowing from the pulpy mass where the digit had been. "Allenby, you are now the brewery manager. Lord Yuse-Uth trusts your deliveries will be complete. Perhaps in time you will wear this very ring."

The woman gulped, stepping away from her former supervisor. "Thank You, my Lord," she quavered. "Andersen, your contract with Mr. Hoppy is terminated. We will talk tomorrow about your future with the brewery. Think about it."

"Y-yes ma'am," Andersen said, his hands trembling.

"Dammit, I had nothing to do with shorting the shipments," Hoppy swore.

"Lord Yuse-Uth thanks you for bringing this matter to Her

attention," the speaker said, turning to the Duke. "She looks forward to continued good relations and trade with Her Brethren in Chicago."

"I appreciate Her Lordship's time," the Duke said.

The Kurian, her speaker, and the Reapers departed, and Valentine found himself able to breathe again.

"Responsibility demands performance, Hoppy," the Duke said. "Personally, I think you were cheating me." The Duke looked at the man with the butterfly knife. "Make him shorter. Permanently."

Valentine watched, his face as passive as the Kurian's mask, as the man with the knife knocked Hoppy to the floor. He savagely hamstrung the screaming man, cutting the tendons at the back of his victim's knees.

"Guess they'll call you Crawly now," the Duke said. "Ms. Allenby, take that trash out with you as you leave. Dump him with the other garbage on the dock. I'll talk to you in the morning and see what kind of understanding we can come to."

None of the Duke's companions looked particularly upset as the brewery people dragged the bleeding, weeping wretch outside. The Duke's craggy face split into a smile.

"Party time. Go get a bottle of something decent, Palmers. And a couple cases of Miller, in sealed bottles. I'm going to get rolling on some of this white gold. Join me, Denise?"

She smiled and reached again into her purse for a mirror. "Tested high blue, Dukey? You bet your ring I am."

Twenty-odd beers, three bottles, and multiple toots later, the Quislings and Valentine were closing down the Bunker. Still behind the wire, Adolph counted out most of the contents of the Duke's purse. One bartender remained. A passed-out merchant marine was being dragged outside, and the waitress sat in the bodyguard's lap. Her bikini top rested on the closed eyes of Butterfly Knife, who had downed almost a whole bottle of the unlabeled house busthead. Behind the toilet curtain, Denise's shapely ankles with the blue dress around them twitched in time to the music. Valentine, who had drunk only a little booze while appearing to drink a lot, sat on the sawdust floor with his back to the jukebox, leaning up against the Duke.

Valentine had discovered a passion in the Duke for bad jokes and dirty songs. The ringholder had announced earlier in the evening, "This bar reminds me of what happens when you cross a German with an Irishman: you get someone too drunk to follow orders." After that the Wolf had dredged his brain for every mossy old chestnut he could remember from his early teens to barracks life. Finally, in keeping with his nautical disguise, he taught the Duke of Rush all the lines he could remember of "The Good Ship Venus."

"The cabin boy, the cabin boy, the dirty little nipper / Put ground glass inside his ass and circumcised the skipper," the Duke sang with him, giggling at the end of each verse.

Eva Stepanicz rested in the arms of the other Quisling, there more to keep an eye on Valentine per the captain's orders than to enjoy herself. A small tower of empties stood next to her, begun when she returned to the bar to find out what had transpired during the Kurian visit. She possessed an almost magical power over liquor, making her the choice for this particular assignment. She pushed the man's face away from her, directing his beer-fumed breath toward the floor.

The bartender returned from dumping the merchant marine, escorting First Mate Silvertongue.

"Okay, Tiny, on your feet. Day's breaking, and the captain wants you and Stepanicz back."

Stepanicz climbed to her feet with a relieved sigh.

Valentine looked up at the first mate from beneath his red Bunker T-shirt, worn pharaoh-style on his head. "C'mon, Silver. No reason she can't wait another hour or two. Shove off," he slurred, more from fatigue than alcohol.

"Stepanicz, let's get him up," Silvertongue ordered. The two women each took an arm and pulled Valentine to his feet. Valentine winked at Silvertongue.

"I said *shove off!*" he shouted, startling the Quislings from their slumber. Valentine grabbed a head of hair in each hand and seemingly knocked their heads together. He arranged it so his hands absorbed most of the impact.

And so began a semidrunken three-way brawl that brought even the passed-out Denise from her toilet-seat nap. The men roared approval every time Valentine knocked one of the women on her ass, and the two females ringside cheered whenever Stepanicz or Silvertongue landed a punch. The bare-breasted barhop had placed her pinkies in her mouth and produced a piercing whistle when Stepanicz brought the fight to a close with a powerful, accurate, and all-too-realistic kick in the proper place. Valentine folded like the Quisling's butterfly knife and dropped to the ground.

The Duke of Rush staggered to his feet, absently brushing sawdust from his garish uniform. He knelt next to Valentine and helped his groin-gripping drinking buddy sit up.

"Better get back to your ship, Tiny. Guess they weren't tiny enough, heh?"

Valentine managed a pained smile.

"Look, next time you port in Chicago, look me up. I'm pretty much in charge of R and R, that's rest and relaxation, you know, for those wise enough to join up with the Kurians. My place is above a group of bars called the Clubs Flush. On Rush Street, it's easy to find 'cause it's the part of the city lit up at night, unless you count the Zoo. I cater to the crème de la crème of Chicago society, you understand. Following orders from these bitches every day, I bet you and that other guy are about dying to get laid. I'll get you some on the house, okay?"

"Thanks, Duke," Valentine said, adjusting his trousers.

"You're my kind of people, Davy. And," he added, more softly in Valentine's ear, "if you can tie up to the big pier with another load of the white stuff as good as this, I'll see to it that even if you dock a swabbie, you'll sail out a captain, you know what I mean? Just stop in and see me first, at the Clubs Flush, like I said. I'll treat you right."

Valentine massaged his aching groin. "Thanks for the tip, sir."

With Silvertongue on one side and Stepanicz on the other, Valentine marched back to the ship, exhausted.

"What was all that about, Valentine?" Silvertongue asked as they climbed back on board. "Why were you toadying up to that ring-carrying clown?"

"He's a powerful man where he comes from. Sometimes just knowing the name of someone with that kind of influence can come in handy."

Later that morning, the *White Lightning* landed Harper and Valentine on a deserted stretch of beach north of where they first rendezvoused.

"Sorry for the kick," Stepanicz said, shaking Valentine's hand. "No hard feelings?"

"No, I don't think it'll be feeling hard for a while," Valentine answered. "But thanks for asking."

The captain presented them each with a fifth of rum brought all the way from Jamaica. "And the Lakes Flotilla is always willing to help you out," she said, handing them each a card with her name written on it in elegant calligraphy. "You can always tell a Flotilla ship because the word *white* is in the name somehow. Or a foreign version of white: *blanc, weiss,* something like that. Just give them this card, and tell them I owe you a favor."

"Thanks, Captain Doss," Harper said.

"Your servant, ma'am," Valentine added.

Each Wolf shouldered a bag of dispatches addressed to Southern Command. As they hopped out of the dinghy, again wetting their feet in the waters of Lake Michigan, the weight of their rifles brought home the seriousness of the journey back.

"Should we tell Gonzo about all this?" Harper asked.

"Why?" Valentine said, responding with a twinkle in his eye. "He just missed a boring evening with some sailors. And what he doesn't know won't piss him off. But I'll make it up to him. He can have my Bunker souvenir T-shirt."

Ten

Central Wisconsin, September of the forty-third year of the Kurian Order: North of the road and rail arc connecting Milwaukee with the Twin Cities, Wisconsin under the Kurians has lain fallow. Dense forests of pine and oak shelter deer, moose, and feral pigs. Four-legged wolves prey on both, and occasionally have to give up their kills to prowling bears and wolverines. A few logging camps dot the area around Oshkosh and Green Bay, taking oak and cedar for use in the south. Menominee trappers and hunters also traverse the woods and lakes, traveling down the Wisconsin River to the Dells Country to trade pelts.

The Kurian Order begins at the traveled belt linking Milwaukee, Madison, Eau Claire, and St. Paul, Minnesota. Rich corn and dairy farms still fill the southern half of the state. Three Kurian Lords, known as the Madison Triumvirate, control the farms, mines, and lines of communication from the outskirts of Milwaukee to LaCrosse. Within the gloom of their dominant hilltop dome in the old Wisconsin State Capitol building, they command Reapers from Fond du Lac to Platteville, Eau Claire to Beloit.

The humans under the teeth of the Kurians endure the New Order, living in the gray area between doing the minimum required for survival and full Quislinghood. Their family farms are self-controlled, very different from the brutal plantations

of the south or the mechanized collectives of Nebraska,
Kansas, and Oklahoma. But recently, a new shadow has
fallen over the region. Rumors spread by milk-truck drivers
and road crews tell of a new Kurian Lord turning the pictur-
esque village of New Glarus into a hilltop fortress. To the
fearful smallholders and townspeople of the area, this means
thirteen more thirsty Reapers taking their human toll by night.

They camped on some hills above the Wisconsin River
near Spring Green. The Wolves could see miles of river valley in either direction. A few electrified farms burned porch
lights, but the prominence Valentine guessed to be Tower Hill
seemed shunned by the residents, for no active farm lay at its
feet, or indeed within miles.

They camped a little below the hill, in the ruins of what
was apparently an outdoor stage in the middle of nowhere.
Valentine had explored the warped and overgrown little
wooden theater nestled in a kettle in the hillside. It reminded
him of a fancy version of the simple outdoor platform at one
end of the public tent in the Boundary Waters, where Bobby
Royce had received a prize shotgun what felt like several life-
times ago.

He paced the footboards in thought. Were the people in the
Freeholds the ones who were crazy? All the loss, all the suffering caused by the never-ending battles. A life, of sorts, was
possible under the Kurians. Perhaps they should weather the
storm, turn it to their advantage by bargaining for some measure of independence, rather than fighting for it. He marveled
at the adaptability of his race: the Lakes Flotilla, for example.
They worked at the edges of the Kurian Order, sowing seeds
of destruction while turning a profit. Then there was Steiner
and his enclave, trying to build something new rather than
keep alive the old. Or the determination of the outnumbered

and outgunned Southern Command, standing in their hilly fastness and daring the Kurians to try to enter even as they carried the fight to the Lost Lands. Even the little clusters of hidden civilizations like the Boundary Waters contributed to the fight by simply surviving.

A tingle interrupted his ruminations upon the stage. With the frozen terror of a rabbit under an eagle's shadow, he sensed a Reaper. He stepped off the stage and padded downhill to the little cluster of cabins below. The Reaper seemed to be moving up Tower Hill, bringing silence to the nighted woods. Even the crickets ceased their chirping.

Valentine entered the Wolves' overnight home. It was a two-room house with small windows that made the absence of glass less of an inconvenience. The Wolves had stabled the horses in the larger room. He placed the fingers of one hand to his lips while making the pinkie-and-forefinger hand signal to his comrades that meant Reaper. Gonzalez and Harper unsheathed their rifles and checked their parangs.

All three concentrated on lowering lifesign, sitting back to back in a little cross-legged circle. The horses would give off no more lifesign than a group of deer; there was enough wildlife in the woods to confuse it even if it passed close, as long as they were able to mask their minds properly. As he quieted his mind and centered his breathing, Valentine found he could feel the Reaper atop the hill to the west. Minutes passed, then an hour, and the Reaper moved off to the west as clammy sweat trickled down Valentine's back.

"That was a little too close," Valentine said to his fellow Wolves. "Anyone want to move camp, just in case it circles around the hill?"

"Fine idea," Harper agreed. "I could walk all night anyway after that."

They decided to move south, treating the Reaper as a tornado that you can best dodge by moving at right angles to its path. As Harper readied the horses and Gonzalez hid evidence of their camp, Valentine cautiously walked up Tower Hill, rifle at the ready. He read the trail left by heavy bootprints. The Reaper had paused for an hour on the overlook. Valentine wondered why. After a word to Harper, he found an unobstructed knoll above the stage and scanned what parts of the horizon he could.

Two or three miles to the southeast, flame lit the clouded night. A pair of buildings seemed to be ablaze behind a screen of trees; he could make out a small grain silo lit by the red-yellow glow. Perhaps the Hood had a better view from the western crown of Tower Hill, but it was unlike a Reaper to just stand and watch a fire for the drama of it. And the blaze seemed unnaturally bright. Valentine wished the winds were favorable enough for him to smell the smoke.

He rejoined Gonzalez and Harper.

"There's a good-size fire," Valentine explained. "I think a barn or a house is going up. You want to check it out? It's on this side of the river, so we can get to it easy."

"Do we want to be there?" Harper asked. "If it's someone's house, neighbors will be coming from all over. It would be just like a Hood to pick someone off in the confusion."

"I thought we were headed south," Gonzalez said.

"Yes, eventually. But I think this Reaper watched what was going on there for a while, for whatever reason. It's not like them to just look at something for the sake of the view. I think it's worth checking out."

Harper shrugged. "It's your party. I don't mind watching a building burn. But I don't like the idea of making a decision 'cause of a prediction about a Reaper's behavior. Sounds like a good way to end up drained."

"It'll be okay, as long as the lieutenant's radar is working," Gonzalez suggested.

"Hope so," Harper said. "Let's get there before the patrols wake up."

They moved through the night, leading their horses. Gonzalez walked out ahead, picking the path, followed by Valentine and Harper, each taking two horses.

As they drew close to the fire, Valentine decided the burning buildings were just another abandoned farm in a region where two out of three homesteads were empty. New forests stood in fields that had once belonged to cows.

The Wolves tied up the horses near a shallow seasonal streambed, and the horses drank from runoff puddles scattered among the rocks. They could see the flames flickering through the thin-skinned trunks of scrub beech and young oaks. They crept up to within fifty feet of the dying fire. What was left of four buildings, one obviously a barn, had already collapsed into burning debris. Without the daily rains of the past week, the conflagration would have turned into a forest fire.

Harper spat cotton. "Okay, Lieutenant, here's your fire. What now?"

"No family, no neighbors," Valentine observed. "Must have been empty. These fields sure don't look used. I haven't seen anything but a few old fence posts around with the wire stripped off. So why's it burning?"

"Maybe a patrol came through, livened up a quiet night with a little arson," Harper mused. "That east-west road we crossed yesterday by the river's got to be up there somewhere."

"Could be," Valentine agreed. "If so, they used a lot of starter. You can smell it from here, kind of like gasoline."

Gonzalez and Harper sniffed. "Reminds me a little of napalm," Harper said. "The Grogs used it at Cedar Creek. They had an old fire truck filled with it. Doused some of the buildings our guys were holed up in and then lit it."

"I'd like to take another look around in daylight," Valentine said. "We can wait a few more hours before moving on. Let's get the horses and find a safe spot to sleep."

Valentine could tell from Harper's expression that he thought getting some rest was the first sensible plan out of his superior's mouth all evening.

Daylight inspection of the ruins told the end of the story but not the beginning. While Gonzalez squatted in cover along the road, ready to run like a jackrabbit back to the fire scene at the first sign of a patrol, only a livestock-laden tractor-trailer passed along the old highway, crawling east at a safe fifteen miles an hour along the potholed road.

"This makes no sense," Valentine said to a disinterested Harper. "We've got four burning buildings, or three buildings and a shed, I guess. But what are those other three burned spots?"

Valentine indicated the blackened brush, circles of fire twelve to thirty feet in diameter, scattered around the buildings on what had once been lawn and garden.

"Weird thing number two. Look how the house is wrecked. The frame's been scattered all to hell, but only westward. Like a bunch of dynamite was set off on the east side of it."

Harper shrugged. "Maybe the Quislings were training with demolitions or something."

"Then where's the crater? And the foundation is in good shape; those cinder blocks would be gone if someone put a charge there. And look at those two saplings. They're both broken off three feet up, but the tops are lying *toward* the house. An explosion wouldn't do that. Weird thing number three. That hole dug in the ground by the barn."

The men walked over to the ruins of the old barn, next to the blackened column of the still-standing silo. A triangular furrow, three feet long and almost two feet deep, was gouged into the ground; a dug-up divot of earth and grass lay nine feet away, in the direction of the barn. "What did this?" asked Valentine. "The patrols brought out a backhoe? This was dug out in one clean scoop."

"You got me, Sherlock," Harper said with a shrug.

"And finally, there's no tracks. Unless that's why they burned out those patches of the scrub—to cover their tracks, or the marks of the weapons that did this."

Valentine kneeled and sniffed at the charred wood. It still retained a faint petroleum or medicinal smell, like camphor.

"Somebody's coming," Harper called, moving swiftly behind the silo, rifle already at his shoulder. Valentine threw himself to the ground, hearing footsteps from the forest. The person was not making any effort to keep quiet, whoever it was.

A middle-aged man in faded blue pants and a striped mattress-ticking shirt emerged from the forest. He surveyed the wreckage, not looking particularly surprised. He removed his baseball cap and wiped his face and neck with a yellow handkerchief. What was left of his hair, balding front and back, was a uniform gray.

"Whoever you are," the man called, "you're sure up early. Come out and show yourselves. I ain't armed."

Valentine hand-signaled Harper to stay concealed. Gonzalez had vanished, perhaps into the overgrown drainage ditch next to the road. He stood up, half fearing a sniper's bullet.

"Good morning to you, too," Valentine responded. "I'm just passing through."

"You mean 'we're passing through,' stranger," the unknown rustic chided. "I saw your buddy behind the silo. Since you're not from around here, I'll ask your name, son."

"David, sir. I'm down from Minnesota. Visiting friends, you might say."

The man smiled. "If that's the case, I'd keep that repeating rifle hid. I don't know how it is in Minnesota, but around here the vampires'll kill you for carrying a gun. Among other things."

"Thanks for the tip. We're trying to pass through without attracting attention. Do you live around here, sir?"

"All my life. My name's Gustafsen. I'm a widower now, and my kids are gone. I farm a little place up the road. Saw the sky lit up and figured it was the old Bauer farm. Don't have much business of my own to mind, so you might say I mind other people's, just to have something to do."

That could be good or bad for us, Valentine thought. "Did anyone live here?"

"No, not since they took over. The Bauers all died of the Raving Madness. No one's wanted to live here since: it's five miles from nowhere."

"I wonder what started the fire? There's been a lot of rain, but no lightning."

Gustafsen chuckled. "I wonder myself. I hear from some of the teamsters, there's been a few mysterious fires this summer. Started right around the time the new Big Boss showed up in Glarus. And things have gone from bad to worse for a lot of folks around here since then. There's been disappearances in almost every town, and I'm sure you know what that means."

"I'm surprised you ask questions, Mr. Gustafsen. Most places that's frowned upon."

"My curiosity is all I've got left, David." Gustafsen thrust his hands in his pockets, speaking to Valentine while standing side by side with him as was the custom in that part of the country. They looked over the wrecked barn and house. "I've lived a full life, considering the circumstances. After my Annie got took, I quit looking for anything else from this life, and I'm settin' my heart on the next."

Valentine liked the man on instinct. He thought for a moment about asking the man to come south with them. They had a spare horse, after all, and the Free Territory could always use another farmer or rancher.

Gustafsen said, "I didn't get much formal education. *They* don't like schools. But I'm smart enough to know that men in deerskins carrying guns and staying out of sight of the roads means trouble for them. So if you boys want to come to my place, I'll share what I got with you. Maybe you need to spend a couple nights in a bed. I've got some spares. I'd appreciate the company."

"We appreciate the offer, Mr. Gustafsen. Really. But we've got to move on east," Valentine lied, just in case. "If you could spare a bag of oats for the horses, we'd be in your debt, sir. I'd really like information about these fires, though. You seem to have your ear to the ground."

"It beats me as much as it does you, son. One old man saw some kind of airship over a fire. I don't know exactly where or when; it's a fourth-hand story. Like the old blimps you see in pictures. He said it moved around with sails. And I got a theory about where it's coming from: somewhere around Blue Mounds. They say it's death to go within five miles of there now. Whatever's happening, they got a lot of troops. The Commissary Patrols are culling stock all over this part of the state, taking good dairy stock and hogs, mostly. It's going to be a hard winter."

"Sounds like. You say this new Big Boss is in Glarus?"

"It's New Glarus on a map," Gustafsen corrected.

"We'd better avoid it," Valentine said, lying again. He had to account for the chance that Gustafsen might be going for a brass ring.

"Smart of you, son."

Two hours later, Valentine rode up to the other two Wolves, two bags of oats for the horses across the Morgan's broad back.

"It went well there?" Gonzalez asked.

"Sure. He gave me the feed, and I looked around his place. He seems a nice enough man. I didn't want him to get a look at either of you, just in case."

"Are we going to move on now?" Harper asked.

"Sort of. It seems like the Reapers have something big going on around Blue Mounds. It's about ten miles southeast of here. Good hilly country, plenty of cover. I want to ride over there and see if we can't get a look at what they're up to."

Harper nodded. "Not too much of a detour, then. Gotta ask you straight, though, Lieutenant, begging your pardon. Do you have something against getting back to the Ozarks? Got a woman in the family way, and you want to stay out of the Territory for a while or something? We could be halfway to the Mississippi by now. We're couriers, not Cats."

"If I knew a Cat in the area, I'd ask her to do it for us. But something that flies and drops firebombs is something Command will want to know about. Especially since whatever this is doesn't make noise. You've seen the little prop jobs the Kurians use on us now and then. They're loud. We'd have heard it. And they can fly at night. Never heard of a plane or a helicopter doing that nowadays."

"Maybe they're trying to train Harpies to fly in teams or carry bombs together," Gonzalez thought out loud.

"Could be. Could be just about anything, Gonzo. The Kurians like dreaming up nasty surprises. But Southern Command is going to want facts. We're all this way anyway. When we get back, we might as well know what we're talking about."

"So what's next on the Lieutenant Valentine tour of southwestern Wisconsin?" Harper chuckled.

Valentine consulted his map and compass. "A short ride thataway. How's your nose this morning, Gonzalez?"

"Wishing it was smelling the masala in one of Patel's pepperpots right about now, sir. But it's working well enough."

"I hope so. We're going to need it."

You have to hand it to the Kurians, Valentine thought at midday, when they struck the line of fence posts. *They know how to send a message with easy-to-understand symbols.*

The Wolves sat their horses before the line of rust-colored pig iron posts. Atop each post, at ten-yard distances, a bleached human skull grinned at them. The warning line extended into the woods to either side of them, each skull facing outward in wordless warning to trespassers.

"Jesuchristo," Gonzalez whispered.

Grimly, Valentine performed some mental arithmetic. Gustafsen had said it was death to come within five miles of Blue Mounds. Thirty-odd miles of perimeter. That worked out to something like five thousand skulls. The one immediately in front of them was a child's.

Valentine dismounted, drawing his rifle from its leather sheath. "I'm going to have a look around. Sergeant Harper, I want you to stay with the animals. If you hear any shooting, try to break a record going west. Gonzalez, this is a one-man job, but I'd like to have your ears and nose along, so I'll leave it up to you."

Gonzalez removed his broad-brimmed hat and scratched the back of his neck. "Lieutenant, after I was invoked, I learned the Way from an old Wolf named Washington. Washington used to tell me, 'Victor, only idiots and heroes volunteer, and you're no hero.' But if I stay behind, it'll mean these skulls worked. I don't like to see anything the Reapers do work." He slid off his horse and began filling his pockets with .30-06 rifle shells from a box in his saddlebag.

"Lieutenant," Harper said, "watch your step now. I can see lot of tracks just behind this picket line of theirs. I'm going to take the horses down to that ravine we crossed and wait for you. Be careful; I'm going to make cold coffee for three, and I don't want any wasted."

"Thanks, Harper. No heroics, now. You hear anything, you just leave. I haven't looked at what's in those mail bags, but it's probably more important than we are."

Valentine and Gonzalez moved slowly through the heaviest woods they could find, zigzagging toward three hilltops they could occasionally glimpse through the trees. They moved in a twenty-yard game of leapfrog: first one would advance through the woods to cover; he would squat, and the other would move up past the first. They used their noses, and when Gonzalez picked up the scent of cattle, Valentine had them alter course to catch up.

It was a warm, partly cloudy day. Occasional peeks at the sun through the cumulus lightened their mood; it would inhibit any Reapers around. The cotton-fluff clouds were beginning to cluster and darken at their flat bases; more rain might be on the way. They found the cows, a herd of black-and-white Holsteins escaping the heat under a stand of trees bordering an open meadow.

"That's what we want," Valentine said. "I don't see a herdsman. Maybe they round them up at night."

"That's what we want?" Gonzalez whispered back. "What, you want cream for your coffee?"

"No. Let's get to the herd. Keep down in the brush."

They reached the cows, who gazed at the Wolves indifferently. The tail-swishing mass stood and lay in the shade, jaws working sideways in a steady cud-chewing rhythm. About a thousand flies per cow buzzed aimlessly back and forth.

"We need a little camouflage. The smelly kind," Valentine said, stepping into a fresh, fly-covered pile of manure. His moccasin almost disappeared into the brown mass. Gonzalez followed suit.

"Is this because of the tracks back at the fence?" Gonzalez asked.

"Yes. I saw dog prints by the hoofprints. Just in case we get tracked. The scent of the cows might confuse the dogs. Step in a few different piles, will you? Ah-ha," Valentine said, moving toward one of the standing milk factories.

The cow had raised its tail, sending forth a jet of semi-liquid feces. Valentine quickly wiped his foot in the body-temperature pool, then put each knee into it. "Keep an ear open, Gonzalez. It'd be great if one of them would take a leak for us."

Valentine's sharp ears picked up his scout muttering, "I don't even want to know, man, I don't even want to know."

Leaving the cows behind, but taking the smell with them, the Wolves began to move uphill, again keeping to the heaviest woods.

"So much for my nose, Val. I've heard of wolves in sheep's clothing, but this is above and beyond."

"Concentrate on your ears then," Valentine suggested.

They cut a trail at the base of the hills. Tire tracks informed him that vehicles passed through this area, circling the hills. Farther up the slope, they could see a metal platform projecting out of the trees, still well below the crown of the hill. It looked like a guard tower, but was missing walls and a roof.

"Maybe it's still under construction," Gonzalez theorized.

They moved up the gentle, tree-dotted meadow sideways, approaching the tower from a higher elevation. After completing the half-circle, listening all the way for telltale movement, they gained the tower base.

Concrete anchored the four metal struts supporting the thirty-foot platform. It was built out of heavy steel I-beams and was well riveted and braced. There was no ladder going up. It was new enough that scars in the earth from its construction were overgrown but not yet eroded away.

"What the hell kind of a lookout post is this?" Valentine wondered. "That's a lot of steel to hold up nothing."

Gonzalez knelt in the dirt beneath the structure. "Look here, sir. These tracks: small, narrow boots with heavy heels. Almost small enough for a woman."

"A Reaper?"

"That's my guess," Gonzalez said.

Valentine's spine bled electric tingles. *A Reaper stands on that platform?* he thought. *Watching what? Standing guard? What the hell is so valuable that the Kurians are using Reapers as sentries?*

He looked at the cross-braces. He might be able to climb it, if his fingers held out. Of course, a Hood would have no problem going up, but it presented quite a challenge to a human.

"I'm going to climb it. See if I can't get a look at the top. Maybe there's some sign of what it's used for up there."

"Sir," Gonzalez said. "I wouldn't advise that. Listen."

Valentine hardened his ears and heard thunderous hoof-beats echoing from somewhere over the hill. A lot of hoof-beats. Valentine suspected that these riders would not be scared off by the symbols carved into the butt of his rifle.

He looked at Gonzalez, meeting his scout's alarmed eyes, and nodded.

They ran.

Trained Wolves running though heavy wood, even down-hill, have to be seen to be believed. They kept up a punishing pace through the thickest forest, a pace no horse and rider could match through this ground. They cleared fallen logs with the grace of springing deer. Their footfalls, like their breathing, sounded inhumanly light. The Wolves hunched their bodies atavistically forward, clearing low branches by fractions of an inch. The sound of the distant riders faded behind them, absorbed by hill and wood.

They reached the cow meadow, over a mile from the metal platform, in less than four minutes. Valentine altered the downhill course, and regained the wood. Still at a flat-out run, they were halfway to the line of skulls when Gonzalez was shot.

The bullet struck him in the left elbow as he brought his arm up while running. He spun, staggered, and continued running, gripping his shattered joint close to his body.

The sniper panicked at the sight of Gonzalez continuing straight for his hiding spot. He rose, a monstrous swamp-troll apparition trailing green threads like a living weeping willow. The sniper raised his rifle again with Gonzalez a scarce ten yards away.

The scout threw himself down at the shot. Valentine, a few

yards behind Gonzalez, was breathing too hard to trust himself to shoot accurately. He shifted his grip to the barrel of the rifle and wound up as he dashed forward.

The long camouflage strips hanging from the Quisling's sleeves caught in his rifle's action. As he struggled with it, Valentine swung his gun baseball-bat style, using the momentum of his charge to add further force to the impact. He struck the sniper full in the stomach, emptying the man's lungs with the harsh cough of a cramping diaphragm. Valentine dropped his gun and drew his parang from its sheath on his belt. As the gasping Quisling writhed at his feet, Valentine stepped on the man's back and brought the blade down on the vulnerable back of his neck once, twice, three times. The blows felt good, sickeningly good: a release of fear and anger. The body, its head severed, twitched as the man's nervous system still reacted to the blow to the midriff.

Valentine moved to Gonzalez, who now sat up, shaking and swearing in Spanish.

"Vamos!" Gonzalez said through clenched teeth. "Get to the horses. I'll catch up."

"I need a breather, bud," Valentine said, and meant it. He listened to the distant horses. They were far off, maybe far enough.

"No, sir . . . I'll catch up."

"Let's get a tourniquet around your arm. I don't want you leaving a blood trail. I'm glad your legs are still working," he said, tearing a rag off the sniper's gillie suit, which served that purpose admirably. His hands flew into action with quick, precise movements, binding the wound. "Now hold this," he said, twisting a stick around the knot. "Does that arm feel as bad as it looks?"

"Worse. I think the bone's gone."

"Just hold it for now. We'll get you a sling once we get to the horses," Valentine said.

"Valentine, this is *loco. Loco,* sir. I can't get far like this. Maybe I can find an old basement or something, hole up for a few days."

"No more arguing, hero. Let's go. The posse is on its way. I'll take your rifle."

They walked, then jogged toward the fence line. *Each step must be agony for him,* Valentine thought. They made it past the skulls and to the ravine.

Two horses waited, reins tied to a fallen branch. Valentine's Morgan had a note tucked in the saddle. Valentine uncurled it and read the soft pencil letters: "Followed orders—good luck—God bless—R.H."

Same to you, Sarge, Valentine thought. He felt lonely and helpless. But it would not do to let Gonzalez see that.

"Harper's moving west. Let's go southwest. If they have to follow two sets of tracks, maybe it'll confuse them. I'm sorry, Gonzo, but we've got to ride hard. I'll help you into the saddle."

He tightened the girths on both horses and lifted Gonzalez into his seat.

"I'll take the reins, Gonzo, you just sit and enjoy the ride."

"Enjoy. Sure," he said with a hint of a smile, or perhaps an out-of-control grimace.

They rode up and out of the ravine, Gonzalez pale with pain.

Of all the strange *dei ex machinae,* Valentine least expected to be rescued by a livestock truck.

Valentine, after an initial mile-eating canter across the hills, slowed out of concern for his scout. Gonzalez could not last much longer at this rate. They spotted an ill-used road, in

bad shape even for this far out in the country, and moved parallel, keeping it in sight.

The pair crested a hill, resting to take a good look ahead
before proceeding farther. Gonzalez sat in his saddle like a
limp scarecrow tied to the stirrups.

Valentine saw a little cluster of farms along a road running
perpendicular to their path. Miles off to the west, a series of
high bare downs marched southward. To his right, a small
creek twisted and turned, moving south to where it crossed
the road under a picturesque covered bridge. The bridge appeared to be in good repair, indicating the road might be in
frequent use.

"Okay, Gonzo," Valentine said, turning his horse. "Not
much farther now. We're going to walk the horses for a while
in that stream. I want to pick us up an engine."

"Are we going to give up the horses?" Gonzalez croaked.

"Yes. You can't go on like this. By the way, do you know
how to drive?"

"Maybe. I've worked a steering wheel a couple of times.
You would have to shift, though. Can't you drive?"

Valentine shrugged. "I used to play in old wrecked cars,
but I don't know what the pedals do."

"Sir, let's keep to the stream for a while. Get somewhere
quiet and find an old house. Lay up for a while."

"They might know by now what direction we went. We
have to assume they want us, even if we didn't see anything.
Remember, we killed one of theirs. They won't brush that off.
According to that old Gustafsen, they've got some manpower
concentrated there, so they have the men to do a thorough
search. We need to move faster than they can get organized,
which won't be easy since they probably have radios. That
means an engine. From the tracks Harper made, and ours,

they're going to be looking for us west. If we turn east, we might get ahead of whatever containment they'll use."

Valentine hated the idea of giving up the sturdy Morgan. His horse had proved a sublime blend of speed and stamina. But the odds against them were also increasing, making a risk the only course of action giving them a chance to escape.

Gonzalez nodded tiredly, unable to argue. His scout believed in cautiousness in any maneuvers against the Reapers, discretion being the better part of survival. Gonzalez feared everything; otherwise he would not have lived so long.

The pair rode downhill. At the stream, its rock-strewn bed barely a foot deep in most places, Valentine dismounted and took both pairs of reins, leading the horses. He hoped none of the local farm children were whiling away the afternoon fishing.

They reached the covered bridge. After scouting the shaded tunnel to make sure it was unoccupied, Valentine tied the horses to a piece of driftwood and helped Gonzalez out of his saddle. The scout sank into the cool shade, asleep or unconscious within seconds of Valentine laying him down, head pillowed by his bedroll.

Valentine scrambled up the brush-covered riverbank. He found a position near one end of the covered bridge where he could see down the road a mile in either direction. The asphalt was patched into almost a checkerboard pattern, as if tar-footed giants had been playing hopscotch along the road. The bridge was a strange bastard construction, obviously a well-made iron-and-concrete span dating to before the coming of the Kurians but now covered with a wooden roof. The added-on planks were layered with peeling red paint, and the warped wood seemed to writhe and bend as if wishing to escape from the bridge frame.

The drone of insects and the muted trickling of the stream

were soothing, and Valentine fought the urge to sleep. He counted potholes in the road, clouds, and bell-shaped white wildflowers to pass the time.

A truck appeared out of the east. It was a tractor-trailer, pulling a livestock rig. It plodded along at a gentle rate so as not to bounce its aged suspension too much over the uneven road. As it grew closer, Valentine saw that the door on the cab was either missing or removed, and the windshield on the passenger side was spider-webbed with cracks.

Valentine readied his rifle and ran to the edge of the covered bridge, keeping out of sight of the truck. He heard the truck slow as it approached the bridge, and the engine noise increased as it entered the echo chamber under the roof. Valentine sidestepped out and into the path of the creeping truck, rifle at his shoulder, and aimed at the driver.

Brakes squealed in worn-down protest, and the truck came to a stop. A head popped out of the doorless side, heavy sideburns flaring out from a ruddy face.

"Hey there, fella, don't shoot," the man called, as if people pointing rifles at him were an everyday irritation.

"Step out of there, and I won't. I don't want to hurt you; I just need the truck."

A pair of empty hands showed themselves. "Mister, you've got it backwards. We've been looking for you."

"What 'we' would that be?" Valentine asked, keeping the foresight in line with the bridge of the man's nose.

"Don't have time to go into it, mister. I know one of you's named David. You're three of those Werewolf fellows from down south, right? You went to take a look at Blue Mounds. The vampires' goons spotted you, and now there's a big net out trying to snare you. I heard it on the radio, except the David part. That came across over the Lodge's code through the telephone wires. I've been crawling up and down this road for the last hour looking for your tracks."

"Who are you?" Valentine asked, lowering his gun slightly.

"Ray Woods is my name. Wisconsin Lodge Eighteen. That guy you talked to earlier today, Owen Gustafsen, he's the Lodge leader here west of Madison. You might say we're like an underground railroad. We get orphaned kids and stuff out of the state."

Valentine wanted to believe him, badly. But Eveready had warned them time and again to look for traps. "Sorry, Ray, but I can't trust you. If you are who you say you are, you'll know why. We're going to take your truck, load our horses in it, and take off. If you are who you say you are, you won't tell anybody for a couple of hours. I could even knock you out so you have a convincing bump, if you want."

Woods plucked at his sideburns, twiddling the curly brown hair. "Maybe you can't trust me. But I'm going to have to ask you to take care of a friend of mine."

The truck driver jumped out of his cab and went to a little door mounted in the side of his truck. He opened it and extracted a toolbox. He then pulled out a metal panel and extracted an eight-year-old boy from the narrow slit like a magician pulling a rabbit from a hat. The boy clung to the driver's leg, watching Valentine with hollow eyes.

"This is Kurt," Woods explained. "He's out of Beloit. His father was taken by a Reaper a week ago, and his mother just up and disappeared. We're trying to get him over the Mississippi to a little town called La Crescent. Maybe you can trust him."

Valentine looked into the eyes of the little boy, and they were filled with the hurt confusion of a child whose world has vanished in an afternoon. Valentine wondered if he had looked that way to Father Max some ten-odd years ago. Woods stroked the boy's hair.

With Gonzalez hurt, Woods was their best chance of making it out of the Kurian Zone. More like their only chance.

"Okay, Mr. Woods. I hope you know what you're doing. Maybe you can talk your way out of getting caught bringing a child from point A to B. But we're armed and wanted. If you get caught with us, the least they'll do is kill you. If you have a family, you'd better think hard about them," Valentine said, looking at the driver's wedding ring.

"Ain't got no family no more, mister," Woods said. "I don't want to be parked out here arguing all day, so what's it going to be?"

"What do you want us to do?"

Ten minutes later, the semi was moving again. Valentine sat in a second secret compartment in the truck's cabin. Concealing himself would be a matter of lying down and closing a steel panel. Gonzalez lay next to the little boy somewhere beneath him behind the false-backed tool locker.

"Of course, if they make a thorough search, we're all dead," Woods said, speaking up over the clattering engine so Valentine could hear his voice. "But I'm on the regular livestock run into Blue Mounds now. Before that, I never caused a day's trouble—at least a day's trouble that they knew about—in sixteen years, except when the old diesel gives me problems, of course."

The horses rode in the trailer, hidden in plain sight next to two other crowbait nags. Valentine hoped the horses looked worn out enough to pass inspection as candidates for the slaughterhouse. Their saddles and bridles rested inside bags of feed. A few cows and pigs also rode in the trailer, adding to the camouflage and barnyard odor.

Woods listened to the Quislings' radio calls on a tiny CB hidden inside a much larger defunct one. He explained that the only place the Quislings never searched for guns or radios was inside the dysfunctional box, its dangling wiring and missing knobs mute testimony to its uselessness. Woods simply popped the cover and turned on the tiny functioning receiver inside. "Only problem is, it's just a scanner, so I can't send. I'm going to get you boys in with a family in LaGrange. Alan Carlson's part of the Lodge, and his wife's a nurse. She'll help your man there. Seems like most of the searchers lit off after your other guy. He dumped one of his horses in Ridgeway, and they seem to think one of you is hiding there. They're tearing the place apart. So hopefully he gave them the slip. Better get hid, we're coming up on some crossroads. They might have checkpoints."

For the next half hour, Valentine rode in darkness, lulled by the gentle, noisy motions of the truck. They stopped at one checkpoint, but all Valentine could hear was the exchange of quick greetings between Woods and a pair of unknown voices.

The Carlson farm was a nice-size spread. According to Woods, Carlson was in good with the local authorities. His wife's brother was some kind of Quisling big shot in Monroe, so he rarely had trouble finding supplies and tools to keep the place up. He even employed another family, the Breitlings, to help him farm the land. Under cover of picking up some livestock for the voracious appetites at Blue Mounds, Woods pulled the truck into the cluster of whitewashed buildings.

"Lieutenant, you can pop the box now," Woods said. "You're on Alan Carlson's place."

Valentine climbed into the passenger seat, an improvised upholstery job mummified in duct tape with a horse blanket tied over it. The door on the passenger side was missing, as well. ("The Quislings got a real bug about wanting to see all of you at checkpoints. Sucks to be me in the winter," Woods had explained.) The Wolf looked around. The truck had pulled around behind a little white house, between it and a well-maintained barn. The two-story frame house was screened from the road by trees and had the small, high-roofed look of a building trying to hide itself from the world. Three feet of foundation showed in the back, and the kitchen door could be reached only by ascending a series of concrete steps. The barn, on the other hand, looked like it wanted to take over the neighboring territory. It had grown smaller subbuildings like a primitive organism that reproduces itself by budding. An immobile mobile home stood beyond the barn, under the shadow of a tall silo. A garage with a horse wagon and an honest-to-goodness buggy parked side by side stood on the little gravel road that looped around the barn like a gigantic noose. Farther out, an obviously unused Quonset hut stood in an overgrown patch of brush, and a well-maintained shed completed the picture. Behind the house, cow-sprinkled fields ran to the base of a pair of tree-covered hills. Distant farms dotted the green Wisconsin hills.

The back door of the house opened, and a man in new-looking blue overalls and leather work boots stepped down the mini-staircase to the kitchen door. He fixed a nondescript red baseball cap over his sparse, sandy hair and turned to wave a boy out from the house. A young teen, in the midst of a growth spurt, judging from the look of his too-small clothes, emerged, as well. He had black skin and closely cropped hair and looked at the truck with interest. Carlson said a few quiet words to the boy, who scampered off to the road and made a great show of poking around in the ditch at the side of the road with a stick.

A golden-haired dog emerged from behind the barn and flopped down, panting in the shade with his body angled to observe the proceedings.

Woods jumped out of the truck and performed his trick with the tool locker again. At the sight of Gonzalez's wound, Carlson hollered back to the house. "Gwennie, one of them's hurt. I need you out here!"

"Mr. Carlson, I don't know what you've heard though this network of yours, but my name's David, and I want—," Valentine began.

"Introductions can wait, son. Let's get your man downstairs."

A red-haired woman came out of the house, moving with a quick, stocky grace. She wore a simple cotton shirt, jeans, and an apron that looked like it had been designed for a carpenter. She pressed two fingers expertly against Gonzalez's throat. Woods held the boy from Beloit in his arms. Valentine and Carlson each took an arm and helped Gonzalez. Gonzalez seemed groggy and drunk, and he mumbled something in Spanish.

They entered the house, skirting the tiny kitchen, and got Gonzalez into the basement. It was homey and wood paneled, with a little bed and some clothing that matched the kind the young teen watching the road was wearing. Mrs. Carslon put a finger into a pine knot on one of the wooden panels and pulled. The wall pivoted on a central axis near the knot. A small room with four cots, some wall pegs, and a washbasin was concealed on the other side.

"Sorry it's so dark," Mrs. Carlson said. "We're not electrified on this farm. Too far from Madison. But there's an air vent that comes down from the living room; you can hear pretty good what's going on above, as a matter of fact. Let's get the injured man down on the bed."

Carlson turned back to the stairs leading up to the main floor of the house. "Molly," he shouted, "bring a light down here!"

Mrs. Carlson extracted a short pair of scissors from her apron and began to cut away at Gonzalez's buckskins. "What's his name?" she asked.

"Injured man of average height," Valentine answered.

"Okay, Injured," she said insistently in his ear. "Can you move your fingers? Move your fingers for me. On your hurt arm."

Gonzalez came out of his trance, summoned by her words. A finger twitched, and sweat erupted on his brow.

"Maybe a break, maybe some nerve damage. I'm not a doctor, or even a nurse, you know," she said quietly to Valentine. "I'm a glorified midwife, but I do some work on livestock."

"We're grateful for anything," Valentine answered. "It looked to me like the bullet passed through."

"I think so. Seems like it just clipped the bone. There's a lot of ragged flesh for a bullet hole, though. Not that I've seen that many. I'm going to clean it out as best I can. I'll need some light, and some more water. Molly, finally!" she said, looking toward the open panel.

A lithe young woman of seventeen or eighteen, with the fine features of good genes fleshed out on a meat-and-dairy diet, stood at the entrance to the secret room. Her hair was a coppery blond and was drawn back from her face in a single braid dangling to her shoulder blades. She wore boyish blue overalls and a plain yellow shirt. The shapeless and oversize clothes made the curves they hid all the more tantalizing. She carried a lantern that produced a warm, oily scent.

"Dad, are you crazy?" she said, looking at the assembly

suspiciously. "Men with guns? If someone finds out, even Uncle Mike can't help. How—?"

"Hush, Molly," her mother interrupted. "I need that lantern over here."

Valentine watched in admiration as Mrs. Carlson went about her business. Mr. Carlson held Gonzalez down as she searched and cleaned the wound. She then sprinkled it with something from a white paper packet. The scout moaned and breathed in short rasps as the powder went in.

"Doesn't sting quite like iodine, and does just as good a job," the woman said as she began bandaging. Valentine helped her hold the bandage in place as she tied it but found himself glancing up at the girl holding the lantern. Molly looked down at the procedure, lips tightly pursed, her skin pale even in the yellow light of the lantern.

Mrs. Carlson tied up the bandage, and Gonzalez seemed to sag even more deeply into the cot he lay on.

Ray Woods spoke up. "Hate to give you another mouth, but this boy Kurt here is on his way across the river. I'm not supposed to go out that far again for a few more days. D'ye think he could have a place here for a little while?"

"Of course, Ray," Mr. Carlson agreed. "Now you better be moving along."

He turned back to Valentine. "Now we can shake, son. Alan Carlson. This is my wife, Gwen. And you see there my eldest, Molly. We've got another daughter, Mary, but she's out exercising the horses. The lookout up the road is kind of adopted, as you might have guessed. His name is Frat, and he came up from Chicago about three years ago. On his own."

"Call me David. Or Lieutenant. Sorry to be so mysterious, but the less you know the better—for both of us."

"Well, Lieutenant, we have to get back to the upstairs. The other family who lives on the farm is the Breitlings. They don't know about this room. Same story: better for us and better for them to keep it that way. Their son is with Mary; he's just a squirt. Tom and Chloe are in LaGrange. I sent them there this morning when word came around about your little scrape. They're due back before dark. There's a chance, just a chance, that the house will be searched. If it happens, don't panic. So happens the local Boss is related to me, and we stay in their good graces in every way. Frat has a way of staring at our local goons; I think he makes them nervous. They never hang around long."

"Glad to hear it. You don't mind if we keep our guns, I hope?"

Carlson smiled. "I'd prefer if you did. And take 'em when you leave. Gun ownership is a one-way ticket to the Big Straw."

"Alan, I wish you wouldn't be so crude about it," Mrs. Carlson objected. "He means the Reapers get you."

Ray Woods put the little orphan, Kurt, down on a cot. "Now, Kurt," Ray said, "I've got to leave you here for a couple of days."

The little boy shook his head.

"Sorry, Kurt. That's the way it's got to be. You can't sleep with me in the cab again, and I can't take you to the place where I live. These people can take care of you better than I can, till we can get you up to the sisters across the Big Blue River. You said you'd never seen a river a mile wide, right?"

"Don't!" the boy finally said. Though whether he was objecting to Woods leaving or going to the river, he did not elaborate.

Woods looked away, almost ashamed, and left. The boy opened his mouth as if to scream, then closed it again, eyes glassing over into the wary stare that Valentine had first seen.

"We'll leave the lamp in here for you. We'll talk tonight if you want, after the Breitlings are in and the lights are out. Now I've got to get your horses hid in the hills. I'd give you something to read, but books are frowned on, too, so we don't have any," Carlson said. His wife and daughter stepped out the door, and Valentine caught the accusing look the young girl gave her mother.

As the door shut, Valentine realized the horrible danger their presence brought to the family. He admired Carlson's resolution. In a way, the courage of Mr. and Mrs. Carlson was greater than that of many of the soldiers of Southern Command. The Hunters risked their lives, armed with weapons and comrades all around, each of whom would risk anything to save his fellows. Here in the Lost Lands, this unarmed, isolated farm family defied the Kurians, putting their children in jeopardy, far from any help. Valentine wondered if even the Bears he had met had that kind of guts.

Hours later, Valentine heard Kurt whimpering in his sleep. He rose from his cot and crept through the darkness to the boy's bed. Valentine climbed in and cradled him until the boy gripped his hand and the sleepy keening stopped. Memories long suppressed awoke, tormenting Valentine. The smell of stewing tomatoes and the pictures in his mind appeared as awful and vivid as if he had seen them that afternoon. As he hugged the boy, silent tears ran down the side of his face and into the homemade pillow.

Eleven

LaGrange, Wisconsin: The town of LaGrange is nothing much to speak of. A crossroads with a feed store and an auxiliary dry goods shop marks the T-intersection of an old state road with a county highway. The irregular commerce that occurs there takes place with small green ration coupons, worthless outside the boundaries of the Madison Triumvirate. Across from the feed store is the house and ringing stable of the blacksmith. The blacksmith and his wife are old work-hard, play-hard bons vivants, and the breezeway between their house and garage is the nearest thing to the local watering hole. One or both seem always ready to sit down with a cup of tea, glass of beer, or shot of backyard hooch. The blacksmith's wife also gives haircuts, and longtime residents can tell how many drinks she's had by the irregular results.

The real LaGrange is in the surrounding farms, primarily corn or bean, hay, and dairy. The smallholds spread out beneath the high western downs that dominate the county. Their produce is transported to Monroe, and the thrice-a-week train to Chicago.

Survival here depends on having a productive farm and not drawing unwanted attention. During the day, the patrols drive their cars and ride their horses, looking for unfamiliar faces. Vagrants and troublemakers disappear to the Order building in Monroe and are seldom seen again. At night the residents stay indoors, never able to tell if a Reaper or two is passing through the area.

The residents live as a zebra herd surrounded by lions. There is safety in numbers and the daily routine, and sometimes years pass before when anyone other than the old, the sick, or the troublemakers gets taken. Their homes are modest, furnished and decorated with whatever they can make or salvage. The Kurian Order provides little but the ration coupons in exchange for their labor, although a truly outstanding year in production or community service will lead to a bond being issued that protects the winner's family for a period of years. The Kurians provide only the barest of necessities in food, clothing, and material to maintain shelter. But humanity being what it is, adaptable to almost any conditions, the residents find a kind of fellowship in their mutual deprivations and dangers. Barn raisings, roofing parties, quilting bees, and clothing swaps provide social interaction, and if they are punctuated with "remembrances" for those lost to the Kurians, the homesteaders at least have the opportunity to support each other in their grief.

Valentine remembered little of his first few days with the Carlsons. Gonzalez's condition worsened, and as his Wolf sank into a fever brought on by the shock of his injury, Valentine found himself too busy nursing to notice much outside the tiny basement room.

For three long, dark days Valentine remained at Gonzalez's bedside, able to do little but fret. The wound had seemed to be healing well enough, though just before the fever set in, Gonzalez had complained that he either could not feel his hand at all or that it itched maddeningly. Then, on the second evening after their arrival, Gonzalez had complained of light-headedness, and later woke Valentine by thrashing and moaning.

Kurt, the little boy from Beloit, had been sent on his way westward, and the Wolves had the basement room to themselves. Mrs. Carlson blamed herself for not properly cleaning the wound. "Or I should have just amputated," she said reproachfully. "His blood's poisoned now for sure. He needs antibiotics, but they're just not to be had anymore."

Valentine could do little except sponge his friend off and wait. It seemed he had been in the darkness for years, but he could tell by the growth on his chin that the true count was only days. Then on the third night, Gonzalez sank into a deep sleep. His pulse became slow and steady, and his breathing eased. At first Valentine feared that his scout was slipping toward death, but by morning the Wolf was awake and coherent, if weak as a baby.

He summoned Mrs. Carlson, who took one look at her patient and pronounced him in the clear then hurried upstairs to heat some vegetable broth. Rubber limbed, Valentine returned to his own cot and lost consciousness to the deep sleep of nervous and physical exhaustion. That evening, with the rest of the house quiet and Gonzalez in a more healthy slumber, Valentine sat in the darkened living room talking to Mr. Carlson.

"We owe our lives to you, sir. Can't say it any plainer than that," Valentine said from the comfort of feather-stuffed cushions in an old wood-framed chair.

"Lieutenant," the shadow that was Mr. Carlson replied, "we're glad to help. If things are ever going to change, for the better anyway, it'll be you boys that do the changing. We're rabbits in a warren run by foxes. Of course we're going to help anyone with a foxtail or two hanging from their belt."

"Still, you're risking everything to hide us."

"That's what I wanted to talk to you about, Lieutenant. A way to reduce the risk."

"Please call me David, sir."

"Okay, David. Then it'll be Alan to you, okay? What I wanted to say was with your buddy sick—"

"He's getting better."

"Glad to hear it. But I spoke to my wife, and she says he should stay for at least a couple of weeks. Between the wound and the fever, it'll be a month before you can do any hard riding, maybe. Your horses could use a little weight anyway."

Valentine gaped in the darkness. "A month? Mr. Carlson, we couldn't possibly stay—"

"David, I don't know you very well, but I like you. But please let a guy finish his train of thought once in a while."

Valentine heard the ancient springs in the sofa creak as Carlson shifted his weight forward.

"What I'm going to suggest might seem risky, David, but it'll make your stay here a lot safer if we can pull it off. It'll even get you papers to get out of here again. I mentioned to my brother-in-law that I might have some visitors in the near future, within the next week. I told him about a guy I met during summer labor camp up by Eau Claire. Summer labor is something we get to do now and then, keeping up the roads and clearing brush and such. While I was there I met some Menominee, and as a matter of fact you look a bit like them. Anyway, I told Mike that I met a hardworking, nice young man who was looking to move down here, marry, and get himself a spread. I hinted that I had in mind that this young guy would marry my Molly and told him that I invited him down to meet her. Of course, he's just made up to fit your description."

Valentine's mind leaped ahead, making plans. "And you think he'd get us some papers? Something official? It would make getting out of here again a lot easier if we had some identification."

"Well, it wouldn't cut no ice outside this end of Wisconsin. But it would get you to Illinois or Iowa at least. You'd have to lose the guns, or hide 'em well. You could keep to the roads until the hills begin; if questioned, you could say you're out scouting for a place with good water and lots of land, and that's only to be found around the borders. Also, I'd like to bring your horses down from the hill corral. I hate having them up there. Too much of a chance of their getting stolen. Or us getting the ax for withholding livestock from the Boss Man."

"If you think you can pull it off, I'm for it," Valentine decided.

"Give you a little chance for some light and air. Also you can get a taste of life here. Maybe someday a bunch of you Wolves will come up north and liberate us. Or just bring us the guns and bullets. We'll figure out how to use them."

Two days later, Valentine found himself standing outside the sprawling home of Maj. Mike Flanagan, Monroe Patrol Commissioner of the Madison Triumvirate. Valentine wore some oversize overalls and was barefoot. Carlson had driven him the twenty-three miles starting at daybreak in the family buggy.

"I don't know about the rest, but the *major* part fits him," Carlson explained at the sight of the little signboard on the driveway proclaiming the importance of the person residing within. "Major asshole, anyway."

Valentine did not have to feign being impressed with the major's home. It was opulent. Half French villa, half cattle-baron's ranch, it stretched across a well-tended lawn from a turret on the far right to an overwide garage on the left. Its slate-roofed, brick-covered expanse breathed self-importance. A few other similar homes looked out over Monroe from the north, from what had once been a housing development. Now the mature oaks and poplars shaded only grass-covered foundations like a cemetery of dead dreams.

"Listen to this," Carlson said, pressing a button by the door. Valentine heard bells chime within, awaking a raucous canine chorus.

The door opened, revealing two bristling black-and-tan dogs. Wide-bodied and big-mouthed, they stared at the visitors, nervously opening and shutting their mouths as if preparing to remove rottweiler-size chunks of flesh. The door opened wider to expose a mustachioed, uniformed man with polished boots and mirrored sunglasses. He wore a pistol in a low-slung, gunfighter-style holster tied to his leg with leather thongs displaying beadwork. Valentine wondered why the man needed sun protection in the interior of the house, as well as a gun.

"Hey, Virgil," Carlson said, nodding to the neatly uniformed man. "I've brought a friend to see the major."

Something between a smile and a sneer formed under the handlebar mustache. "I guess he's in for you, Carlson. Normally he doesn't do business on a Saturday, you know."

"Well, this is more of a social call. Just want to introduce him to someone who might be a nephew someday. David Saint Croix, meet Virgil Ames."

Valentine shook hands, smiling and nodding.

Ames made a show of snapping the strap securing his automatic to its holster. "He's in the office."

"I know the way. C'mon, David. Virgil, be a pal and water the horses, would you?"

Carlson and Valentine passed a dining room and crossed a high-ceilinged, sunken living room, stepping soundlessly on elaborate oriental rugs. Valentine hoped he could remember the details of the story Carlson had told his brother-in-law.

The major sat in his office, copying notes into a ledger from a sheet on a clipboard. The desk had an air of a tycoon about it; carved wooden lions held up the top and gazed serenely outward at the visitors. The dogs padded after the visitors and collapsed into a heap by the desk.

Mike Flanagan wore a black uniform decorated with silver buttons and buckles on the epaulets. He exhibited a taste for things western, like a string tie with a turquoise clasp and snakeskin cowboy boots. He looked up from his work at his guests, drawing a long cheroot from a silver case and pressing a polished metal cylinder set in a stand on his desk. An electric cord ran down the front of the desk and plugged into a wall socket, which also powered a mock-antique desk lamp. Bushy eyebrows formed a curved umbrella over freckled, bulldog features.

"Afternoon, Alan. You look well. How's Gwen?"

Carlson smiled. "Sends her best, along with a pair of blueberry pies. They're outside in the basket."

"Ahh, Gwen's pies. How I miss them. Siddown, Alan, you and your Indian friend."

The electric lighter on the desk popped up with an audible *ping*. Flanagan lit his cheroot and sent a smoke ring across his desk.

"How are things in Monroe, Mike?"

Flanagan waved at the neat little piles of paper on his desk. "The usual. Chicago's pissed because the Triumvirate is diverting so much food to that new fort up in the Blue Mounds. I'm trying to squeeze a little more out of everyone. I'm thinking about upping the reckoning on meat out of the farms. Think you can spare a few more head before winter, Alan?"

"Some of us can," Carlson asserted. "Some can't."

"Look at it this way: Your winter feed will go farther."

"Well, it's for you to say, Mike. But I don't know how it will go down. There's been some grumbling already."

"By whom?" Flanagan asked, piercing Carlson with his eyes.

"You know nobody tells me anything on account of us being close. Just rumor, Mike. But this visit isn't about the reckonings. I want you to meet a young friend of mine, David Saint Croix. I mentioned he'd be visiting and helping me with the harvest."

"Pleased to meet you, David." Flanagan did not look pleased. In fact, he looked perturbed. "Hell, Alan, first you take in Little Black Sambo, and now a mostways Indian?"

"He's a helluva hard worker, Mike. After I teach him a few things, he could run a fine farm."

"Let's see your work card, boy," Flanagan said.

Valentine's mind dropped out of gear for a second, but only a second. "Sorry, Major Flanagan. I traded it last winter. I was hungry, you know. It didn't have my real name on it anyway."

"Dumb thing to do, kid. You're lucky Alan here has connections," Flanagan said, putting down his thin cigar. He rummaged through his desk and came up with a simple form. "Fill this out for him, Alan. Just use your address. I'm giving him a temporary work card, six months. If he improves an old spread, I'll give him a permanent one."

"I need two, Mike. He brought a friend. There's a lot of guys in the north woods looking for something a little more permanent."

"Don't press me, Alan. Jeez, these guys are worse than Mexicans; another one is always popping up outta somewhere."

Carlson leaned forward, spreading his hands placatingly. "With two men helping me this fall, I can clear off an upper meadow I spotted. I was also thinking of building a pigpen across the road and raising some hogs, since meat is becoming such an issue. These men can help me, and I can be ready to go in the spring."

"Fine, Alan, two work permits. Your place is going to be a bit crowded."

"It's only temporary. Thanks a lot, Mike. Gwen and I really appreciate it. So does Molly, of course. Stop by anytime."

"Yeah," Flanagan mused, "you're a fortunate man, David. She's a real beauty. Some of my patrollers say she's kinda standoffish, so I wish you luck." The major pulled out a seal punch, filled out the expiration dates, signed both cards, and punched them with a resounding click. "You're lucky I take this with me. I don't trust my secretary with it; she'd probably sell documents. She can forge my signature pretty good."

"I'm in your debt, Michael," Carlson said, handing over the work cards.

"You've been in my debt since I let that little Fart or whatever his name is stay with you."

"Frat."

"Whatever. That big place and nothing to work it but women; I pity you. I'd offer you lunch, but I'm too busy to make it, and Virgil's hopeless. My girl is out at her parents' place this weekend."

"Thanks anyway, Michael, but it's going to be a long way back. The horses are tired, so they'll have to walk most of the way."

"Thank you, Major Flanagan," Valentine said, offering his hand. Flanagan ignored it.

"Thank my brother-in-law and his wife, not me. Guess they want a bunch of little half-breeds as grandchildren. Up to me, I'd take you to the Order building and let you wait for the next thirsty blacktooth, seeing as you don't have a work card and you're in Triumvirate lands."

Carlson made a flick of a motion with his chin. Valentine moved past the sleeping dogs and out the door, followed by his benefactor. Flanagan tossed away his cheroot and returned to the papers strewn across his desk.

Outside, the horses were very thirsty. Ames was poking in the picnic basket.

"Virgil, please take that in, will you? We'll water the horses ourselves. The pies are for Michael, and Gwen put in a jar of preserves for you. She remembers your sweet tooth."

The smile-sneer appeared again. "That was kind of her. You know where the trough is. I'll bring the basket back out to you."

As Carlson and Valentine brought the horses over to the trough, Alan spoke softly to Valentine. "See what I mean by Major Asshole?"

Valentine clucked his tongue against the roof of his mouth. "Seems like he's trying hard for a promotion to colonel."

That evening, after the long ride back, the Carlsons celebrated the "legitimate" arrival of their guests. Even the Breitlings attended, filling the dinner table past its capacity. As they made small talk, Valentine drew on his memories as a forester in the Boundary Waters to flesh out his David Saint Croix persona.

Valentine ate at Mrs. Carlson's end of the table, across from Molly, grateful for the room the corner chair gave his left elbow. Frat sat on his right, eating with the single-minded voracity of a teenager. The Breitlings were next to Mr. Carlson at the other end of the table, with the younger Carlson girl, Mary. Gonzalez stayed in his bunk in the basement, still too weak to socialize. Mrs. Carlson explained his absence to the Breitlings as being due to illness and a fall from his horse during the journey south.

During the dinner, Carlson told stories about his summer labor, mixed with fictitious ones about how he came to know "young Saint Croix here." Valentine played along as far as he dared but worried that the younger girl might say something about the Wolves or their horses that would blow the story. Mary kept her eleven-year-old mouth shut; her only comment during dinner was a request to ride Valentine's Morgan someday.

"Of course, once he's rested. Any time I'm not using him, that is. Of course I'm going to do some riding, looking for some nice land to get a farm going."

"Maybe Molly can show you around the county," Mr. Carlson suggested.

Molly focused her eyes on the plate in front of her. "Sure, Dad. Since you went to all this trouble to find me a husband, it's the least I can do. Glad you've given me so much say in the matter. Should I get pregnant now, or after the wedding?"

"Molly," Mrs. Carlson warned.

The Breitlings exchanged looks. Valentine figured that discord was rare in the Carlson house.

Molly stood and took up her plate. "I'm finished. May I be excused?" She went to the kitchen without waiting for an answer.

Valentine could not tell how much of the byplay was real, and how much was acting.

Two days later, he and Molly Carlson rode out on a fine, cool morning with a hint of fall in the air. Valentine's indomitable Morgan walked next to Molly's quarterhorse. She wore curious hybrid riding pants, leather on the inside and heavy denim elsewhere, tucked into tall rubber boots, and a sleeveless red flannel shirt. They chatted about their horses as they headed west toward the high, bare hills.

"Lucy here is great with the cows," Molly said, patting the horse on the neck affectionately. "They'll follow her anywhere. It's like she can talk to them."

"I've always wondered if animals talk to each other," Valentine ventured.

"I think they can, sort of. In a real simple way. Like if you and I had to communicate by just pointing at stuff. We couldn't write the Declaration of Independence, but we'd be able to find food and water and stuff. Warn each other about enemies. Hold it, Lucy's got to pee."

Molly stood up in her stirrups while the mare's stream of urine arced into the grass behind her.

"You know horses," Valentine observed. "Those are fine riding pants. Do you ride much?"

"No, too much to do at the farm. My sister's the horse nut. But I did make these breeches. I like working with leather especially. I used to have some nice riding boots, but some creep in the patrols took 'em off me. These rubber ones are hotter than hell, but they're good for working around the cows. I sewed a leather vest for Dad, and when Mom does her calving, she's got a big leather apron that I made."

They trotted for a while. Watching the up-and-down motion of Molly posting left him desperate to switch the conversation back on.

"I get the feeling you don't like us staying," he finally said when they slowed to cut through a copse of mixed oaks and pines. The sun had warmed the morning, but Valentine was flushed from more than the heat of the day.

"Oh, maybe at first. Still don't know what you're doing here—"

"Just passing through. I tried to find out what was going on up at Blue Mounds," Valentine explained.

"You probably wouldn't tell us the truth anyway. I don't know much about the insurgents, but I know you wouldn't tell what you were doing so they couldn't get it out of us, just in case. Or is it because I'm just a girl?"

"It's not that. We have plenty of women in the Wolves. And I hear over half of the Cats are women, too."

"We've heard about you. Werewolves, always coming in the dark, just like the Reapers. Don't you guys go into Kansas and Oklahoma and kill all the people there, so the Kurians have nothing to feed on?"

"No," Valentine said, somewhat taken aback. "Nothing . . . quite the opposite. Just this spring my company brought over a hundred people out of the Lost Lands. That's what we call places like this."

"Lost Lands," she said, rolling her eyes skyward. "I'll buy that. We're lost, all right. How would you like to spend your life knowing it's going to end with you being eaten? I've developed a lot of sympathy for our cows."

"Your uncle seems to be watching out for you all," Valentine said, trying to reassure her.

"My uncle. I should tell you about him. No, my uncle doesn't mean shit. A hungry vampire could still take us any night of the week, good record or no. Uncle Mike has done everything in his life exactly as the Kurians want, and he still doesn't have one of those brass rings. And even if you get it, any Kurian can still take it away if you screw up. And if I'm all testy over the husband thing, it's just because it makes me think about something I'd rather not think about. Let's go up this hill. The view's pretty nice from up top."

They walked their horses toward the grassy slope. They crossed a field with a herd of the ubiquitous Wisconsin Holsteins in it, and Molly waved to a man and a boy mending a fence.

"That's the Woolrich place. The poor woman who lives there is on her third husband. The first two got taken, one while doing the morning milking, and the second when a patrol came through just grabbing whoever they could get their hands on because a bunch of Reapers dropped in for a visit."

They rode to the top of the hill and dismounted, loosening the girths on their wet animals. The horses began to nose in the tall, dry grass at the top of the rolling series of hills. Farmland stretched below in all directions, crisscrossed with empty roads. A hundred yards away, an old highway running along the top of the hills had degenerated into a track cleared through the insistent plant life.

"Is that why you don't want to marry?" Valentine asked. "You're scared of becoming a widow?"

"Scared? I'm scared of a lot of things, but not that in particular. If you want to talk about what really scares me . . . But no, to answer your question, I don't want the life my mother has. She's brought two children into the world, and is taking care of another, and for what? We're all going to end up feeding one of those creatures. I don't want any children, or a man. It just means more fear. It's easy to talk about living your life, trying to get along with the system, but you try lying in bed at night when every little noise might mean something in boots and a cape is coming in your house to stick its tongue into your heart. The way I see it, the only way for us in the Madison Triumvirate to beat these vampires is to cut off their food supply. Quit pretending life is normal."

"I see."

"My grandmother on my mother's side, Gramma Katie Flanagan, she was a teacher or something in Madison before everything changed. When I was about eleven, we had a long talk. She was getting old, and I think she felt her time was coming. As soon as the old people slow down, the patrols show up, sometimes with some bullshit story about a retirement home. She told me about in ancient times there were these Jewish slaves of the Romans who rose up and fought them from a fortress on top of a mountain. The Romans finally built a road or something so their army could get up to the fortress, and all the Jews killed themselves rather than be slaves again. Gramma said if everyone were to do that, it would cut off their power, or whatever they get from us."

Valentine nodded. "I heard that story, too. It was a place called Masada. By the Dead Sea, I think. I always used to tell Father Max—he was my teacher—that I wouldn't have killed myself if I were up there. I would have taken a Roman or two with me."

"If it had just been another battle, would anyone have remembered it?" Molly asked.

"That's a good question. Maybe not. I think Gandhi, you know who he is, right? I think he suggested that the Jews should have done something like that when the Nazis were exterminating them. To me, that's just doing the enemy's job for them. Maybe some of you should try to sell your lives a little more expensively."

"That's easy for you to say. You have guns, friends, other soldiers to rely on. About all we have is a broken-down old phone system and a set of code words. 'John really needs a haircut' for 'We have a family at our place that is trying to go north.' Not much help when the vampires come knocking."

Strange how her thoughts mirror mine. I was thinking the same thing the night I got here, Valentine mused.

"Maybe we can't all commit suicide," she continued. "But for God's sake, we should quit helping them. We feed the patrols, work the railroads, keep the roads repaired. Then when we get old and sick, they gather us up like our cattle. They got it pretty good just because it's human nature to ask for another fifteen minutes when you're told you have an hour to live."

"Brave words," Valentine said.

"Brave? Me?" She sat down in the grass and plucked at the burrs clinging to her jeans. "I'm so scared at night I can barely breathe. I *dread* going to sleep. It's the dream."

"You have nightmares?"

"No, not nightmares. A nightmare. It's only one, but it's a doozy. Wait, I should tell this properly. We have to go back to Gramma Flanagan again. She told me a story about when the Triumvirate had first got things organized in Madison. I think it was in 2024, in the middle of summer. They had a group of men—well, some of them were Reapers, too—called the Committee for Public Safety. About two hundred people were working for this committee, in charge of everything from where you slept to where you went to the bathroom. The three vampires on the committee were kind of the eyes and ears of these Kurians who were dug into the State Capitol building. I don't know how much you know about the Kurian Lords, but they sure love to live in big empty monument-type buildings. I bet a bunch of them are in Washington. But back to the story my Gramma Katie told me. There was this woman, Sheila Something-or-other, who got caught with a big supply of guns: rifles, pistols, bullets, equipment for reloading, all kinds of stuff. I think even explosives. One of the vampires said her punishment was up to the people who worked for the Committee, and if it wasn't to their liking, they'd kill every last one of them and get a new bunch.

"So with that incentive, the whole committee goes over to where she's being held. And they tore her to bits. With their bare hands. They took the pieces and stuck them onto sticks. Gramma said the sticks looked like pool cues, or those little flagpoles from school classrooms, stuff like that. They put her head on one, her heart on another, her liver, her breasts, even her . . . you know . . . sex parts. They made streamers out of her intestines, and painted their faces with her blood. Then they paraded back to the basketball court at the university where the Committee met and showed what they did to her to the vampires. Some of them were drunk, I guess. The Reapers looked at it all and told them to *eat* the bits, or they'd be killed. Gramma said there were fistfights over her liver."

She sat silent for a moment. "Maybe I was too young to be told that story. It gave me a nightmare that night, and pretty often ever since. I'm always dreaming that I've done some-thing wrong, and the crowd is coming for me. They're all around, and they grab me and start pulling me apart. That's when I wake up, cold and sweaty. Mary says I sometimes say 'no, no' in my sleep. She calls it the 'no-no' dream. It seems silly in the daylight, but try waking up from it at two in the morning on a windy night."

"I have a dream, or nightmare, I guess, that keeps coming back," Valentine began. "Never told anyone about it, not even Father Max. My mom and dad and little brother and sister got killed by a patrol when I was just a kid. I come into the house—I remember it smelled like tomatoes in the kitchen that day, but that's not in the dream—and there's my mother, lying in the living room, dead. Her legs were . . . Well, I guess they had raped her, or started to anyway. They shot my dad in the head. But in my dream, it's like they're still alive, and I can save them if I just could fix the bullet wounds. I press my hands against the blood that's coming out of my mom's throat, but it just keeps pulsing and pulsing out, while my little brother is crying and screaming. But I can't save them. Can't . . . ," he said, voice trailing off. He looked up at the clouds to try to get the tears to go away. High white cirrus clouds painted the blue sky with icy white brushstrokes.

"I guess everyone has their own set of nightmares," Molly said.

"Well, we're getting plenty of help. Whatever happened to your grandmother?"

Molly Carlson wiped tears from her own eyes with the back of her hand. "Oh, she injured her back and got taken away. The vampires got her in the end, I'm sure. She got driven away by my uncle Mike. Her son. Her own fucking son."

The following Saturday, Molly taught Valentine how to drive the four-wheeled topless buggy. The thicker reins felt funny in his left hand, the buggy whip held up in his right. Valentine was used to riding English-style with split reins, although he mostly used his legs to control the horse while riding. Driving was a completely different skill.

"You're doing great, David, really great," Molly said, beaming for a change. They were driving well ahead of the family cart, which held the rest of the Carlson clan as well as the Breitlings. "Of course, normally we drive the buggy tandem, which is tougher to manage, but they need the two horses for the big cart. And remember, if you ever have a load to carry in back, to place it evenly in the bed and secure it if you can. An unbalanced load will exhaust a horse faster than anything."

The combined families of the Carlson farm were on their way to Monroe. Mr. Carlson explained that there was a speaker in town, a visitor up from Chicago to give a lecture for the New Universal Church. A Kurian organization, the New Universal Church did not demand weekly assemblies but rather encouraged people in the Kurian Order to come to the occasional meeting to catch up on new laws and policies. But now and then a true "revival" took place, and attending them was a way of keeping in the Order's good graces.

The clouds piled up and darkened, threatening rain. Carlson opined that some would use it as an excuse not to attend, but this made him all the more determined to go. Showing up in spite of precipitation would just make their presence all the more notable, considering the long round trip to and from Monroe. "If we're going to play their game, we should really play it," he added, stowing tarps in the two horse-drawn vehicles and reminding everyone to bring rain slickers and hats.

Only Gonzalez—much improved but still not up to a long trip in the wet—and Frat stayed behind. The young man wanted to keep an eye on the stock and said he felt like he stuck out like a sore thumb in a sea of white faces.

So it turned out that Molly and Valentine ended up together in the buggy, bearing four baskets full of lunch, dinner, and gifts of food for Mrs. Carlson's brother, with the rest following in the larger wagon. Valentine's Morgan trotted along behind the buggy, brought along as the equine equivalent of a spare tire.

At lunch, a few miles outside of Monroe, the first sprinkles of rain came. When they climbed back into the buggy, Valentine draped the tarp over himself and Molly and drove on, the heavy raindrops playing a tattoo on the musty-smelling oiled canvas. They used the buggy whip as an improvised tent pole and peered out from a cavelike opening, their faces wet with rain. Valentine felt the warmth of her body against his right side, her left arm in his right, helping him hold up the tarp. The rich, seductive smell of femininity filled his nostrils without his even using his hard senses. She also had a faint, flowery smell of lavender.

"You smell good today," Valentine said, then felt himself

go red. "Not that you smell bad normally . . . I just mean the flowery stuff. What is that, toilet water?"

"No, just a soap. Mrs. Partridge, the blacksmith's wife, she's a wonder at making it. Puts herbs and stuff in some of them. I think she started doing it in self-defense; her husband picks up animals that have died of disease or whatever, turns them into pig and chicken feed. Dog meat, too. I guess he smelled so bad after working with the offal, she went into scented soaps as a last resort."

"It's nice. Hope I'm not too bad. This tarp kind of reeks."

"No. For a guy who traipses around in the hills, you're really clean. Some of the county men could take a lesson." Valentine felt a stab, remembering Cho's near-identical joke. "A lot of them are going to use this rainstorm as an excuse to skip their Saturday bath." She turned her face and pressed her nose to his chest. "You just smell kind of tanned and musky. Like the saddle from a lathered horse. I like it."

Valentine suddenly felt awkward. "So who exactly is this we're going to hear?"

"My dad says he's a speaker from Illinois, someone affiliated with their church. Kind of a bigwig. This church the Kurians run, it's not like you worship anything. The Triumvirate doesn't discourage the old churches, but they do listen to what gets said. As long as the ministers stick to the joys of the afterlife, and God's love in troubled times, they're fine. Anyone who speaks out against the Order is gone real fast. Most of them get the hint. No, this New Universal Church is more designed to get you to like the Kurian Order. They are always trying to recruit people into the patrols, or to come away and work their machinery, railroads, factories, and stuff. The real slick ones try to convince you that the Kurians came as the answer to man's problems. Some answer."

"So we just sit and listen, then go home?"

"That's about it. They try to recruit people right then and there. Take them up on stage, and everyone is supposed to applaud. Just clap when everyone else claps, and don't fall asleep. You'll be fine. I've got a feeling today's topic is going to be the importance of motherhood. They want more babies in Wisconsin."

The tent they eventually reached dwarfed the old public tent in the Boundary Waters. From a distance it resembled a sagging pastry. But as they grew closer, the mountain of canvas turned into an earthbound white cloud, complete with festive little flags atop the support poles that jutted through the material to either side of the center arch.

Horses, wagons, and vehicles of all description including cars and trucks were parked in the fields of the fairgrounds. Most of the people were already sheltering from the intermittent rain beneath the tent. The Carlson wagon pulled up, and the families all got out and released the horses from their harnesses. Tied to numerous posts in the field, the horses munched grain from their nosebags and stamped their unhappiness at being left in the weather. Carlson nodded to the uniformed patroller navigating the field, wearing a poncho that also covered much of his horse against the rain.

"Major Flanagan is inside. He's got some seats lined up for you, Carlson," the patroller called.

"Thanks, Lewis. Are you gonna get a chance to come in out of the rain?"

"Naw, we had our meeting this morning. All about how duty isn't the most important thing, it's the only thing. Your brother-in-law gave a pretty good speech. Be sure to tell him I said that."

"Deal. If you get real desperate out here, we got a thermos

with some tea that might still be hot in the buggy. Help yourself."

"Thanks, Alan. Enjoy."

True to the patroller's word, Major Flanagan had some seats set off right up in front. There was a main stage, with a little elevated walkway going out into the crowd connecting it to a much smaller stage. The Carlsons, with the addition of Valentine and the subtraction of the three Breitlings, sat in a row of folding chairs lined up parallel to the walkway. A few hundred chairs formed a large U around the peninsular stage, and the rest of the spectators stood.

As part of the day's festivities, a comic hypnotist warmed up the crowd. His show was already in progress when Valentine sat at one end of the row. Molly sat to his right, then her sister, with Mr. Carlson next to her. Mrs. Carlson took the seat in between him and her brother, and they chatted as the hypnotist performed. He had a pair of newlyweds on stage; the young groom was hypnotized, and the wife was asking him to bark like a dog, peck like a chicken, and moo like a cow. The audience laughed out their appreciation for the act.

"I saw this guy in Rockford," Major Flanagan explained to his guests. "I recommended him to the Madison Bishop, and he got him up here for this meeting. Funny, eh?"

The young woman finished by having her husband lie down with his head and shoulders in one chair and his feet in another, four feet away from the first. The hypnotist then had her sit right on his stomach, which did not sag an inch. "Comfortable, yes?" the hypnotist asked.

"Very," she agreed, blushing.

The audience cheered for an encore, so she had her husband flap his arms and be a bird. As he flapped and hopped around the stage, the hypnotist finished off with a final joke, "Most women, it takes ten years till they can get their husbands to do this. How about that, ladies, after only two weeks of marriage?"

The audience laughed and applauded. "Let's hear it for Arthur and Tammy Sonderberg, all the way from Evansville, ladies and gentlemen."

After the befuddled Mr. Sonderberg came out of hypnosis, and his wife told him what he had been doing on stage, the hypnotist gave a good imitation of him to further laughter before they left the stage and returned to their seats.

A heavyset man in a brown suit that was simple to the point of shapelessness came onstage. He applauded the hypnotist as the latter backed off, bowing. Valentine marveled at the man's hair, brushed out at the temples and hairline until it looked like a lion's mane.

"Thank you, thank you to the Amazing Dr. Tick-Toc," he said in a high, airy voice.

"That's the bishop of the New Universal Church, David. From Madison," Mr. Carlson explained quietly across his two daughters.

The bishop stepped to the podium on the small stage at the end of the runway and picked up the microphone. "Thank you all for coming out in the rain, everyone," he said, looking at the speakers mounted high on the tent poles which broadcast his voice. "The Harvest Meeting is always a serious occasion. We have a lot more fun at Winterfest, and the Spring Outing. But I know everyone has all the coming work on their minds. Well, today we have an expert on hard work on loan to us from the flatlands in the south. Won't you please welcome Rural Production Senior Supervisor Jim 'Midas' Touchet, visiting us all the way from Bloomington."

A middle-aged, hollow-cheeked man strode out on stage, dressed in a red jumpsuit. He had thinning hair combed neatly back and held in place with an oily liquid, giving it a reddish tint. White canvas sneakers covered his feet. He took the microphone out of the bishop's hand with a flourish and a bow to the audience. He exuded the energy of a man younger than his years.

"Can you all see me?" he asked, turning a full 360 degrees. "I know it's hard to miss me with this on. You see, we're all color-coded in downstate Illinois. Red is for agricultural workers, yellow for labor, blue for administration and security, and so on. In Chicagoland, you can wear whatever you want. I mean, *anything* goes up there. Any of you guys been to the Zoo? You know what I mean, then."

A few hoots came from the audience, mostly from the patrollers, Valentine noticed.

"Oops," Touchet continued. "I forgot we have children present."

Valentine shot a questioning glance to Molly, who shrugged. He suddenly noticed how charming she looked with her wet blond hair combed back from her face. It accentuated her features and the tight, glowing skin of a vital young woman.

"Never mind about that. I bet you're out there wondering, 'Who is this guy? What does he have to show me, other than what not to wear, ever?' Anyone thinking that? C'mon, let's see your hands."

A few hands went up.

"I bet you're thinking, 'How long is he going to speak?' Let's see 'em!"

A lot of hands went up. Major Flanagan, smiling, raised his, and the Carlsons followed suit.

"Finally, some honesty. Okay, since you've been honest with me, I'll be honest with you. I'm nobody, and to prove to you what a big nobody I am, I'll tell you about myself.

"I'm from Nowhere, Illinois. Actually, more like South

Nowhere. Just off the road from Podunk, and right next to Jerkwater. Typical small town, nothing much happened. I grew up quick and brawny. You wouldn't know it to look at me now, but I used to have a nice set of shoulders. So I ended up in the patrols. And the patrols in downstate Illinois, let me tell you, they're really something. I didn't have a car. I didn't even have a horse. I had a bicycle. It didn't even have rubber tires; I rode around on the rims. The highlight of most days was falling off my bike. It's a little better now down there, but back in the thirties, we were lean when it came to equipment. In the winter, I walked my route. We didn't get paid back then, just got rations, so there was no way I could even get a horse at my rank.

"I spent ten long, empty years riding that bike. Farm to farm, checking on things. I carried mail. I delivered pies and pot roasts to the neighbors. 'Since you're going that way, anyway,' they always used to say when they asked me. I was bored. I started reading a lot. I was curious about the Old World, the good old days, people called them. Do they call them that up here, too?"

A couple of "yeps," quietly voiced, came from the audience.

"It was lonely in the patrols, and when you're lonely, you need friends. So when I found a little hidden pigpen or chicken coop on someone's farm, and they said, 'Be a friend, forget you saw this, and we'll let you have a couple extra eggs when you come by,' I went along. Hey, everybody wants to be a friend. So I went along, got a friend and a few eggs in the bargain. On another farm, I had another friend and a ham now and then. On another farm, some fried chicken; down the road, a bottle of milk, a bagful of corn. I had tons of friends, and I was eating real good to boot. I had it made."

The red figure paced back and forth, microphone in one

hand and cord in the other, first facing one part of the audience and then another.

"Eventually, I got caught. Like I told you, I'm nobody special. And I wasn't especially bright. One day my lieutenant noticed me wobbling down the road with a ham tied to my handlebars and a box of eggs in the basket in back. I think I had a turkey drumstick in my holster, I don't remember.

"Boy, it all came crashing down in a hurry. I think I died the death of a thousand cuts as my lieutenant walked up to me. I made the mistake of asking him to be a friend, and I'd give him everything I was collecting from the farms. He didn't have any of that.

"So within six hours of my lieutenant spotting me, I was sitting in the Bloomington train station, waiting for my last ride to Chicago. I was bound for the Loop. I was very, very alone. All those friends on all those farms, they didn't come get me, or turn themselves in and take their share of the blame. They weren't my friends after all.

"Well, it's a good thing for me I got caught in the spring of forty-six. I'm sure you remember the bad flu that went around that winter. It killed thousands in Illinois, and thousands more got so weakened by it, they caught pneumonia and died just the same. So we had a serious labor shortage in Illinois. I got put to work shoveling shit. I'm sure many of you know what that's like. But that's all I did, every single day. I worked at the Bloomington railroad livestock yards, taking care of the hogs and cows bound for Chicago's slaughterhouses. Of course, I was just on parole. Any time they felt like it, they could throw me on the next train to Chicago, and no more Jim Touchet.

"The first day shoveling, I was happy as a dog locked up overnight in a butcher shop. The second day, I was glad to be at work. The third day, I was happy to at least have a job. The fourth day, I began to look for ways to cut corners. By the fifth day, I was trying to find a nice spot to maybe take a nap where my boss couldn't find me.

"Of course, my boss noticed me slacking. He was a wise old man. His name was Vern Lundquist. Vern had worked at the railroad station in the olden days, and he still worked there. He didn't threaten me, not really. He just called me into his office and said that if I wanted to stay in his good graces, I'd better come in tomorrow and give an extra five percent effort.

"Even though he didn't threaten me, I got scared. That night I couldn't sleep. I was worried that I'd show up at work the next day, and the boys in blue would throw me on the first train to Chicago. I could be in the Loop in less than twenty-four hours."

He stood still, next to the lectern, wiping his sweating brow. His eyes passed over the Carlson family, and he smiled at Valentine. His face took on a scaly, cobralike cast when he smiled.

"That twenty-four hours changed my life. All that night, I thought about giving another five percent. How hard could that be? Vern wasn't asking me to work seven days a week, which is what most of you out there do on your farms.

"The next day, I gave the extra five percent. It was easy. I just did a little extra here and there. Did a job without being asked, fixed a loose gate. If old Vern noticed, he didn't say anything. I got worried; what if he wasn't noticing the extra five percent?

"So the next day, I did just a little bit more. Spent an extra fifteen minutes doing something I didn't have to do. Cleaned some old windows that hadn't been washed since Ronald Reagan was president. I found it was easy to give that extra five percent.

"It turned into a game. The next day, I gave another five

percent. I was compounding my interest, to use an old phrase. In tiny little baby steps I was turning into a real dynamo. Jim Touchet, the guy who leaned his bike against a tree for a two-hour lunch, who always rode home on his route faster than he ever rode it while patrolling, was trying extra hard even when no one was looking.

"Vern was real happy with me. After a month, I took the job of his assistant. Within a year, I was old Vern's supervisor. I always gave that extra five percent no one else was giving. I always did more than my boss, and usually within two years I had his job.

"I said the same words to people under me. I asked for an extra five percent. That's all. An extra five percent, when you have a whole bunch of people doing it, can turn things around.

"Before I knew it, they were calling me 'Midas' Touchet. Everything I turned my hand to seemed to turn to gold. Me, the guy who never learned his multiplication tables as a kid, who couldn't stay upright on his bike, went from shit-shoveler to production senior supervisor. I'm responsible for farms from Rockford to Mount Vernon, Illinois. I answer to the Illinois Eleven. You think you have tough quotas? What are they called up here, *reckonings?* I've seen the figures; the Illinois Eleven are a lot more demanding than your Triumvirate up in Madison. And last year, we were over production. I know what you're thinking; we broke quota by five percent, right? Wrong. We *doubled* the quota. That's right, doubled. The New Universal Church is handing out brass rings to my best people like lemon drops. See mine?" Touchet asked, holding up his hand. The coppery-gold ring glinted on his thick pinkie. He passed it through his oiled hair, removed it, and flicked it into the crowd before the platform. A woman caught it, screamed, and almost fainted into her husband's arms.

"Oh my God, oh my God," she blubbered, shoving it onto her thumb as the audience gaped.

"It's no big deal, that ring. I'll get another one this fall. Not that I need it. If I could have your attention back, I'll let you in on a secret. I've already given you one secret, the secret of the extra five percent. I'm a generous man. I'll give you a twofer.

"The secret is that you don't need a brass ring. That's the beauty of the New Universal Order," he said, lowering his voice.

Valentine looked around, trying to shake the feeling of being almost as hypnotized as the young Mr. Sonderberg.

"All the Order demands is production. Efficiency. Good old hard work. The things that made this country great before the social scientists and lawyers took over. I see some old-timers out in the audience. How was it when the lawyers ran the show? Did they make things more efficient, or less?"

"Are you kidding? Anytime lawyers got involved, things got cocked-up," one old man shouted.

Touchet nodded happily. "In the old Order, how far you went depended on going to the right school. Getting the right job. Having the right degree. Living on the right side of the tracks. Being the right color. Ten percent of the people owned ninety percent of the wealth. Anyone want to disagree?"

No one did.

"And not just the society was sick. The planet was sick too. Pollution, toxic waste, nuclear contamination. We were like fruit flies in a sealed jar with an apple core. Ever done that little experiment? Put a couple flies in with some food, knock some tiny holes in the lid, and watch what happens. They eat and breed, eat and breed. Pretty soon you'll have a jar filled with dead fruit flies. Mankind removed every form of natural selection. The weak, stupid, and useless were breeding just as fast as the successful. That isn't in nature's plan. And there's only one penalty for a species that breaks the laws of Mother Nature.

"Now you can drink out of any river, and you fishermen know the streams are full of fish again. The air is clean. It sounds crazy to say, but I'm one of the people who believes the Kurians were a godsend. The scale is back in balance. We're a better people for it. The Kurians have winnowed out the useless mouths. They don't play favorites; they don't make exceptions. They keep the strong and productive and take the slackers."

A few, perhaps surprisingly few, murmured disagreement.

"I'm not asking you to agree with me. Just hear me out and go home and think about it. And do one more thing. Think about how you can give that extra five percent. I know you all work hard. But I bet each of you can do what I did: figure out some way to do another five percent. You'll feel better about yourself, and your life will be more secure. Like me, you'll find you've got a brass ring in your pocket and not even need it because you're going the extra mile. How many of you slaughter your best milker for steaks? None, right? The Kurians are the same way. They're here, they're staying, and we've got to make the best of it.

"You've heard my story. You know I wasn't born special. No great brain, not much drive. Not even good-looking. But I've got a beautiful house—I've got pictures if any of you want to see it afterwards—a real gasoline car, and a nice house picked out down south for when I retire. So I guess that brass ring is worth something after all. Napoléon used to say that every private of his carried a marshal's baton in his knapsack. Each of you should carry a brass ring in your pocket.

You can do it. Any of you out there spend ten hours a day shoveling shit? No? Then you've all got the jump on me. You're already way ahead of where I was when I decided to give that extra five percent. Whether you're sixteen or sixty, you can do what I did, believe me. Give the extra five, and it'll happen to you, too.

"Now, before I leave for the flatlands, as you call my home, I gotta do the usual recruitment drive. We're looking for young men and women, seventeen to thirty, who want to take some responsibility for public order and safety. I won't give the usual gung-ho speech or list all the perks: You know them better than I do. I will guarantee that you won't be mounted on a bicycle with no rubber on the tires. And don't forget, even if you go to boot camp and flunk out, you still get your one-year bond, no matter what. So who's going to be the first to come up on stage and get the bond? Okay, moms and dads, aunts and uncles, now's your chance to tell those kids to come up and get the bond."

Valentine listened to the forced applause as a few youths took to the main stage, then joined in. It seemed safest to do what everyone else was doing. He wondered how many in the audience believed the story, and how many were just going along to get along.

Touchet shook hands with the bishop who'd introduced him. The bishop patted his back and said something in his ear. Touchet returned to the microphone.

"Before you leave, I have a couple of announcements. The Triumvirate has changed your quotas, or reckoning, I mean. They'll be discussed individually with you by your local commissary officials."

The audience knew better than to groan at the news, but they did quiet down and stop filing out of the aisles.

"On the good news side, there's an exciting announcement

from the New Universal Church and the Madison Triumvirate. Any couple that produces ten or more children in their
lifetime automatically wins the brass ring."

Valentine and Molly Carlson exchanged a significant look,
and she tweaked up the corner of her mouth at him.

"The New Order recognizes the importance of motherhood
and family life," the snake oil salesman continued, "and
wants to get the northern part of the state repopulated. Any
children already born to the family count, so you big families
with five or six children are already well on your way to the
brass ring."

Some more applause broke out, probably from the bigger
families.

"And finally, we've had some problems with insurgents
and spies recently. The standard reward of a two-year bond
has been upped to a ten-year bond in exchange for information leading to the capture of any undocumented trespassers
in the Triumvirate's lands. Thank you for your cooperation."

"Thank you for your cooperation," Molly whispered.
"Now go home and start making babies. God knows what
you're going to feed them, since they are upping the reckoning."

"Now, Molly," Mr. Carlson said quietly. The tent was emptying fast, save for a few people with questions for either the
bishop or Touchet. Valentine escorted Molly to the exit, following her parents, and paused to look back at the podium.
Touchet was looking at him and speaking to the bishop. The
Wolf smelled trouble at that look. He hurried out of the tent,
racking his brain as he tried to remember if he'd ever seen the
Illinoisan's face before.

What was there about him that would draw the golden
touch?

                    *   *   *

Back at the wagon and buggy, the Carlsons ate a quick dinner out of their baskets. Flanagan joined them, helping himself to a choice meat pie.

"He left a few things out, you know, Gwen," Flanagan said, treating them all to a view of half-chewed food. "In his lecture to the patrols, he elaborated a bit about how he got out of the jam after he was caught helping those folks hide animals from the commissary. While he was sitting in the depot, they offered him his life back if he would turn in each and every farmer who withheld so much as an egg or a stick of butter from the commissary. Turned out he had a real good memory," Flanagan chuckled.

"It was all part of the talk he gave on duty this morning. Oh, and the brass ring he threw out into the audience is a phony. But don't tell anyone I told you. Don't hurt nothing to have those folks believing they got it made, as long as they stay in our good graces."

"Duty, Mike?" Mrs. Carlson said. "I bet you could tell Mr. Midas there a thing or two about devotion to duty. Like putting it before family. You're an expert at that."

"Don't start, Gwen. That's in the past. I've done plenty for you since, even a few things that would get me on the next train to Chicago. Oh, shit, it's starting to rain again," Major Flanagan grumbled, looking at the sky. "Bye, kids. Stay out of trouble. Glad to see you showed up for the meeting, Saint Croix. Maybe you're smarter than you look."

On the ride back, Molly drove the buggy. Valentine was unsure of himself on the rain-wet surface, and they decided a pair of experienced hands on the reins would be best. Valentine and Molly sat together under the tarp again, but he couldn't recapture the half-excited, half-scared mood of the trip down when he first felt her close to him.

"You didn't fall for any of that baloney, did you?" Molly asked.

"No, but he did know how to tell a good story. He had me spellbound for a while."

"Yes, he's one of the best I can remember hearing. That's what you'd expect right before they increase the reckoning." She paused for a moment. "You seem a million miles away."

"I didn't like the way he looked at me. At the end, when he was talking to the bishop. Almost like he was asking about me. Funny, because I've never seen him before in my life."

"Well, according to Uncle Mike, he really is from Illinois. You ever been there?"

"I passed through it on the way here, but we stayed in the uninhabited part. Or mostly uninhabited, that is. Sorry if I seem preoccupied. You sure pegged the baby thing. How did you know?"

She smiled at him. "Just because I'm eighteen and hardly been more than twenty miles from home, you think I'm ignorant. There's a fresh batch of vampires up in New Glarus. Nobody knows when they came in with their Master exactly, but it seems like they're here to stay. That's more hungry mouths. How often do they need feeding, anyway?"

"That is one of the many things we don't know about the Reapers. According to the theories out of this group that studies them down in Arkansas, how much they need to eat depends on how active they and their Master are. We think a lot of times the Kurians have about half their Hoods shut down. This is just guesswork, but the fewer Reapers a Kurian has to control, the better he can control them. Sometimes when he's trying to work all thirteen at once, they just turn into eating machines and do stupid stuff like forget to get in out of the daylight. But the Kurian can't control too few, either. He takes a risk when he does that. If the link for feeding vital auras to the Kurian Lord gets shut down, like say if he's got only one Reaper left and it gets killed, we think the Kurian dies with it."

Molly rewrapped the thick reins in her hand. "That's interesting. It's funny to just be able to talk about them with somebody. Discussing the Kurians is a taboo subject here. Too easy to say the wrong thing. So a Reaper can be killed?"

"Yes," Valentine said, "but you need to put that at the top of your 'easier said than done' list. I've seen six trained men pump rifle bullets into one at a range of about ten feet, and all it did was slow it down. Of course, those robes they wear protect them a lot. If they're hurt, you can behead them. A lot of times we're satisfied just to blow them up or cripple them so they can't move around much and they're easier to finish off. But again, even catching one where you can gang up on it is hard. They're usually active only at night, and they see better than us, hear better than us, and so on."

"So how do you do it?"

"It's a long story. Kind of hard to believe, too, unless it's happened to you. Now I know I've told you there are also people like the Kurians, but they're on our side."

"Yes, the . . . Lifeweavers."

"Good, yes, you have it. Long time ago, I think we worshiped them, and made them out to be gods. But they have the ability to awaken latent . . . I don't know, I guess you'd call them powers . . . within a human. About four thousand years ago, they made it very totemistic so the people would accept what these gods or wizards or whatever were doing. 'The spirit of a wolf is in you.'"

"Can they do it with anyone?"

"I don't know. The Lifeweavers select you for it, I know that much. Down in the Ozark Free Territory, they have three kinds of warriors they create, each named for an animal.

Maybe they use different animals elsewhere, like lions in
Africa maybe. We're called the Hunters. We all carry a blade
of some kind to finish off the Reapers. In the Wolves we just
use a short, broad-bladed knife. It's a very handy tool in the
woods, too. The Wolves are like the cavalry. We move fast
from place to place, scout out the enemy troops, and fight
guerrilla actions, mostly. There's lots of Wolves. Those Cats
are spies, assassins, and saboteurs. I don't know about the Cat
training, seems like they're just really, really good Wolves
who prefer to work alone. I've known only one Cat. They go
into the Kurian areas and mess with the Reapers. Maybe
there's one around here somewhere. But if there is, he or she
probably doesn't know I'm around. As I told you, I was just
running the mail up to Lake Michigan. Then there are the
Bears. They're the meanest bunch of bad-asses in the Southern Command, I can say for certain. I don't know what the
Lifeweavers do to the Bears to make them the way they are,
but I've heard of a single Bear taking on three Reapers and
killing them all. They're like human tanks. We Wolves always
make room for them at the bar when they come in."

They listened to the *clip-clop* of hoofbeats. Luckily it was
an asphalt road, with only a few gravel stretches. The Morgan
trotted steadily behind at the end of his lead, enjoying his exercise. Molly slowed the buggy to a walk and let the horse
breathe, to give the rest of the family a chance to catch up a
little in the plodding wagon.

"Do you win often?" Molly asked. "I mean, actually go out
and beat the Reapers?"

"Sometimes. The Ozarks are still free, aren't they? But it
costs people. Good people," Valentine said, remembering.

"Don't think about that too much," she suggested. "It
makes you look all old and tired. You're what, twenty?"

"I feel older. Maybe it's all the miles."

Now it was Molly's turn to be lost in thought. "You beat them," she ruminated. "We've always been told you just hide out up in the mountains. Starving to death in winter, stuff like that. Even the lodges, our organization for getting people out of the Triumvirate's reach, discourage anyone from going down there."

"It's a long trip," Valentine agreed. "Long and dangerous."

"You must really trust us, David. I could turn you in and get a brass ring for sure. A Wolf, an officer even, they'd love that. Uncle Mike would shit himself to death if he knew. He even gave you a work card." She giggled.

"At first I didn't have much of a choice except to trust you. Seemed like we were going to get caught anyway. Gonzalez wanted me to leave him, but I couldn't do that. Now I'm glad I gambled."

She cocked her head and smiled. "Why?"

Valentine shook his head and averted his eyes. That smile was irresistible. "Father Max used to say, 'Women and six-year-olds never run out of questions.'"

"Only because men and four-year-olds never have the right answers," she countered.

"Listen to you," Valentine laughed.

"C'mon, I mean it, David, why are you glad? Do you like this little charade we're playing, the courtship thing?"

At the word *charade,* Valentine felt a glass splinter pierce his heart. He forcibly brightened his voice. "It's been fun, sure. I've enjoyed talking to you, being around your family. I haven't had a family since I was little."

Molly started the horse again at a slow walk. "I've had fun, too, David. Sometimes I can't tell if it's a role that I'm playing or not. I'm almost sorry it has to end. Not that I want to bring a baseball team of your kids into the world to win a brass ring, of course."

"Of course," Valentine agreed. *I'm sorry it has to end, too,* he added mentally.

Back at the Carlsons' home that night, Valentine and Gonzalez talked in the basement. Valentine told him about the pep talk that took place at the tent and the funny look he received from the speaker.

"I don't know, Val. All the more reason to get out of town soon. You don't think it's going to look suspicious if we just disappear?"

"No, I already talked about that with Mr. Carlson. He's going to say Molly and I didn't get along, and we took off for parts unknown after a big argument. How's that arm—can you ride yet?"

Gonzalez removed it from the sling. His fingers were curved, and the skin looked dry and unhealthy, like an octogenarian's arthritic hand. "It's bad, Lieutenant. I think the nerve is gone. It kind of burns and itches sometimes. I can still ride, but it'll be one-handed."

"You can't shoot one-handed. Looks like you're heading for a well-deserved retirement."

"I'll use a pistol."

"That's for Captain LeHavre to say. Speaking of which, I haven't had a good dressing-down in weeks. I'm ready to go home and get yelled at again. How about you?"

"Say the word."

"I want to wait another day or two. You still look kind of pale, Señor Gonzalez. I want to cook us some biscuits and see to the horses' shoes. Anyway, how was your day holding the fort with Frat?"

"He's a tough kid. We could use him in the Wolves."

Valentine was intrigued. He could not remember the last

time Gonzalez had called anyone tough. "What do you mean?"

"We got talking while you were away. I told him where I come from, and he told me about Chicago. When he was little, he got put in the worst part of town with his mom and dad. In the center of the city, inside the river, there's this place called the Loop. It's got a river to the north and west, and the lake to the east. A bunch of those frog-Grogs live in the shallows. In the lake, you know? Then to the south, there's a big wall made out of an old expressway.

"According to Frat, trains still run people in, but no one can come out. The buildings are so tall, it's like being at the bottom of a canyon. No lights. The people there live on rats, birds, garbage that gets dumped in the river. He said they eat each other, too."

"You sure he wasn't just making it up?" Valentine said.

"If he is, he's good at it," Gonzalez argued. "The only people that go in are the Reapers. All the bridges are down, but they use a tunnel system under the city to get in and out. That whole Loop area is like the happy hunting ground for the Chicago Reapers. They just leave the bodies for the rats or those frog-Grogs."

"That's how the kid got out. Through the tunnels. Can you believe it, crawling in the dark through a tunnel the Hoods use? I couldn't do it, that's for sure."

Valentine shuddered at the thought. A pitch-black tunnel, Reapers maybe at either end. Of course, maybe the kid's bravado came from ignorance of how easily the Reapers could spot him.

Engine sounds from outside the house penetrated their refuge. Valentine's heightened hearing detected a vehicle slowing as it approached.

"Hey, sir . . . ," Gonzalez said, startled.

"Shh, I hear it, too." Valentine identified a car engine with a bad muffler. It pulled into the Carlsons' yard, and he heard two car doors open and shut. Muffled voices came from upstairs.

Valentine gestured toward the hidden room. Gonzalez kept watch at the stairs, and Valentine worked the pine knot that allowed him to pull open the door. The secret room was a little more spacious with their cots out in Frat's part of the basement. Their packs and weapons were still concealed within.

The ventilation duct let him hear the voices in the living room loud and clear. Mr. and Mrs. Carlson received Major Flanagan and his assistant Virgil in the main room. Even the squeaks of the old chairs could be heard through the air vent.

"What brings you out tonight, Major?" Carlson asked.

"It can't be a second helping of meat pie," Mrs. Carlson added. "I'm all out, and with the rain, there's no rabbits in the traps today. I can roast you a potato, if you want."

"It's a social call, Alan," Flanagan said. "Well, fifty-fifty. It's about the meeting at the tent today."

"What, did we miss an encore?" Mrs. Carlson asked. "Pull himself up by his bootstraps so hard he flew out of the tent?"

"Gwen, your sense of humor needs a good curb bit," Flanagan growled. "But it does have to do with Jim Touchet. He saw someone in your family who really intrigued him. Wants a personal interview, you might say."

Valentine reached for his rifle. It felt comforting in his hand.

"Who, Saint Croix? I'm not sure he's even going to be in the family yet, Mike."

"No, Alan," Flanagan said with a sardonic laugh. "It was Molly. He wants your daughter."

There was a silent pause in the room above. After a full ten seconds, Mr. Carlson's voice echoed forcefully down the vent. "Fuck you, Mike."

Valentine smiled with approval. He had never heard Mr. Carlson say anything stronger than *heck* before, but the occasion deserved it.

"Are you going to take—?" Virgil's voice demanded.

"Fuck you, too, Virgil."

"Now just wait—"

Flanagan interrupted his lieutenant. "Okay, before we get into a pissing contest, which you'd lose and you know it, Alan, just think this deal through. Listen to what I have to say. Not only would you be doing me a big favor, and I think you owe me one after all these years, but you'd be helping your family, too. They're offering the whole family a two-year bond. Actually it's a five-year bond; they said I could go up to five if I had to. Don't look at me that way, Virgil, she's my niece and they ought to get everything they can out of it.

"Alan, I'll be honest with you. The next five years are going to be tough. You know there are new Reapers in Glarus. I've already got orders to make up lists of who is going to make the cut and who isn't. Your farm is doing good now, but what if you have a bad year? What if the cows catch something? You'd be damn glad you had that bond if something like that happens. And even if you're not on the list, maybe a vampire is passing through and happens to get hungry by your place. You know it happens as well as I do. The lists don't mean shit when they're prowling, but bonds do."

After a moment to let the threats, spoken and unspoken, sink in, the major continued. "It ain't like she'd be gone permanent. I have that from the bishop himself. Touchet is giving talks in Platteville, Richland Center, and Reedsburg, then going back through Madison. Three weeks, she'd be gone. He said he wanted some companionship on the trip. And the bond starts as soon as she shows up at the Church Center in Monroe, so she'll be safe in Madison, even. What can I say, Alan. You've got a real honey of a daughter. She caught his eye."

"Quite a time for this to happen," Carlson said. "I wonder how Saint Croix would like her disappearing with that old lech. So much for them settling down."

"Don't worry about him. Worry about your family, Alan. Saint Croix might understand, after all. I'll have a word with the bishop. Since Saint Croix is practically family, maybe we can offer him the bond, too. Even make getting married to her a condition. That might close the deal. If he's a smart kid, he'll know five years is just what he needs when he's trying to get a farm up and running."

"He's a smart kid, all right," Valentine breathed. "Smart enough to blow your ass off through the floor."

"Let's talk to Molly tomorrow," Mrs. Carlson suggested, obviously to her husband. "And maybe David, too."

Valentine counted twenty heartbeats.

"Okay, Gwen. Listen, Mike, I'm sorry I got riled. You, too, Virgil. I was just a little surprised is all. When you're a father, your little girl is always six years old. She's a grown woman; I forget sometimes. But why her? There were prettier girls at the meeting."

"Not according to Touchet. Virgil, go wait outside. Alan, if you don't mind, I'd like a private word with Gwen."

"Okay, Major. I'll sleep on it. Call you tomorrow. Good night."

"Night, Alan."

Valentine listened to the footsteps move about as Virgil was escorted to the door and Mr. Carlson retired to the kitchen. Valentine thought he heard him exchange a few words with Frat.

"Now listen, Gwen," Valentine heard Flanagan say to his

sister, keeping his voice low enough for it not to travel out of the room. *Not quiet enough for my ears, though,* Valentine thought.

"You know I'm not the law. The law is whatever the Triumvirate says it is. This Touchet is a big wheel in Illinois, one of the biggest outside of Chicago. The New Church wants him happy, and I'm going to see that he's happy. I'm making it look like Alan has a choice in this, but he doesn't. Neither does Molly. You follow me?"

"I follow you," Mrs. Carlson said in a low tone. Valentine picked up the anger in her brittle voice. He wondered if her brother did.

"Touchet's going to have her one way or another. I know what you have to say cuts a lot of ice with Alan. So you might as well profit from it and get that bond."

"Is there a bond in it for you, too, Michael?" she asked.

"Can't fool you, can I, Sis? Maybe there is. This is pretty important. I think the Kurians want Touchet to consider moving here permanently. That is, if we can pry him away from the Illinois Eleven. They want him running the Wisconsin farms like he does in Illinois."

"*We*, Michael? Are you a we with the Kurians?"

"Always have been. I know which side of the bread my butter is on. I always figured I got Mom's brains. I think all you got was Dad's stubbornness."

Mrs. Carlson sighed. "Okay, Michael, you're right. I'll see what I can do."

"There, that wasn't so hard now, was it?"

"Harder than you'll ever know."

"Wow, man, you're losing it," Frat exclaimed, eyeing the mountain of cordwood.

Valentine was turning logs into firewood with his usual

vigor. He stood outside one of the many little buildings budding from the barn's walls, filling the woodshed with fuel. During his stay with the Carlsons, he had chopped a little every day to keep himself exercised. Valentine did not use an ax. He preferred a saw to reduce the trunks into manageable two-foot lengths, which he could then split with a wedge. He followed his routine with robotic precision. He grabbed a length of trunk and placed it on his chopping block: an old stump that had no doubt served in this capacity for years. Then he picked up the wedge in his left hand and the twenty-pound sledgehammer in his right, gripping the latter right up under the rounded steel head. A vigorous tap seated the triangular metal spike. Then he'd step back, shift his grip on the sledge by letting gravity pull the handle though his callused fingers, and whirl it in a sweeping circle behind him, up and then down to the wedge. He would then stack the halves and quarters in a nice, tight pile.

The day's woodcutting began after a halfhearted appreciation of one of Mrs. Carlson's epic breakfasts. Everyone ate with a preoccupied detachment, as if the family dog had gone rabid and no one wanted to talk about who would have to shoot it. Molly looked drawn, her mother pale and tight-mouthed, and Mr. Carlson sported a dark crescent under each eye. Frat gobbled his breakfast like a starving wolf and fled to the backyard and his chores, taking the dog with him. Even young Mary seemed to pick up on the tension; she shifted her gaze from her sister to her parents and back again.

Valentine decided Frat had the right idea, cleared his plate, and went outside. He had played the role of a forester the past few days and brought down several likely looking trees from the wooded hills to turn into split-rail fences and fireplace fodder.

He lost himself in the chopping, thinking about how to improvise a pack for his Morgan and some spare saddles. He could tie together a sawbuck rig, and there was enough worn-out leather and canvas in the old tack trunk to strap it to his horse. By having the Morgan carry feed for itself and Gonzalez's horse, and with Valentine loaded, as well, they should be able to get within striking distance of the Ozarks before the oats and corn ran out. He planned to cross the Mississippi farther north and move quickly across Iowa, returning to the Free Territory somewhere southwest of St. Louis.

But despite the hard work and plans to get his crippled Wolf home, thoughts of Molly continually shifted his train of thought to emotional sidings.

Frat's comment brought him out of his sledge-swinging meditation.

"What was that?" Valentine asked.

"You've been chopping wood almost every day since you got here; you're a regular Paul Bunyan. We've got enough to get us through two winters. It's going to rot before we can use it."

"Well, maybe your dad can sell some of it."

Valentine realized his back and arms ached. He looked at the sun; the warm September afternoon had already begun. Even better, his mind was relaxed, tranquil.

"Hey, David, why are they watching the house?"

Valentine put down the sledge, leaning the handle against his leg. *So much for tranquillity.* "Who is watching the house?"

"The patrols. There's a car down the road toward La-Grange. One guy in it, so his partner is probably in the hills somewhere with binoculars or a spotting scope." Frat shaded his eyes and looked up into the hills and shrugged.

"How do you know there are two?"

"They always go in pairs. Uncle Mike talks about it. They

switch around the partners a lot so no one gets used to working with anyone. Keeps them honest, I guess."

"You're pretty sharp, Frat."

"Naw, it ain't that. It's just when it's the same thing day
after day, you notice the patterns. Like you—anytime you're
worried about anything, you cut wood."

"I do it for the exercise."

Frat shook his head, a triumphant grin on his face. "You
sure needed a lot of exercise before meeting Uncle Mike. And
when you and my mom talked about the damage to Gonzo's
arm, you cut a lot then. Before you went riding with Molly,
too. And that same day, after you got back and cleaned up
your horse, you chopped until dinner."

Valentine sat down on the stump, staring at the youth.
"Hell," was all he could think to say. He looked over at Frat.
"Do you know about the deal with your sister?"

"Yeah, Mom and Dad were up most of the night talking
about it. They talked about packing up and asking you to lead
them out of Wisconsin. My mom said that wouldn't work because Mike was having us watched. Turned out she was right.
They woke Molly up early and talked about it upstairs first
thing this morning."

"Did they decide anything?"

"I don't know. Molly started crying."

Valentine concentrated on keeping his face blank.

"Frat, do me a favor. You have a few rabbit snares around,
don't you?"

"Uh-huh. There's a warren up in one of the pastures, and
there's rabbits in the hills, too."

Valentine scanned the hills. "Go up and check your traps.
See if you can see where that other patroller is. Can do?"

"Sure. Can do."

"Come and look for me in the stable if you spot him. But

first of all go in the house for a few minutes. Like you were just sitting around, and your parents came up with something to get you out of their hair. Now get going."

Frat scampered off toward the house.

Valentine forced himself to put away his tools for the benefit of the hidden observer. He wandered to the stable, in no particular hurry. The ancient stalls, missing their doors, enclosed the horses with short lengths of rope. The rich smell of horse sweat and manure filled the warm afternoon air.

Five horses, he considered. *Three belong to the Carlsons, then his and Gonzalez's. Mrs. Carlson on one, the girls on the second, Gonzalez sharing the third with Mr. Carlson, taking turns riding it. He and Frat could walk; the boy looked lean and capable. They're farm and riding horses, not packhorses. Best keep the load under 150 pounds for travel up and down hills. Blankets and tenting, rope and equipment. Farrier supplies for the horses, or losing a shoe means losing a horse. Maybe a week's food for man and beast. Would a week get us out of reach? God, the lifesign. Extra Reapers in Glarus to think about, they'd cover the thirty miles to LaGrange between dusk and midnight, running. Shit, we'd be drawing to an inside straight. And Gonzalez can't shoot.*

"Hi, David," a scratchy voice said.

Molly.

"Phew, you're sweaty. Frat said you were cutting wood."

"Oh, yeah. Well, I thought I'd leave your dad with a good supply. Or he could sell it, help pay for all the food we ate. Don't know how to pay him back for saving our lives. Are you okay?"

She ran her hands through uncombed hair, pulling the sun-kissed blond strands behind her. "So you know, then."

No point in lying, he thought. "Yes. I sort of eavesdropped last night through the basement air vent. None of my business, I know, Molly. Your uncle painted a pretty ugly picture. What did your parents say?"

"They just told me to do some thinking, and we'd talk about it more today. But I've already made up my mind."

"Not the Masada solution, I hope."

A hint of her old smile crossed her face. "No." She took a deep breath. "I'm going to do it, of course." It came out as a single word: *I'mgoingtodoit.* As if by saying it faster, it would be over with all the more quickly.

Valentine had a feeling all morning that would be her decision. What alternative did she have? Perhaps he could offer one.

"Did you tell your parents?"

"Not yet. I , . . wanted to tell you first. I know that sounds dumb. I mean, it's not like you're my husband, but—"

"Molly," he interrupted, "I've been thinking about getting your family out of here. And not just since yesterday, either. It's a slim chance, I'll admit. Here's what we do—"

"David, don't start. It's okay."

"No, listen to what I've—"

"No, I want you to listen to me. Your slim chance, it involves us trying to slip out, becoming runners, right?"

"Not just us, everyone. Your parents, the horses, even the dog."

"Listen, David, you're crazy. None of us are in shape to ride or walk for days and days. And they're watching us. If my uncle's letting us see two men, that probably means there's six more all around somewhere. He's no doubt let the Breitlings know that if we try something stupid, they can get the five-year bonds just for calling the patrols.

"They're only giving me an illusion of choice in the matter. My mom didn't say it, but I think that one side of the coin has the promise of the bond, but the other has a threat. If the bishop says *frog,* my uncle jumps. He's not going to let something like family get in the way of orders."

Valentine opened his mouth, but she stepped toward him and gently cupped her hand over it. "David, I'm glad you were thinking about getting us out. Before this stuff with Touchet, it would have worked, I'm sure. No one would have expected us to up and disappear. We could have done it with you guiding us. You know, almost nobody has maps anymore. None of the roads have signs. I couldn't find my way to Madison if I wanted to, or anywhere else outside a twenty-mile circle." She pulled her hand away and hugged him. He put his arms around her, strangely unhappy at the embrace. "You're being good and brave," she said. "But let's face facts. I'm not a damsel in distress, and there are too many dragons anyway. This guy is a big shot. He's going to get what he wants. I see a few cow farms I've never seen before, and some backwater towns. I get a trip to Madison. Maybe he just likes having a girl on his arm to impress people, who knows. So I sleep with him. One thing's for sure, I don't want a baby. My mom said there's a way—"

"Molly, don't say it. I don't want to think about you doing that," Valentine said, twisting his mouth in disgust.

"What, pregnancy? Well, you're a man. I guess you don't have to think about it if you don't want to. You seem a little old not to know the facts of life, but women have to consider the possibility."

"No, I've just heard things. About women dying that way, you know."

She looked down the aisle of horses and patted Lucy on the nose. Valentine looked at her, in an old pair of her father's pants cut off at the knee, breasts swelling under a T-shirt. In her disheveled state, she looked younger than her eighteen years, too young to be cold-bloodedly discussing abortion.

"Well, with luck, the old fart's incapable," she said, closing the discussion. She walked down the line of horses. "Great, the hay nets are empty. Mary only wants to ride and groom horses; she leaves the mucking out to Frat and me. Poor things! Sorry, guys, we can't turn you out in the new field until the fence is done! These two new horses ate up what grass you guys left in your pasture. Do me a favor, David. Can you get two bales from the loft? I'm going to water these two."

Valentine crossed to the barn and climbed into the hayloft. He liked the sweet smell of hay and alfalfa up there, masking the cow odor from beneath. A couple of sparrows hopped and played in the air, and spiderwebs caught the sunlight like little silver flowers.

He heard the ladder rungs creaking. Molly joined him in the loft, a determinedly cheerful smile showing off her good teeth. She had washed her face at the horse-pump, her T-shirt had a wet, face-shaped patch over the belly where she'd used it to dry herself.

"Thought I'd give you a hand with the bales. They're really loose. Sometimes they're hard to handle. But if you bale hay tight, it gets all mildewy and rots. We can't afford to waste anything."

Valentine sniffed a bale. "Hey, you're right. I didn't know that. All the hay I've ever seen has been packed too tight. Doesn't smell as good as this."

"That's the clover. We grow that on the other side of the road."

She cut a bundle and spilled it onto the floor of the loft.

"Very funny," Valentine said. "How are we going to carry it now? Or do you want to make a scarecrow?"

"Sure, David," she said, her eyes big and bright. "We can

use your clothes. Why don't you take them off and give them to me."

"What's that?" he said.

She knelt in the hay. "Too shy? Okay, I'll start."

With a quick, graceful movement she pulled her T-shirt up and over her head. Her shapely young breasts bobbed enticingly as she leaned back into the hay. Valentine stood and gaped, feeling his groin swell, otherwise utterly dumbfounded.

"David, do I have to spell it out for you? Let's make love. I need you to do this for me."

"Molly . . . I mean, we've never even kissed, this is kind of—"

"Sudden?" she finished. "Well, yes, I suppose you're right. Actually, I've only kissed a couple of guys. And one, he was in the patrols, I didn't even want him to kiss me. But he did, and he put his hand on my chest. I yelled, pushed him away, and ran for it. That's the sum total of my sexual experience.

"David, I'm a virgin. I'm going to be with this guy, and the thing that bothers me the most about it . . . well, other than that I'm being forced to do it in the first place . . . the thing that bothers me the most is that he'd be my first time. Not a memory I want to have for the rest of my life. I know you, I like you a lot, and I think you like me. You're nice. You're better-looking than some, and brighter than most. You're an officer. A gentleman, too, otherwise you'd already be on top of me."

"It's not like the thought hasn't crossed my mind, Molly."

"Just go slow, okay, David?" she said, scooting her hips up off the floor of the loft and slipping the oversize shorts down to her feet. She kicked them off with the flick of a leg.

Valentine sank to his knees beside her, placing his mouth on hers. He was also inexperienced, his innate shyness and quiet manner made even youthful kisses and pettings few and far between. Molly Carlson, perhaps the most beautiful girl he had ever known, was in his arms and his for the taking. Animal instinct came to his rescue. His young, demanding lust took him where his self-confidence feared to tread. He felt her probing hand reach the hardness in his pants. She fumbled with his belt. He wanted to take off his shirt, but her soft, yielding mouth felt so exquisite against his, it was impossible to break contact. She undid his belt and the worn-out stitching of the fly gave way to her hearty pull; skittering buttons flew in all directions. He managed to tear his mouth away from hers, laying a series of gentle kisses across her face and down her neck. She giggled and squirmed, thrusting her breasts against his chest. He pulled his shirt up and off his head and thrashed out of his pants.

She came up to his mouth, pressing him with a hard kiss that went all the way down to his soul, and he lost balance, falling onto his back with her on top of him. Coppery-blond hair tickled his face and neck like tiny dancing fingers as she kissed him. Her hand trailed down across his stomach and found him, first touching, then exploring, and finally gripping his hardness. His own arms traced the muscles on her back and caressed the soft skin of her buttocks. She responded, rubbing herself against his thigh, one of her hands playing with his black hair as the other stroked him below.

"God, Molly, that's good," he groaned, a deep and sensual rasp in his voice. He returned the favor, his gentle hand tracing the outlines of her sex, from the curly triangular mat of pubic hair to the soft folds of flesh between her legs. Their kisses became a rapid staccato, and he felt a rush of moisture come to her.

"Please, David. Slowly, okay?" she breathed in his ear. She turned over on her back, and he followed her movement as if in time to a waltz. She gazed up at him, pupils dilated in the dimness of the loft. He suddenly wanted this moment to be forever, Molly in his arms and the smell of womanhood and clover and a hint of lavender-sweet nepenthe in his nostrils. He pressed himself against her, kissing her softly and slowly as she guided him inside, and they were one. He took her in a series of slow strokes, each one slightly deeper than the last. A wince of pain washed across her face and then turned, as an ebb tide gives way to the flow, into a flush of passion. Her hands alternately clawed and caressed his rippling back with each deep, slow penetration. They lost themselves, together and yet apart, until at last he climaxed, emptying himself into her as spasm after spasm racked his body, mouth gaping open as if in a scream, but producing only an intense, unintelligible moan.

Afterwards she lay in his arms, drowsing away the afternoon. He teetered on the pleasant point between exhilaration and exhaustion.

"Are you okay?" he asked.

"Wonderful," she said, drawling out the word. She reached between her legs and brought up her fingers. A smear of blood coated her forefinger and thumb.

"Funny. I figured it would be gone after all the horse riding," she mused.

He kissed away the blood from her hand. The girl named Molly who walked into the barn that afternoon would have been disgusted at the gesture, but the woman in her lover's arms thought it touching.

"Ha, fooled you. My time of the month," she said.

He glanced up at her, eyebrows lifted.

"Joke," she said, twitching her nose at him and rolling her eyes.

"Well, since this chore is done, I really have to look into making a pack for my horse," Valentine said, not letting her get away with it. She restrained him, tightening her grip around his neck.

"Chore indeed! When I took off my shirt, you about passed out."

"Yeah, the blood drained out of my head, all right," Valentine agreed.

"I know where it all went. I'm going to be walking funny for a while, I think."

They kissed, laughing into each other's mouths.

"Seriously now, David. This whole thing actually helps you, too. If you and Gonzo pack up and go right after I do, it will fit perfectly. I'm sure they're expecting you to get pissed and leave. You can keep the story about looking for a place to farm west of here. Your work cards are legit. Even if they call Monroe to check it out, your story will stand up."

He rolled onto his back in the hay with a sigh. He did not want the afternoon to end.

"When are you going to Monroe?"

"Tomorrow afternoon. Touchet is leaving for Richland Center the day after tomorrow. Tuesday morning, I guess. That's what Uncle Mike told my dad on the phone today. Is this guy that important that they kidnap young ex-virgins for him?"

Valentine shrugged. "You'd know better than I. But if he gets production out of the farms, I suppose he's pretty important. Their army has to eat, too. Speaking of eating, I wonder if Frat found any rabbits. Your mother makes a great game pie. Oh, God! Your parents . . . I'm going to have a hard time acting normal in front of them."

"You and me both. But—what do we have to feel guilty about? You're my fiancé, right?"

He chuckled, nuzzling her with his chin. The shyness had magically vanished. Or perhaps it had been exorcised by a far stronger and more ancient magic.

"Molly Valentine," she mused. "Ugh!"

"Hey!" he objected.

"No, I just hate the *Molly* part. I love *Valentine*. Melissa Valentine? That's better. Nobody ever called me Melissa. Molly is way easier to shout."

"Put your pants on, Melissa. Or we'll be here all night," he said, looking out at the setting sun.

"That wouldn't be so bad. I wonder if the patrolman watching the place got an eyeful."

Dinner passed self-consciously, but Valentine found he could talk to her parents without feeling too uncomfortable. Her parents seemed to have other things on their minds. All Valentine could do was look at Molly's red, raw lips. *How could they not notice that?*

Gonzalez noticed something else in the basement as they got ready for bed.

"Hey, Val, what happened today?" he asked.

"Split a lot of wood."

Gonzalez snorted. "You stuck your wedge into something."

Valentine turned around. "What's that supposed to mean?"

"Well, your fly's been unbuttoned all night, and your back looks like two alley cats went about fifteen rounds on it. Unless you've been rolling in barbed wire, I'd say someone was moaning in your ear."

"Just go to sleep, funnyman. I was just doing some chores for the family, really. Molly had something she needed fixed, so I took care of it for her."

Gonzalez shook his head and turned over, carefully positioning his injured arm. "You officers get all the good jobs," he observed.

Valentine awoke in the middle of the night to a light tread on the stair. In the dim light shining down from the kitchen, he saw Molly cautiously entering the basement.

"David?" she whispered

"Over here," Valentine breathed back.

"No, over here," Gonzalez answered.

"Shut up, you," Valentine said, throwing his pillow at the scout.

"I wanted to talk to you. Sorry, Gonzo," she said.

Gonzalez swung his feet to the floor with a groan and pulled on his pants with his good arm. "I just remembered how long it's been since I've watched a sunrise. Don't make too much noise 'talking,' you two."

"Thanks, Victor. I mean it," Valentine said.

"You owe me one. See you at breakfast."

He moved soundlessly up the stairs.

Molly scuttled into Valentine's arms. He kissed her, grateful for her surprise.

"Did you want to talk?" he asked.

"Sort of," she said. "But not anymore. Let's go into the secret room. It's dark, and we can make a little bit of noise. But just a little."

Valentine opened the panel in the wall, and they nipped into the deep shadows, holding hands.

"Hey, you used one of those soaps," Valentine whispered, smelling her clean skin.

"Yes, this one's—"

"Roses," Valentine said, caressing her hair. "Beautiful."

She shut the door, and they were in blackness so total there was nothing but touch, and the faint smell of roses.

They kissed and kissing, lay down together. They melded in the darkness, learning new ways to please each other, delight each other, and, finally, love each other.

They said good-byes in a steady, spirit-sapping drizzle. As Flanagan and his ubiquitous shadow waited out of the rain in the patrol car, family, friends, and lovers shared a few parting hugs. Valentine, Molly, and her parents all wore the same air of false cheerfulness that appears at a funeral, after a septuagenarian drops dead in perfect health. "Never knew what hit him," one relative will say to another. "Yes, I'd love to go that way. No pain, no suffering, no illness. Lucky man," the other will agree, jointly looking for the tiny patch of sunshine among the dreary clouds.

The same forced tone was present in Mr. Carlson's voice as he said good-bye to his daughter. Molly wore her oldest cow-mucking work clothes, clean but nevertheless permanently stained. "Country girl he wants, country girl he gets," she had said to her mother after turning down the suggestion that she wear her prettiest dress, a blue-checkered barndancer that matched her eyes, to cheer herself up. "No, give that to Mary. Something to remember me by," she said, leaving the room before her mother could ask what she meant.

"Take care of that arm, Victor," Molly said, shaking his left hand. "My turn to see the big city, Frat. At least Madison isn't Chicago, thank God. Mary, there's more to horses than riding and brushing them. I'm putting you in charge of the stables while I'm gone, and you'd better keep it clean."

Her words to Valentine, in hindsight, also hinted at her dark mood under the steel-gray clouds. "David, you're going tonight, right? When it gets dark?"

"That's the plan. I'm still working on that pack for my horse. We'll be miles away by morning."

She smiled up at him, satisfied. They wandered to the side of the house, where they could kiss without watchful eyes on them. "I'll think of you fighting Reapers, David. You know, now that I've thought of it, maybe your Masada solution is the better one. Take a few of them with you."

"Molly, don't get so grim. You'll look back on this in a couple of years and laugh. Or maybe throw up. But it's not forever. It's really kind of pathetic of him if you think about it. Sending your butt-kissing uncle out into the woods to bring him a dinner date at gunpoint."

"That's the first thing I'll tell him," Molly said, beaming at the thought.

"Come back and work the farm. And just because my plan won't work right now doesn't mean it won't three years from now. Some night a team of Wolves will show up at your back door. We'll get your whole family out."

"If my dad will go. He's pretty committed to smuggling people out of here."

"Well, I owe your family a very big favor. You're going to collect on it. I'll come for you someday in the fall, if I can."

She looked into his eyes. "I think three years from now, you'll have more important things to worry about. Be careful with promises. You know that saying, 'Tomorrow is promised to no one,' right? That's like the law of the Kurian lands."

"You've got five years promised to you and your family."

"We'll see, David. That bond might be as worthless as the ring he tossed into the audience. Just go tonight, okay? But can you tell me one thing, David? Was I your first time . . . you know . . . lovemaking?"

Valentine owed her the truth. "Yes. I hope you liked it. I've never been very . . . lucky with women."

"Good. You'll remember me, then."

"I'll remember you as the Wisconsin beauty who was really good at pointing out the obvious," he said, giving her nose a gentle tweak.

They embraced, kissed, and touched each other's faces as if trying to record memories with their fingertips.

"Believe it or not, I'll come for you. It's a promise, Molly." He read hurt disbelief in her eyes. "No, not a promise: a vow." Now only the hurt remained.

"Don't," she said, unable to look at him. "A lot can happen in three years."

"A lot can happen in three days. Like falling in love, Melissa."

"David, stop. You're just making this hard, making it painful. This is an end. I don't want you to talk like it's a beginning."

He kissed her, trying to win a concession through sheer sensual power.

"No," she said, lowering her eyes from his. "I can't. Not when I have to . . . go like this."

She turned and fled.

At dinner that night, Valentine and Gonzalez decided to leave with the first light of dawn. A morning departure, with a quick good-bye to the Breitlings, would seem less suspicious than a midnight escape.

After a final farewell talk with the Carlsons, Gonzalez and Valentine lay in the basement, their guns and packs stored for the last night in the secret room. Gonzalez hid his anxiety about his injured arm well, but Valentine knew the worry dragged at his scout. Gonzalez worked best when the only thing worrying him was what might be around the next bend or over the next hill, so he talked frankly about how they would accommodate his injury on the trip home. The rest of the household had long since retired, and they burned only a foul-smelling tallow dip for light.

"You'll ride," Valentine said after rolling his maps back up into their tube. "I wish we could hang around longer, but it might be months before your arm is totally healed."

"You think it will get better?"

"Of course, Gonzo. Nerve tissue just takes forever to heal."

Gonzalez moved two painful fingers. "I don't know about that. Might never grow back."

"Well, you can move your hand a little. I think that's a good sign. In fact . . . Hey, an engine."

Both Wolves used their hard ears. It sounded like a truck engine. Perhaps one of the semi drivers was passing through with another foundling. But it stopped in the road, idling with thick coughs of exhaust.

Valentine and Gonzlalez exchanged looks. Without another word, they got up and moved to the secret door. They carried the tallow lamp behind the false wall with them and shut the panel behind. They ignored their packs, grabbing knives and guns. A crash sounded from above through the air vent, the house-shaking sound of a door being kicked in.

A whisper came from the other side of the secret door.

"Guys, are you in there?" Frat whispered.

Shouts from upstairs, a man's voice issuing orders to search the house.

"Yes," Valentine answered softly.

"Two men in a big van and two more in a patrol car. They're all armed and coming in. Gotta go," Frat said. Valentine finished tying his parang sheath on his leg and picked up his rifle.

"Hey, kid," an unknown voice barked. "Get outta that bed and get up here."

"I'm coming," Frat answered, voice cracking from strain. "Don't point that shotgun at me, okay?"

Gonzalez blew out the tallow dip in case the smell was wafting up to the living room.

They heard Mr. Carlson's voice, angry and scared, as he descended the stairs from the second story into the living room. "What in the heck is all this, Toland?"

"Orders. You're wanted for questioning."

"Orders? We'll see what Major Flanagan has to say about that!"

"He gave the orders, pard," the harsh voice answered. "Think your days of being under his wing are over. Your little girl stuck a steak knife into Mr. Brass Ring's neck—"

"Oh, my God!" Mrs. Carlson gasped.

"—a couple of hours ago," Toland continued. "Your brother is fucked, and he knows it, and he thinks the only way out of the jam is to arrest everyone here."

"Can I at least tell my hired help to take care of things while I'm gone?"

"The Breitlings? We're supposed to arrest them, too. Where's those two from up north, the guy who was seeing your daughter? The major wants him brought personal to his office."

"They left after dinner," Frat volunteered. "David was pissed about the whole thing with Molly."

"Shuddup, Sambo. If I want your opinion, I'll slap it out of you. Carlson, is he right?"

"Yes, you searched the house, didn't you?" Carlson said, voice still tremulous.

"Which way did they go, and when?"

"After dinner. They didn't even eat with us. I think they went north, but I dunno. I've had other things on my mind today than watching them leave. You should leave us alone and go after them; they probably put her up to it."

A rattling came from above. "I got them leg irons, Sarge. Should we link 'em up now?"

"Yeah. Pillow, go out to the car and radio that we got the Carlsons in custody. Also put out a general call to pick up two men on horseback. One's got a bum hand. You other two get busy with those shackles."

Valentine touched Gonzalez on the shoulder in the darkness, and they felt for the door. They cut across the shadowed basement, listening to the rattle of chains as the patrollers fixed the family into the leg irons. Valentine led the way up the basement steps, keeping to the edges to lessen the sound of boards creaking. They padded through the kitchen barefoot, Valentine with his repeater to his shoulder and Gonzalez with his held against his hip. Valentine paused for just a second to listen at the corner between the kitchen and the front living room, attempting to place the occupants by sound. All he could hear was a frightened crying from young Mary Carlson and the sounds of shackles being clicked closed and chains passed through steel eyes. He gestured to Gonzalez, who moved to the kitchen door of the house.

With a quick sidestep Valentine rounded the corner, gun tight to his shoulder, a shotgun-wielding man already in his sights. "Nobody move," he said, in a low tone. "You with the shotgun, put it on the floor, holding it by the barrel. You two with the chains, facedown on the floor!"

As he spoke, Gonzalez opened the back door, holding the rifle in his armpit, and disappeared into the darkness.

The patrollers, conditioned by years of practice in using their guns to bully unarmed farmers and townspeople, complied with alacrity. The Carlsons, dressed in their bedclothes, kicked the weapons away from the uniformed Quislings.

"Okay, you with the stripes, facedown, too. Good. Spread eagle, gentlemen. I've got eight shots in this repeater; the man who moves gets the first one. Frat, get the guns away from them, before they get any ideas."

Frat began collecting pistols and shotguns. "This'll cut it, Carlson," Sergeant Toland said, speaking into the floor. "Before, you were just wanted for questioning. This means you're all dead within a day or two. Not an easy death, either, if the Reapers—"

A pistol thrust into the sergeant's mouth cut off the imprecations. "Shut up, Sarge. When I want any of your lip, I'll blow it off," Frat said, cocking the revolver.

"Mr. and Mrs. Carlson, start putting the shackles on them, hands and feet, please," Valentine said.

The screen door swung open, and the fourth patroller entered, his fingers laced behind his head and the muzzle of Gonzalez's gun pressing him behind the ear.

"Pillow here just reported the situation as being under control," Gonzalez said. "Is it, sir?"

"Seems to be. Where are the Breitlings?"

"They hadn't gotten around to them, yet," Mr. Carlson said. "They're probably still asleep."

"Mrs. Carlson, after you've finished, do you think you could go get them?" Valentine asked.

"Could I get some more clothes on first?"

"Of course." The patrollers were now securely shackled and handcuffed. *They're scared,* Valentine thought, looking at the sweat stains on the blue uniforms. He was also pretty sure that the one named Pillow had pissed himself. *Scared people confuse easily.*

"Boy, that major is fucking things up, Carlson," Valentine said, winking at his benefactor. "Hey, Sarge. Do you know what you've stumbled into?"

"You're a corpse, boy. You're a corpse that happens to be walking and talking for a few more hours."

"Don't think so, Sarge. Look at this," he said, thrusting his rifle butt under Toland's nose. "You've just busted in on a Twisted Cross double-secret blind operation."

"What the fuck is the Twisted Cross? 'Double secret' bull-shit!" Sergeant Toland said, unimpressed.

"You wouldn't know, would you? We wanted Touchet dead, but we couldn't get at him in Illinois, because he's bought off so many of the people around him. But why am I telling you this? He was trying to spy out the operation at Blue Mounds."

"Bullshit," the sergeant responded. "Bangin' the Carlson girl ain't going to accomplish that, nor giving speeches, nei-ther."

"Sarge, you don't have to believe me. But let me give you two facts. One is that you're still alive, and the other is that all this is way over your head. Something's gone wrong with our operation, or you wouldn't have gotten those orders to bring these folks in. I suggest that in the future you have Madison confirm everything before doing what Major Flanagan says. Gonzalez?"

"Yes, sir," his scout replied.

"We're switching to plan Red Charlie."

"Er . . . you're in charge, sir," Gonzalez said. Valentine hoped the patrollers would interpret Gonzalez's confusion for reluctance.

"Let's go outside and discuss it. Mr. Carlson, Frat, keep an eye on these four."

In the cool night air, Valentine patted Gonzalez on the back. "Good job with Pillow, Gonzo. You still haven't lost your touch, injury or no."

"Sir, what's our next move? Are we going to leave now?"

Valentine nodded and walked down the road toward the vehicles. A dirt-covered patrol car and a delivery-van-type truck stood in the blackness. The clouds had still not dispersed.

"Gonzo, I'm going to have to give you a lot of responsibility. Maybe it will take your mind off the pain in your arm. I want to get the Carlsons and the Breitlings out of Wisconsin. All the way to the Ozark Free Territory."

"We can do it."

"Maybe we could. But, Gonzo, it's not going to be a *we*. It's going to be a *you*. I'm going after Molly."

Gonzo's eyes bulged with surprise. "My friend," he said finally. "She's probably dead already."

"If she is, she's going to have some company. That asshole of an uncle, for one."

"What is more important, getting you and me and these people back safely, telling about what we saw behind all those skulls, or killing one Quisling? I hate to tell you your duty, but—"

"Fuck my duty," Valentine said. Just the words themselves could subject him to a court-martial and firing squad, but he might as well be hanged for a sheep as a lamb. "I've had too many people I care about die. Not this one, not this girl."

"I've already forgotten what you just said, sir. But you will still have to explain this if you get back. What am I supposed to do with these civilians? The prisoners? I'd have a tough time making it back to the Ozarks, just me and my horse, let alone all these people."

"Here's the plan . . . ," Valentine said. Gonzalez listened as his lieutenant gave his final orders.

An hour later, everything was ready. The patrollers were locked in the feed shed, still shackled. The feed shed had the best lock and was the only all–cinder block construction on the farm. The delivery van waited with its ramp brought up and rear liftgate closed; horses were saddled and tied to the rear bumper. Inside the spacious interior, empty except for numerous eyebolts for fixing prisoners in position, were the Breitlings, Mrs. Carlson, and Mary Carlson, clutching a few blankets and some travel clothing, along with the family dog. Mr. Carlson was at the wheel, and Gonzalez rode shotgun. Both were dressed in blue patroller uniforms taken from the Quisling captives.

Valentine and Frat stood outside the passenger door. Valentine wore the best of the uniforms and carried the identity papers of the patroller who most resembled him, the pants-wetting Pillow.

"We meet south of the bridge outside Benton, okay, Frat?" Gonzalez asked, rolling Valentine's map back up and returning it to the tube. Frat nodded.

"Mr. Carlson, if I can't get your daughter, I'm going to leave one hell of a trail of dead Quislings," Valentine said. "They'll come after me with everything they've got. Should make it a little easier for you."

"No one's asking you to do this, son," Mr. Carlson said from the driver's seat. "Molly's probably already dead. Maybe she used the knife on herself after killing Touchet." Carlson's lips trembled as he spoke.

"I don't think she'd give up that easy, Alan. If she's alive, I'm going to get her back. I'm coming back with your daughter, or not at all." He turned to Gonzalez and shook his friend's good hand. "Gonzo, I know you can do this," Valentine said quietly. "You've got the brains and the skills. Just keep them moving. Eat the horses one by one if it helps. When you get back, tell them everything you remember, even if it doesn't seem important. They've also got to get a

Cat or two up here to find out what's going on at Blue Mounds. One other thing: Get Frat into the Hunters, or at least have him posted as an Aspirant. He'll make a better Wolf than either of us, at least someday. Take every buckchit I've got and draw it to get the Carlsons started. I've got some friends in a little place called Weening."

Valentine racked his mind, searching for another suggestion to increase Gonzalez's chances. There was always one more order to give, one more contingency to consider.

"I will do it, all of it, sir. *Vaya con Dios, jefe.* And I'll be praying for you, sir. Every day."

"Back to praying, Gonzalez? I thought your mother was in charge of that."

"She's in charge of my soul. I'll take care of yours."

"You're going to have plenty to take care of in the next couple of weeks without my soul thrown in. But thank you anyway; I'm honored."

Carlson started up the truck, and Valentine hopped to the ground. Gonzalez gave a little salute from his perch. "Good luck, Lieutenant."

"Send my respects to the Zulus, Gonzo!"

The truck rolled off into the darkened west. Hours to go before daylight.

"Okay, Frat. You and me now. I wish I had learned how to drive better."

"It's okay, Lieutenant," Frat said, moving around to the driver's side. "I know the way, so it's just as well."

"You can call me David, bud. Drive slow and careful. Keep the headlights off."

"I know, I know. You told me. Where to?"

Valentine checked the contents of his pack and a spare feedbag, which held extra restraints and a few packets from the Carlsons' kitchen. "Your uncle's house. You can tell me everything you remember about it on the way."

Frat covered the twenty miles in just over an hour, switching to tractor trails and cattle paths as he drew close to Monroe. The roads were empty, and the night seemed to be waiting for the curtain to go up on the last act of the play. The radio squawked occasionally, reporting from the patrols looking for two men on horseback. Valentine mentally prepared himself for a tragic ending to the drama. As Frat drove, leaning far forward as if the extra foot and a half of viewing distance made a difference, Valentine applied a hacksaw to the double-barreled shotgun, taking off the barrels from the edge of the wooden grip onward. He then filled the pockets on its leather sling-bandolier with buckshot shells. A second pump-action shotgun lay on the wooden backseat of the car.

"Okay, we're in the fields behind his house. It's right beyond that line of trees there," Frat informed him. "We've stayed over here a few times, back when he had a wife."

"Whatever happened to her?" Valentine asked.

"Don't know. Nobody does. One day she was just gone, and we learned not to ask."

"So he's not much for answering questions, then?" Valentine stepped out of the car and took the pump-action shotgun, pocketing shells into his stolen uniform. "I'll try to change that. Keep the scattergun handy, Frat. Don't be afraid to use it, and pull out if something comes after you. Keep alert."

"I will, sir. You be careful."

Valentine walked silently up to the line of trees, listening and smelling for the guard dogs. Their scent seemed to be everywhere across the lawn. Perhaps they were around front.

The extravagant house had bright security lights mounted high up just under the roof, angled out to bathe the lawn in white light. Their brilliance threw the surrounding terrain into harsh, black-and-white relief, blazing white wherever the lights touched and utter black in the shadows. Valentine whistled softly.

One of the great black rottweilers appeared from around the garage corner. Valentine reached into his feed bag and placed a few strips of meat on the flat of his parang. He whistled again. The dog growled and took a few steps closer. Valentine stayed very still, offering the meat from the brush at the edge of the woods.

"Good dog, good dog," Valentine said soothingly. The dog licked its chops and padded forward. Valentine lowered the blade to the grass, and the dog began eating. Flanagan obviously used the dogs only for show; a real guard dog would be trained not to take food from anyone but its keeper. Having made friends, Valentine stood for a moment patting the hopeful-looking dog.

Valentine watched the sleeping house for a few moments then jogged across the lawn to the back door. The rottweiler trotted along happily. The second hound, curled up on the mat at the door fast asleep, startled at their approach. Seeing the other dog, it came forward to greet the late-night visitor. Valentine issued more tidbits to the dogs and began feeling along the top of the windowsill to the left of the door for the key Frat said was hidden there. He found it, placed on a small nail hammered into the top of the windowsill.

The key fit the dead bolt on the back door, but Valentine was able to open the door only an inch or two. A heavy chain across the inside of the door barred further progress. He reached into his bag of tricks for the rusty crowbar from the patrol car's trunk, fixed it to the chain near its mounting on the doorjamb, and pulled. The chain parted with a loud *ting*.

Valentine entered the kitchen behind the business end of the shotgun. The tabletop was a mess of dirty dishes and paperwork. The main light over the table was still on, bathing the littered octagonal surface in a puddle of yellow. A heavy electric typewriter sat before a chair, a cold mug of coffee next to it, nestled like a small brown pond in a forest of empty beer bottles. A raspy snoring echoed from the living room.

He looked at the typed report on the table, flipping to the second page. Apparently it was a statement by the one patroller standing sentry outside Touchet's VIP suite door at the New Universal Church building. A paragraph caught Valentine's eye.

> When the cook entered with Mr. Touchet's nightcap of coffee, I heard him scream. I drew my gun and entered the bedroom. Mr. Touchet was facedown on the bed, nude except for a pair of socks. The young woman was trying to force up the window of the bedroom, not knowing that it was nailed shut. As I entered, she smashed it with an ashtray but I was able to restrain her.
>
> After she was handcuffed and held down by the cook, I examined Mr. Touchet for a pulse. He was dead. He had a steak knife handle sticking out of the back of his head right were the neck meets the skull. His back was coated with some kind of oil and he lay on a towel. There was very little blood on the towel. Mr. Touchet's brass ring had been removed from his finger and was placed around the handle of the knife.

The young woman was screaming obscenities at us, so I hit her. She had not been injured by Mr. Touchet; the bruise on her face was from me.

Valentine walked to the living room and looked in. Virgil Ames lay stretched out on a leather sofa, sunglasses finally off, pistol belt looped around his arm. The air around him smelled of beer breath and stale flatulence. Beyond, in the glass turret-room, he could make out Maj. Michael Flanagan. The major slept in his chair, phone in his lap, widespread feet propped up on his desk.

The prowling Wolf shifted the shotgun to his left hand and took up the parang. *No making friends with this dog,* he thought, putting the wedge-shaped point just above Virgil's Adam's apple. At the swift inward thrust, the late Virgil Ames opened his eyes. Valentine wiped his knife on the rich leather sofa and moved toward the office.

Major Flanagan woke when the blued steel of the shotgun barrel poked him between the eyes. As Flanagan sputtered into surprised wakefulness, Valentine changed the angle of the shotgun barrel, pointing it between Flanagan's outstretched legs.

"You wanted to see me, Major?" he asked.

"What the—? . . . Virgil!" Flanagan shouted.

"Dead, sir," Valentine reported. "Better speak up, or you'll be joining him in five seconds. Tell me, is Molly Carlson still alive?"

"Virgil!" Flanagan cried.

Valentine stuck the shotgun toward Flanagan's screaming mouth. "Major, your screaming is not doing you any good, and it's giving me a headache, so cut it out. Or I might cut your tongue out and have you write down your answers."

"Fuck you, Saint Croix. We don't just have Molly, we've

got all the Carlsons, as of eleven this evening. If you back out of here and never let me see your face again, they might live. You might even live."

The powerful, spearlike thrust of the shotgun shattered two incisors and left a worm-tail of lip dangling as it hung from a thin strip of bleeding skin. The major's hands flew to his wounded mouth, and Valentine clipped him on the side of the head with the shotgun butt. The major fell over, knocked senseless. Valentine busied himself with handcuffs and rope.

The house was dark when Major Flanagan came to. Valentine splashed cold coffee into his face. Groans rose from the Quisling just before he vomited all over himself. The paroxysm showed how securely he was tied into his office chair.

Handcuffs fixed his wrists against the arms of the chair, and heavy lengths of rope cocooned his chest and shoulders into the back. His legs were tucked under the chair and secured by ankle shackles with a short length of chain winding behind the central column that attached the chair itself to the little circle of wheels below.

No hint of morning could be seen through the windows of the office. Valentine stood next to the desk, a breathing shadow.

A metallic *ping* sounded, and Valentine picked up the silver cigar lighter, waving the lit end hypnotically in front of Flanagan's face. Its dim red glow reflected off piggish, angry eyes. "Okay, Uncle Mike, do you want to talk to me, or do I have to use this thing?"

"Talk about what?"

"Where Molly is."

"She's in the Order building in Monroe."

Valentine grabbed his pinkie and thrust the cigar lighter

over it. An audible *hiss* was instantly drowned out by the major's scream. Valentine pulled away the lighter and stuck it back into its electric socket, pushing it down to turn it back on.

"Wrong answer. I read some of the papers in the kitchen. According to your report, you put her in a car for Chicago."

Ping.

"Why Chicago, Major?"

"We called the Illinois Eleven as soon as it happened. That's what they told us to do, send her to Chicago."

"Where in Chicago?" Valentine asked, extracting the lighter.

"How should I know? The Illinois Eleven don't like being questioned any more than the Madison Kurians," Flanagan said, watching the lighter wave back and forth in the darkness. "No! God, Saint Croix, I don't know."

This last was addressed to the approach of the lighter to his left hand. Valentine forced Flanagan's fist open and inserted his index finger into the cigar lighter. The smell of burnt flesh wafted up into his nostrils as he ground the glowing socket home. Flanagan screamed again, and Valentine withdrew the lighter. He pressed it back into the socket, re-heating it.

"The pain will stop as soon as you tell me where she is in Chicago. You want me to stick your dick in this next?"

The tip of Flanagan's forefinger was a blackened lump of flesh and blisters. Even the fingernail was burned back.

Ping.

"I think they're putting her in the Zoo," Flanagan gabbled, seeing Valentine's hand move to pick up the lighter. "I've been there, it's on the north side of Chicago, near the lake. Lots of boats tied up permanent."

"Why there? I thought they just put everyone in the Loop when they wanted to do away with them."

"They knew Touchet. They asked me if she was a real looker. I told them about her. I mean, if she weren't my niece, one of the patrollers would have raped her a long time ago. Saint Croix, you haven't been around much. I've risked my job—my life even—to help my sister and her family. Molly was never going to be hurt." Sweat coated Flanagan's face, wetting his bushy eyebrows and running down his neck in rivulets.

"So what's this Zoo?"

"It's in a place called Lincoln Park. I've got a little map of Chicago in my desk, bottom drawer. Even has phone numbers for cab companies. The Zoo is . . . a big brothel, that kind of thing. There are a lot of bars there; they do sports, too. Kind of a wild place, anything goes, like Old Vegas."

Valentine popped up the lighter and left it resting lightly in its socket. "Good enough, Flanagan. There's one more thing I want before I go. I need a travel warrant made out for one Private Pillow. Giving him a week's leave or whatever you call it to go to Chicago. And some money to spend."

Flanagan's massive eyebrows rose in surprise. "Madison paper's no good there. Our guys bring things to barter. Jewelry, beer, food, stuff like that. But what you're thinking is nuts. I'd like to see Molly alive as much as her parents, but it ain't going to happen. There're hundreds of soldiers from Illinois, Indiana—Michigan, even. I've heard of officers coming all the way from Iowa and Minnesota to go to the Zoo. Even if you can find her, you'll never get her out. The Black Hole's a one-way—"

"Black Hole?" Valentine asked.

"I dunno where she would go for sure. But the Black Hole is kind of a prison. Women don't last long there. They're used . . . treated badly. Some of the men like that kind of thing. Never went there myself, but you hear stories."

"Just tell me where to find the papers to fill out."

Flanagan gave detailed instructions, and soon Valentine had his travel warrant. The major applied his seal and signed it; Valentine had freed the man's uninjured right hand to do so. The major wiped his face with his good hand. "You're tough, Saint Croix. I had no idea."

So he thinks fawning is his ticket to safety. Interesting. Has it gotten him out of jams with the Kurians? Valentine thought. He put his new papers and the folded map in one of the front pockets of his shirt. He then walked over to the front of the desk. The shotgun leaned up against one of the carved wooden lions.

"Take my car. It's in the garage, and the keys are in my breast pocket here. I'll tell them you went north. I'll keep the Carlsons under lock and key for a few days, then release them. We'll shout questions at 'em for a few hours; don't worry, they'll be fine. Of course, Molly can't ever come back here, but I'm sure you can get her somewhere safe up in the woods if your plan works. Watch yourself in Chicago, though. Must be a hundred Reapers there, easy. But if . . ."

The major stopped in openmouthed amazement as Valentine brought up the shotgun, pointing it at his head. "No, Saint Croix. Be fair! I gave you everything . . ."

Valentine put the butt tightly to his shoulder and placed his finger on the trigger. "You once said that if it were up to you, you'd hand me over to the Reapers for not having a work card. Well, now that it's up to me, I'm going to follow a little rule we have in the Wolves. I call it Special Order Twelve, section Double Ought. Any high-rank Quislings bearing arms against their fellow men shall suffer death by firing squad."

"You said you wouldn't kill me!" Flanagan shrieked, holding out his hand, palm outward.

"I said the pain would stop," Valentine corrected, pulling the trigger. The dark room exploded in noise and a flash of blue-white light like an old-fashioned flashbulb. At the last instant, Flanagan flung his arm across his face, but the blast of buckshot tore through his arm, head, and the back of the chair. Bone, blood, brain, and wood from the chair splattered the brick wall behind the chair.

Valentine went through the house, filling a pillowcase with anything of value he could find: Virgil Ames's sunglasses and beaded pistol belt, Flanagan's cheroots and electric lighter, a solid silver cigarette box, gold jewelry belonging to the missing Mrs. Flanagan. The liquor cabinet contained two bottles of bonded whiskey. They joined the other contents of the pillowcase.

He went into the furnished basement and flicked on one of the electric lights. A pool table filled one end and a small workshop the other. Three rifles hung from an ornate gunrack, set between two eight-point deer heads. Valentine's eyes lit on an old Remington Model 700. He shouldered it. Then he crossed to the workshop and found a tin of kerosene. He opened it and splashed it along the pool table, carpet, and wood paneling. He struck a match and tossed it into the puddled liquid on the pool table. Flames began to race across the green baize surface. Sure that the fire was well on its way, Valentine climbed back up the stairs.

Frat pulled the car out of the field and onto the little path leading back to the road. "Now what, Lieutenant?" he asked. Oddly enough, Frat had asked no questions about what had transpired in his uncle's house.

"Where can I catch the next train to Chicago? Not a station, though. I mean to jump on."

Frat considered the problem. "The line connecting Dubuque goes right through Monroe. A train goes along that every day. Takes you right into Chicago, or the meatpacking plant, that is. You'd be in the city by tonight. You'll know you're close when you go through this big stretch of burned-out houses. Reapers burned out a huge belt around the city. Great Suburban Fire, it was called. Happened before I was born. Then they did something to the soil so nothing but some weeds grow. Mile after mile of old street and rubble. Of course, I was pretty young when I saw it. But you'll never find Molly in the Loop. You could look for days. How you gonna get her out again?"

"They didn't put her in the Loop. She's in someplace called the Zoo."

Frat smacked his head. "Zot me! I shoulda thought of that! They would put someone who looks like her there. My momma used to tell my older sister, 'What you trying to do, get a job at the Zoo?' whenever she didn't like what Phila was wearing."

"What else can you tell me about Chicago?"

Frat turned the car onto a road heading south. "It's big, really big. But what you got going for you is that there's people from all over, so strangers don't get noticed. If you cause any trouble, they grab you and throw you in the Loop. They use the old United States money there, too, but it has to be authorized. The bills they've authorized have a stamp on them, kind of like the stamp on our work cards. I'm pretty sure some of your people who fight the Kurians are there, but I don't know how you would ever find them. And I'd hide that big curved knife of yours. Too many of the soldiers know about those."

They reached a bend in the road. Frat pulled the patrol car
to the side.

"Frat, you've been a great help. You know what to do
now, right?"

"Drive fast with all the lights on, like I'm hurrying
somewhere," Frat recited. "Put the car in a ravine and then
walk to that bridge. Go cross-country and keep out of sight.
I think I can manage."

"I'm sure you can."

"All you have to do now is go south, and you'll hit the
railroad tracks. They curve where they run along the Sugar
River, and I bet they'll slow down. Lots of guys bum rides.
As long as you got identity papers, you're okay getting into
Chicago. Just take my advice and don't cause any trouble
until you're sure you can get away with it. Getting out again
isn't so easy. They check the trains heading out for runners."

Valentine offered his hand, and Frat shook it. "Listen to
Gonzo on the way back, pup. You can learn a lot from him."

"Yeah, he's cool. He thinks a lot of you, by the way. Says
the Wolves in Zulu Company call you the Ghost."

"The what?"

"The Ghost. On account of you walk so smooth and
quiet, like you're floating. And there's another reason: Mr.
Gonzalez says you can tell when there are vampires around.
He says it's spooky, but kinda comforting."

"The Ghost, huh? Well, have Gonzo tell them to keep their
rifles clean and oiled, or I'll come back and haunt them.
Good-bye, Frat."

"Good-bye, Lieutenant Valentine. Don't worry, I'll get
everyone out, if Mr. Gonzalez just points the direction. You
ain't the only one good at smellin' out Skulls."

*   *   *

While Valentine waited for the train in the morning shade beneath a willow, he ate from a bag of crackers and a brick of cheese he had taken from Flanagan's kitchen. He had already improvised a shoulder strap for his pillowcase of loot and admired the manufacturing on the stolen Remington rifle; he figured it would bring enough money for a bribe or two, or serve as one itself. He studied his map of Chicago, memorizing as many of the street names as he could. *It must be quite a city, he thought. Over a hundred Reapers. Great place to visit, but I wouldn't want to die there.*

Twelve

Chicago, October of the forty-third year of the Kurian Order: The Second City is still a town on the take. A resident twentieth-century Pulitzer Prize-winning journalist once suggested that the motto for the city should be "Where's Mine?" Nowhere is the art of bribery, corruption, and widespread beak-wetting more common than in the Kurian-controlled, Quisling-run City of Big Shoulders. No one is even sure exactly how many Kurian Lords run the city, as the Kurians divide it not by geography but by business and property ownership. A Kurian Lord might control a steelworks in Gary, an automobile-parts plant on the West Side, several apartment buildings on the Gold Coast, and a few antiquated airplanes that fly out of O'Hare. His Reaper avatars will travel among holdings, going into the Loop for regular feedings.

To prevent the Reapers from taking too much of an area's vital labor force, the Loop system was developed after twenty years of fractious and chaotic rule. The Kurians had little use for the high-rise business centers of the downtown, and after emptying the assorted museums and stores of anything they fancied, they created the walled enclave as a dumping ground for undesirables. Here the Reapers could feed without worrying about taking a vital technician or mechanic and starting a series of inter-Kurian vendettas that might escalate into a full-scale feud.

The workers of Chicago enjoy a security that few other communities under the Kurians know. But their existence depends on paying their way in old federal greenbacks. The destitute receive a quick trip into the Loop. But the elite Quislings who run the city for the Kurians amass sizable fortunes in a variety of barely legitimate ways.

One might wonder what the point of wealth is with the Kurians in control, but the Kurians have become infected with the viruslike corruption that seems to thrive in Chicago and are often bought off by their ostensible slaves. The top Quislings use their money to bribe the Kurians not with cash, but with vital auras, the one thing the vampiric Kurians prize above all else. The Quislings buy captives from a soulless body of men and women called the Headhunters, who in turn buy them from wandering bounty hunters who lurk on the fringes of the Kurian territory, grabbing everyone they can. These latter-day fur trappers pick up strays in a circle moving clockwise down from northern Michigan, across southern Indiana and Illinois, and then up the eastern shores of the Mississippi to the northern woods of Wisconsin.

When a wealthy Quisling has turned over enough vital aura to the Kurians, a brass ring is awarded. Only in Chicago is this practice of "buying" brass rings allowed. With the security of cash and a brass ring, these robber-baron Quislings then retire to Ringland Parks, a twenty-mile stretch of stately homes along the shore of Lake Michigan just to the north of Chicago, the only large area of suburbs to survive the flames that desolated greater Chicagoland. But as brass rings cannot be passed down to sons and daughters, their progeny are left with the tiresome task of doing it all over again.

Chicago has become what Vegas was to the pre-Kurian world: an anything-goes city where anything, including human life, can be bought or sold if the price is right.

*   *   *

The Chicago skyline looked to Valentine like the bones of a titanic animal carcass. His position atop the freight train gave him an unobstructed view as the train bore southeast, straight as an arrow in flight, toward the city. He would have felt naked and defenseless riding the rocking platform, clattering across the uneven points on the rail line, but for the companions scattered across the last few boxcars. Now and then other hitchers made the run-and-vault onto the line of cars.

He first spotted the skyline in the blackened ring of former suburbia that encircled the city like a burned-out belt. It reminded him of a picture of the town center of Hiroshima after the atomic bomb: nothing but rubble and cracked pavement. He wondered what the Kurians had done to the ground to poison the plant life; just dry-looking brown weeds and the occasional withered sapling grew from the bare patches of soil. He wondered why the Kurians wanted to create this vista of desolation. He asked an Illinoisan, a thirtyish man who had hopped on as the train left the hills north of Rockford.

"The Chicago Blight?" the man said, looking at the expanse as if seeing it for the first time. "You got me. My brother is in the Iguard, and he says it's a no-man's-land between the Chicago Kurians and the Illinois Eleven. They depend on each other, but they had a big fight back when I was just five or six. Anyway, the Blight makes them refrain from wandering out of their territory to feed. Then I got a sister-in-law in Chicago, and she says it's to make getting out of Chicago harder. Guess burning everything was easier than building a wall that would have to run for fifty or sixty miles. But I've still heard of a few people managing to run across it in daylight. If they get lucky and dodge the Security Service and make it out by nightfall, I've heard of people escaping

Chicago just using their legs. A lot of times they run right back, though; it's more dangerous downstate. I've been trying to get a good-paying job in Chicago for years, but I don't have the toke for a good position."

"You don't have the *toke?* What's that?" Valentine asked.

"You must be on your first trip to Chicago, blue boy. A toke is like a tip, but it's more of a bribe. Money's the best, but it's got to be their authorized stuff. You try to palm off a bill you picked up in Peoria, and you're asking to get your face smashed in. Cigarettes are good tokes, too. And if you are doing anything major, like getting a cab ride or checking in to a hotel, you toke twice, once when you arrange it and again when you're done. If the first one is too small, they might blow you off and look for someone else. If the second is too small, they'll just swear at you, but you'd better not expect any more favors. I've seen fistfights over too small a toke at the end of a cab ride, so be careful. But getting back to my point: For me to get a decent factory job, I'd have to toke the doorman, the union boss, and the manager. Maybe a couple of managers. And those would be big tokes, in the thousands. Hard to scrape up that kind of money on the farm."

Valentine reached into his bag and extracted one of the major's cheroots. "Thanks for the tip," he said, handing it to his fellow traveler.

"Hey, you catch on fast. Listen, if you want, you can come with me when we get off. I know a good route out of the railroad yard. That's a fine rifle, and some Chicago Security Service officer is gonna quote regulations and take it off you if you go through channels. Unless you can cough up about a hundred bucks worth of toke, that is."

"You're a pal. My name's Pillow," Valentine said, using the name on his identity papers.

"Norbu Oshima. Most of the guys call me Norby. Pleased to meet you, Pillow."

"My friends call me Dave. It's my middle name."

They made small talk as the city grew steadily larger. At last the train pulled into a bustling rail yard spread out over several square miles and dominated by a thick concrete tower. The train eventually switched to a siding near a series of livestock pens. Produce trucks and horse-drawn carts waited nearby, ready to accept the contents of the boxcars as the shipping clerks sorted them.

"C'mon," Oshima said as they jumped off. "Through the cattle crushes. There's a storm drain to the Halsted Bridge."

Other figures were hopping off the train and scattering, pursued by a few police in navy blue uniforms. A corpulent CSS cop jumped out after them from between two cars, but Valentine and his guide vaulted over a series of fences as they ran across the pens, and their pursuer gave up after mounting the first two bars, settling for yelling a few obscenities after them.

"Fuckin' yokels," the distant voice protested. "Where's my toke, you bastards!"

They rolled under a chain-link fence and slid into the concrete drainpipe, dragging their bags after them. "Welcome to Chicago," Oshima said, panting and slapping dirt from his clothes.

"Looks like he lets his uniform do his fighting for him," Valentine observed.

"Yes, those CSS guys got it made. Everybody tokes them. He's had one too many free burgers and beers at the Steak and Bun. Speaking of which, I'm starved. After I drop my stuff off at my sister's, you wanna eat?"

"Thanks, but I have to find someone. You know where I

can find a bunch of bars in a row called the Clubs Flush? On Rush Street, I think."

Norby whistled appreciatively. "You must have some good barter in that sack. Those are some nice places. Never been in 'em myself. They take up a whole block. Rush is easy to find; it runs at an angle to the rest of the streets. Watch yourself around the vacant lots. I'll get you to Division Street and point you in the right direction."

"Thanks," Valentine said, and meant it. He handed Oshima two more cheroots.

"Don't worry, David. You'll do fine. As long as those cigars hold out, anyway."

Valentine walked down the street, consulting his tourist map. Even in the afternoon, there were more people on the street than Valentine was used to seeing in the most populated parts of the Free Territory. Despite the people, he felt strangely alone. The city smelled noxious; a mixture of tar and garbage assaulted his nostrils. Sewage odors wafted up from the storm drains, and trash overflowed from Dumpsters in the alleys. Public sanitation was not a priority with the Kur.

"Hey, blue boy, want a ride?" a man in a straw hat called from the front of a carriage. A horse stood patiently in harness. "Take you to the Zoo. I got a friend at one of the entrances, let you in half-price. Your buddies in Wisconsin won't believe their ears when you get back."

"Maybe later," Valentine said.

Cats seemed to be everywhere, especially in the rubble of the empty blocks. Hungry-looking stray dogs prowled the alleys, sniffing the gutters.

Valentine spotted the Clubs Flush. Had it been night, he would have seen it from farther off; electric lights on the building illuminated a ten-foot mural of a hand holding four kings and a joker. In sight of his goal, Valentine realized how tired he was. His last night in bed had been interrupted by Molly's visit, and he had been active ever since. He unbuttoned his shirt and smelled his chest. Molly's rosebud-soap scent still clung to his skin. The memories gave him new strength, even as he considered the hopeless task ahead of him. How could he have imagined a city this size?

He reached the bars, but there seemed to be no way to get inside. Nor could he see through the dark-tinted glass windows to get a hint of what waited within. He passed a woman wearing a dirty smock, standing out of the wind and smoking a cigarette.

"Entrance is around the side," she informed him, pointing her thumb over her shoulder. She took a long pull on a cigarette. "I work there, three-to-eleven shift. Good luck getting past Wideload. You looking for a job?"

"No, just a little fun. Thanks."

"Hey," she said conspiratorially, removing a brown-paper-wrapped package from under her smock. "Check it out. Sixteen-ounce porterhouse, right out of the Diamonds' cooler. Twelve bucks, what do you say?"

"No, I'm fine for food. "

"Eight bucks. Can't do better. You can sell it for at least twenty on Michigan Avenue."

Valentine turned the corner and found the entrance. It was a decorated alley, with a brick arch above, wide enough to allow a wagon inside. Red and black painted wooden double doors with the Clubs' hours stenciled on showed that it must still be before six, as they were closed and locked. A smaller door was fitted into right side of the gate, and Valentine knocked.

A face that would not encourage casual conversation scowled out from a crack in the door. "What?" it said in a deep, monotone bass.

"You Wideload? I want to see the Duke, if he's in."

"Not for you, hick. Beat it."

"I'm forgetting my manners," Valentine said, reaching inside his pack. Looking at the fleshy face, he opted to hand over the brick of cheese he had snacked on earlier.

"That's more like it," the heavy-framed man said, opening the door and engulfing the three-pound brick in a paw that resembled a gorilla-hand ashtray. Valentine watched Wideload as he sampled the Wisconsin dairy gold. Both of the Wolf's legs would have fitted in the man's shirtsleeve, and he and Gonzalez could have slept out of the rain in his trousers. "Mmmm, not bad, blue boy. Go up the spiral staircase. There're two doors at the top. One's marked 'office.' Go in the other one."

Valentine nodded and entered the courtyard. Plants sprouting through a mulch of cigarette butts decorated the brick-paved enclosure. Beautiful brass and glass doors, one facing in each direction, indicated the locations of the four bars. Each was named for a suit of cards.

Curious, Valentine looked in each door. The one marked SPADES seemed to be devoted to gambling; the kidney-shaped green baize tables could mean little else, and brightly lit slot machines filled the walls. The Diamonds bar looked like a dining room. Valentine had heard about, but never before seen, white tablecloths, polished silver, and flowered centerpieces. All were in opulent abundance inside the restaurant. The Clubs room was the only one open for business. Comfortable leather chairs lay scattered around next to small tables, and the bar appeared as devoted to cigars and pipe tobacco as to alcohol. A few men, some even wearing suits and ties, lounged around, reading newspapers or playing cards. Most were smoking. The Hearts bar looked like a glitzy brothel. It was the largest, taking up two stories, and had an open space in the center that featured the traditional stripper's pole mounted on a circular stage. Valentine counted three bars within the mirror-decorated main room.

"Hey, Tori," Valentine heard Wideload say from his door.

"Hey," a bored female voice answered, and a woman who seemed mostly made of blond hair and legs strode into the courtyard, carrying an angular purse over her shoulder big enough to sit in and paddle down a river. She glanced at Valentine with an appraising eye and disappeared down a narrow hallway branching off from the central area.

Valentine shrugged to the cheese-eating doorman and climbed the metal spiral staircase. He went to the unmarked door and knocked.

"It's open," a familiar female voice sang out.

He entered, and recognized the Duke's escort sitting behind a desk larger than the one in Flanagan's office but somehow more delicate and feminine in its rich glossy sheen. *Debby? No, Dixie.* Valentine's mind cast about for her name. *Denise, of the revealing décolletage dress,* he remembered. Today she was wearing a simple gray sleeveless outfit.

"Hi, Denise. Can I see the Duke?"

She looked up at him, puzzled. "Does he know you?"

"Sort of. We met at the Bunker in Madison. He said to drop by if I was ever in Chicago. David Tiny, remember?"

"That's it. I thought I saw you before. You're the guy with the nice hair. The Duke says some wild stuff after a few drinks, but you might be able to see him for a minute before we, er, he goes to dinner. Hey, you wouldn't have an extra toot of that happy-dust, would you?"

"I'll see what I can do later," Valentine said.

"Great, thanks. If you want to sit, there're a couple of chairs. He's meeting with the guy who brings in the drinks and eats. They've been at it all afternoon, so they should be done soon." She favored him with a smile.

Valentine offered Denise a cigarette. Her smile widened, and she tucked it away in her desk. He sat, trying to stay alert. Faint, muffled voices came from the inner office behind a door painted with a king of clubs. Trust someone with the Duke's taste in clothes and women to carry an idea too far.

Needing something to occupy his mind to prevent himself from dozing off, Valentine hardened his ears and listened to the voices inside the office.

"I tell you, it's hell, Duke. The whole Kurian system would work better if they just formed a New Order bank or something and had a currency that was good everywhere. This business of shuttling around boxcars full of people is just ludicrous. 'All I've got is a two-hundred-pound male, can I get a hundred-pound woman and a fifty-pound kid as change?' "

Valentine heard the Duke laugh.

"Okay, I'm exaggerating again. It's a little better organized than that. It's one thing for the Kurians here to send a few boxcars full of people up to Milwaukee and then bring the cars back here loaded with beer. But let's say I want to buy beef in Texas. If it's hot, some of the 'currency' is going to drop dead on the trip. Plus you got the local Reapers in Tennessee and points south looking to take some people off you in exchange for riding their rails."

"Well," the Duke countered, "you got to look at it from their point of view. Money doesn't mean much to them. Some of them like art and stuff, but auras are the only recognized currency. They're like a bunch of damn junkies."

"Yeah, you're right. But it still makes me nuts. Plus the people know what's coming at the other end of the ride, which makes them tough to control. And finding good men to do the work of keeping them in line ain't easy. Most of the ambitious ones are in the military. Leaves me with the idiots and thugs who just want to push people around."

"I hear that," the Duke agreed. "Listen, if the side meat is a little late, we're okay. I'll just do a special on pork chops or something. But you gotta get home to those pretty wives of yours, and my stomach is growling. Call me tomorrow and let me know if you've made any progress."

They said their good-byes, and the man, richly dressed in a matched set of pin-striped pants and a vest, walked out and waved at Denise. She picked up the telephone and pressed a button.

"Hi, big guy. Can you see someone really fast? It's that sailor with the black hair, David Teeny. . . . No, we met him in Wisconsin last month. . . . Yeah, at the buy . . . I dunno, he said he might have some later. . . . Okay."

"You can go in, Dave," she said, getting up and opening the door. The empty eyes of the pale painted king stared into his.

The Duke, who seemed to draw his fashion inspiration from Elvis Presley, wore a white silk jumpsuit with the four suits of cards printed as racing stripes going down his arms and the seams of his pants, which were tucked into white leather boots. His office was all business, save for a rug made out of a polar bear. Its snarling mouth pointed at the door.

The Duke was putting away papers and clearing his desk. Valentine noticed a gleaming revolver in easy reach used as a paperweight.

"Well, well, well. David Tiny, right? Didn't expect to see you so soon. I heard a boat from the Fleet was in, but it wasn't yours. What are you doing in Wisconsin blues? You jump ship?"

"Bull's-eye," Valentine said with a smile. "There was some bad blood with the captain. I'm searching for fairer horizons."

Valentine reached into his bag and pulled out one of the bottles of bonded whiskey. "Here you go, Mr. Duke. A little token of my esteem. Thanks for the great party that night at the Bunker."

"Hey, thanks, Tiny, you're two flavors of all right," the Duke said, reading the label. "So you're seeking a new opportunity. Ambitious fellow. Good for you. Hey, you wouldn't have another load of that high blue, would you?"

"Sorry, sir. But if I did, you'd get it." *All of it,* Valentine thought. *Wonder how you'd look after swallowing a pound of cocaine?*

The Duke seemed to lose interest. "Too bad. So, you gave up life on the waves and are toting a gun in Wisconsin. Any other plans?"

"Just a brass ring."

"Well, I wish you luck. Here's a card; you can get an evening's drinks at any of my clubs. And here's a backstage pass for the Hearts room. You're good-looking. One of the girls might take a shine to you. You'll find they're a lot more fun than those would-be dykes on that ship. Have Denise endorse it on your way out, would you?" the Duke said, putting his hand significantly on the phone.

"Sir, I'm new in town. I've got some barter I want to turn into cash. Where won't I get ripped off?"

The Duke's interest returned. "Sure, buddy, I can give you an opinion on that. What you got?"

Valentine placed the contents of his sack, save for his parang and Virgil Ames's pistol belt, on the Duke's desk, finishing by laying the Remington carefully on top. The Duke picked up the gun and worked the action. "Not bad, Dave. How'd you come up with this stuff after only a month in uniform?"

"Same way as I got the pass to come down here for three days. I did my captain a big favor."

"A favor? What kind of favor?"

"I promised not to say."

The Duke smiled. "I get it," he said, flicking the side of his nose with a finger. "I bet you took out the captain's rival. Or did the colonel get shot by insurgents and the captain take his place?"

"You're warm, but I can't tell you, sir. Sorry."

The Duke examined the rest of the loot. He plugged in the silver cigar lighter and worked it. "Hey, that's aces. Look nice down in the Club Room. Tell you what, since you're an old friend and all, I'll buy it all off you. Make it three grand, plus free drinks in the Hearts room while you're on your pass. This your first trip to Chicago? You can have a lot of fun on three grand."

"Yes, it is, Mr. Duke. But I think I can do better on Michigan Avenue."

"Hold on, son. Okay, five grand. I wish I could do better, but jewelry just isn't worth what it used to be."

"Mr. Duke, some patrollers told me about the Zoo. What's that?"

The Duke laughed. "The Zoo, huh? I guess your balls are working again after that kick you took. Well, the Zoo is the place for you, then. It's pricey, but it's a blast. Every night is anything-goes night. Ever seen a Grog fuck a woman? They got one there with a dick like your forearm. Hey, Tiny, tell you what. Just to seal the deal, how about I give you a three-day pass to the Zoo. Save you a grand right there."

Valentine reached into his pocket and pulled out the mirrored sunglasses. "You do that and give me a place to crash while I'm in town, and I'll throw these in."

"Let me see those," the Duke said. Valentine passed the

shades over, and the Duke looked at the wire-thin frame. "These are twentieth century, maybe." He gently flexed a bow. "Hell, real titanium. Okay, Dave, you got your place to sleep. Have Denise set you up in one of the rooms above the Club Room. There's even a shower down the hall. You can get yourself all squeaky clean for your night at the Zoo."

"And my five grand?"

"Coming, coming. Gotta hit the old bank."

The Duke walked across his office to the rear and swung a velvet painting of a grinning jester's face away from the wall. A gray, formidable-looking safe sat in the wall behind. Whistling, the Duke spun the combination and opened the door, which was layered with multiple panels of steel. He extracted a pad of bills with a thick rubber band around it and walked over, handing it to Valentine.

"Five thou, my friend. Pleasure doing business with you."

Valentine pulled up the first bill and flipped through the others. "Hey, most of these aren't authorized!" he objected.

The Duke slapped him on the shoulder. "Good eye, Dave, good eye. I knew you were sharp! That was just a test to see what kind of an edge your mental blade has. Here, give me that back, I'll get you the real stuff."

The Duke wandered over to a decorative roulette table stacked with bottles of fine liquor. He spun the wheel to a point Valentine could not determine and pulled up the spinner. He reached into the space beneath the wheel and took out a sheaf of bills. He hurriedly counted.

"Okay, all this is authorized, Dave. Scout's honor. But spend it all—that stamp's good only for a couple more weeks. Then you gotta stand in line for a new issue. Counterfeiters make it tough on us hardworking smugglers."

Valentine checked again, seeing the red circle with cryptic squiggles stamped over the face of Ben Franklin on each bill.

He picked up the now almost-empty sack. "Thanks, Duke. I want my first trip to Chicago to be a memorable one."

"Don't mention it. If you decide to move here, I might be able to connect you to a job. For, say, fifteen percent out of your first year's paychecks. I could even need a favor myself someday. You might be able to help me with that, and I'd be able to give you a hell of a lot more in return than your captain, or whatever he is. And Chicago beats the hell out of living up in Cheeseland."

"It's my kind of town," Valentine agreed.

Valentine arranged for his room with Denise. The room was small and clean and had a mattress to die for. Valentine inspected the late Virgil Ames's pistol again. It was an old army Colt automatic, firing the powerful .45 ACP cartridge. It wouldn't necessarily stop a Reaper, but it would give it something to think about. The gun belt also held four spare magazines, all of which were full. With the ammunition in the gun, that gave him thirty-five rounds. More than enough, as he did not want to use the weapon except as a last resort.

Valentine stretched out on the bed and forced himself to sleep for two hours. He showered and put the gun belt and his knife back in his pillowcase sack.

He ate downstairs in the Club room. The food was simple, satisfying, and overpriced: He paid twenty-five dollars for an overloaded sandwich and a pot of tea. He looked at an employee working on a case that held smoking paraphernalia and had a thought.

"Excuse me, sir," he said to the server behind the counter. "Do you have any waterproof matches?"

"Huh?" the waiter asked, flummoxed.

"He means the big matches in the tins," the man arranging cigars in the display case said. Valentine noticed a tattoo with a dagger stuck through a skull on his arm. "They work good even in the rain."

"Yeah, that's what I'm looking for," Valentine agreed. "I'm outside a lot, and it's a bitch to light a cigar in wet weather."

"Here's what you want," the cigar man said, putting a circular tin in front of Valentine. Valentine unscrewed the lid and extracted a three-inch match. The entire thing was lightly coated with a waxy substance. Valentine struck one on the strip at the side of the tin, and it flared into a white light. He could feel the heat on his face. "That's magnesium," the man explained. "It'll get a cigar going in any wind, unless your tobacco is soaked, of course."

"Hey, thanks. Can't find these in Wisconsin. How much for a tin?"

"They ain't cheap. Fifty bucks for a tin of ten matches."

"If I buy five tins, will you give them to me for two hundred?"

"Sure, seeing as you're a friend of the man upstairs."

"Done," Valentine agreed, and toked the man the other fifty.

"You must not get to Chicago often."

"No, there's lots of things here that you can't get in Wisconsin. Like the Zoo."

The tattooed man looked wistful. "Yes, but I can't afford to go there often. Once in a while I buy a cheap pass off the Duke."

"Ever been to the Black Hole?"

"Oh sure, I've checked it out a couple of times. I've got a strong stomach for that kind of thing. Some of it even turned me on."

"Do they ever let regular guys get at the girls, or is it just shows?"

"Oh, if you've got a couple thou in cash, they got these

rooms in the basement. Soundproofed, you know. And you can do anything you want. Anything. After all, the women and men in the Black Hole, well, they're the people that the Kur decided deserved something worse than the Loop."

"You don't know anyone who works there, do you?"

"Nahh, sorry. Wish I did. But you seem to know how to toke. Just get the money in the right hands, and you'll be fine."

Valentine paid for his matches and took his leave of the eatery. He approached Wideload, still on duty, blocking the door like a parked dump truck.

"Leaving?" Wideload said, stepping aside to open the door after a glance outside. "Fun starts soon."

Valentine squeezed past the human obstacle and entered the street.

He turned and looked up the sidewalk in the direction of Lake Michigan. A black van, its windows reinforced with wire, stood on the curb in front of him. The initials *CSS* and a small logo were stenciled in white on its side. *The Chicago Security Service?*

Two grubby youths leaning on a corner stubbed out their half-smoked cigarettes.

A silent siren went off in Valentine's head. Tobacco in Chicago wouldn't be wasted by street punks. He heard footsteps behind him.

For a moment his body betrayed him: His legs turned to bags of water. When the handle on the back door of the CSS van turned, he knew the trap was being sprung.

Two massive arms enveloped him. Wideload locked his hands in a deadly variation of the Heimlich maneuver, but instead of pushing up into his diaphragm he pulled Valentine to him in a rib-squeezing embrace. Valentine's breath left him.

A second pair of men approached from across the street.

One, tall and thin wearing a red tank top and pair of chain-mail gloves, removed a pair of familiar sunglasses as he ran toward Wideload and his victim.

"You're—," Wideload started to say, when Valentine brought his booted heel down hard on his captor's instep. He thrust back his head, and felt a solid *thunk*. The bear hug ceased.

The four men closing on him were trying to trap him between the Clubs Flush wall and the CSS van. Its rusty back door swung open. He lashed out with his foot, kicking the door closed again. It shut on something, fingers or a foot; muffled howls echoed from inside the van.

He ran across the street, accidentally spilling a pair of riders on bicycles as they turned on their rubberless wheels to avoid him. The four pursuers tried to triangulate in on him, but he called on his speed and his legs answered. He cornered around a parked horse wagon so fast his feet skidded on the pavement. But he maintained his balance . . . just.

With open sidewalk ahead of him he broke into a loping run. A few loungers on doorsteps stared as he passed. He chanced a glance over his shoulder; the four were sprinting to catch him.

Thirty seconds passed, and the four became three. In another minute, the three were two. By the time Valentine turned a corner, running up a series of short cluttered blocks, the two had become one: the tall man with the chain-mail gloves. His red tank top was dark with sweat.

Valentine turned down an alley and found breath in his body to do one more sprint. He zigzagged around fetid mountains of refuse, scattering rats with his passage. His pursuer just managed to start down the alley as Valentine turned the corner at the other end. To the east down this street he saw an end to the buildings. *I must be near the lakeshore . . . and the Zoo.*

He pressed himself up against the corner and listened to his pursuer's heavy breathing and heavier footsteps as he trotted up the alley. The man slowed, sucking wind as he approached the alley's exit.

When he knew the man was about to come around the corner, Valentine lunged. He brought his knee up into the winded man's groin. Chain-Mail Gloves managed to avoid the blow, but Valentine's thick thigh still caught him in the stomach. The blow was just as debilitating: The Chicago air left Chain-Mail Gloves's lungs in a gasp, and he bent over in breathless agony. In no mood for a fair fight, Valentine grabbed his assailant by his hair and brought his knee up again. Cartilage gave way with a sickening crunch. The man went down, now out of what wasn't much of a fight to begin with.

The Wolf shuddered, still keyed up. He pulled the gloves from the unconscious man and added them to his sack of weapons, then trembled again. But for a different reason.

A Reaper. Coming, and already so near.

Valentine tried to clear his mind, make it as empty and transparent as a paneless window. He stepped back into the shadows of the alley, moving away from the Reaper. At the other end, he dug himself into a pile of trash, burrowing on his knees and elbows into the filth. He felt cockroaches crunch and crawl as he joined them at the bottom of the sodden refuse pile.

The alley grew colder.

up, you, up, Valentine heard a Reaper say, seemingly in his ear.

The Wolf almost leaped to his feet, ready to fight and die, when he realized the voice was at the end of the alley with the Duke's thug.

Center, center, I've got to center or . . ., David thought frantically.

you, foodling—where is the terrorist?

"Murfer . . . motherfucker jumped me," the man groaned, in the sharp honking tones of a man with a broken nose. "I dunno . . . speak clear, willya? Who? Ohmygod!"

awake now?

"Yessir . . . umm, I think he went . . . toward the lake? That's where he was running. Sorta."

you were supposed to follow him, not take him.

"The Duke said—"

the duke isn't here, or he would be taken . . . instead of you!

A motor at Valentine's end of the alley drowned out the Reaper's low hissing voice. He looked out from beneath his garbage and saw a gleaming red car stop. One of the punks who had dropped out of the footrace sat on the hood, directing it. Rats scattered again as the man jumped off and the passenger door opened.

Valentine heard screaming, the terrible gurgling sound of a man being fed on, from the other end of the alley. The cold spot on Valentine's mind marking the Reaper swelled and pulsed as it conducted the aura to its Master Vampire. All around the neighborhood Valentine heard doors slamming and windows closing.

From beneath a mass of flattened cardboard Valentine watched the Duke, in all his gauche splendor, blanch as he looked down the alley. The Duke gulped, and slunk into the alley toward the scene. His henchman trailed him for two steps, then thought better of it and returned to the car. The Duke rubbed the brass ring on his finger. Valentine wondered if he sought comfort in its touch, or perhaps imagined what having his finger pulled off would feel like. The Wolf read mortal fear in the Duke's eyes before he passed. He let his ears take over, afraid to shift his position. The Reaper had senses other than that which allowed it to read auras.

the good duke, the Reaper whispered, slowly and thickly. *eight years with a brass ring courtesy of his aura-drunk lord. dealer of powder-white chemical joy. harborer of terrorists.*

"How was I to know, sir?"

you are too ready to do business first and ask questions not at all. you have tap-danced close to the edge of the law too many times: others in the order are beginning to take notice. like this fiasco. my instructions were not clear?

"I just thought—"

you're kept alive to do, not think, the Reaper hissed.

"Well, why should that damn renegade get my money anyway, sir? He's up to no good; throw him in the clink and be done with him."

that "damn renegade" is something special. one of my clan sensed him coming into the train yard. we want to know, who he is going to meet, what they know, and what they plan. his kind do not just wander into town to look around. he's one of that breed our foe-kin use for their dirty work. clean up this mess and return to your club. we will take over the search.

"He said he was going to the Zoo."

a cover story. or perhaps . . .

"What shall I do with my man?"

throw the corpse to the snappers. i go now, to find what you have lost. i felt his aura hot and clear for a moment as he fought with your man, i can find him again.

The chilling spot in Valentine's mind moved away. He waited while the Duke had another henchman carry the corpse to his trunk. By the time they left the alley, it had grown dark.

Valentine emerged from underneath the garbage and left

the alley. He concentrated on keeping lifesign down, casting about for somewhere to get some clean clothes. He found a used-leather-goods store and purchased four cheap belts and a long leather trench coat that was missing some buttons. He put the black coat on after paying for it. In an alley, he put on the gun belt and the parang and filled his pockets with the tins of matches. He tucked a belt up his left sleeve and rolled the others up and put them in his pants pockets. His remaining cash lay folded in his breast pocket, next to his identity papers and a small white card.

Well, I'm as ready for the Zoo as I'll ever be, Valentine thought. *Pray God the Zoo isn't ready for me.*

Thirteen

The Zoo: Lincoln Park, a green oasis between the shores of Lake Michigan and the shattered city, is considered the premier entertainment tract of Chicago, and indeed the Midwest. From what had been the oldest zoo in the United States at the south to the Elks' temple in the north, Lincoln Park as run by the Kurians is a mixture of Sodom and Mardi Gras. Along with its adjacent gambling ship tied up at the old Chicago Yacht Club in Belmont Harbor, it offers diversions to suit the most jaded palate. From late March to November, "Carnalval" is in session. This nonstop party provides much-needed relief for the favored Quislings who are allowed to attend. During Chicago's dreary winters, the action is limited to the indoors but remains just as wild. With good behavior, a Midwestern Quisling can expect a trip into Chicago to visit the Zoo every few years. They are released in groups, and anywhere from two to a hundred go to Chicago together, with the direst warnings about what will happen to the rest should any desert. Parties from places as far away as Canada, Ohio, and even Colorado and Kansas visit for up to a month. But as the money runs out to the point that even shoes are sold to pay for unholy delights, the trips are ended early by mutual consent. Everyone knows the destination for those left penniless in a city where there is no such thing as a free meal or room.

Within the confines of the Zoo, there is no curfew as there is everywhere else in the city. There is ample if poor-quality food and drink to be had at any hour from street vendors, tented cantinas, and permanent restaurants. Mounted officers, equipped like the statue of Phil Sheridan with sword and pistol, patrol the area from their headquarters in the old Chicago Historical Society building. They do very little to break up disturbances, and only a fistfight that threatens to grow into a riot will cause them to do anything but pause and sit their horses to watch. Everyone from magicians to three-card monte operators to street musicians tries to make a living on the streets, but nothing can be sold on the grounds of the park save food, drink, tobacco, drugs, and flesh.

It is this last that is the real attraction of the Zoo. Under every lamppost, at every corner, and inside every barroom, women, a few men, and the occasional child can be found for a price. At the top of the carnal hierarchy are the showgirls, performing everything from stripteases in the clubs on Clark to variegated sexual displays behind the bars of the Zoo that would make those performed in pre-Kurian Bangkok seem tame. Next come the geishas. These women, found in some of the better bars, act as short-term girlfriends to the Quislings on vacation who want more than just sex, providing a sympathetic ear as well as other favors. The full-time companionship of a geisha for a week or two is out of the price range of all but the wealthiest Quislings, but bar girls in the saloons will do the same as long as the soldier keeps buying them watery drinks. Finally there are the colorful streetwalkers in a variety of flavors, offering their services anywhere from alley and bush to the little flotilla of old boats anchored in the park's Lake Michigan–fed waterways.

The careers of the Zoo women are short, and most come to a sad end in the Loop. A few make enough money to retire to Ringland or open an establishment of their own. A few more

*leave the Zoo permanently in the company of a Quisling. But
for most, it is a degrading road that leads to servicing the
most perverted and violent customers before the final trip
downtown.*

*As for the Quislings, like carnivorous flowers attracting
insects with bright color and perfume, only to trap and devour
them within, the wanton joys of the Zoo leave many too broke
to get home and, unless they are smart or lucky, they become
prime candidates for the Loop.*

The night breeze no longer blew just cool, but downright
cold. Scattered clouds crossed the full moon like inky stains.
Below, the color had drained from Chicago's streets, leaving
a world of low-contrast black and white. As Valentine drew
farther away from Rush Street, the streetlights became irregular, and those that still functioned gave light to a few square
yards around the pole. Scattered figures clutched their coats
or thrust hands deep into their pockets, shoulders hunched
against the wind as they brushed past Valentine without a
word or a glance. Beater cars and small trucks chugged along
the streets, most without benefit of headlights, as clattering
bicycles dodged out of their way. Valentine could hear the
clopping sound of hoofbeats on pavement down a nearby
alley. He cast about with his nose; the city seemed overwhelmed by an oily petroleum smell and dusty coal smoke.
The gutters reeked of urine.

Valentine glanced up again at the moon. Its chalky white-
ness comforted him somehow. *Full moon, good night for a
Wolf.* But a sudden wave of fear passed through him, leaving
his back running with cold sweat and his hair bristling. He
paused under a light, ostensibly to check his map, when motion ahead caught his eye.

Pedestrians parted like a school of fish swerving to avoid

a cruising shark. A Reaper garbed in a shirt, trousers, boots, and a cape—rather than the usual robes—moved toward the dead heart of the city. It ran with great multiyard leaps, like a deer bounding through the woods. Valentine's hand fell instinctively toward his gun, but he managed to change the gesture into a simple thrust of his fist into his coat pocket. The Reaper passed without a glance in his direction, its sickly yellow eyes blazing like tiny lightbulbs. Valentine turned and watched it go. It reached the back of a slow-moving car, a ramshackle vehicle with wood planks where the panels and roof used to be. The Hood leaped over it in a single bound, cape flapping like bat wings in the night, and disappeared out of sight as the startled driver stood on his squealing brakes.

Somewhere to the east, Valentine could hear Lake Michigan lapping at its breakwaters. He sensed lights and music somewhere to the north, a mass of noise that could only mean the Zoo. To either side of him, ruined blocks of rubble sprouted shanties like wooden toadstools. Some buildings still stood and showed signs of irregular maintenance—everything from glass to iron bars to wooden shutters covered the windows, and the smells of cooking wafted out into the street. He could make out trees in the lights ahead, and now several figures had joined him in moving toward the Zoo. Most of them had brightly colored cards dangling from thin beaded chains around their necks.

He noticed a line at a kiosk on the edge of the park and joined the cluster of waiting men, almost all of whom wore assorted uniforms. An elephantine redheaded woman sold the white cards on chains to the lined-up men under the supervision of a cigar-smoking baldie with the watchful, sullen air of a pit boss. Valentine looked at the prices, which started at five hundred dollars a day. He extracted the pass he'd obtained from the Duke and passed it to the meaty hand of the redhead.

"Three-day pass, huh, boy?" the woman said, reaching under her counter for a card on a chain. "You one of the Duke's couriers?"

The supervisor's eyes narrowed as he evaluated Valentine.

"Sort of," Valentine said. "What do I get with the pass?"

She did not really smile so much as smirk, but her eyes favored his with a friendly twinkle. "About anything your heart desires." She peeled a covering off the paper and began to recite the rules in almost a singsong manner. "This card will stay green for seventy-two hours; that's guaranteed. When it turns red, you gotta leave the premises. But while it's green you can see any show, go in any bar, and get free coffee or iced tea on the *Lady Luck of the Lake* if you're playing. That's the gambling boat," she added, breaking out of the recitation. "Real plush carpets and more lights than you've seen at once in your whole life, I'll bet."

A gruff voice broke in from over Valentine's shoulder. "Hey, there's people waiting."

"Shut your trap, you," she barked, "or I'll start readin' to him outta the '22 yellow pages." She turned her attention back to Valentine, drawing close enough for him to smell the beer fumes on her breath. "You take my advice; just spend your three days here. The food's cheaper than most anywhere in Chicago, and when you want to sleep just pay one of the girls for an all-nighter. You'll get a woman and a bed for what you'd pay for a bed alone in one of them ripoff hotels by the Michigan Avenue Market. And a guy with your looks will maybe get another tumble in the morning, free of charge."

Valentine slipped her a bill. She slid the toke into her udder-size bosom with a deftness that belied her size. "You got a map?" he asked.

"Listen to him," the voice from behind grunted. "Kid thinks he's in Dizzyland."

"Naw, it ain't that big a place. You'll find your way around. Why, you lookin' for something in particular?"

"The Black Hole. I heard it's really weird."

She did not look surprised. "It's always you nice-looking, quiet ones," she mused. "You can't miss it. North side of the Zoo, a big lit-up pit with walls all around. Last night the Grogs worked over this little beauty from Michigan. By the time they were done, she didn't have enough blood in her to fill up a Reaper's tongue. I hear the main attraction tonight's gonna be some real cute young thing from your Wisconsin. Enjoy."

"Nattie, you got other customers," the cigar-chomper said.

"Okay, okay. Just talkin' to the Duke's friend. The Duke would want us to make sure he got happy here. Geez, where'd he go?"

Valentine heard her expostulation as he strode off across Clark Street and into the Zoo, but the noise of music and shouting soon drowned her out. Bars lined the road on Clark, marching up north toward darkened high-rises. He glanced at a few of the names: Paradise Found, Jack Off With Jill On, the Gold Coast Grotto . . . Heavily made-up women enticed customers inside, strutting and promising greater delights within. He ignored the twinkling tableaux and moved into the cluster of old Zoo buildings. Women in assorted stages of undress challenged him with everything from a throaty "Hi, there," to a bellowed "Best head in the Zoo, twenty bucks!—Over here, handsome." A sickly stench struck him, and he stepped around a pool of vomit half covering the sidewalk. A shoeless drunken shape in bright orange overalls leaned against a boulder with the words EVERYTHING GOES scrawled in white paint across its chipped surface.

There seemed to be nothing preventing people from coming and going as they wished, but security troops mounted and on foot wandered the grounds, mostly looking at the colored cards dangling from the revelers' necks. One of them motioned to an apelike Grog, pointing at the shoeless drunk. Valentine watched as the Grog hoisted the man into a wheelbarrow cart and trotted off, pushing the drunkard south on wobbly wheels.

A long lagoon filled with little boats bordered the Zoo. Couples got on and off in a steady stream. Far to the north, Valentine spotted a glittering wedding-cake shape of light, obviously the *Lady Luck of the Lake*. He circled back into the Zoo's cluster of buildings from the north. A couple of small Grogs were picking up trash from the sidewalks and grass. Valentine walked up to them and pressed some very special toke into their hands before moving off toward another crowd.

A domed cage the size of a tepee stood in the center of a little depression. A ring of twenty or thirty laughing soldiers stood around it, hurling small stones and pieces of fruit through the bars. An extraordinarily tall man, dressed in a simple khaki uniform, stood before the crowd with a long pole with a metal club on one side and what looked like a noose on the other.

"Hey, let's have him change shape again," one of the men called, throwing a small rock into the well-lit center of the cage. He passed some bills to the khaki-uniformed man.

Valentine craned his neck to look within the bare cage. A single tree, barkless and dead as a piece of driftwood, decorated the twelve-foot circle within. A serpent lay coiled around the tree, hiding its head in the crotch between two branches.

"I can get him to switch, no fail," the keeper said, and poked the metal end of the pole into the cage. He rapped the snake twice on the head.

A shiver seemed to course up the body of the snake, a shiver that turned into a blur. Before Valentine's astonished eyes, the snake transformed into an orangutan, which hung from the tree by one long arm and then dropped to the ground. It thrust a rotten apple in its mouth and worked its jaws hungrily.

"How the hell did you do that?" a voice called from the crowd.

"I didn't do it, he did," the keeper explained. "What you have here is a relative of the Kurians. It's the only one that's been captured and put on display. They can change their shape at will, and they can practically go invisible. They're the masters of some of the terrorists and rebels that hide out in the hills. The rebs worship them as gods. Only way to please them is to bring scalps, and the rebs aren't particular about whose hair they take. They tell me this one had fifteen, twenty little blond scalps. God knows what the rebs did to them before lifting their hair."

"Motherfucker," one of the soldiers said, throwing a stone in at the seated figure. The rock made an impact in the sand next to the orang, kicking dirt up onto it.

The orang's eyes gazed sadly over the crowd. A few more stones flew in, some hitting the illusory ape on its broad back. Its eyes met Valentine's, and he jumped as if shocked by the spark that passed between their eyes.

Lee . . . Lee Valentine, a voice said inside his head. *Please let this not be the madness again. Oh, Lee, is it you, can you be here? It's Rho, the Ancient. Of the firstwalkers. By the Bonds and by the Gates, have you come to end my torments? Please say Paul Samuels is with you somewhere, and Ghang Ankor. The years . . . the years have sung their songs and moved the earth itself since we last met. Please say I will be finally free of their smacks and stares.*

All this passed through Valentine's mind in a flash. He responded. *No, I am not the Valentine you knew. I am his son, David. My father has been dead for over ten years.*

Son? Son? I can sense you are a Hunter. I do not know what brings you here, but I feel it is not I. You are anxious to be gone and fearful and worried and hateful and hopeful and . . . in love. Oh, I would cast myself into oblivion if I could, but they watch, always watch, with their dull eyes. You cannot know what I've been through. Years of abuse and bad weather and no food and torment. The orangutan stared at Valentine. Please just kill me if you cannot get me out. If my life runs its course, I could be here for hundreds of years until these bars turn to rust and new ones replace it.

Something sought his mind. Valentine pulled back and into himself.

I'm sorry, so sorry, Valentine thought, breaking out of the ring and filling his mind with *sorry* over and over again. The agony of the trapped Lifeweaver had been palpably transmitted through its thoughts. Valentine could not let despair overtake his mind with Molly waiting in some cage and a Reaper hunting for his lifesign.

He hurried past the converted animal displays. Inside one, a nude woman cavorted upon an artificial tree, alternately hiding and exposing herself to the whistling admirers. A few men threw money into the cage, and she picked up a thick green cucumber and sucked on it. More bills littered the floor of the cage, and she began to move one end of the spit-moistened vegetable down across her breasts and belly.

He reached an open pit. Black paint covered the stone barriers surrounding it and forming the deep walls of a large hollow. A uniformed Zoo patroller sat on the wall, idly smoking a sharp-smelling cigarette. Valentine approached the pit and looked in. A central mound, built up to the point that it was almost level with the ground outside the pit, sported two stone lions facing each other. From the mouth of each dangled a long leather strap, and the ground between the opposing lions had badly stained rugs spread out, covering the dirt. A Grog was scrubbing at the broad back of one of the lions, trying to remove bloodstains. To the far south in the pit, a gallowslike structure had a pair of ladders leaning against it and numerous hooks embedded in the posts and lintel. To the far right on the north end, a simple pole lay buried in the ground, with four sets of shackles dangling from the top. Valentine took in this three-ring circus of de Sade and moved over toward the smoking patroller.

"Is there going to be a show tonight?" Valentine asked, handing him one of the few remaining cheroots.

"You bet your ass. In a couple hours. You lining up for a good view?"

"Maybe. What do they do?"

"Make the ladies here scream themselves to death," the patroller said, putting the cheroot in his mouth and lighting it with the end of the hand-rolled cigarette. The scrubbing Grog paused in his work and watched the glowing red tip of the cheroot as the patroller inhaled.

A group of soldiers, civilians, and hookers walked by. Half-empty bottles dangled from their hands. While passing the pit, one of the prostitutes whispered something into her escort's ear. "Yeah, I seen a Black Hole show before," her john answered. "I've even seen Reapers in the audience."

"I heard that private parties can be arranged," Valentine ventured, after the party passed on.

The officer blew out the rich smoke with an air of approval. "If you've got the cash, just about anything is possible."

Valentine slipped the officer a hundred dollars. He glanced

at the bill for a second before it disappeared into his shirt pocket. "I'll get you in to see the Head Keeper, sport. Wait here. He agrees to talk to you, you gimme another toke the same size."

"Fair enough," Valentine agreed. The patroller moved off toward a long brick building with a busy rooftop eatery.

Valentine looked at the Grog, who was similar in size to the one at the Miskatonic University. He lit a match from the tin and waved it back and forth. The Grog applauded with a childlike, patty-cake motion and waddled down toward the edge of the pit by Valentine. It looked up at Valentine expectantly.

"You want to see more?" Valentine asked. The Grog cocked its head from side to side like a woodpecker looking for termites. Valentine looked around, but the few Zoo patrons close by were paying no attention to the empty Black Hole.

The Wolf took out one of his tins of matches and rattled it for the Grog. The Grog held out both of its hands, just like the inhabitant of the Institute's catacombs. Valentine tossed the tin down to it. The Grog gave a little hoot of pleasure and thrust the matches into a pocket in its tattered trousers. Valentine made a slow circle of the Black Hole and found another Grog changing lightbulbs on a lamppost. He tried to hand a few more matches to the low-caste worker, but it shook its head and put its hands behind its back. Perhaps it had been punished in the past for something to do with matches.

Valentine's patroller, still smoking the long cheroot, returned. "You're golden," he said. "It's getting toward the end of the year, and they're not so busy anymore. You want to visit before or after the show? Sometimes it gets a little crowded after. Plus, there's a few less girls to choose from, you know?"

Valentine forced a smile. "Thanks. I'll see him now, if that's okay with you." Valentine handed over another hundred dollars in toke.

"Wise choice. After the show, Burt's usually drunk and ornery anyway. He tries, but he's just not smart enough to come up with new ways of killing people every week. Plus, he's pissed 'cause they're making him do a show tonight. He'd rather wait until the weekend, advertise it a little bit and work up a decent crowd. They toss in money and tell him what to do. But I guess the management wants this girl done fast and dirty . . . ho now, button up a sec," the patroller said, looking up at a Reaper moving down the path. It felt similar to the one who had pursued him to the alley. David assumed it was still searching for him. Or perhaps it was one of his siblings, animated by the same Master Vampire.

Valentine breathed slowly and deeply, letting his eyes go out of focus. Death passed in silence.

The officer led Valentine though a wooden fence screened by trees and overgrown shrubbery. The patroller rapped on the door and called, "Open up, Todd, it's me. I've brought a customer for Burt."

The brown-painted door swung open, and Valentine followed the patroller past a shotgun-toting guard and into a long brick building with a green peaked roof. It was half barn, half fort. The patroller brought Valentine to a metal door and opened it with a key from a small ring on his belt. He entered, holding the door open for Valentine.

They walked down a hallway and entered a linoleum-floored room. An unshaven man sat in a chair, legs extended and arms dangling tiredly. A few more chairs stood against the walls, and an empty desk at the corner shone under a hooded light. The cop gestured toward one of the open chairs.

"Take a seat. Looks like there's not much action tonight. I'll go get Burt."

Valentine sat down opposite the rag-doll figure. The bedraggled man wore a jumpsuit, new and shiny, made out of what looked to Valentine like nylon. He had long, unkempt black hair and a mustache. A prisoner-like pallor made his skin seem anemic against his dark beard. A pair of comfortable-looking black sports shoes with new soles covered his feet. Obviously a favored Quisling, if a tired and dirty-looking one. The jumpsuit had a high collar, almost a turtleneck, and Valentine had to look twice at the insigne in silver stitching just under the man's chin: a reversed swastika. *The Twisted Cross?* Valentine thought.

The man, noticing Valentine's stare, yawned and looked across the room at him.

"Howdy, pal," the man in black said. "Burt's kinda slow tonight. He's probably in one of the bars on Clark drinking. I've been waiting almost an hour." He had a drawling accent which Valentine identified as more western than southern.

Valentine looked at the pattern on the linoleum floor. It resembled a cross section of sedimentary rock strata. "I'm in no hurry. Got a three-day pass, and it's my first night."

"You in the Service?"

"Yes. In the patrols. Madison Triumvirate. How about you?"

"I get around. I'm on the General's Staff."

Valentine hazarded finesse. "You're Twisted Cross, right? You guys work pretty tight with the Reapers. Where are you operating now?"

"Some people up here call us that. Can't discuss it, though. You know, security."

"Oh, I hear you. Looks like they work you pretty hard."

The man smiled. "Depends on your definition of work. But it is exhausting, in its own way."

Valentine nodded. "You look kind of sick or something."

"This is nothing. You should have seen me when I first got out of the tank. I'd been connected for six days. Couldn't even stand up until they got some orange juice in me."

Valentine nodded. "Sounds like tough duty. I'm sure it's more interesting than driving around in an old car, though, making sure nobody's hiding milk cows in the hills."

"Funny, I've never been to Wisconsin, but damn if you don't look familiar," the man mused.

"You been up in the north woods?"

"No."

Valentine fought the urge to lower his face, but he looked the man square in the eye. "Then I don't know where else you might've seen me. I've never been south of Indianapolis."

The man shrugged. "I dunno. I never forget a face, and—"

A heavy tread echoed from the hallway, and the cop returned, escorting a shuffling man with the bulky build of a power lifter. He had a battered face that looked like he drove railroad spikes with it. "Burt, this guy wants to do some business with you," the patroller said.

"Sure, sure. Be with you in a minute, kid. Hey, Jimmy King, you look tuckered. You need the usual?"

"A nice juicy one, Burt."

There was a look of raw lust in the man's eyes like nothing Valentine had ever seen. It sickened him, but he was glad of it; the mystery of Valentine's face was plainly the last thing on Jimmy King's mind at the moment.

Burt grinned. "Then follow. Pickings are a little slim this time of year, but I know you ain't particular. Some of your friends have been through, and I have a lot of empty cells."

As Burt and Jimmy King left the room, Valentine toked the cop yet again. "Thanks again," he said.

"Have fun, kid. Pleasure doing business with you."

As soon as the cop had passed out the metal door to the yard, Valentine hardened his ears. Burt and the Twisted Cross man seemed to be going down some stairs.

"Got the old thirst, huh?" Burt asked.

"You know it," King said, his rubber-soled feet squeaking a little against the stone stairs.

"Your bro recovered from that shotgun blast yet?"

"Yeah, sure. He won't win any dance contests, but he gets around well enough. For a while there, I was limping even when I wasn't in the tank."

"How long were you hooked up this time?"

"Almost a week. Fucker fed three times. Made me want it so bad I almost bit the guy pulling me out. But the general was happy with what we did; gave the whole team two weeks off. We wiped out a whole nest of rebs in the Smokies."

Valentine heard keys rattling and the sound of a door being opened somewhere below.

"General shouldn't make you pull such long shifts. I heard some of your guys went nuts after . . ."

The clang of the door shutting echoed loudly enough for Valentine to hear with soft ears. The voices were gone.

He waited fifteen minutes before the basement door opened again, and Burt's ponderous step ascended the stairs, key ring jangling. Burt returned to the linoleum-floored room, and Valentine rose to meet him.

"My name's Pillow, sir. First visit to the Zoo."

"Burt Walker. Chief of One-Way Exhibits."

"One-Way?"

"Now and then we get troublemakers the management

wants to make an example of. Don't matter how they die, as long as it's ugly. Whatcha lookin' for, Pillow? Something the girls out there can't handle?"

"You might say that. It's something I don't like talking about."

"Hey, kid, I heard it all, believe me," Burt said, in a rich, world-weary tone. "But I respect people's privacy. You just gotta let me know one thing. . . . Will she still be alive when you're done? 'Cause if you kill her, I gotta charge you big-time."

"She'll live, Mr. Walker. That's a promise."

"Okay, then, but remember what I said and don't get carried away. I gotta see the cash, though."

Valentine flashed his breast-pocket wad. "I want to see the girls first. I'm willing to pay, but I don't want anyone whose already used up. Someone kind of innocent and fresh," Valentine said.

"Hey, Pillow, you want innocent and fresh, you have to come to the special show tonight. When I saw her, I almost decided to come out of retirement. But I'll let Clubber and Valkyrie and my two best Grogs do her."

Walker took Valentine to the basement stairs.

"This'll be private, right?"

"Kid, there's curtains on the cells. Don't worry about noise; no one's going to disturb you."

They came up against the metal basement door. Walker thumbed through a ring of keys and opened it. They passed though to a spacious lower level.

It reminded Valentine of a stable, except for the dirty white tile everywhere. A series of cells with barred doors lined the walls. Valentine smelled blood, urine, and feces without even using his hard sense of smell. Another man in a khaki uniform sat at a desk, talking animatedly over a phone.

"Hey, Burt! There are problems up top. There's a fire in the Grog pens, and the stables. Can you believe it?"

"Oh, fine," Walker said, disgusted. "Stupid Grogs. 'Cause they're cheap and eat anything, we gotta employ 'em. They're more trouble than they're worth. Find Clubber and go help out at the stables. I don't give a shit if the Grog pens burn right to the ground. They can spend the winter under Lakeshore Drive for all I care."

The man nodded and disappeared up the stairs to the first floor.

"Okay, kid. Check out the cells, and then we'll talk price."

One of the doors slid open, and Jimmy King staggered out. He was nude, hollow chested, with spindly arms and legs. His face was covered in blood, and it ran down his chest into a mat of sticky black hair. He wiped blood from his eyes with slow, tired movements.

"Hey, King," Walker called. "Go use the hose, will ya? You're dripping all over the place."

The Twisted Cross man went to a washbasin with a floor drain beneath and began to hose himself off. Valentine walked up and down the cells, looking at the battered, pathetic figures behind the bars. Most of the stable-stall-size rooms were empty, and one held the remains of King's purchase, lifeless legs spread wide and throat torn messily open. Valentine reached a smaller hallway, empty of cells with another gate at the end of it, and wandered down it. The sliding barred door blocked his way, and he could see a long, poorly lit tunnel on the other side of the bars.

Something from down the tunnel tickled at his nostrils. He hardened his sense of smell and sniffed at the air. His heart skipped a beat as he recognized the odor of rose-petal soap. He returned to the tiles of the wide central hallway.

King had dressed again and was leaving, almost scuttling

out the door to the upstairs. Walker shook his head and hefted
his bulk up from behind the desk.

"Okay, boy. I'm a busy man. Which one? King's left me
with a mess for the Grogs to clean up."

"Sir, how about you let me have the one for tonight's
show? I won't even bruise her."

"Naw, sorry, kid. I'm already in Dutch about her. One of
the guys got a little rough when she first got here, and I caught
hell. They want her with a lot of energy for the show, you
know? The guys always like it better if they aren't half-dead
to begin with."

Valentine looked in one of the pens at a curled up, sleeping black woman. "This one looks unspoiled. But I think she
might be dead. I can't see her breathing."

"Eh? What's that?"

"I don't see anything moving. And her head's at sort of a
funny angle."

Walker came over to the cage, reaching for an old-
fashioned key. He looked inside.

"What the hell are you talking 'bout, junior? I can see—
graak!"

Walker's last choked cry came as Valentine whipped the
thin leather belt, wrapped tightly in each fist around the man's
neck. The chief's massive frame heaved, and latissimus muscles the size of halved watermelons bulged against his shirt.
Valentine leaped onto Walker's back, wrapping his legs
around his thick waist, and pulled on the leather garrote until
his muscles flamed in agony. Walker crashed over backwards
onto Valentine, trying to crush him with his weight, but the
Chief of One-Way Exhibits weakened. Valentine rolled him
onto his stomach with a heave, digging his knee into his op-
ponent's kidneys. Walker flapped like a landed fish as the
muted crackling of his throat's collapsing cartilage sounded

through his gaping mouth. Valentine continued pulling until he could no longer hear a heartbeat. Then he stood, the odor of Walker's feces and urine rank in his nostrils.

He turned the chief over, avoiding looking into the bulging eyes. Removing the key ring and a club from Walker's belt, he pulled the body feetfirst into an open stall, closed the curtains, and slid the door shut, locking it. His hands shook as much from nerves as from muscular exhaustion as he went to the smaller corridor. The rose smell calmed him as he tried the barred gate. It did not yield until after he tried several different keys.

Perhaps the corridor had been brightly lit once, but now only a dank gloom filled his eyes. He used his nose to guide him, following the homing beacon of the rose smell to a cell door. The sound of quiet breathing behind the door reassured him.

"Molly, it's me, David . . . I'm here to get you out," he whispered, trying the keys. She did not respond, and he grew frantic. The lock finally yielded. He pushed the squealing door open. The cell was bare and dark, the cracked cement floor sliding down to a drainage hole.

Molly Carlson lay curled up in a corner, arms around her drawn-up legs, head resting sideways on her bare knees. She wore the tattered remnants of her white shirt from yesterday—*yesterday,* he thought, *or a year ago?*—and blood smeared the side of her face where it had dried from a bloody clot of pulled-out hair. Valentine's heart ached at the purple bruises on her face and in her eye sockets. He knelt next to her.

"Molly, Molly! *Molly,*" he almost shouted, gripping her hand. He patted the side of her pallid cheek and futilely searched for a response. He felt a strong, steady pulse under her wrist. *Was she drugged?*

He reached around her shoulders and under her knees. "I'll carry you out, then, Melissa," he said, lifting her into his arms.

Like a jinni summoned by the use of its name, her eyelids fluttered open. "David?" she croaked. "No . . . yes . . . how?"

He bore her out of the cell and down the tunnel, away from the basement. "Explanations will have to wait. We're both in a fix. But we're getting out of here," he said, quietly but with all the confidence he could muster.

Tearing himself away from the smell of roses on her skin, he caught the scent of fresh air and followed it like a blood-hound on a trail. Soon they reached a small corridor, jutting off from the main one at an empty doorframe. Following the now stronger odor of the outdoors, Valentine reached a short set of stairs.

"Can you walk?" he asked.

"I think so, David. I thought I was dead. I made my mind die."

Valentine looked into her battered features. He wanted to kiss her, but something in her haunted eyes held him back.

"Did they hurt you? Were you—?"

"Don't ask, David. Maybe I'll tell you someday. Now . . . now it's out of my mind, and it's staying out for a while. Where are we?"

"Chicago. The Zoo."

"That's where they said they were taking me. They said some big shots from downstate were going to come here and watch me . . . die."

"You're going to disappoint them, Molly."

"But you can't get out of Chicago. Not with me, anyway."

"Watch us."

"David, just shoot me. Shoot me and go, because after . . . I want you to get out, no matter what."

He looked down at her, shaking his head. "Oh, no . . . 'promises to keep, and miles to go before I sleep.' We'll be out of their reach by midnight, one way or the other."

"But how?"

"A Reaper is going to help us."

The arena of the Black Hole glowed under bright arc lights. Valentine heard distant fire bells and smelled smoke; the Grogs had made good use of their matches. He covered Molly with his leather coat and took her wrist, then brought her out into the bright lights of the pit. Giving her a boost up the side of one of the walls, he followed, taking her offered hand.

The cool night air chilled his skin, and Molly gripped the coat around her as her teeth chattered. Confusion hung in the air along with the smoke from the fires. Through the scattered trees, Valentine could see two fires burning, and noisy crowds clustered around, perhaps helping, perhaps simply enjoying the excitement. Valentine got his bearings and hurried along the deserted sidewalks, ignoring the knots of people rushing to and fro. He sensed Reapers searching near the fire.

In the little dome-shaped cage, the Lifeweaver now wore the shape of a large sloth. The audience that had been present earlier was gone now save for two drunks passing a greasy bottle back and forth. Ignoring them, the tall keeper snapped shut a final shackle to the sloth's curved paw and rapped it across the nose with a short black club similar to the one Valentine had taken from the body of the strangled chief. "Looks like you're done for the night," he said. "Everybody's watching the Grog Quarter go up in flames."

Valentine brought Molly around to the low cage door. "Hello, in there," he called, flashing a handful of bills. "When you're done, I need a favor."

A look of tired distaste came over the keeper. "Hey half-breed, beat it. Go get your Big Medicine elsewhere. Just 'cause it looks like an animal doesn't mean it actually is. It's just a trick. If you're looking to fuck an ostrich or something, you're outta luck."

The keeper fastened the last cuff to the dried-out tree limb and approached the door. Valentine passed him the bills with his left hand, casually holding the right behind his leg. The keeper grabbed the money, counting it with his eyes. "Okay, okay, you got my attention. Now what—," he began, bending almost double to squeeze his frame out of the low door to the cage.

The keeper never ended his sentence; the hard wooden shaft of the club crashed into the back of his skull with a *kraak.* The keeper dropped, unconscious or dead.

Valentine added the keys to his growing collection and hurried to the tree. The ones for Rho the Lifeweaver hung from a second, smaller ring. *If we make it, we live. If we don't, nobody's going to be an exhibit,* he silently promised himself, and Molly. And Rho. As he unfastened the leg irons on the sloth, he patted it gently on the head.

A Hunter? The other mind inside his head asked. A fleeting mental touch. *Valentine, it's you.*

The shape blurred again as it fell to the ground, released from its bonds. Valentine knelt and grasped it by the shoulders. He found himself looking into the rugged face of his own father.

"Dad?" Valentine found himself saying without even thinking about it.

The shape blurred again and became a hawk-nosed, deep-eyed old man with a tuft of white hair at the temples. "Sorry, Valentine the Younger. I was thinking of your father. My control isn't what it was," it said in a croaking voice.

Molly grabbed at the bars behind him. "David, we don't have much time. Those two drunks just took off!"

Valentine helped the Lifeweaver to his feet. "Sir, we have to move. Can you walk?"

"I would love to walk. Run even, Valentine. But I fear I won't be able to go far."

"I'll see what I can do. Now let's see what you can do," Valentine said, explaining his plan. "But we have to hurry."

Somewhere, somehow, the Reapers knew. He felt them coming.

Following a Reaper through the crowds made negotiating the press of humans a simple task. People parted for the Reaper like the Red Sea before the Israelites. Valentine and Molly only had to stay a respectful distance behind the flowing cape.

"Open your stride a little more," Valentine said in a low tone. The Reaper complied, almost goose-stepping into the street. "That one, the cab," Valentine added.

A dirty yellow lump of dented metal sagged to one side on a broken suspension. The Reaper stepped to the driver's side, reaching up to tap at the window, and paused, finding no window to tap on.

i need your ride, the Reaper breathed down at the driver. The grizzled driver looked up and lost perhaps two pounds while staring at the death's-head face gazing down at him.

Valentine and Molly climbed in, and the young woman sagged against Valentine the instant they were seated on the badly sprung bench. The Reaper joined them, squeezing into the backseat. The driver did not offer to have the Reaper sit up front.

"Where to, sir?" the driver asked, the effort to sound normal sticking in his throat.

the great pier, the Reaper said as Valentine pointed to his small map, which was illuminated by the streetlights shining into the car.

"Be there in five minutes, sir." The driver started his car. Valentine wondered if the man's hair had always been that gray. The taxi began to roll, engine sputtering as diesel fumes leaked into the car.

The Lifeweaver switched to his telepathy. It gripped Valentine's hand to make a more secure connection. *Valentine, you have saved me. In ways you cannot imagine.*

Don't fool yourself, he thought back. *We're not out of it yet.*

The audacity of this . . . It is worthy of your father. Once a Cat passed through the Zoo, but she was so sickened by the goings-on she barely touched my mind before hurrying away.

How well did you know my father?

I trained him, Valentine the Younger. I invoked him as a Wolf and saw in him the potential to be a great Bear. He and others forged Southern Command out of a few camps in the mountains. The worst days. But the Kurians grew to know and hate your father. He killed five of them. Not Grogs, not Reapers. Kurian Lords. They had a fortress in Saint Louis, suspended from the arch like a spider's egg sac. He stole a small plane and parachuted onto it. When he finished, no Kurian within ever drank another aura.

I never knew this, Valentine thought back after a moment.

He was the best of men, beyond our design.

Design?

He once had a family in the Free Territory, but they were swallowed in a battle that raged years before your birth. He sought solace in the remoteness of the north, and I never met him again. I hope he found some measure of happiness before he died.

He did, Valentine responded.

*   *   *

They made their way through the pier, checkpoints and all, with the same simplicity granted by Rho's Reaper aspect. Guards looked busy elsewhere, and port officials sprang into action, driving their work gangs into greater and greater efforts. Valentine urged them on, sensing a Reaper approaching from behind.

What had been Chicago's Navy Pier was now only an ill-lit and deserted utilitarian warehouse for merchandise moving into and out of Chicago by water. The great concrete pier sprouted wooden docks like leaves from a branch. Valentine found a responsible official by searching out the most well-maintained uniform.

"You there," he said, stepping from behind the Reaper. "Is there a ship here, the White-something-or-other?"

"*Whitecloud,* sir?" the officer said briskly. "She left this evening. Just under two hours ago. Probably halfway to Milwaukee by now."

Valentine's disappointment may have helped with the act. He thought for a moment. "Is it possible to still catch her?"

"Yessir. We have a fast motorized patrol boat. She could catch up in an hour."

bring it, the Reaper said, searching the dark horizon of the lake.

"Uh, follow me, sir," the man stammered. "There's only a skeleton crew. If you want more men for boarding, the *White-cloud* is pretty big, crew of a dozen or so—"

"I think we'll be enough. The woman there just needs to go on board and identify someone. There's a terrorist on board," Valentine explained.

The port official walked them down a long, narrow wooden dock extending into the lake, held up by thick wooden pilings. The warped wood creaked under their feet.

Ahead they could see a long, low shape. The aged speedboat gleamed in the distant reflected light of Chicago. Valentine prayed that they would still get away with no one questioning a Reaper's orders.

The Reaper.

The real Reaper was somewhere close.

Valentine tried to hurry the other three along by trotting out ahead toward the boat, his hackles rising like a wary dog's. Rho seemed to blur, but his Reaper aspect re-formed.

They've found me. They are homing. I give off lifesign like a firework, Valentine the Younger, the Lifeweaver thought to him.

The Reaper grew closer. Valentine knew it was just behind them now.

The port official scuttled up the gangway. He began speaking to a pair of figures on board. Valentine pressed the pistol into Molly's hand. "Keep this in your coat pocket," he whispered. "Don't let them take you alive."

The Reaper approached. Its cold shadow was at the jetty, moving down the boards.

Valentine drew his parang, turned, and went to meet it.

When Valentine was fourteen, he had read Livy. Tonight his was the role of Horatius at the Sublician Bridge. What had seemed heroic now felt suicidal, with two meters of genetically engineered death moving toward him at cheetah speed.

At first he was afraid that the Reaper, coming out of the dark like a bounding tiger, would simply leap over him to tear and toss his charges lifeless into the lake. But Valentine stood, legs planted with the balanced blade of the parang resting in his hand against the back of his thigh.

The Reaper stopped.

It regarded him, drawn skull-face expressionless and yellow eyes sunken in bony sockets.

ahh, the foodling stands, curious after the long chase. it is your nature to run, human, it breathed. *did you think you could steal and escape with our bauble? you would not get out of sight of this pier.* It crouched, froglike.

Valentine tried to keep the fear out of his voice even if he couldn't banish its shadow from his mind. His bowels suddenly seemed made of water, and his tongue was thick and dry.

"Your time is up," Valentine said, speaking quietly to keep his voice from cracking. "In a few seconds, your Master is going to have one less drone."

Go, Rho. Take Molly and haul out of here, he mentally implored.

The Reaper did not laugh, did not smile. It pulled back its lips to reveal obsidian pointed teeth.

oh, no, foodling. it is high night, and your world is mine. soon you will be as cold and empty as the moon, your woman, too. all you have done is spit into a hurricane.

Behind him Valentine heard the motorboat sputter into life. The thing looked for a moment at the vessel. *ahh, a boat, i thought so. your luck has run out.* It reached into its robes and pulled out a short, thick gun. Valentine took a step back in confusion; he had never heard of a Reaper using a gun, but it fired into the air, in the direction of the speedboat. A parachute flare opened, bathing the pier in red light.

"Do you know me, creature?" Valentine asked.

i know your kind, boy. weak and easily emptied. i feast on your fathers at will, as i shall consume you, the Reaper hissed, rising and opening its arms for the deadly embrace.

Valentine brought his blade up. "Not my father. My name is David Valentine. Son of Lee Valentine. Have you met my kind, creature?"

The thing's face lost animation. Perhaps the Kurian Lord at the other end knew dismay.

Valentine attacked. He lunged, hitting it with a backhand swipe that narrowly missed its neck. His blade struck the skull, cutting and glancing off its face with a resounding *thwack.*

It lashed out with a foot, almost caving in Valentine's chest. He fell backwards onto the dock, gasping for air, his parang teetering at the edge of the wooden jetty.

With a soft *plop* it dropped into Lake Michigan.

And David Valentine knew he would die. The vampire-avatar advanced four steps, then bent to take him up in its long arms. But Valentine would meet it on his feet. He rolled away in a blur and got up with the balance of a judo champion recovering from a throw. Exhilarated, he felt a rush of power, a presence that lifted the fear away.

With him stood a phalanx of spirits who had also faced the Kurians. His father and mother, holding hands. Steve Oran and Gilman DelVecchio formed an unflinching wall to his right and left, and behind him Gabriella Cho went on tiptoe to reach his ear.

Go on, Davy. He's not as tough as he seems, she seemed to whisper in his mind.

A terrible strength filled Valentine as the rush infused his belly with fire. The thing paused to wipe sticky black blood from its eye, and Valentine was upon it. The force of his leap knocked it over. Valentine clawed at its back, pinning an arm that tried to tear him off. He wrapped his arms around it. The Reaper flopped and rolled like a netted fish.

It rose, bearing Valentine like a backpack. It began to totter down toward the boat, which seemed to Valentine bathed in a red mist. It tried to shrug him off, but Valentine's arms had turned to steel cables.

Molly Carlson stepped out of the darkness, sighting down the pistol's barrel with tear-streaked eyes. The Reaper moved toward her, no longer struggling with Valentine but reaching for the woman. Valentine shifted his grip and tore open the Reaper's robes at its chest, baring the rippled surface of its rib cage.

"Shoot! Molly, shoot!" he yelled.

She fired, putting bullet after bullet into the vampire's chest. Valentine felt the impact against his own body as the heavy slugs tore into the Reaper's flesh. Black blood fountained out of its mouth.

He slid off the thing's back to avoid the bullets, falling to the ground. It turned its armored back to Molly and staggered toward Valentine, leaning over him as if it sought to at last crush and smother him under the fall of its body. Its deadly jaws opened wide, revealing the pointed tongue behind its fangs.

Valentine brought his knees to his chest and grabbed at the Reaper's sleeves. He brought the creature's weight to the soles of his feet, using its momentum against it. Now almost standing on his head, Valentine kicked out with both legs.

The hissing nightmare flew, thrown upside down into Lake Michigan, arms clawing at empty air. It splashed into the water.

Valentine rolled onto his stomach, looking at the circle of waves emerging from where the robe-weighted Reaper sank from sight. Turbulence broke the water; perhaps the thing was still struggling as it descended into final darkness. . . .

Now it was Molly's turn to help him up. The pair returned to the motorboat, where the fake Reaper still glowered at the two-man crew.

"What the hell was that back there? Who called the Snap-

pers to the pier, of all places? They'll kill us all!" the port officer yelled as they climbed on board.

nothing for you to know about, if you wish to see the dawn,
Rho said in imitation of a Reaper's breathy hiss. *return to
your duties, and let us catch the* whitecloud.

The port officer ran.

Molly sat next to Valentine, leaning against his shoulder.
He watched the two men nervously casting off the boat under
Rho's glowing eyes. Just in case, he reloaded the gun. While
moving out of the slip, the boat hit something and rocked to a
halt.

"What the—?" the man at the wheel said.

The engine sputtered and died.

"You have more guns?" Valentine asked. They ignored the
question and stood looking out at the water around them in
confusion, He fired a bullet into the windscreen. It spider-
webbed, and the men turned to him.

"Get your damn guns!"

The pilot grabbed a shotgun, and the other followed his example and took a revolver from the map case. The boat
rocked, and Valentine lurched toward the side. Molly threw
herself down, pulling him into the bottom of the boat. Rho
clutched at the throttle levers.

Humanlike hands and a dripping face appeared over the
side. The Reaper. Valentine fired the pistol and missed, but
the face disappeared nevertheless.

"Grenades on this boat?"

"We have a few," he said. He reached into a locker.

"Drop them over the side."

"Can't we get away?" Molly asked.

"The propeller's wedged," the pilot shouted.

"Here!" the man at the locker said, finding a canvas bag
with soup-can-style grenades.

Valentine handed his gun to Molly and grabbed a sharpened boathook. He listened and tried to guess where the Reaper would appear next while the mate yanked the pin of a grenade and turned to throw it overboard.

An arm lashed up out of the water, catching the man in the temple. The unpinned grenade fell into the bottom of the boat, bounced and rolled toward Valentine.

Molly scrambled for it on her hands and knees. She scooped it with a shoveling motion, as if it were a hot rock. The grenade spun into the water. It exploded, sending a column of water into the air.

The Reaper climbed onto the front of the boat. It had shed its robes and boots. Bullet wounds showed as black patches on its chest like three extra nipples.

"What the hell?" shouted the man at the controls.

Valentine raised the boathook and leaped onto the bow of the speedboat, but the Reaper knocked him aside. It went straight for Rho, jumping into the back of the boat. The Reaper struck the Lifeweaver with a raking blow across his chest.

Rho's masquerade blurred for a moment as he fell, giving Valentine a glimpse of an amorphous blue-green shape. Molly reached for Valentine's gun.

His vision blurred from pain, the Wolf grasped the boathook in both hands. He moved toward the Reaper as it bent to take up the Lifeweaver, a hungry light shining in its eyes.

now, i take—

Valentine buried the curved prong into the thing's back. It reared up, and reached for the boathook in its back by using its elbow joints in the opposite direction from how they worked on a human being.

shoot him, stupid foodling, the Reaper hissed at the pilot, pulling at the hook.

"Don't," Molly shrieked. She pointed the Colt at the pilot.

The Reaper lunged at Valentine. The blow sent him flying. He landed on the prow of the boat. Something hard poked him in the back: he had fetched up against the anchor.

The thing launched itself in the air, landing astride him. It bent, yellow eyes blazing.

Blue-white light flashed, and a shotgun blast tore through the side of the Reaper's face. Skin and stringy black hair exploded in shreds from the skull. A second shot caught it in the back, toppling it over Valentine and into the water.

"Always wanted a crack at one of those sumbitches," the pilot said, breaking open the shotgun to reload it.

Valentine could only lie and watch as a pair of ghostly white hands gripped the tube-steel of the low front rail of the boat.

"No, goddammit," Valentine said. "You're through." He put the pain away and unclasped the anchor, making sure the line was not attached.

Mechanically, the Reaper pulled itself onto the boat. Its face had lost all animation, its limbs moving in uncoordinated jerks.

Valentine lifted the Danforth anchor by the shank, and turned it so the twin flukes pointed down. He brought it down on the Reaper's spine, burying the steel into its torso. Still holding on to the anchor, the Wolf strained every muscle and picked up the Reaper. He heaved and threw the weighted abomination into Lake Michigan.

Beyond the splash, he saw gray humps in the water moving toward the boat.

"Shit, the Snappers are coming," the pilot said.

Rho rose to his feet, the Reaper disguise gone. His human

form looked like a wind-bent old tree, white hair streaming in the lake breeze. A misty patch at his chest throbbed with a faint blue light.

"I'm so tired," he said. "But perhaps I can help."

The Lifeweaver closed his eyes and gripped the boat. It began to move.

The boat picked up speed. Valentine saw more humps closing in from the sides. But they avoided the boat, gathering around the turbulence where the Reaper had disappeared in its final plunge.

"I've got the other grenade," the pilot said.

"We won't need it," Molly said, looking out over the stern. "Whatever they are, I hope they have strong stomachs."

Once clear of the harbor, Valentine and the pilot went over the side and unwound the Reaper's robe from the propeller.

"You two just helped three terrorists escape Chicago," Valentine told the Quisling as Molly helped them back into the boat. His friend was still unconscious, under a blanket in the forward cabin. "You can come with us and be set down somewhere, or join the fleet if they'll have you. It's the least I owe you for your help. That is if you don't want to paddle back and have a talk with the Reapers."

"I think we'd better come with you, sir. The name's J. P., by the way. My mate's name is Cal Swanson."

"Thought you might, J. P."

With the powerful motor again in action, they spotted the two-masted ship's lights before dawn. The speedboat tied up against the *Whitecloud* in an easy swell. The sailors, a mixed group of ten men, women, and children, came on deck to look at the visitors.

Rho stood still as a carving for a moment, looking at the new faces, then sank to his knees.

Valentine rushed to his side. He turned the Lifeweaver's face to him, but Rho did not react.

"I'm exhausted, Valentine the Younger. You are among your kind now?"

"Close enough," Valentine said. "We're safe, if that's what you mean."

The masklike expression did not change. Valentine looked into eyes filled with thousands of years of memories. "I will go in peace, then." Something that might have been a smile appeared on his lips. "I escaped them after all."

"Maybe you just need rest and food, sir. I'll help you up."

The Lifeweaver's mind touched his.

Too tired to talk. You've helped me more than you know. They would have dined long on me, but now I'll fly away free in death. Bring me to the cabin, the others should not . . .

"Molly, you and J. P. clear out the cabin, would you?" Valentine said.

He picked up the featherweight Lifeweaver. The former Quisling dragged his comrade Cal out into the night air.

"Help us, please," Molly implored to the faces above. Two sailors from the *Whitecloud* swung down.

Valentine took Rho into the dim compartment. A pair of tiny bunks angled together into the sharp prow of the vessel. He laid the Lifeweaver down.

Thank you, Lee . . . David. You have a strong aura. It might be best if . . . the others didn't see me, after . . . The mind's touch faltered.

"It's not over, sir. Just rest."

It . . . , Rho began, but never finished. He flickered one final time, before shifting back to his natural form. The thing he knew as Rho collapsed into a rubbery mass the size of a teenage boy. Rho sagged—there was no skeleton to support his body—into something that looked like a blue octopus with

a bit of bat in the evolutionary tree. Leathery fins ran the sides
of his tentacles, the longer limbs at the back of his body
joined by the veiny membranes almost to the sucker-tipped
ends like a ribbed cape, the shorter ones at the front unat-
tached and with smaller, more delicate suckers. His aqua-
colored skin, more blue around cephalopod skull, changed to
sea-foam green along his limbs, with a latticework of delicate
black lines covering the skin that he found eerily beautiful,
though if they were decorative or functional Valentine could
not say. Spicules and flaps formed a band under the brain-in-
a-bag of its head, but whether they were noses, ears, breathing tubes, or even sexual organs was anyone's guess. The
bulging eyes, lids opening wider and wider as it relaxed into
death, drew Valentine's gaze back every time he looked elsewhere. They were like yellowish crystal balls flecked with
red, with a black band running across the middle.

God, it was ugly for an angel. Or a devil, for that matter.

Valentine hugged the moist, limp form to himself. He
owed his and Molly's life to the dead Lifeweaver. When the
warmth had left the body, he covered it with a blanket.

He should stuff Rho's body in a bucket or a big jug, preserve it with alcohol, and get it back to the Miskatonic. The
researchers there might be able to find a weakness, some flaw
that would allow them to kill the Kurians without blasting
into their lairs and blowing them to bits. Duty, and loyalty to
his species, demanded it.

He exited the cabin and went to the engine.

"Take any gear and fixtures you want out of her," he said
to the crewmen of the *Whitecloud*. "But don't go in the
cabin."

He found a hose and siphoned some gasoline up into a
water bottle. He took the fuel down into the forward compartment and splashed it on the carpet and wood paneling. He

repeated the process until the gas was gone and the speedboat reeked of fumes. He followed his shipmates into the sailing vessel as the sailors pulled the powerful outboard up out of its mount with a block and tackle.

Valentine reached into his pockets and found one more tin of matches. He struck them all at once, and tossed the flaming handful into the cabin. Flames raced through the boat, and the *Whitecloud* sailors cast it off.

He watched and waited until the lake consumed the flaming wreck. The smoke dissipated into the fresh breeze.

Sailors are used to the unexpected. A woman with a long, thin-boned face introduced herself as Collier, the captain of the *Whitecloud,* and offered them blankets and hot coffee.

She invited them below to the cramped galley. Valentine showed the captain his card, the chit given him by Captain Doss of the *White Lightning.* She agreed to take them north, where they could transfer to another ship, which could take them anywhere in the Great Lakes they wished to go. "I'd do it anyway, even without Dossie's card. Something tells me you went through a lot to get here."

He, Molly, and J. P. discussed their options on the coming voyage. They decided to winter in the familiar (at least to Valentine) reaches of the Boundary Waters. He would see Father Max again. Only when spring came would he have to make new decisions.

A very weary David Valentine took Molly into the clean, cold air of the Lake Michigan morning. They looked west as the shoreline slowly became distinct and the sun penetrated the clouds. He thought of all the doomed souls beyond the distant, mist-shrouded shore. He had saved Molly, but how many others had died to feed the Reapers in the last three days?

He remembered a story that Father Max used to tell, and a quote he had to memorize from the green blackboard, of a tireless nun named Mother Teresa. She and her Sisters of Mercy had worked with the multitudes of impoverished, disease-stricken people in India. A journalist had asked her how she managed to keep her spirits up, when despite her unceasing labors there would always be more suffering than she could possibly cure.

Mother Teresa had thought for a moment, and then said: "You start with one."

David Valentine turned to watch the dawn, Molly's hand in his.

One.

This ends the first volume tracking the career of David Valentine. He will return to face the mysterious Twisted Cross in Choice of the Cat, *the second book in the* Vampire Earth *series. For more information on it and other tales of* Vampire Earth, *please visit the author's Web site at www.vampireearth.com.*

Glossary

Aspirants: Teenagers, often sons and daughters of those in a particular caste, who travel with the Hunters and perform assorted camp functions.

Bears: Hunters and the most fearsome of the Lifeweavers' human weapons. The Bears are proud to take on anything the Kurians can design.

buckchits: The plastic currency of the Ozark Free Territory, they are doughnut-shaped coins of various denominations.

Cats: Trained by the Lifeweavers, these Hunters act as spies, saboteurs, and assassins in the Kurian Zone. Some work in disguises; others work openly.

Grogs: Any of the multitude of creations the Kurians have designed or enhanced to help subjugate man. They come in many shapes and sizes; some are intelligent enough to use weapons.

Hunters: Human beings who have been enhanced by the technomagic of the Lifeweavers to cope with the spawn of Kur.

Interworld Tree: An ancient network of portals between the stars, the doors of which allow instantaneous transportation across the light-years.

Kurians: Lifeweavers from the planet Kur who learned

how to indefinitely lengthen their lives by absorbing vital aura. They are the true vampires of the New Order.

lifesign: Energy given off by any living thing in proportion to its size and sentience. The Reapers use it, in addition to the normal senses, to track their human prey.

parang: A short, fat machete with a slight curve at the tip. Its three cutting edges can be used to skin game, chop down small trees, or even dig.

Pre-entities: The Old Ones, a vampiric race that died out long before man walked the Earth. From their knowledge the Kur learned how to become vampires by living off vital aura.

Quislings: Humans who assist the Kurians in running the New Order.

Reapers: The Praetorian Guard of the New Order, they are in fact avatars animated by their master vampire. They permit the reclusive Kurians to interact with humans and others, and more important, absorb the vital aura through a psychic connection with the avatar without physical risk. The Reaper lives off the blood of the victim, while the aura sustains the Master Kurian. Also known colloquially as Capos, Governors, Hoods, Rigs, Skulls, Scowls, Tongue-Tong, Creeps, Hooded Ones, and Vampires.

vital aura: An energy field created by a living creature. Sadly, humans are rich in it.

Wolves: The most numerous caste of the Hunters, their patrols watch the no-man's-land between the Kurian Zone and the Free Territories. They also act as guerrilla fighters, couriers, and scouts.

*Read on
for a special preview
of E. E. Knight's
next volume of the
Vampire Earth:*

CHOICE OF THE CAT

Available from Roc.

Lt. David Valentine looked back down into the gully. His platoon, numbering thirty-five in all, rested against leafing trees, using their packs to keep their backsides off of the rain-soaked earth. They had covered a lot of ground since skirting the northern edge of Lake Oologah that morning, moving at a steady, mile-eating run. The Wolves held rifles in their laps. Their leather uniforms were cut in variegated styles. Some Wolves still wore their winter beards, and no two hats matched. The only accoutrement his three squads shared were their short, broad-bladed machetes known as parangs, though as would be expected of the individualistic Wolves, some wore them on their belts, some across their chests, and some sheathed in their moccasin-leather puttees.

Valentine signaled with two fingers to the men waiting in the gully, and Sergeant Stafford climbed up the wash to join him in the damp bracken. His platoon sergeant, known as "Gator" off-duty because of his leathery skin and wide, toothy grin, worked his way slowly to Valentine's overlook. Wordlessly, the lieutenant passed Stafford his binoculars. Stafford examined the compound as Valentine worked another inch off of the grass stalk clamped in his teeth.

"Looks like that last sprint was for nothing," Valentine said. "The tractor trailer pulled in here. We wouldn't have intercepted anyway. This must be a pretty good stretch of road."

"How do you figure that, sir?" Stafford said, searching the compound in vain for any sign of the tanker truck they had spotted crawling through the rain that morning. Using a map, making some guesswork, and trusting to luck, the platoon had dashed cross-country to ambush the tanker, hardly a forlorn hope given the terrible state of the roads in this part of the Kurain Zone.

"Look at the ruts by the gate, turning off the road. They've got to have been made by an eighteen wheeler," Valentine said.

"Could have been from yesterday—even the day before, Lieutenant."

Valentine raised an eyebrow. "No puddles. Rain would have

filled in something that deep. Those were made since the shower ended, what, a half hour ago?"

"Err, okay, yeah. So the truck's in one of those big garages getting worked on. We get in touch with the captain, the rest of the company is here in a day or two, and we burn the compound. I figure fifteen or twenty guarding this place at most. Ten's more likely."

"I'd like nothing better, Staff. Time's a problem, though."

"Val, I know food's short, but what else is new? There's enough game and forage in these woods."

"Sorry, Gator," Valentine said, taking the binoculars back. "I misspoke. I should have said time's running short for *them*."

Stafford's eyebrows arched in surprise. "What, those four tied up down there? Okay, it's ugly, but since when have we had much control over the punishment handed out by these little Territorial commandants?"

"I don't think it's just punishment," Valentine said, his eyes now on the two-story house.

"Hell, sir, you know these collaborator creeps—they'll flog a woman for not getting the skid marks out of their skivvies. These four probably were last out of the barracks for role call or something. God knows."

Valentine waited for a moment, wondering whether to give voice to a feeling. "Staff, I think they're breakfast. There's a Reaper in that house, maybe more than one."

Sergeant Tom Stafford blanched. "H-how d-do you figure that, sir?"

Valentine read the sergeant's terror with a species of relief. He wanted a subordinate in mortal fear of the Reapers. Any man who did not tremble at the thought of facing a couple of Hoods was either a fool or inexperienced, and there were far too many inexperienced Wolves in Foxtrot Company. Whether or not the whole lot, officers included, were fools was a question Valentine sometimes debated with himself on long winter nights until his thoughts became too much for him.

"Look at the first story of the house, Sergeant," Valentine said, passing the binoculars back. "It's a nice day. Someone is letting in the spring air. But that second story—shuttered. I think I even see a blanket or something stuffed between the slats. And that little stovepipe coming out of the wall—that's got to be for a bedroom, not the kitchen. See the vapor? Someone has a fire going."

"Dark and warm. Hoods like it like that," Stafford agreed.

"My guess is that after the sun's down, the visitor will rise and go about its business. It won't feed till almost morning. It wouldn't risk taking them before it could sleep safe again. You know how dopey they get after feeding."

"Okay, sir, then that's the time to hit 'em. Tomorrow morning." Stafford couldn't keep the excitement out of his voice. "Maybe the captain could even get here by then. That refinery he's scouting can't be more than thirty miles away. They feed, dawn comes, and they button up in that house. We burn them out, even if it rains again, and have enough guns to knock 'em down and keep 'em down till we can get in with the blades."

"That would be my plan exactly, Sergeant," Valentine agreed. "Except for one thing."

"What, you think that house won't burn if it rains again? Those phosphorous candles, I've seen them burn through tin, sir. They'll get the job done."

"You missed my point, Staff," he said, spitting out the thoroughly chewed blade of grass. "I'm not going to let the Hoods get their tongues into those poor bastards."

Valentine knew the word "incredulous" was probably not in his platoon sergeant's vocabulary, but Stafford's expression neatly illustrated the meaning of the word. "Er, sir, I feel for them too, but hell, it's too much of a risk."

"Having thirty Wolves within a mile of the Reapers is a risk too. Even if we all concentrate on lowering lifesign, they still might pick up on us. Then we'd be faced with Reapers coming from who knows where in the dark. The sun isn't waiting. I've made up my mind. We're going to hit them now with the platoon while most of the guards are off in the fields. That's all there is to it, Sergeant. Keep an eye on the camp up here. Whistle if anything happens."

The lieutenant returned to his platoon, scooting backwards on his belly until he reached the cut in the hillside. He gathered his three squads around him.

"Heads up, Second Platoon. The captain detached us with orders to raise a little hell if we get the chance, and we just got it. There's a pretty big civvy compound on the other side of this hill.

Looks like farm workers and maybe some mechanics—there's a couple of big garages behind the wire. Two guard towers with a man in each. I figure most of the able-bodied are out in the fields to the north, and most of the garrison is keeping an eye on them. Chances are there are only a few left in the compound, counting the two in the towers. But it looks like there could be Hoods in there too."

Valentine gave them a moment to digest this. Newer Wolves comprised the majority of Foxtrot Company, which had been re-built after being bled white in action east of Hazlett, Missouri, in the summer of '65. Each of his three squads had only one or two reliable veterans. Most of the experienced men were with the captain or leading smaller patrols on similar scouting forays into the Gulag lands north of Tulsa. While all of Foxtrot had gone through arduous training by Southern Command, the gulf between training and experience had been crossed by only a handful of his men. But they were eager to prove themselves as true Wolves, and all had reason to hate the Reapers and the Quislings assisting them.

Valentine searched the expectant eyes for a pair of almost cherubic young faces. "Jenkins and Oliver, take a map and head south. Sergeant Stafford will show you where the captain's headquarters is supposed to be. If he's not there, go back to sum-mer camp south of the Pensacola dam and report. If you do find him, tell him we're about to hit some Reapers. I expect the Territorials'll react, and there'll be columns from all over con-verging on this spot. Maybe he can bushwhack one. We're going to run east and wait at camp. Got it?"

Marion Oliver held up her hand. "Sir, can't we be in on the at-tack, *then* go find the captain?"

Valentine shook his head. "Oliver, I could sure use you, but just in case this goes to hell, the captain would want to know what we found, where we were when we found it, and what we were going to do about it. Getting that information to the captain might save our lives.

"When it was raining earlier, I saw a few of you with those new rain ponchos you lifted outta that storehouse we broke into a cou-ple days ago. I need to borrow three of them, and two volunteers."

An hour later Valentine walked down the empty road towards the camp, watching clouds build up again to the southwest. He hoped for more rain overnight. It would slow pursuit.

He wore a green rain slicker, an oily-smelling poncho borrowed from one of his men. Behind him two of his best snapshooters walked down the road, brisk and bold in the open daylight, also wearing the rain gear stolen from the Quisling Territorials. Valentine had his sleeves tucked together like a Chinese mandarin he'd once seen in a laminated placemat pinned to an eatery wall.

As the trio approached the camp, the guard in the south tower near the road waved lazily and called something down to the cinder-block guardhouse below. Valentine smelled concentrated humanity ahead, along with the odors of gasoline and oil.

Thanks to the Lifeweavers, humanity's allies in the battle against their fallen brothers, Valentine, like all Wolves, possessed an almost feral sense of hearing and smell, superhuman endurance, and remarkable reflexes. Valentine made use of his hearing as he approached the camp, focusing on the two guards walking up to the gate.

"Guy in front looks Injun if you ask me," one uniformed figure commented to his associate. Valentine, still a hundred yards away, heard every word as if from ten feet. "Mebbe he's Osage or something."

"Didn't ask you, Gomez," the older of the two replied, scratching the stubble on his chin in thought. "Better go tell the Looie, strangers comin' to the gate on foot."

"Franks is having a beer with that truck driver. Any excuse for that pisser. They've been through six by now, prolly."

"You'd better tell him or he'll have you stripped. He's jumpy, what with the Visitors."

Valentine worked the safety on the pistol in his left hand. The gun in his right hand was a revolver; he covered the hammer with his thumb, so it would not catch when he pulled it from the baggy sleeves that covered his arms and hands. The seconds seemed to stretch as the Wolves approached the gate. The Territorial named Gomez returned with a tall thin man who threw away a cigarette as he exited the gatehouse.

"Shit, four at the gate," Alpin, the young Wolf behind him, muttered.

"Stick to the plan. I just want you two to get the guy in the tower," Valentine said, quickening his step. "Hi there," he called. "I'm supposed to see a Lieutenant Franks. He's here, right? I got a message for him."

The bored guard at the southern tower leaned over to hear the exchange below, rifle held ready but pointed skyward. Valentine took a final glance around the compound. Back towards the barracks, a few women and children squatted on the steps or peered out of tiny windows at the visitors.

The tall lieutenant stepped forward and eyed Valentine through the wire, hand on his stiff canvas holster. "I don't know you, kid. Where's the message, and who sent you?"

"It's verbal, Lieutenant," Valentine answered. "Let me think. . . . It goes like this: you're a shit-eating, traitorous, murderous disgrace to the human race. That's about it."

The guards inside the gate froze.

"What?" Franks barked. Franks seized his side arm, the Velcro on the clasp making a tiny tearing sound, but Valentine had his two pistols out before the Quisling's hand even got around the grip. Valentine squeezed off two shots from the automatic and one from the revolver into the lieutenant's chest, spinning the man in a full 180 with the impact.

Behind him, the two Wolves raised their carbines. One had some trouble with his poncho, delaying him for a second, but Alpin aimed his gun up and put a bullet through the guard's chin while the sentry was still shouldering his rifle. The other Wolf got his gun clear in time to put another shot into the lurching figure even as the magazine-fed battle rifle fell out of the tower.

In the time it took the guard's rifle to smack into the wet dirt twenty feet below, Valentine emptied his two pistols into the other Quislings at the gate. The three Wolves dived for the roadside ditch, splashing into puddled rainwater. Valentine abandoned the empty revolver and slipped a fresh magazine into the automatic, sliding the action to chamber the first round. A shot fired from the northern tower whizzed overhead.

Alpin slithered along the ditch as Valentine popped his gun arm and one eye over the crest of the depression, gun following his gaze as he checked the door and windows of the old guardhouse. An unlatched metal screen door with the word "Welcome" worked into the mesh squeaked in the gusty breeze. Valentine ducked back into the ditch.

"Should I make a try at the gate, sir?" McFerrin asked, muddy water dripping from his face.

Valentine shook his head. "Stay put and wait for the Sarge."

Farther down the ditch Alpin popped up to swap shots with the northern tower.

"Alpin, stay down, dammit!" Valentine yelled.

The young Wolf brought his gun up again, and a bullet burrowed into the ground right in front of this face. Dirt flew, and with a pained cry Alpin dropped his gun and brought his hands up to his right eye. Valentine crawled toward the youth, swearing through clenched teeth, when he heard a wet smack followed by the report of the shot. Alpin toppled backwards into the ditch. Valentine risked a dash to Alpin, whose one good eye fluttered open and shut next to the bloody ruin of the other.

A distant, challenging wail reached Valentine's ears as he pulled Alpin along the ditch, seeking to put the gatehouse between them and the rifleman. Stafford had the platoon attacking the northern fence. Valentine heard a shot and the sound of breaking glass. His other gunman was shooting at God knows what in the guardhouse.

Valentine found the wound in Alpin's arm and pressed hard to stop the bleeding. Thankfully, the sticky flow welled up underneath his palm in a steady stream rather than short arterial bursts. He called the other Wolf over.

"McFerrin! Alpin's hit!"

"Someone came to a window there—I missed," McFerrin gabbled.

"Keep your head down. C'mere and put a tourniquet on Alpin right now," Valentine barked. McFerrin scuttled over, but seemed at a loss as soon as he looked at Alpin. First-aid training always took place in a quiet meadow with plenty of space, not stretched out in a wet ditch with no elbow room. Valentine blew out an exasperated breath. "Never mind. Just put pressure right here," Valentine said, placing McFerrin's hand on the underside of Alpin's arm just below the armpit. "Press hard. Don't worry, he's in shock; he doesn't feel anything."

Valentine ripped material from the flimsy poncho and used the revolver's barrel to wind the tourniquet tight. Valentine popped his head up again—still no sign of the other Wolves, although no more shots came from the direction of the northern tower. The guard had either run or been shot. McFerrin seemed to catch on and took control of keeping tension on the tourniquet.

"Mister, mister," someone yelled from the guardhouse. "We surrender—I surrender, I mean. I'm coming out, no gun. I got a woman with me."

"I'm just a housekeeper. I ain't one of the Territorials!" a woman's voice added.

He cautiously looked out of the ditch. "Come on out, then!" Valentine called. "Hands up in the air!"

The "Welcome" door opened, and a young man in camouflage fatigues emerged, followed by a woman in a simple smock. Valentine aimed the pistol at the Territorial. "You in the uniform—face down on the ground. Now!"

The Territorial complied. No more shots came from the other side of the compound, but Valentine could see Oklahomans running from the barracks toward the north fence. The Wolves must have reached the compound.

"Open the gate, please," Valentine said to the woman, who rushed to comply. The unlocked gate swung easily on its hinges, and Valentine entered the camp. He walked up to the Territorial, still on the ground, face turned sideways and fearfully eyeing Valentine.

"Okay, Terri, unless you want to piss off the man holding the gun, you better tell me who's in the house with the big porch."

"Mister, it's four Skulls and some administrator guy out of Tulsa. And I ain't really a Territorial, I just wear the uniform because I'm in the transports. I drive trucks. I just drive trucks, I swear."

"Did you drive a tanker in here today?"

"Yes, sir—that was me. They got a pump for the road vehicles and the tractors. I'm s'posed to spend the night here at the Rigyard, then—"

"I found the lieutenant," called a Wolf pointing his gun around the corner of the guardhouse.

"Sarge, Lieutenant Valentine's here. He's okay," another Wolf added.

"Keep an eye on these two," Valentine ordered. "Sanchez, help McFerrin carry Alpin in." McFerrin's head and shoulders popped up like those of a curious prairie dog. Wolves rushed to help McFerrin with their wounded comrade.

THE VAMPIRE EARTH
series by

E.E. Knight

Louisiana, 2065. A lot has changed in the 43rd
year of the Kurian Order. Possessed of an unnatural
hunger, the bloodthirsty Reapers have come to
Earth to establish a New Order built on the
harvesting of human souls. They rule the planet.
And if it is night, as sure as darkness,
they will come.

This is the Vampire Earth.

Don't miss Book Two:
CHOICE OF THE CAT
0-451-45973-3

Available wherever books are sold or at
penguin.com